The Winter Spirits

The Winter Spirits

KIRAN MILLWOOD HARGRAVE
LAURA SHEPHERD-ROBINSON
ANDREW MICHAEL HURLEY
IMOGEN HERMES GOWAR
NATASHA PULLEY
ELIZABETH MACNEAL
BRIDGET COLLINS
STUART TURTON
JESS KIDD
CATRIONA WARD
SUSAN STOKES-CHAPMAN
LAURA PURCELL

SPHERE

First published in Great Britain in 2023 by Sphere

3 5 7 9 10 8 6 4 2

A CIP catalogue record for this book is available from the British Library.

ISBN 978-1-4087-2758-4

Typeset in Garamond 3 by M Rules
Printed and bound in Great Britain by Clays Ltd, Elcograf S.p.A.

Papers used by Sphere are from well-managed forests and other responsible sources.

Sphere
An imprint of
Little, Brown Book Group
Carmelite House
50 Victoria Embankment
London EC4Y 0DZ

An Hachette UK Company
www.hachette.co.uk

www.littlebrown.co.uk

CONTENTS

HOST

Kiran Millwood Hargrave

The second candles of Advent burn on the capital's church altars, though the days are all the same to Mary. Her birthday was yesterday, but she doesn't know that, no mother nor father to tell her so. Her brother Abel older but not by enough to remember. They are lucky to be together: this is repeated on the Island, where it is common to have breaks in the limbs of your family tree, oozing tender sap.

Jacob's Island is a sprawl of a rookery, stuck between two confluences of effluence. They were pitched, Abel and Mary, out of the workhouse in Whitechapel and into this new freedom-that-is-no-real-freedom three years before, finding lodgings over a knocking shop on Edwards Street that by day claims to be a grocer with wilted cabbage and goggle-eyed potatoes and at night lays wilted women beneath goggle-eyed men and won't scrub the tables in between.

It is no longer a bewilderment to her, the Island. She knows it well enough now, where to lift her skirts, where to keep to the middle to avoid slop, where the rookeries' worst thieves are more active and likely to target even a child, but something is stalking her now, as she weaves with fresh hides in her hands, heading for the small, slumped dock where deliveries carry all the skilled work out to better areas. She cannot see it, nor nose it, but it knows her in some bone-deep, soul-certain way, is relentless as hunger or desire – *is* hungry, desirous – and so there is no escaping. Poor Mary, head down. If she did not look so much like prey, perhaps she could have been luckier.

It is not all bleakness. Christmas brings some relief, with the rich from across the river feeling a burr of conscience, sending gifts of money to the old leper hospital, the grubby church. Some of it even reaches those it was intended for, and there are clementines, bright orange as lit coals, handed out at Advent services, studded with cloves. Mary had her first clementine at such a service last year, and the memory of its sweetness haunts her still, like a phantom limb.

She is thinking about it now, as she weaves closer to the dock, more than she should. She should have half a mind on her way, an eye on what's about her. Then she'd notice, maybe, how the man behind her now has boots of shiny leather, at odds with his patched and darned overcoat, the stubble on his face.

Mary is spat by the alleys onto the jetty, once wood rotting underfoot and now slick stone built haphazard from the riverbed, wide enough for a dozen boats to dock and so the busiest part of the Island at any time of day. Teirney's barge is always moored in the same place. The man drops back here, and watches as Mary carries her hides to the woman smoking on deck. It reminds him to smoke too, the pipe he purchased for when his pursuit would require a watch-and-wait, something to do with his hands and face. He tamps tobacco into the clay and lights it, puffs awkwardly as the girl speaks with Ma Teirney.

'And how's tha t'day?'

'Good, Ma.'

'Keepin free of the yellowin, you and your brudder both?'

'Yes.'

'Tha's good, girl.' Ma Teirney inspects the hides, finds them as always a little wanting, but pays in full nonetheless. It is more than she'd admit to anyone, least of all herself, but Mary is the reason she comes to this godforsaken island for her hides at all. The girl has thick, dark hair, fierce pale skin and dark, liquid eyes. A gentle spirit.

'Same again next week, Ma?'

'Closed for Christmastime.'

'Christmas next week, Ma?'

'Aye. An' here's sommit for the occasion.'

Ma brings out the peg doll from her pocket, dressed in a bright twist of leftover taffeta taken from the sewing floor. Peacock blue, formed by Ma's skilled fingers into a bodice and full skirt of the current fashion – she has even lined the hem and cuffs with lace. The peg's face itself is rubbed nearly smooth by cherishing, but the wood is a lovely pine.

'Ma.' The word is gasped. Mary has never had a gift before. She can't even bring herself to reach for it lest it be snatched away. 'It can't be for me?'

'Why can't it? Take it so.'

Mary does so, in trembling fingers. She sees her fingers

grubby against the bright azure of the skirt, but her shame is forgotten by the wonder of the fabric, soft one way and rough the other, and so thick it keeps the dents of her touch. She crushes the doll to her chest in ecstasy.

They part, Ma feeling sadder and lighter, Mary in love with her new and first toy, and the man peels off from the wall and follows Mary, back into the warren.

The yellowing sweeps the Island the next week, and the third Advent candle is lit to half-empty pews as bodies are shipped out for paupers' graves. Cholera outbreaks are nothing new in places so packed and reeking, but this is especially virulent, coming as it does so hard on the heels of that year's influenza.

Abel and Mary keep indoors, as Ma Teirney told Mary they must in such times, and survive off boiled peelings from the grocer's. Mary doesn't much mind. They have been hungrier. She likes her brother and loves her peg doll, who she has named Clementine. She and Clementine attend balls and brush their lips against knots in the wood of the rotting door frame, that when squinted at could have beards and kind eyes. Abel frets at the work going begging, but he listens to his sister's pleas to stay put.

No one else stops their business, including the man with leather boots and trimmed nails, whose business is to keep watch over their one way in or out, waiting for Mary to emerge. He leaves the Island only at night-time, takes the boat he has hired west to Waterloo Bridge, where his coach waits to take him across the bustling Strand, skirting

St Giles and Soho, those thin ribbons of streets he once frequented, and through Bloomsbury where he was born in a house with high ceilings and crystal lamps. On to their quiet house set before a Regent's Park that stretches out dark as a sea.

Now the streets are empty, the lampers long left and only the occasional coachman waiting outside houses lit golden with candles and the bright chatter of dinner parties. They used to throw such soirées in their dining room, the walls hung with damask and twelve courses created by their cook, poached from the Corinthian in his prime. Now that room stands stripped to its plaster and the heavy carved table is sold too, alongside its twenty high-backed, silk-cushioned chairs. Heavy draped curtains always drawn, and candle-light: they remain beside shadows, and a round table moved from the unstaffed kitchens with four matchstick-legged chairs of unknown provenance. And it is there that his wife waits for news, with a woman who talks with the dead.

By a system of shadow casting between the gas lamps of the fine street and the smallest chink left in the drapes hung at the leaded windows, Mrs Flint's assistant Violet can alert her to the exact moment Mr Ezra Griffiths's coach turns into the square. It is this cue that rouses Mrs Flint from her trance and tells her to turn dark green eyes on her quarry and say, 'He's home.' Mrs Edith Griffiths will go to the window and gasp at the accuracy, adding this to her wisps of evidence, built up frail as a nest, that this is after all the right thing, that this woman squatting in her home is real in her promises. It is easier to sweep aside her unease at the plan.

She opens the front door, which they keep freshly painted as though that would ward off the street's gossip, and takes Ezra's stinking coat, his flat cap, takes in his exhausted eyes, kisses his stubbled cheek and holds her breath against the whiff of poverty that steams off him. She doesn't know, but the house smells just as bad to Ezra: closed-up misery and waiting.

'Well?'

'Still inside.'

Edith turns from him and hangs the coat carefully next to his good cloak, the flat cap atop, and goes dazed back to the dining room. Ezra reluctantly follows, rubbing his eyes and swallowing a yawn.

'Still inside,' he hears Edie tell Mrs Flint, and both women look at him as he enters. He feels the now familiar shiver of revulsion when the older woman's eyes fix on him. She is handsome, strong boned, and the green of her irises is deep as a pond, thick streaks of white hair framing her pale face, the rest a rich brown. She is powerful, so unlike his dear Edie, and it disturbs him quite as much as the fact he believes everything she says. But she is their link, their hope. She has a plan for them.

'We can't wait longer,' says Mrs Flint. 'Who knows when the sickness will end. Every day we wait now, the threads are fraying. I cannot keep them tethered for ever. And the girl must be willing, remember that.'

'I know,' says Ezra, keeping temper from his voice. 'But

she lives with her brother, well built and rough. And you said no fuss.'

'The woman with the doll. Turner?'

'Teirney,' he says, recalling the name on the barge.

'Can she write?'

Ezra shrugs. 'I doubt the girl can read.'

'But a letter may do it anyway. Something signed. A letter, summoning her for work. She is clearly fond, it would not be unusual.' She looks expectantly at him, and he realises he is being dismissed to look for paper, a pen.

He silently fumes as he leaves the musty room for his study on the first floor. The bare steps creak, and he wishes he could move stealthily, could hear what the witch says when he exits. He hates leaving Edie with her in the day, and when Violet is there it eases him only slightly, for the girl is as under her spell as his wife.

It began at one of their dinners with Alistair and his wife Maude, both devout attendees of electric shows and mesmerists, mentioning a particular establishment in Holborn, where there are no tricks or mirrors, just a woman with green eyes who sees through the veil of life to the other side. When the spiritualist was mentioned – a Mrs Stone, or Mrs Slate – Edie went very still. The muscles clenched in her jaw since that terrible night softened, and her eyes went bright. It was an expression, almost, of ecstasy, one that he had sometimes seen when they lay together. He should have closed down the chatter, but how could anyone who loves someone refuse them such pleasure?

And when she came to him the very next day in his study,

him stowing the bottle hurriedly in his bottom drawer, she had the same calm gleam to her, the address in Holborn clutched in her palm. He still did not close it down. The truth was, he needed the hope too.

Through the coachman Thomas, they organised an appointment a week hence. Edie seemed soothed. He drank less, and they moved around the house balancing their secret between them, like the early days of her pregnancy, and when the day came dressed with the care of attending the opera. If Thomas thought their attire strange for a night in Holborn, his face, as usual, gave nothing away.

The house was small and neat, unobtrusive in a way he instantly approved of. It put him in mind of the better sort of bawdy houses, where you could be served tea alongside other services. No signage proclaimed what sort of establishment it was, only a small brass sign engraved *Mrs Flint*. He knocked twice, Edie hanging from his arm, her breath slightly misted in the cold air.

A girl they would come to know as Violet opened the door. She wore a frilled cap and black uniform, like a scullery maid, unruly blonde curls and unruly twisted teeth tucked out of sight. A pointed, clever face, he'd thought it even then.

'Mr and Mrs Griffiths.' It was not a question. She stood aside in the narrow hallway. 'Come in. Back room, please.'

The corridor was lit softly, a closed door to the left, two to the right, a staircase leading up to second-floor darkness. The shabby wallpaper seemed pleasantly faded rather than squalid, and there was a heavy, floral scent pervading as they approached a door set at the back, where a kitchen would usually be in a terrace such as this.

Before they reached it, the door opened though there was no one standing the other side. Edie gave a shiver, of excitement or fear, as beyond was revealed a small round table set with candles, a seated woman framed in the doorway. She could only be Mrs Flint. Perhaps it was a pseudonym, it suited her so well. The hard gaze, the sharp cheekbones, the perfectly pressed widow's weeds – she was forbidding, far from his visions of floaty scarves and plump, waving forearms.

Violet ushered them inside, and Mrs Flint offered them the seats either side of her.

'Please, sit. It is good to meet you both.'

They sat, and Ezra scanned the room. There were, as Alistair and Maude had said, no mirrors. It had once been a kitchen – that was obvious from the size of the hearth, the cupboards, the smoke stains on the wall – but there were no cooking smells any more, only that floral heaviness everywhere. A large curtain concealed a window, and another longer curtain covered a door through which leached some of the September night's chill.

'Tell me,' said Mrs Flint, 'why you are here?'

'Our daughter,' said Edie, her voice already cracking, at the same time Ezra said, 'Our friends—'

'Well, yes,' he continued, as Edie fell silent. 'Both. Our friends told us about you. The Wallaces?'

'Oh,' said Mrs Flint, and there was little warmth in her voice. 'They thought it all a great game.'

'They said you were the real thing. That you really can speak . . .'

He couldn't bring himself to say it.

'But you must say it,' said Mrs Flint. 'The time for hesitation is past. Leave it at the door. Here, you must believe. Your daughter?'

'Yes.'

'When?'

'This winter past. Influenza.'

'Her name?'

"Eleanor.'

'Age?'

'Seven,' said Edie. 'And two months. And ten days.'

Mrs Flint clucked her tongue. 'A great shame, a great waste. Children, though, they are often harder to coax out. The transition – it frightens them. Like a game of hide and seek they have taken too seriously and convinced themselves of danger.'

'We do not want to frighten her,' said Edie, mortified.

'Transition?' asked Ezra.

'The place between. The mist. Children often get stuck there, waiting. So you are doing the right thing to contact her, guide her. And you will have brought what I asked?'

'Her hair,' said Edie, slipping off her mourning ring. 'And her favourite doll.'

This Ezra drew from his overcoat. A china-faced, glass-eyed girl the length of his forearm, with tight chestnut curls and a sage green hat, a sage green umbrella hanging from a plump cloth arm.

'Pretty,' said Mrs Flint damningly. She took both objects and placed them carefully on the table where they cast strange umbras. 'Violet?'

Ezra stifled a start as her assistant moved out from the shadows by the door. She had closed it unnoticed, and now the room felt very small, any sounds from the street very far away. Violet extinguished the lamps around the walls, moving close past the chairs, and brought a black candle from a high shelf, placing it in front of Mrs Flint.

'I prefer not to explain too much, but there are some rules. We do not break the circle. One knock, yes; two knocks for no. We keep our focus on Eleanor. Do not dwell on darkness, but on light.' She struck a match, lit the black candle. 'The candles are for that, to bring you back. This place is where what we think is made manifest, and that is perilous. When Violet tells you, you may ask questions. Otherwise please do not speak out of turn. I may fit, or shake, and you must not be alarmed. Keep hold of my hand – you are my tethers. Understood?'

'Yes,' breathed Edie, but Ezra felt a swell of misgiving. She had not told them what to expect, not really. Will they hear Eleanor, see her? He was not ready for any of it.

But Mrs Flint was holding out her hand to him, and Violet, seated his other side, was too, and Edie already had tight hold of them. He complied, noting how strong Mrs Flint's grip was, how cool Violet's skin. It was strange to hold women's hands like this.

Violet began to count, very slowly, down from ten. 'Ten . . . nine . . . eight . . .'

Ezra fixed his gaze on the candles, but at 'five' Edie's sharp gasp pulled his attention up. His wife was staring at Mrs Flint. The woman was unnaturally still, shoulders lifted close to her ears, green eyes wide as the doll's on the table.

'Four . . . three . . .'

Her shoulders slumped, her head flopping forward like a puppet with cut strings.

'Two . . .'

Ezra found himself fearing the final number, but it came anyway.

'One.'

A gust of cold wind filled the room, guttering the candles and causing all but the black one to extinguish. Mrs Flint's grip was iron, Violet's ice. Edie whimpered as Mrs Flint slowly, slowly raised her head.

'Mrs Flint?' asked Violet. Her voice did not so much as waver. A knock, definite as his own had been on the front door, echoed around the room. His heart was beating, galloping, racing. A second knock.

'Eleanor?' asked Violet.

Knock. Ezra held his breath. Surely it could not be so easy? His little girl could not have been waiting so long for them to come for her, stepping so simply forward from death? *Knock*. No.

'Who are you?'

'A guide,' said Mrs Flint, and her voice was a man's.

'Are you of God?'

'Light only.'

'Do you know Eleanor?'

'I know the girl you seek. Dark hair, like her father. Small hands, like her mother. Loved horses and her china doll. Clary – the doll? Clary.'

'Clary, yes!' exclaimed Edie, but Violet threw her a warning look.

Wait, she mouthed, and then, aloud, 'Can you let her through?'

'Do you mean to bring her home?'

Violet's voice was troubled. 'What do you mean, guide?'

'She wants to come home.'

Tears sprang into Ezra's eyes, and he fixed his gaze on the ceiling, to stop them falling.

'Let me speak with her,' said Violet.

'Let her come home, poor lamb.' Mrs Flint's voice had something uncomfortably close to malice in it. Lit by the trembling candle, her eyes seemed full of flame. 'Little lamb, soft and taken so soon.'

'Are you of God?' repeated Violet, and there were definite nerves in her now. Her hand was vibrating in Ezra's, and he resisted the urge to stroke it, to soothe her. What was she, sixteen? Barely more than a child.

Mrs Flint leant forward, pulling Edie's and Ezra's hands closer to her, hovering over the candle. Her breath made it dance. 'Light, only.'

'Let Eleanor through,' said Violet. 'Let her past.'

Mrs Flint rocked back violently onto two chair legs, hauling Edie and Ezra sideways, yanking Violet across the table.

Ezra's arm strained, he felt his grip slipping, and then the chair legs banged square onto the terracotta tiles once more.

'Mama?'

Ezra's body began to shake, and somewhere deep within his sternum a white-hot point of pain opened and spread – longing, sharp enough to cut. The voice was not a child's parody, but a child's. His child's. Their child's.

Edie convulsed. She was weeping silently, her face frozen in anguish, and Ezra opened his mouth to speak but Violet shot him a warning look.

'Is that Eleanor Griffiths, of Cambridge Gate?'

'Is my mama there?'

'Your mama, Edith?'

'Edie. Mama.'

Violet nodded at Edie, but she shook her head. Ezra understood – he felt a lump in his own throat. Violet looked instead to him, and he swallowed it down.

'Eleanor, it's Papa.'

Mrs Flint cocked her head towards him, like a dog listening to its master.

'Papa?'

'Here, sweet girl. I'm here. Me and your mama both.'

'I'm cold, Papa.'

'My girl. You mustn't be afraid.'

'Will you come and fetch me?'

Edie choked on a sob, and for the first time Ezra realised what a fool he'd been, allowing this. What possible good was there in any of it?

'It's all right, dear one. You can go. You can cross over.'

'I don't know the way.'

'The guide.' He tried to keep the question out of his voice, looking at Violet. 'Can they show you?'

There was a long, long pause.

'Eleanor? Are you still there?'

'Papa?' It was a whisper, and of such urgency Ezra was catapulted back to the previous Christmas, their last together, her hot breath on his cheek. *Papa, can I open one more gift?*

He looked for the first time since she started speaking with his daughter's voice at Mrs Flint, and immediately wished he hadn't. Her staring eyes, the crags of her lined and handsome face were as far from Eleanor's smooth cheeks as it was possible to be.

But she jerks her head to move him closer, and he obeys. 'Papa,' she whispers. 'I don't like him. He's trying to keep me here.'

Terror floods Ezra's belly. 'He?'

'Help me, Papa. Bring me home.'

Another terrible gust of cold, and the black candle goes out.

They saw Mrs Flint weekly after that. Each time, they had to go through the guide, Violet asking if he was with God, and he claiming light, only. But once Mrs Flint's trances ended and they discussed what was said, the parents and spiritualist and her assistant all agreed that something had a hold on Eleanor, and it was darkness.

Constant, jittery anxiety seized Edith and Ezra, a deep

and endless terror of what their child was experiencing. Was she in a struggle for her soul, lost in purgatory? Was this guide a demon? It was possible, even likely. Though Mrs Flint explained Eleanor had no body to corrupt, it was the fleshy possibilities of what may be happening to his daughter that consumed Ezra day and especially night. In those days he still could afford his weekly visits to the oriental dens of Harley Street, but he found himself unable to perform or enjoy the enticements of these young women, girls really, thinking of his daughter stuck in the inbetween with her hellish guide. For the first time, he considered his effect on these women with clear eyes, heard the emptiness of their laughter and saw his casual, even gentlemanly caresses as something tolerated, not invited.

Things took a desperate turn at one session, their eighth, when Mrs Flint as Eleanor had her head knocked forward against the table with a vicious and unnatural force. A red welt appeared, and with his own eyes Ezra saw something move within the rapidly swelling lump, like a burrowing insect rippling its way into the spiritualist's brain.

'This cannot stand!' he howled, forgetting himself. 'This cannot stand!'

It was Edie who suggested the spiritualist and her assistant move in, so they could talk daily with their daughter. The rates were steep, but they could afford to host them easily, at least at first. And when they began having to sell first some ornaments, then some rugs, a couple of solid gold and ugly old rings Edie never wore – what did it matter? Eleanor was afraid, and stuck with a low-voiced man none of them trusted in a place only Mrs Flint could reach. There was no price her parents would not pay.

Mrs Flint took the best guest rooms, and Violet the servants' floor. Violet was a queer fish, her narrow body slipping through their cavernous house. Her gold head dipped whenever they passed each other, but he sensed no true coyness in her, only the performance of it. When his brain allowed him brief relief from nightmares, he dreamt of her instead and woke hot and throbbing, repulsed by his desire.

It did not take long, after the cook and the maids and the manservants were dismissed, and the weekly Fortnum and Mason food deliveries cancelled, and the dining room stripped, and Ezra's father's desk carried away to a pawn shop, for them to lose any sense of what the value in anything at all was, even a stranger's soul.

Mrs Flint had been living with them two months before she acquiesced to discussing their options beyond speaking with Eleanor. She had Violet go to their house in Holborn and return with a small red-bound book embossed with a symbol that seemed inherently unholy. A book, she said, brought from Germany where it was seized from a witch's estate hundreds of years before. It was block-printed in byzantine script that Ezra understood only parts of despite being trilingual, but it was enough to convince him that it was genuine, or at least written by someone who believed what they wrote to be genuine.

The thought that Mrs Flint may not be genuine herself had long since vanished if it had been there at all. She knew too much, was as wise about their daughter as they were, and the voice – it was Eleanor who came to them, of that there was no doubt. Any scepticism was replaced by awed respect in Edie, and something close to loathing in Ezra. He hated that this woman was their only channel with Eleanor, that without her they would never have known of her torment. He even sometimes resented knowing about it at all, though that was a heartless thing to feel. What was a parent for, if not to feel their child's pain as keenly as the child themself?

The difficulty, Mrs Flint explained, was that even when they spoke with Eleanor directly, it was clear the guide was listening. Ezra envisaged a man in a dark coat and beard standing at his daughter's shoulder, his skin fearsomely pale, eyes feverishly intent.

'So whatever the plan, Eleanor cannot have knowledge of it.'

'But there can be a plan?' asked Edie, twisting her handkerchief, soiled with many days of tears. 'We can move her on.'

'We can.' Mrs Flint paused, eyes flicking between husband and wife. 'Or we could try . . . it is perhaps possible . . .'

'To bring her back?' croaked Ezra. Edie looked startled a moment, then hungry.

'We can have her back?'

'She is not yet a year gone. I have never done it,' said Mrs Flint, as uncertain as he'd ever seen her. 'I have never seen it done. But it *has* been done, in America, in Central Europe.' She tapped the blood-red book. 'In Germany.'

'That book tells you how?'

'Yes.'

'Then we must try it,' said Edie.

'But it is of course not without risks,' said Mrs Flint, eyes darting to Violet, who looked wan and strained. 'There is a reason we do not attempt such work. It takes expertise, an incredible level of knowledge and preparation—'

'We can pay,' burst out Edie, and Mrs Flint held up a hand and inclined her head in an *of course*.

'Most delicately, there is the requirement of a host.'

'Here,' said Ezra stupidly. 'We can host it, do whatever you need to, here.'

Mrs Flint looked at him pityingly and he hated her even more. 'A host for her *soul*, Mr Griffiths.'

A silence.

'I'll do it,' said Edie.

'It must be a child, around her age.'

It was a mark of how deep they were inside that black pit that Ezra did not so much as flinch.

'Willing, too. Or at least not unwilling.'

'How would we find such a child?'

'Perhaps tell them a half-truth?' said Mrs Flint. 'Not five miles from here are a dozen slums filled with children barely surviving. There are children who would like to live in this sort of luxury.'

Ezra avoided looking around at his hollowed-out dining room, shuttered and thick with their dust.

'But what do we do with them,' said Edie in a whisper. 'Does it . . . would it hurt them?'

'No,' said Mrs Flint with unearned certainty. 'Possession only pushes the individual aside. Buries them deeper. Or else we could move them over.'

'Move them?'

'Encase them, in an object. Such as a doll. Many of those coarse sorts barely have will as it is.'

Violet twitches, but only Ezra sees.

'A workhouse then,' said Edie. 'Say we are hiring a maid? Or adopt a child, from an orphanage?'

'There are paper trails, with both those routes,' said Mrs Flint. 'There is no law that addresses this directly, as there was in the witch's day. But it concerns the occult—'

'Is it Satan's work?' said Edie, who is true in her faith, believing every word when she prays each Sunday.

'Of course not. We are saving her, aren't we? It can only be to the good.'

Her voice echoes in the empty room, and none of them answer.

He begins his work. It is silently agreed that no one else can know, that their group of four is where the plan must stay, and so it is out of the question that anyone but Ezra can find the girl. He buys a jacket, a cap from a pedlar, lets his stubble grow.

Thomas, the coachman and last of their staff, takes him to Waterloo Bridge, where Ezra hires one of the various boats and takes it to one of the slums lining the river like rotten teeth. He has no luck in the snake pits behind Bankside, nor the congested gullet between Paradise Street and the water. His view of the poor, in keeping with others of his class – pity and a near-fondness for their strange ways of talking and dressing – becomes something calculated and disturbing, not that he recognises it as such. He assesses with the eye of a merchant, weighing wares, and finds no one suitable.

He passes over Jacob's Island four times, the bustling dock keeping him at bay until he asks that day's boatman, with calculated ease, where the worst of London can be found. The boatman does not think it an odd question, is well used to the poverty tourists come from the north and west. He is as happy to take their money as he would be to drown one of them.

'The Island, sir, no doubt. A cesspit. Venice of the drains.'

Ezra heads there the next day with a different boat, and he sees Mary within a half-hour of watching. That first day, he follows her home, a tingle of rightness under his breastbone. He had been waiting for someone with a sweet face and the same height, he now realises, as Eleanor. When he returns home, the four of them raise a glass of port to his success. Violet does no more than sip, and Edie brings the leftover glass to bed, her lips stained red, and when they kiss he imagines she is Violet beneath him.

The host – he eventually learns her name but tries to forget it – becomes more suitable with scrutiny. She has no parents, only a brother a few years older who works long hours. She is small, as Eleanor was, surely within months of her in age, and with all her own teeth. Her only regular appointment is with a gypsy woman of advanced years who smokes and seems half blind. The moment with the doll gives him pause – a gift suggests fondness – but he reasons that it is nearly Christmas and maybe that is a gypsy's way, to give out worthless trinkets. If she truly cared, she would surely take her away from this place. It is the worst of anywhere he's ever been other than his own grief, the stench alone like breathing the breath of a devil's dog, and his nightmares soon have Ada running through the twisting paths with the guide on her heels.

Abel answers the door. Mary sits with Clementine, weak with hunger, her games entirely in her head now. She hauls her head up, and sees a man standing there, removing a handkerchief from his face. Black overcoat. Dark beard. Pale, pale skin. She shivers though she does not know why. The man speaks low and holds out a piece of paper to Abel, who has a few letters and shows it to Mary.

'It's for you, Mary.'

She nods as though it is usual for her to receive a letter, and Abel opens it, reads the contents carefully to himself.

'It's from that traveller, Teirney. She has . . .' He pauses, looks from the man to Mary, back at the letter. 'Sent for you. Says she has work in her shop.'

Mary blinks slowly. Her stomach is so empty it has bloated.

'Is this honest?' asks Abel of the man. 'Why did she send you, not wait until the new year?'

'She trusts me,' says the man. He has the Island lilt, but it sounds oddly forced. 'She said she hopes you are enjoying your peg doll, Mary, and that there will be more treats like that. She knows the cholera is here, and wishes to have you safe and away.'

'Abel . . .'

'Your brother can follow if you do good work.'

'It says so, here,' says Abel, looking back at the letter. There is excitement in his voice, alongside suspicion. 'Is she a woman of her word?'

'A woman of honour,' says the man.

'She is,' says Mary, but she does not know why she says it. She does not want to go with this man. But he is looking around their room and Abel invites him in. She feels shy of him, though Abel has the same height, the same breadth. It is then Mary notices his boots – nice boots, clean and solid with unbroken laces. This rings wrong in her starving mind, but then he has pulled something from his pocket and she smells ham only a day or two past its best.

'Something from Teirney, to settle your stomach before our journey.'

Abel watches the meat like a stray dog as Mary takes it, tears it in half, and offers her brother half of her own before trying to return the rest to the man. He shakes his head. 'It is all for you.'

The siblings eat. Mary tries not to moan with the joy of salt and something to chew. Abel smiles at her sleepily. 'We are made, Mary. You have done us proud.'

She knows then that he has decided, and that she will agree because she trusts her brother above all else. He would not send her with this man unless he believed him. There will be more ham, more warmth at Ma Teirney's, and though this is nothing but good news, she wants to cry. Her life here has not been easy, but she does not want to leave the world of the two of them and Clementine. Whatever people say about the Island, it teaches you to value your own above all else, and Abel is all she has.

'Can he not come now?' she asks, choosing to focus on the man's coat, not his boots.

'I'm sorry, Teirney was quite clear, and you know how she gets. It will not be long, and we will come back.'

'You will stay inside?' asks Mary. 'Until we fetch you?'

'Here,' says the man, and pulls cheese from his other pocket. 'This will keep you. I'll come back, or another of us, as soon as she sends us.'

Abel helps her bundle her dress and vest into a package. There is nothing else to take but Clementine, whom she holds tight to her chest. Her brother is beaming at her, but his lip wobbles.

'Your letter, Mary,' he says, holding it out.

'You keep it. It's Ma Teirney's promise,' she replies. He hugs her briefly. She breathes him in, familiar sweat. He makes to follow them to the dock but Mary shakes her head.

'Inside,' she says. 'You promised.'

He sighs, and shakes the man's hand.

'Take care of our Mary, sir.'

It is not until they are out of sight, a few steps down the unlit street, that Abel, as tired and hungry as his sister, realises he didn't ask the stranger's name. The letter, though – he grips it in his hand – that is solid, written on thick paper in a crisp hand. It speaks of officialdom and promises, and both these Abel, wrongly or rightly, trusts despite the many disappointments of his short life. It is better she is off the Island, with Ma Teirney who has always been kind. He will see his sister again soon. He kisses the letter. He gives it his word.

Ezra cannot believe his luck, their gullibility. He did not even need to use the chloroform. It makes him feel powerful after so many months of erosion. He leads Mary back to the dock, to the boatman waiting.

'Who's this?' asks the man, himself a father to three girls.

'This is Mary,' says Ezra, roughing his voice as he had with the brother. 'She's coming to stay while the sickness is about.'

'Are you now, Mary?' asks the boatman. 'You know this man?'

Ezra bristles.

'I know his mistress,' says Mary, but she is alarmed not to recognise the boat, nor the boatman. Why would Ma Teirney hire one when she has a barge?

'Can we set off?' asks Ezra. 'I want to get her away.'

The boatman chews his tongue, looks at the dock as though someone will come forward and tell him what to do.

'There are a dozen other boats would take us,' says Ezra, feeling sweat prickle under his cap.

'Yes,' says the boatman, thinking of the price the man had named, generous even for this time of year. He could take

Christmas Day off, even. He takes up his oars, and pushes off from the dock.

Mary's unease mounts as they arrive at Waterloo Bridge to find a coach waiting for them. She cannot imagine Ma Teirney having a coach, but there is a propulsiveness to their journey now, the man's hand on her upper arm, not tight but certain. The coachman doesn't look at her, and the boatman turns his back as soon as he is paid. She feels like a coin slipped into a pocket and forgotten. She holds tighter to Clementine. *The letter*, she tells herself. *The letter.*

The man has not spoken directly to her since leaving their room. She has never been alone with a man before, nor ridden in a coach, and she notes that the leather of the seats feels buttery as she'd imagined when playing going to balls with Clementine. She watches the window, screened by thin drapes, and knows enough to know they are not going to Ma Teirney's in Clapham. Wrong side of the river, wrong sort of streets – getting wider and quieter, more exclusive, until they are in the other world of London that she has never had cause to visit. She feels herself shrinking, no longer a coin but a piece of lint, and when they pull up outside a grand house on a grand street, it is not even terror she feels, but exhaustion, a learned helplessness at being tossed from place to place all her life. Without Abel to steer her, she feels rudderless.

She steps from the coach and stumbles. A woman's hand steadies her, a slim, well-dressed woman with tangled hair and tired, kind eyes, who slips a hand around her shoulders and guides her towards a shiny painted front door, and into a huge and empty hallway lit sparsely with cheap tallow so it smells like the grocer's downstairs. The door closes behind and it is much darker. The man and woman speak in whispers.

'She is perfect.'

'I told you so.'

'Did you use—'

'No, no need.'

'She seems . . .'

'Hungry only.'

'Are you hungry, Mary?'

How does the stranger know her name? How do both these strangers know her name? But she nods, because to be held like this woman is holding her is soothing, reaching back into some deep and primal need.

She is taken to a large and dirty kitchen, pans piled around the sink, and carved more old ham. She eats and eats, and it brings her slightly to herself. The two strangers watch her, the woman's arms wrapped around her own narrow waist, the man very still.

'Is that your doll?' asks the woman.

Mary snatches Clementine up from the table.

'I won't take her from you. You're very quiet, Mary? Were you taught not to speak to strangers?'

The woman sits across from her. The table is too small for the room, Mary notices, and just like the man with his fine boots and horrid overcoat, this woman and her pearl buttons and unbrushed hair, the whole place has the sense of abandonment.

'That's good if so,' continues the woman. 'But my name is Edith, and this is Ezra, and this is our home. So now we are not strangers, are we?'

Mary chews.

'You'll be wondering why you are here. The first thing you must know is we will not hurt you. We are parents, to a much-loved girl your age, and we would never hurt a child.'

Mary is not comforted. She eats more.

'We want to look after you. We have a gift for you.'

She nods at Ezra and he fetches something from the dresser. It is a doll in a green dress with a painted china face and tight chestnut curls. She knew a girl in the workhouse with curls like that, who sold her hair. Perhaps this doll has it, perhaps this is that girl's hair. The woman clearly expects her to take the doll, but it makes her feel sick. Edith sets it down on the table instead.

'Her name is Clary. She can be friends with your doll. What's her name?'

'Clementine.'

'A lovely name.'

Mary looks into Edith's face. She does seem very kind. Mary is good with faces, and just as she does not like Ezra, she does like Edith.

'Thank you.'

'You have very good manners, Mary.'

'Thank you.'

'Now, I know it is always scary in a new place. But we have a room, a lovely room for a girl. You will sleep there tonight and tomorrow we can talk more, all right?'

Mary is sure it is not night-time yet, but she is so tired. She lets Edith lead her up a winding wooden staircase – Ezra stays behind, thanks be – and into a room with a high ceiling and thick curtains at the windows. This room seems untouched by the purge evident elsewhere. There is a bed, big and soft, and a wardrobe of clothes, and a nightdress draped over a child-size chair.

'Would you like me to help you change? To put you to bed?'

Mary shakes her head.

'Very well.' She sounds disappointed. 'There is water there, for washing. Milk there, for drinking. Sleep safe.'

She sets the doll down on the bed, and closes the door. Mary hears a soft *click*. A key turned in the lock. The milk tastes sour, thick on her tongue. She looks at the nightdress – it is too small for her, she can see at a glance, and too white and frilly. She would not want lace around her neck while she sleeps.

She moves the doll off the bed onto the chair, and lies down atop the covers fully dressed, Clementine tight against her face. She has never slept without Abel beside her, or, in the workhouse, one of the girls. Despite this, despite it all, Mary sleeps.

'Broth only, I said,' snaps Mrs Flint, downstairs in the repurposed dining room. 'She must be kept pure.'

'She was starving,' says Edie. 'Ham was fastest.'

'So much the better. It must be easy to conquer her spirit. It is kinder for all involved. The chloroform would have helped too.'

'I thought it best—' begins Ezra.

'Please,' says Mrs Flint. 'Do not falter now. If you had given her broth and chloroform, we could even have done this tonight.'

'I thought she must be willing. I thought you wanted her to become close to the doll. She would not touch Clary, only that peg doll.'

'We can spare a couple more days. But it must be before a year since Eleanor's passing. Broth only, and a little chloroform at night. Did you place the doll in bed with her? Good.'

'Drugging a child—'

'Whatever means necessary, yes, Mr Griffiths?'

He had used those words. He has come this far, done this much. The adrenalin of his success has not left him. He nods.

'Is she well?' asks Violet, speaking for the first time in days, it seems.

'Hungry, but healthy,' says Edie. 'She has a sweet face, a sweet nature. You did so well, Ezra.'

He blooms under her praise, is able to ignore Violet's look of distaste. She is the weak link here, he knows it. And more than that, he has seen her leaving the house at night. Does she have a fancy man, another place of work? But whatever Mrs Flint has over her, even if it is just a portion of the considerable wage they are paying, has held her tongue so far.

'Can we speak with Eleanor?' asks Edie.

'Not tonight,' says Mrs Flint. 'We will have one attempt at this. The guide must not be wise to what we are planning. The merest hint, and he may keep Eleanor from us.'

'Won't he guess something is amiss, if we do not speak?'

'Time does not pass the same way in the spirit world. A day or two will make no difference.'

Edie's eyes fill, but Ezra grasps her hand. 'Not long, my love. Not much longer now.'

The next two days are a haze to them all. The house becomes encased by snowfall, thick and cushioning, and Mary feels encased too, because of the broth and the chloroform. She falls asleep holding Clementine, and wakes with Clary tight in her arms. She does not fully understand what is happening to her, but she resists as far as she can, pushing the doll away and holding only Clementine willingly, eating as little as possible and not wearing any of the outfits Edith offers her.

She meets Mrs Flint and Violet on her third day in the house. They visit her in the kitchen while Mary, still groggy from her mid-morning sleep, is taking tiny, birdlike sips of broth. She tries to concentrate on Edith's introductions, but her head feels full of wool. The woman has very green eyes, and the girl will not look at her.

'It is lovely to meet you, Mary. Did you know what a lucky girl you are, to be chosen by Mr and Mrs Griffiths? They had a daughter, and they want to make a new one. Wouldn't you like that, Mary, to live in this fine house with these fine and loving people?'

No, thinks Mary. 'I want my brother.'

'Your brother will be well. He can look after himself. It is always easier for boys. And that doll, Mary, what a fine doll!' She taps the china-faced doll that Edith has placed on the table next to her. 'Don't you love Clary?'

Mary shakes her head. 'I want Abel. I want my brother.'

'That's not polite, is it, Mary?'

But Mary doesn't want to be polite. Her hand shakes, and she drops the spoon. Broth splatters Clary's fine sage gown, and Edith whimpers.

'All right,' says Mrs Flint, wiping her palms on her skirts. 'I think this may be the best we can get. Violet?'

The girl crosses to the sink and does something out of Mary's sight. She senses, like a cat, an approaching attack, but is too heavy-limbed to so much as stand. She feels something cover her mouth and nose, smells a sweet sharpness, and fades faster than a snuffed candle.

Mary is in a dark, dark room, and the adults all have very bright eyes, like animals in a forest. Her arms are so heavy, her legs rubber. She is sitting upright in a chair, is being held by rope, the way they slept in the worst of the boarding houses. She tries to speak but her tongue is a stone.

Violet sits one side of her at the round table, Mrs Flint the other. Clementine lies on the table before Mrs Flint, and Clary is beside her, laid out as though ready for burial. She sees how small and shabby her peg doll looks next to the china one, and feels a pang of love for her, for Ma Teirney who gave her to her. Edith and Ezra sit across from her, and she hates them as much as she hates the woman and the girl and the chestnut-haired doll.

There are other things on the table. A red book, white powder in a pattern, a small glass bottle of water. Another glass bottle full of something thick and shadowy – is that blood? As if in answer, the crook of her arm itches. Is that *her* blood?

'Ready? Mr and Mrs Griffiths – your places please.'

The couple stand, and move around the table. Each places a hand on Mary's shoulders, and she has not the strength to shrug them off.

Violet lights another candle. This candle is black, lights with a hiss. She looks like she is swallowing down vomit. She and Mrs Flint join hands around the three of them.

'Ten . . .' she counts, 'nine . . . eight . . .'

At 'one', Mrs Flint begins to twitch, to shake. Her head rolls in a slim figure of eight, and when she opens her eyes, there is something new in them. Something hard, and dancing. Sly.

'Hello.'

'Hello,' says Violet. 'May we speak with Eleanor?'

'No parents today?' asks the voice, which is a man's. Mary goes very still, a rabbit listening for a fox.

'Just us,' says Violet.

'Eleanor might not want to talk to just you.'

'Can we ask her?'

'You're very polite today,' the voice purrs.

'Is Eleanor there?'

'She's always here.'

'Mama?' A girl now, speaking through Mrs Flint. Mary nearly swoons.

'Mama will come.' Violet speaks the next words quiet and quick. 'Eleanor, I need you to say something, all right?'

Violet nods at Mr Griffiths, who opens the red book and holds a page down, his other hand still on Mary's shoulder. Mrs Griffiths responds to the same cue, licking her finger and dipping it first in the white powder, then pressing it to Clementine's smooth face, then Mary's forehead. Some grains trickle down to her lips, and Mary tastes salt.

Violet begins to chant. *'Te rogo, qui infernales partes tenes—'*

Almost instantly, Mary feels herself fading again. It is not like before, with what she is sure they added to her broth and certainly what Violet used in the kitchen, but rather a splitting, a peeling. She remembers putting her fingernail into the Christmas clementine, the waxy shell coming off. She is being shucked from herself, and her vision splits.

She sees the room, and she sees mist. In the mist there is a girl with Edith's eyes and Ezra's dark hair, and behind her stands a man who looks like Ezra had in their doorway. The girl is mouthing words that Mary can't hear. She feels herself pooling away, like someone has pulled a stopper on her essence, and she floods into something wooden and smooth and known. *No.* She is weaker, weaker.

The man behind the girl is becoming monstrous. He is so pale, and his eyes are stretching wider, wide as mouths, eyelashes pointed teeth. She cannot hear Violet any more. The man is reaching out to her now. He is loosening his grip on

Eleanor – for this is who this is, Mary realises – and Eleanor is becoming fainter while Mary is stronger here in the mist. It hurts now, like forcing through some tough fabric that won't give.

In the other place she is, she sees herself. She is fitting. There is blood on her chin – she has bitten her tongue. Edith and Ezra are grim and holding her down in the chair, and Mrs Flint's head is whipping back and forth, her hands free and flying through the air – Violet is not there. She is ripping the curtains from the window, running outside. She calls over her shoulder, 'I will fetch him, child, I will find Abel!'

'Broken!' shrieks Mrs Flint. 'Broken!'

A wrench in her soul. Pain unlike anything earthly, a deep, deep sorrow. Eleanor screams in the mist, a high, unyielding sound, and it is Mary screaming too. Now Edith, and Mrs Flint. Mrs Flint's sleeve is aflame.

'He is loose,' she says, and slumps forward, the flame catching her hair. In the street outside, Violet is screaming bloody murder. Mary is stuck between Clementine and the mist and herself, and she can see in thirds:

the ceiling with a corner of burning hair
the man fading from the mist as Eleanor weeps
and her own face in the bare window, a man
behind her with a black beard and pale, pale skin

Mrs Flint is not stirring, and the holy water Edith throws over her hair does nothing to quell the flame. Edith snatches for the book. It too is alight, her hand burns, but she searches for the words that will bring her daughter back.

'Help me, Ezra!'

But her husband is staring, horrified, at his reflection in the window, at his hand on Mary's shoulder – for it *is* still Mary, but where is her Eleanor? In the doll? In the other place?

'Eleanor!'

There are people outside. Neighbours' servants, neighbours not far behind, staring in at the whole sorry tableau. Edith drops the book, properly alight now, and picks up Clary, whose hair is starting to singe. She runs outside with the doll, rolls her in the snow.

'Eleanor?' she asks it, as her neighbours crowd around. Her china face is cracked, one glass eye stuck open, but Edith holds her tenderly, looks up at the window.

The whole room is aflame. She hears a child coughing, sees Mary brought out and wrapped in a blanket. She wants to tear the girl's heart out and pour in whatever wisps of soul are caught in Clary, stuff her full of her daughter like a straw mattress, and lie down in the snow with her and never let her go. Where is Ezra?

There is a man in the window. He has Ezra's height and his beard. Ezra's pale skin and his black hair But his eyes are stretched wide as mouths, and with all his teeth, he smiles.

INFERNO

Laura Shepherd-Robinson

I

Jasper Godolphin climbed out of the hired carriage, alert for any sign of impending ambush. It would be just his luck to wind up dead in an Italian ditch. He could see nobody lurking in the shadows, only the coachman on his box, and the guard who had just opened the carriage door. *Must have given them the slip back in Brescia.* He grinned at his own cunning. Maybe at last his luck was about to turn.

Lake Garda in the moonlight was flat as a beaten silver coin. About three hundred yards from the shore, a large white villa clung to the side of a small island. Max had said in his letter that it had once been a monastery. Jasper made out a tower and what looked like terraced gardens.

The guard dragged his trunk down to a wooden jetty. Fixed to the top of one of the red-and-white-striped poles was a large bronze bell. The guard pulled on a length of rope and the bell tolled mournfully. Then he hurried back towards the carriage, without waiting for his tip.

'Hey,' Jasper cried, not wanting to be left alone in the dark and the cold. If his enemies caught up with him out here, he wouldn't stand a chance. But the driver and the guard seemed in great haste to be off, and Jasper watched in dismay as the carriage rattled away down the road. He stood shivering on the jetty for some minutes, his breath coming in silver clouds, until eventually he glimpsed something moving out on the lake. A queer sort of boat: long, thin and black, with an ornate prow. A figure stood upon the stern, sculling the craft by means of a single, long-handled oar.

As the boat neared the jetty, Jasper called out to him. 'My name's Godolphin. I'm a friend of Maximillian Cavendish-Green. You are expecting me?'

'*Signore*,' the man answered in a low, guttural voice, his face concealed within the deep folds of his hooded cloak.

With some pushing on Jasper's part and pulling on the part of the boatman, they manoeuvred his trunk into the vessel, and Jasper clambered in after it. Sitting back on a fur-lined seat, his relief assuaged the knife-edge of the December air. *Good luck to his enemies finding him out here!*

The boatman was short, but strong, his deep strokes steadying the vessel against the deceptive currents. As they drew closer to the island, Jasper observed that the villa was in a sorry state of repair: the paint cracked and blistered, the statues mildewed, the gardens overgrown. But it was cheap, Max had said, a good place for a man in a spot of bother to lie low for a time.

A flight of lichened waterstairs led up to the villa's grand portico, and the moment the boat drew alongside them Jasper bounded out in his eagerness to find his friend. The doors of the villa opened, and the slender figure of a woman stood framed in a glow of light.

'Signor Godolphin?' Her English was lightly accented.

'My name is Luciana Mondragone. Welcome to the Villa Principe.'

Jasper kissed her hand, making a surreptitious assessment as she ushered him into a wide hall lit with lamps. Max had said that the mistress of the house was a hot little piece, descended from a long line of minor Venetian nobility. She was about twenty-five, Jasper judged, her dark hair coiled and pinned, her forehead sloped like a leopard's, her eyes serene. He approved of her simple lawn gown with its low, scooped neckline, a jewelled crucifix nestling between her rather fine breasts.

Jasper removed his fur-trimmed cloak, smoothed his duck-egg blue frockcoat, and gave her the famous Godolphin grin. He was rising forty now, a little greyer than he'd like – but ageing well, unlike this hall, with its fading frescoes.

'Have you ever visited the lakes before?' Luciana asked.

'Not since my Grand Tour, back in 1762. Max and I did the lot. Venice, Florence, Rome.' He looked about him. 'Where is the old rogue? Don't tell me he's already in bed? It's not yet eleven.'

Luciana stepped back as the boatman staggered past with Jasper's trunk. He was older than Jasper had anticipated: lean, brown and gnome-like, his muscles bulging beneath his dun woollen coat.

'I regret to say that Signor Cavendish-Green was called away for a few nights on urgent business,' Luciana said. 'He asked me to look after you until his return.'

What business could Max possibly have here in Venetia?

The news disgruntled Jasper. He'd been looking forward to piquet and port. Knowing Max, he was probably chasing a woman. Stealing another glance at his hostess, he wondered if his friend had already tried his hand there and been rebuffed. The thought made him smile, his disgruntlement already forgotten. A day or two alone with Luciana need not be a chore.

She opened a door. 'Come into the library, sir. You must be tired after your journey. Giovanni will bring wine.'

The library had a barrel-vaulted ceiling, the shelves holding many thousands of old volumes. Jasper was relieved to see a handsome blaze of logs in the vast blackened fireplace. Above it hung a painting in the style of the Italian masters: a concentric spiral of hellfire, burning sinners and grinning demons.

'By one of my ancestors,' Luciana said, noticing his interest. 'It depicts the Nine Circles of Hell.'

'Dante!' Jasper cried. 'I read *The Divine Comedy* at Oxford. I suppose that fellow there is the ferryman of the dead?' He pointed to a hooded figure, and declaimed dramatically: 'Abandon all hope, ye who enter here!' He studied her face to see if the quotation had impressed her.

She inclined her head gravely, as Giovanni, the same old fellow who had rowed him across the lake, limped in with a bottle. Jasper drank greedily, the wine cold, yellow and sweet.

'All that dwelling upon sin,' he said, rising to study the painting more closely. 'I always thought old Dante must have had a fondness for it, deep down. Perhaps your ancestor did too?' He raised his eyebrows at a sea of naked figures, writhing and burning in what he presumed to be the Circle of Lust.

'All are tempted by sin.' Luciana touched her jewelled cross. 'The Lord sends such trials to test our resolve.'

Intriguing. Jasper relished the prospect of a battle for her virtue. How delicious it would be to have her in his bed by the time Max returned.

'As for the artist,' Luciana went on, 'my ancestor was acquainted with sin only too well. There is a sad story connected to this painting.'

Jasper cocked his head invitingly. 'Oh? Tell me more.'

But the light seemed to dim in her eyes. 'Perhaps tomorrow.'

II

Jasper awoke to a strange sense of melancholy. It took him a moment to realise that he had been dreaming about Helen, his first love. She had been sitting on the floor weeping – so very vivid, he half-expected to see her sitting there now. Helen had cried like that on the day they had been so cruelly parted, her wide blue eyes brimming with reproach.

As Jasper lay there, lamenting this ancient injustice, the events of the previous night flooded back to him. After their conversation about her ancestor's painting, Luciana had retired to bed. Jasper had stayed to finish the wine, and then that odd gnome of a manservant had shown him upstairs to this bedroom at the pinnacle of the villa's tower. And very sumptuous it was too. A Persian carpet upon the freshly scrubbed boards. A vast four-poster bed with lace curtains. And an ornate desk with a silver inkwell and marbled Venetian paper for his letters. Jasper rose from the bed to open the curtains. Shivering in his nightshirt, he drank in the views of the lake in the morning mist.

He took his time over his toilette, thinking of Luciana's smile, and then hastened downstairs in search of her. Rather to his disappointment, he discovered a note addressed to him on a table in the hall. Luciana wrote that she was busy with engagements that day, but would see him later at dinner. In the meantime, he should feel at liberty to explore the house, and would find refreshments laid out in the blue salon.

Feeling ravenous, Jasper went looking for this repast, wandering through a series of palatial yet shabby rooms. There was no sign of Giovanni, and nor did Jasper encounter any other servants. It was decidedly odd. A house of this size should have a dozen servants at least. He presumed Luciana too must be down on her luck.

In the blue salon, he discovered a basket of fresh bread and Italian sausage, a sheep's cheese sitting in a dish of green oil and herbs, and a bowl of black olives, shiny as iridescent beetles. Jasper devoured everything, washing it down with several glasses of the yellow wine.

Sated, he imagined his enemies searching the Brescian countryside for him in vain. It brought a broad smile to his lips. When Max returned, they'd depart for the isle of Capri, where they hoped to find their long-lost friend, Old Chum. The triumvirate reunited! Visions of lemon groves and sybaritic delights had kept Jasper going on that cold, uncomfortable and at times – though he'd admit it only to himself – rather frightening journey from London to the villa. Now his luck seemed to be looking up. The villa might have seen better days, but Luciana was a perfect peach. Jasper sat there imagining all the different ways he might set about the plucking.

How delightful Luciana looked when she appeared downstairs that evening, three red silk roses woven into her hair. The dining room had Tuscan red walls, and a table that might have seated twenty. Giovanni brought in a platter of suckling pig and roasted artichokes, and Jasper had to concede that the old fellow was not a bad cook.

Luciana smiled at him across the table, the candlelight catching her jewelled cross. 'I hope you were not too lonely today.'

Jasper met her gaze boldly. 'I should have enjoyed it rather better in your company.'

'Forgive my neglect,' she said. 'At this time of year, I like to spend my days at prayer.'

'What? The whole day?' Jasper was all for religion, but this was a bit much. Then a happy thought occurred to him: perhaps she'd been wrestling with a sudden feeling of temptation?

'It is the second day of the Christmas Novena,' she said. 'The Italian Advent is a time for reflection and prayer. Nine days to think about one's obligations – both to the living and the dead.'

Well, that was hardly cheerful. Max had presumed in his letters that Luciana was a widow, and Jasper wondered if she was still mourning her husband. As a widower himself, he was familiar with grief. And yet he felt that dwelling overly upon one's loss was an insult to the dead, to whom a man owed a determination to go on living.

They ate in companionable silence and when they had finished, Giovanni brought in bowls of China oranges and walnuts.

'Signor Cavendish-Green told me that you are heading for Capri?' Luciana said.

'That's right. Our friend Cholmondeley is living there. Do you remember him? He stayed at your house a couple of years ago. That's how Max knew where to find you.'

'I remember Signor Cholmondeley,' Luciana said. 'He sold houses in London, only the houses didn't exist, and everyone who'd invested in his company ended up poor.'

'He was unlucky, that's all,' Jasper said uneasily. It was unlike Old Chum to be so forthcoming about his affairs. Hastening to change the subject, he suggested that they retire to the library. 'Weren't you going to tell me the story behind that painting of yours?'

They sat in the same chairs as they had the night before, looking up at the painting.

'My ancestor was a devout Christian, as well as a talented artist,' Luciana said. 'His wife died young, leaving him to raise their daughter alone. He loved the girl dearly, but he was also obsessive about his work. For days, he would shut himself away in his studio, that same room in the tower where you are presently staying. The summer he worked upon this painting, a young man, a distant cousin, came to visit. The daughter caught his eye and over the weeks that followed, she fell in love. When her suitor departed for his home in Florence, she believed he would soon return to ask for her hand. Only it transpired that he was engaged to another woman, and by that time, she knew she was carrying his child.'

'What a blackguard!' Jasper exclaimed – and he meant it. Hadn't he often taken Max and Old Chum to task for just this sort of scrape? Widows and actresses were one thing, but a man who'd ruin an innocent girl of good family deserved the horsewhip!

'When she confessed her shame to her father, he was overcome with guilt and rage. He strangled his daughter, and then threw himself to his death from the tower. His penultimate act was to paint himself and his daughter into his painting.' Luciana rose and pointed to one of the dozens of contorted figures suffering torment. 'Here you see the poor girl, burning in the Circle of Lust, cradling her unborn child. And here is her father in the Circle of Violence, enduring the eternal damnation of the murderers and suicides.'

Jasper didn't like this nasty little story and he was sorry he'd asked. 'All this happened in my room? It's a good thing I don't believe in ghosts.'

He'd been attempting to lighten the mood, but Luciana gazed at him rather earnestly. 'There is a chapel on the north side of the island, should you feel afraid.'

'Afraid?' he exclaimed. 'It'll take more than a dark tale to scare old Jasper.'

His words seemed to disappoint her. 'Be sure to ask me for the key to the chapel, should you change your mind.'

III

Rosamond was sitting on the end of his bed, weeping. She had her face in her hands, but Jasper recognised her red ringlets and pale skin. He reached out a hand to touch her shoulder, and she turned to look at him in outrage. 'Why did you do it?' she said. 'Why, Jasper?'

He was stammering an explanation, how none of it had been his fault, when she drew back her hand and slapped his face. The shock of it startled him awake, and it took him a moment or two to come back to himself. He had been dreaming again – and yet it had felt so damn real! His cheek smarted from the slap even now.

He'd liked Rosamond, a young widow he'd met at the theatre in Chichester, back in '76. She'd had a waist only a little larger than the span of his hands, and soft pink nipples he'd liked to kiss. How strange it was to have two such similar dreams in as many nights, when normally he hardly gave old affairs of the heart a second thought.

He dressed and went downstairs, again finding the villa deserted, more food laid out in the blue salon. From somewhere outside, he could hear the sounds of carpentry and went to investigate. A door from the rear hall led out onto a terrace overlooking a herb garden. Most of the plants were dead, their skeletal remains casting odd shadows in the pale light.

Three buildings along the island's shore were separated by clumps of sorry-looking palm trees: a boathouse, a ramshackle outbuilding, and the little white chapel Luciana had mentioned. Jasper followed the sound of sawing to the outbuilding, where he discovered Giovanni hunched over a carpenter's bench.

'*Signore.*' The manservant did not look pleased to see him.

'That town over there.' Jasper pointed to a lakeside settlement in the distance. 'What's it called?'

'Bardolino.'

'Is that where you go to buy provisions? Or do they bring them out here?'

'*Signore?*'

'Keep an eye out for me, will you, the next time you go ashore?' Jasper said. 'Any redcoat officers hanging about, making a nuisance of themselves. Asking questions about me, that sort of thing.'

Douglas Hamilton was a persistent fellow. Jasper had learned that to his cost. He wouldn't make the same mistake again.

Giovanni stared at him unblinking. 'You want to find friends? English soldiers?'

'They're not English, they're Scottish, and they're no friends of mine. If anyone asks, you never heard of me. You got that?'

Giovanni inclined his head. '*Signore.*'

'Good man.' Jasper fished in his pocket for a coin and when the manservant made no move to take it, placed it on the end of his bench. He had taken a few paces back towards the villa when a troubling thought occurred to him. 'I say, could those men find a boat for hire in Bardolino? Or somewhere else? Might they come out here to the island?'

Giovanni shook his head. 'Nobody give them boat. Not to come here.'

'Good then,' Jasper said, both relieved and a little puzzled by the man's conviction.

The Romish interior of the chapel, a riot of frescoes and coloured marbles, stood in stark contrast to the plainness of the building outside. Several giltwood pews faced a marble altar and a painted statue of a weeping virgin. In the tortured expressions of the martyred saints upon the walls, Jasper thought he recognised the hand of the same artist behind the painting in the library.

He'd hoped to find Luciana here, but there was no sign of

her. Deciding to await her return, Jasper circled the chapel, admiring the murals, rehearsing a few favourite lines he thought might amuse. After about ten minutes, Luciana came through a door to the left of the altar. A broad smile broke over her face as she caught sight of him. 'You came.'

Her evident delight spurred him on. 'Do you invite all your guests to chapel?' he asked, with a flirtatious lilt. 'Or only the dreadful sinners, like myself?'

She had turned to lock the door behind her. 'All are welcome, but I regret to say few come.'

They sat side by side in one of the pews, Luciana's head bent in prayer. A chapel was an odd place for a tryst, Jasper reflected, but then Luciana was no ordinary woman. She possessed grace and intelligence, and she seemed genuinely to care about the health of his soul. For a moment, Jasper entertained the possibility of marrying again, playing the Italian count out here on the lake. There were worse ways to live.

'How long have you lived here all alone?' he asked. 'Apart from Giovanni, I mean?' It was a polite way of enquiring about her husband.

'For too long,' she said, and Jasper thought he glimpsed a trace of yearning in her eyes. She wanted him, he thought, even if she couldn't yet admit it to herself.

Carpe diem and all that. Jasper pulled her towards him, covering her mouth with his own. She struggled a little, but he could tell it was half-hearted. He was enjoying the taste of her lips, still waiting for her to surrender to her secret longing, when he was seized roughly from behind and thrown to the floor, his head striking the flagstones with a crack. Dazed, a trickle of blood smarting one eye, Jasper looked up into the furious face of Giovanni.

Following his mistress's curt instructions, Giovanni helped Jasper to the sofa in the library. Luciana joined them there with a basin of water and a towel, but disappeared again before Jasper could ascertain her feelings about what had just happened in the chapel. He dabbed ineffectually at the cut on his head, while Giovanni poured him a glass.

'I wouldn't have hurt her,' Jasper said, seeking to mollify the fellow. 'You know what women can be like. Sometimes they don't know what they want. But I'd never have forced her.'

Giovanni's face, when he turned, held an expression of such startling malevolence it took Jasper's breath away. He half-feared that the manservant might strike him again, but Giovanni simply hobbled from the room.

Jasper took a gulp of port. Surely he hadn't misread the signs? Luciana was probably just embarrassed that their moment of passion had been witnessed by her servant. Nevertheless, he thought, perhaps he should take dinner in his room tonight. Give everybody a chance to cool off. His head was pounding remorselessly, and he closed his eyes.

He must have drifted off, because when he opened them again it was nearly dark outside. The room was cold and dim, and as Jasper debated whether or not to call Giovanni to light a fire, he was startled to realise that he was not alone.

A young woman was seated upon one of the chairs by the fireplace. Even in the half-light, Jasper could see that she was a pretty little piece. Her hair the colour of lemons with a natural curl; a skinny waif of a thing, but still rather lovely. He presumed she must be a friend of Luciana's.

'Madam,' he said. 'I don't believe I've had the pleasure.'

She turned. 'You don't remember me, Jasper?'

An English accent. Jasper studied her, confused. She was toying with the end of something tied around her neck, flicking it back and forth, distracting him. There was something familiar about her, but he couldn't quite place it.

'Forgive me,' he said. 'Have we met before?'

'On a day I'll never forget,' she said. 'It was supposed to be the happiest of my life.'

The way she said it gave Jasper pause, and a memory suddenly surfaced: a girl standing in a church, tiny and fair, just like this one. What had been her name? Emily? Amelia? But it couldn't be her. She was . . .

The girl rose and came towards him, swinging the thing around her neck, which he now saw was a length of rope. 'Why did you do it, Jasper? Why didn't you warn me?'

Jasper let out a faint moan, burrowing his face into a cushion. When he dared to look again, she was gone. He shuddered with relief. That whole wretched business with Max and the girl made him feel sick to think of it even now. Dear God, but she had looked so damn real! Muttering a prayer beneath his breath, he drained his port.

IV

Jasper ran his fingers through Luciana's unpinned hair. They were lying upon his bed, her eyes glazed with desire. Hot and primed, Jasper couldn't wait any longer. As he pushed inside her, she moaned, moving against him. So warm and so wet – and yet that wetness was suddenly everywhere, thick and viscous and unnatural. Startled, Jasper pulled away, gazing in horror at the blood that coated her thighs and the sheets and his member.

'Luciana!' he cried.

Only the girl in his bed wasn't Luciana, it was Angelica. Her pupils were unnaturally still, her skin so very grey, and when Jasper touched her face, it was cold as a tomb.

Wrenching his hand away violently, he lost his balance and toppled out of the bed. He lay there dazed on the floor for a moment, and then grabbed the sheet to wipe the blood from his body. Except there was no blood. Not on him. Not on the sheet. Summoning the strength of will to look, he examined the bed. No Angelica. No Luciana. No sign that any woman had ever been there.

Those damn dreams! Visions! Whatever you wanted to call them. Jasper had never known anything like it before.

He grimaced at his bloodshot eyes and bloated face as he attended to his toilette, all sorts of outlandish thoughts running through his mind. Had he been seeing ghosts? Had someone laid a curse on him? Had Douglas Hamilton paid some Scottish hag to do it?

Yet as the day progressed, fortified by several glasses of wine, reason prevailed. His humours must be unbalanced, he decided, probably due to the dampness of the lake air. Then that blow to the head yesterday – what did they call it? Concussion? It was hardly surprising that his sleep had been disturbed.

By dinner, he was in markedly better spirits, determined not to let a few bad dreams put him off his stride. He gazed across the table at Luciana, trying to gauge her mood. 'That business in the chapel yesterday. I hope I didn't overstep the mark. The truth is, my judgement momentarily deserted me. My only excuse is that I've not been sleeping well.'

She gave him a long, considered look. 'Bad dreams?'

'As it happens, yes,' Jasper said, relieved, not to say encouraged, by her evident sympathy.

'This island can have a strange effect upon a person's soul,' Luciana said. 'Our seclusion sometimes prompts an examination of the conscience. Prayer can be a great consolation, I find. If you like, we could go to the chapel now.'

Scene of yesterday's humiliation? Not bloody likely. Besides, his conscience was clear. With Helen, his first love, it was her father who'd been at fault. He'd heard some unkind stories about Jasper in London and put a halt to their engagement – all deuced unfair. The fellow had shown not one ounce of gentlemanly understanding.

Whereas with dear Angelica, it had been nobody's fault, least of all his own. Hadn't he stepped up gallantly when she'd discovered she was with child? Offered to take full responsibility for her and the baby? As women do, she'd wanted to be married, but at that time he'd had expectations from an uncle on his mother's side, who would have cut him off if he'd wedded an actress. When Angelica had died in childbirth – inwardly Jasper shuddered, remembering the blood from his dream – he had mourned her and the baby honestly, for several weeks.

When it came to Rosamond, the pretty widow from Chichester, Jasper conceded that perhaps he bore some part of the responsibility. Yet all he'd done was let Old Chum read her letters. She'd had a way with words, and it had all been rather a jape. Only somehow – his memory of the day was a fog – those blasted letters had got around their club. The first he'd known of it was when poor Rosamond had confronted him in tears, saying she was no longer welcome in polite society. He'd felt wretched about the entire episode and had apologised profusely, but it wasn't as though her shame had ever been his intent.

Then there was Max's girl. Emily? Amelia? There was no denying that had been a bad business. Yet Jasper hadn't known what the other two had planned. He'd merely shown up at the church to find Max and the girl before the altar, and Old Chum got up like a parson. He'd not wanted any part of that deceit, and yet Max had put him in a tricky spot. Sometimes Jasper wondered if he'd been unlucky in his choice of friends. As for what the girl had done to herself afterwards, it could hardly be laid at his door. Jasper drank deeply from his glass, irritated that his thoughts had strayed so far from the point.

To Jasper's great disappointment, Luciana retired to bed shortly after dinner. Not wanting to be left alone with Giovanni, he asked him to leave the bottle and dismissed him for the night. Hopefully everyone would be in better spirits tomorrow. He had been too forward with Luciana in the chapel. He saw that now. She needed a gentler hand to coax her towards her desires. Tomorrow he would speak of fresh shoots and new beginnings. Learning to love again after loss, that sort of thing.

His wine was thick with sediment, and Jasper wondered if Giovanni had chosen the bottle deliberately. The man was clearly jealous of any man who even looked at Luciana! Rising, he went to the bureau by the fireplace and opened a few drawers at random, looking for a funnel or some blotting paper. As he rooted through a jumble of old pipes and sticks of sealing wax, something caught his eye. A letter addressed to Max. It must have arrived at the villa after his friend's departure. Presumably Luciana had put it here for safekeeping until his return.

Oh ho! Jasper thought. *Bet it's from a woman!* He decided to take a peek. Max had opened enough of his own letters back when they were students at Oxford.

Returning to his chair, Jasper soon discovered, to his disappointment, that the letter was not from a woman at all, but from a London physician named Doctor Lockwood.

As a curative for nightmares, I am reluctant to recommend laudanum, due to its liability to form a habit in the user. A forbearance of alcohol is advised, though I can imagine how you will take that! As for your hallucinations, I venture to suggest that they are caused by your disrupted sleep, and should you successfully counter the one ailment, you will attain respite from the other.

Of far greater concern to me are your melancholic thoughts – particularly the direction in which they pertain. Not least, because they seem so out of character. Improved sleep will undoubtedly help, as will a daily constitutional, but I wonder if you are also in need of bleeding and a dose of arsenic. I advise you to consult a local physician post haste.

Jasper frowned. Max had been having bad dreams and visions too! And what was all this about melancholic thoughts? 'Out of character' was putting it mildly. Max had never had a melancholic thought in his life! Was that why he'd changed their plan? Had he gone to seek out a local physician? But then why hadn't he returned?

As Jasper sat there, mulling these questions, he came to the uncomfortable conclusion that he had been more than a little complacent about the well-being of his friend.

V

Jasper barely slept that night, tossing and turning, fretting about Max. His headache was compounded by a relentless scratching in his room, which he put down to mice or rats or owls in the roof. At least he was spared any more bad dreams.

In the morning, he rose with a fierce determination to *do* something. If Max was in trouble, disordered in his mind, then he might need help. Jasper wondered if there might be some clue to his whereabouts in his room.

He wandered the upper floors of the villa for nearly half an hour. Yet every bedroom he entered appeared to be uninhabited: the shutters barred, the furniture draped in bedsheets. Convinced he must have missed a staircase or a door that led to another part of the house, Jasper retraced his steps until he came to a narrow door that he had at first taken to be a cupboard. Inside, he discovered a little room stacked with travelling trunks and boxes. To his surprise, the trunk nearest the door had a brass plaque set into the lid engraved with Max's initials: MCG.

Kneeling, Jasper unbuckled the straps and lifted the lid. Everything inside was neatly ordered: Max's embroidered frockcoats, his silver brushes, his bottles of scent, and the polished mahogany box in which he kept his duelling pistols. Jasper frowned. Normally, that box went everywhere with Max. He opened it and discovered both pistols inside, one primed and loaded, the other discharged.

Jasper next turned his attention to the pockets in the

lining of the trunk. In one, he found a golden locket, which he recognised at once. It was Max's most treasured possession, containing a miniature of his mother and a lock of his father's hair. Jasper had once witnessed his friend run into a burning tavern to retrieve his coat, simply because it was in the pocket.

It seemed inconceivable to Jasper that Max would have left the locket here so carelessly, no matter how disordered his spirits. And what were his things even doing in this boxroom in the first place?

That night, he decided to seize the bull by the horns. His plan of seduction be damned. Some things were more important than a pretty woman.

'Now look here,' he addressed Luciana. 'This business with Max. Something's not right. I went looking for his room, only to find his trunk shut away. He's left his pistols behind and his mother's locket. I read one of his letters, and I find he wasn't well. Having bad dreams, consulting a doctor, having visions.'

'I told you such dreams were not uncommon out here on the lake,' Luciana said. 'Your friend's certainly caused him some agitation. Perhaps he went to consult a doctor in Venezia.'

'Why didn't he take his trunk? Why was it shut away?'

'He said he wished to travel lightly, and I was to look after his things until his return. He had been staying in your room in the tower, but as it is the finest in the villa,

I suggested that I give that room to you, rather than leave it unoccupied during his absence. Signor Cavendish-Green was amenable to this plan, but he made it very plain that he wished to take possession of it again upon his return. I believe his precise words were: "Don't let that bounder Godolphin get too comfortable."'

Jasper could certainly imagine Max saying that. 'He talked to you about his dreams?'

Luciana nodded. 'He was troubled by visions of his past. All the duels he had fought. He told me that he had not always behaved as a man of honour.'

That was putting it mildly. Tampered pistols. A metal plate worn over the heart. Covert ditches dug on the field of honour to trip his opponents. Not Jasper's way, but Max used to say with a laugh: 'Better a devil on this earth than a saint in the grave.'

Again, Luciana retired to bed early, but this time Jasper made no effort to persuade her to stay. He paced the library, still fretting about Max. Luciana's answers hadn't satisfied him. Quite the contrary. Especially the part about Max unburdening his soul, telling her all sorts of unwise things. Not like him at all.

Coming to a halt before the fireplace, one of the figures in the painting caught his eye. The man was naked, half-submerged in a river of boiling blood and fire in the Circle of Violence. His arms were thrown into the air, an agonised expression contorting his saturnine features. Jasper stared, sweat crawling down his face. From his angled black brows and widow's peak to the duelling scar upon his cheek, the desperate sinner bore more than a passing resemblance to Max.

VI

Jasper struggled to sleep, all manner of suspicions crawling around in his mind. Why was Max in that devilish painting? Who had put him there? Luciana? Giovanni? What did it mean?

Scratch. Scratch. Scratch. The noise was louder than last night, as if whatever creature was making it was right there in his room. Not a rat, please God. Jasper wasn't sure his heart could take it after everything else. His frustration getting the better of him, he fumbled for the tinderbox on his nightstand and lit a candle.

Turning, Jasper started violently. A dark-haired woman in a nightgown was sitting at his desk, writing with the quill from his inkwell. *Scratch. Scratch. Scratch.*

'Luciana?' he said, his voice tremulous. Yet he already knew that it wasn't her.

Alice turned and regarded him coldly. 'Well, Jasper,' she said. 'Here we are.'

Jasper pressed a hand to his temple, speaking firmly to himself: 'She's not really here.'

'But I am here,' his wife said. 'What else was I supposed to do? Write? You never answered any of my letters.'

'You're dead,' Jasper told her. 'I've been to your damn grave.'

'Once,' she said. 'When you came to sell my house.'

In the face of her hostile stare, every rational thought abandoned him. He pressed his face into the bolster, which had dispelled his vision in the library – only this time when he looked again, Alice was still there.

'You are so near to it now,' she said. 'Can you not feel it? Can you not smell it?'

'I don't know what you're talking about,' Jasper cried.

'Eternal fire,' she said, a chilling conviction to her tone. 'Without the blood of the lamb, you will burn.'

Jasper stared out at the icy waters of the lake, listening to the ominous bang of Giovanni's hammer. He shuddered, remembering Alice's stare.

A new theory had occurred to him. What if Max's judgement too had been affected by his dreams and his visions, and he'd also made amorous advances to Luciana? He remembered how Giovanni had thrown him roughly to the floor. Might Max have had a similar confrontation with him, only worse? Max had always been a forceful character in his dealings with women. Might Giovanni have killed him, and then painted him into that scene of hellfire as some sort of macabre act of celebration?

Even thinking about it made Jasper's throat close up. What to do? Leave at once? Make his own way to Capri? And yet how could he face Old Chum alone, without knowing the truth about what had happened to Max?

'Signore.'

Jasper almost jumped out of his skin. Giovanni was standing behind him, holding out a little blue bottle. 'For bad dream.'

Luciana must have told him. 'What is it?' he snapped.

'Henbane,' Giovanni said. 'To help sleep.'

'Henbane?' Jasper exclaimed. 'Isn't that poison?'

'Before bed, five drops. If you wake, five drops. Never more.'

It occurred to Jasper then that Giovanni might be responsible for the dreams and the visions in the first place. Had he been slipping something like this tincture into his food? Yet he held out his hand for the bottle, not wanting to betray his suspicions, watching darkly as Giovanni returned to his workshop.

For the next hour or so, Jasper walked every inch of the gardens and beaches, looking for any sign of disturbance in the frost-hardened ground. His search proved fruitless, which brought him a slight feeling of relief – until his eye fell upon the chapel. He remembered Luciana emerging from that door to the left of the altar. The chapel didn't look large enough to contain another room of significant size. Did that door lead to a staircase and a crypt? What better place, after all, to hide the victim of a murderer than amongst the dead?

If Jasper was right about Max, then Luciana had told him a pack of lies. It made his blood boil just to think of it. He longed to shake the truth out of her – and if his worst fears were realised, then he'd put a bullet in Giovanni's head!

And yet if Max was a forceful creature, then Jasper was a subtler man by far. At dinner, he gazed into Luciana's duplicitous eyes, betraying not a hint of the turmoil behind his smiles.

'Did you dream again last night?' she asked.

'Rather more than a dream. I would call it a vision – of my late wife. She was angry with me.' He gave a heartfelt sigh.

'Do you know why?'

If Luciana wanted a confession, then he'd give her one! 'Before our marriage, Alice had inherited a thousand pounds and a small manor house in the north of England. I was determined to turn that money into a fortune, and my investments demanded that I spend a lot of time away from her in London. Regrettably, my luck took a turn for the worse and I was forced to mortgage the house. Then I decided to recoup my losses at play. After that,' he made a hopeless gesture, 'I was too ashamed to go home. My creditors were circling, and my wife had an unpleasant visit from the bank. So I took to ignoring her letters. Which is why I never realised quite how bad things got. Most of the servants left, Alice couldn't afford to heat the house, and then she fell ill. Her physician was owed a sum of money and the blackguard just stopped coming. Which was when Alice turned to some damn quack, whose medicine killed her.'

Luciana dabbed a napkin to her lips and regarded him solemnly. 'Who are those soldiers you feared might be looking for you in Bardolino? You told Giovanni they were not your friends.'

'Alice's brother and two of his fellow officers. He was serving in the colonies when she died. On his return, he questioned Alice's maid, who had never liked me. Now he blames me for everything. Wants to fight me to the death.'

'So you ran away, and your sins brought you here.'

Sins was a bit much. Mistakes rather. But remembering his objective, Jasper nodded. 'I should like to find a way back to God, but I am not sure that He would have me.'

Luciana took the key to the chapel from her girdle and held it out to him with a smile. 'Tell it to Him,' she said. 'Let the Lord see that you are worthy of redemption.'

VII

The fog had rolled in off the water and Jasper could barely make out the darkened gardens around him. Faintly, on the distant shore, he heard a church bell striking two. In his hand, he clutched a selection of tools he'd just pilfered from Giovanni's workshop. Reaching the chapel, he entered, locking the door behind him.

He walked along the aisle and set his candelabra and the tools down on a pew. Seizing a chisel from the pile, he wedged it into the crack of the door to the left of the altar and heaved. The frame splintered, and after a little more digging with the chisel, Jasper got the door open. He'd worry about the consequences later.

Beyond the door was a flight of steps leading down into

the darkness. Jasper descended slowly, his heart thudding in anticipation of what he might find down there. He emerged into a large chamber lined with marble tombs and shelves of coffins. So many coffins! He shivered violently, telling himself it was just the chill.

Some of the coffins appeared to be very old, the wood dark and warped. Others were much newer, their piney, resinous scent filling the air. Selecting one of the latter, Jasper inserted his chisel into the narrow gap beneath the lid. Putting his weight behind it, he levered out the nail. Sweat beaded his forehead as he slowly worked his way around the coffin. When the last nail came free, and Jasper lifted the lid, an ancient, primal smell – not rot as he had feared, but a scent of wax and leather and old bones – rose up to greet him.

The man in the coffin wasn't Max. Jasper could see that right away, the shrunken, leathery face of the corpse astonishingly well preserved. The poor fellow had clearly died young, and Jasper bowed his head for a moment, before turning to the next coffin.

It did occur to him, as he worked, to wonder about the sheer number of coffins in that crypt. He supposed some of them might have dated from the villa's time as a monastery – and yet so many of them were clearly of much more recent provenance. A plague, perhaps, which might explain the lack of servants upon the island? Could a man catch a plague from a corpse? He didn't know. The lid of the second coffin was trickier than the first, and Jasper laboured away at it for half an hour. Once he froze in terror, hearing a faint scrape against stone somewhere up above. He listened hard, his senses prickling, but when he didn't hear anything more he put it down to the wind and resumed his work.

When Jasper slid the lid off the coffin, he stood back, startled, covering his mouth. The body had no head, or at least not very much of one. There was hardly any desiccation, and Jasper took in the man's embroidered coat and large hairy hands. On one finger was a signet ring – a dark bloodstone on a band of gold. A bilious gasp of recognition arose from his throat.

Oh Christ, oh no, oh poor Max! The chisel fell from Jasper's hand as grief and horror overwhelmed him. *Run!* he told himself, all his plans of revenge and derring-do abandoned in the face of this cruel reality.

Yet something drew him back – not Max's mutilated corpse, but the man in the first coffin. There was a wound in the side of his neck that Jasper hadn't noticed at first. Black stains had stiffened the front of his green silk coat. Another gentleman. Another violent death. And from the look of the corpse, not long before Max had died. What were the odds? Jasper turned again to study the piles of coffins. He thought of Giovanni in his workshop, hammering and sawing away. All those trunks piled up in the boxroom.

Gripped by a terrible new fear, Jasper stooped to snatch up his chisel. He set about opening another coffin, working in a frenzy of desperation. Then another. And another. Each coffin held the body of a man, finely dressed, of varying ages and states of preservation. One had horribly broken limbs. Another what looked like a gunshot wound to the chest. Another was missing his head, like poor Max. Only one appeared to have died a quieter death, though he had a curious green stain around his mouth and an expression of terror contorting his leathery features.

Heaving the lid off yet another coffin, Jasper emitted a strangled cry. The dead man's face was unrecognisable, the skin shrunken and brown, a few brittle strands of sandy-coloured hair clinging to his scalp. He had a jewelled pin in his cravat, and his coat was blackened with old blood. Jasper didn't recognise the jewelled pin, but he knew the family crest embossed on those silver buttons only too well. He remembered sitting in a tavern, a day of wine and dice and good cheer, watching Old Chum scribble away at this very design. 'You'd be surprised at how much faith people place in a family crest.'

As Jasper stared down at the body of his long-lost friend, panic broke over him in waves. Grabbing the candelabra, he ran for the stairs.

Jasper's feet skidded on the gravel paths, the icy dampness of the mist a shock after the dry air of the crypt. How long had he been down there? Several hours, by his reckoning. Would Luciana and Giovanni be awake yet? The fog was so thick, Jasper couldn't judge the hour. But it was also thick enough to mask his departure from the island from anyone who happened to be gazing out at the lake.

How many had they killed? Jasper was now convinced

that Luciana must be in on it too. Hadn't she been down there in that crypt? He had little doubt that he was intended to be next.

Reaching the boathouse, he unbolted the door and untied the strange black boat from the dock. He clambered into it, nearly falling overboard in his haste. Retrieving the long oar from the bottom of the vessel, standing unsteadily in the stern as Giovanni had done, he awkwardly manoeuvred the boat out onto the black waters of the lake.

Fog pressed in around him, only a few feet of water visible ahead. It unnerved him, not being able to see where he was going, but he pulled hard against the currents in his desperation. The further he rowed, the more his feeling of disorientation increased. His limbs soon tired, the bitter air chilling his hands to the bone.

After about fifteen minutes of this labour, he guessed he must be nearing the shore. The water grew choppier, rocking the boat more violently. As he struggled to maintain his course, a great swell hit the boat side on. Jasper staggered, dropping his oar into the water. Making an instinctive lunge for it, he lost his balance and tumbled in. The water hit him like a stake of ice through the heart. The weight of his boots and cloak dragged him down, the water closing over his head. *This is it*, he thought, *this is what it is to drown.*

Then his boots hit the bottom of the lake, and he pushed himself up hard. His head broke the surface, and he vomited water. He drew in a lungful of air, just before he sank again. Once more his boots hit the bottom, and once more he pushed himself back to the surface. Surely he must be very near to the shore? Tearing off his cloak, he began to swim and soon found he could stand on tiptoe, keeping his head above the water. Slowly, he waded up the steep bank of the lake, before collapsing upon a stretch of gravelly beach.

Hot tears came to his eyes. He was safe! Yet shivering violently, each breath cold as a blade. He needed to get help, to find shelter, or he would freeze out here. How ironic that would be, after everything.

He attempted to rise, but his strength seemed to have deserted him. Gazing around, all he could see was fog. Then he heard the sound of nearby voices.

'Who's there?' he called. 'Please, I need help.'

Through the fog, he made out a ghostly figure coming towards him. If it's Douglas Hamilton himself, he thought, I'll embrace him after that trip to hell and back.

But the man who emerged from the fog to loom over him was not the Italian villager of his prayers, nor Douglas Hamilton, but the short, wiry figure of Giovanni. Letting out a cry, Jasper tried to scramble away, but Luciana appeared behind him, wrapped in a fur cloak, a look of consternation upon her face.

He was back on the island – must have got turned around in the fog. Jasper began to weep in earnest. 'Please,' he said, looking from one to the other wildly. 'Don't hurt me.'

VIII

Jasper was burning in hellfire, submerged in a boiling river of blood. Pain seared through him, and he screamed. Yet he could still feel the icy chill of the lake deep in his bones, and he didn't understand how he could be shivering while he burned. The light kept changing around him, one moment bright as quicksilver, the next black as Charon's cowl. In those darker moments, a bleak terror contorted his body into crab-like shapes, and he imagined himself crawling across the stony beach. Yet the ground beneath him was soft and white, like his mother's cheek.

'You have a fever,' Alice said.

He was in his room in the tower. The women were clustered around his bed: Alice, Helen, Rosamond, Angelica and the other one – Max's girl. Helen and Rosamond were weeping again.

'Stop it,' he begged. 'Leave me alone.'

Angelica, who had always been argumentative, glared down at him. 'You cannot take our grief. You own it now.'

And he did. Jasper felt it. Crushing, soul-destroying. Unable to face them any more, he burrowed beneath the counterpane, desperate only to sleep. Yet when sleep came, it brought more dreams, more rivers of blood and hellfire. Men writhing in pain, begging for salvation. The flames licked his flesh, the agony unendurable. He screamed like an animal, awakening suddenly to find Luciana standing over him.

'Get away,' he cried, retreating in a huddle of bedclothes.

She poured him a glass of water from a jug and held it out to him. His thirst was powerful, and despite his fears, he snatched the glass and drank. Luciana refilled it and placed it upon the nightstand, next to Giovanni's little blue bottle and a pistol. The weapon looked very much like one of the pair from Max's box. Jasper made a grab for it, and Luciana made no move to stop him.

'Tell that rogue Giovanni that if he comes near me, I'll kill him.'

Luciana smiled sadly. 'I shall leave you now.'

When the door closed behind her, Jasper breathed a sigh of relief. The other women all looked at the pistol in his hand.

'Do it,' Angelica said.

'It won't hurt,' Rosamond added.

'It would be a kindness.'

'To the world.'

Hearing these words, Jasper was consumed by an overwhelming urge to put the pistol in his mouth and pull the trigger. His hand was halfway there, before he caught himself. He stared down at the pistol. Dear God, what was wrong with him?

Appalled, he swung his legs out of the bed, and staggered to the window. He threw it open and hurled the pistol out. Gazing down at the rocks below, he remembered that broken body in the coffin.

'For a moment, it will feel as if you are flying,' Alice said.

Jasper turned and tried to stagger to the door. But it was

too much, and he sank to his knees, forced to crawl back to his bed, while the women jeered. He craved sleep, and yet he couldn't bear the pain again. Couldn't bear to smell his burning flesh as the fire consumed him.

His eye fell upon the tincture. Five drops, Giovanni had said – but Giovanni was a killer! Yet the bottle was already in Jasper's hand, cold and hard and comforting. He unstoppered it with his teeth, and with a trembling hand added five drops to his glass.

It was dark when Jasper awoke. No fever, no hellfire, no dreams. The tincture had worked.

Outside, the mist had lifted and he could see the stars. He tried to come up with a plan of escape, but the mere act of thinking exhausted him.

'You need to sleep,' said a voice in his ear. 'You need more tincture.'

Jasper turned to see Angelica lying next to him in the bed. She brushed a damp lock from his forehead.

'Don't touch me,' he cried, jerking away.

'You never used to say that,' she said, reaching beneath the counterpane to fondle him.

'Leave me alone,' Jasper begged. 'I'm sorry.'

They all laughed at that.

'Sorry? Now there's a word,' said Max's girl. She'd been silent up until now, simply toying with the rope around her neck.

'He always said sorry,' Alice said. 'It doesn't mean a thing.'

'So many words,' Angelica agreed. 'There was a time when I believed them.'

'At least you got words,' Max's girl said. 'He doesn't even remember my name.'

'Please believe me,' Jasper said, weeping again. 'It wasn't my fault.'

Helen helped him with the bottle. 'Five drops,' she said. 'You'll wake in an hour or so, and you'll need five more.'

IX

Christmas Eve. Luciana opened the door to the tower bedroom. The window was ajar, the room very cold. Jasper was lying in the bed, staring up at the ceiling. The green stain around his mouth had leached onto the bolster, and would take some scrubbing to get out.

It had happened quickly this time, as it often did when a man had a conscience lurking somewhere beneath his sin. Her father had thought that Jasper would be weak at the end, the sort to blow his own brains out, or open his jugular vein, but then he always took a dim view of the seducers. She remembered his face in the chapel, as he'd thrown Jasper to the floor. As if any amount of anger at these men could ever erase his original sin.

Forcing her mind from such ancient resentments, she wiped away a tear. The ones at Christmas always upset her more.

Going downstairs, she found her father in the library – up

on a stool before the fireplace, his palette in hand, painting Jasper's face onto one of the sinners in the Circle of Lust.

'It is done?' he said, without looking around.

'The tincture,' she said. 'He fought until the end.'

The beads of her rosary were smooth beneath her fingers. Turning, she went to the window, seeking respite from her desolation in the lake's beauty. The sun was dazzling upon the water, like the dawn of Creation. On days like this, if she stared very hard into the light, she could almost remember how it felt to be alive.

THE OLD PLAY

Andrew Michael Hurley

He'd lost his watch, but he knew that he was late – very late. It had to have gone eleven by now, thought Morgan, as he knocked on the stage door and waited under the lintel to keep out of the rain. It had been falling all day with a briny, decayed smell, as if the surface of the North Sea was being swept up and thrown over the town. The alleyway streamed with water as the gutters and downspouts choked and spewed. It was a dismal end to December. A cheerless end to an ugly decade.

The blustering wet wind found him however much he tried to huddle himself away and, pounding on the door with the flat of his hand, he finally summoned Rennie, the stage manager.

She ushered him inside with the sardonic, aggravated look he'd been expecting.

'I know, I'm sorry,' he said. 'It's the weather. The high street was flooded.'

He shook his coat and went off to get ready before she could smell that he'd been in the pub.

'Bobby's here,' she called after him.

'Bobby?'

'His mother left him at the door.'

'And you let him in?'

'What was I supposed to do, make him stand out in the rain?'

'Well, he can't stay. I don't want him to stay.'

By her expression, Rennie had just caught the tang of brandy on his breath, and perhaps deciding that the drink was making him belligerent she softened her tone.

'Look,' she said. 'He's here now. Just let him get dressed up with the other children. Then he won't be under your feet.'

'Dressed up? No. I'm taking him home.'

'There's no time for that,' said Rennie. 'We've only got twenty minutes. Nineteen, in fact. And the Committee wants to see you before curtain up. Get ready, please. You know what they're like.'

She gestured beseechingly and he went off down the stairs to his dressing room in the basement.

The door was ajar and inside Bobby was there in his duffle coat and scarf, reading a comic.

'Hello, Dad,' he said, looking up and blinking spasmodically behind his glasses. The lad didn't know whether to be ashamed or excited about being here.

'What happened?' said Morgan, knowing that it was unlikely he'd get anything close to the whole truth.

'Nothing.'

'Your mother must have brought you here for a reason. Did you fall out with her over something? Where is she?'

'Aunty Mary's.'

Right on the other side of town.

'What did you do to make her so cross, for God's sake?'

Bobby shrugged as he usually did whenever he was faced with questions he didn't want to answer, and Morgan tried something easier.

'How long have you been waiting?' he asked.

'An hour,' said Bobby. 'I don't know.'

'An hour? Down here?'

The basement of the theatre was like something hewn out of the earth by a race of troglodytes. The walls sweated, especially on nights like this, and the musty crypt-like smell brought on headaches and nausea. The stagehands threw down rugs but they did little to take the chill off the stone floors. Still, it wasn't surprising that the cold and damp were so hard to shift when the theatre was closed for eleven months of the year.

'Aren't you freezing?' said Morgan.

'I don't mind it,' Bobby replied, which was probably true. For him, the thrill of being backstage more than compensated for the squalor. He'd been hankering after coming to see the Old Play all year. Being dumped here by his mother was hardly a punishment. She knew that well enough. She was really punishing Morgan. *He's your son too. You deal with him.* As if it was his fault that he hadn't been there at home when this argument or fight or whatever it was had flared up with Bobby. But she seemed to forget that she'd been the one who'd thrown him out two months ago. *Drinking like that. It's no wonder you've no work. It's no wonder you have nightmares.*

'Here, make yourself useful,' said Morgan, handing Bobby the enamel bowl from the dressing table. 'There's a sink at the end of the corridor.'

'All right, Dad.'

It was Dad these days, not Daddy.

Now aged twelve, he'd started to pupate. Every time Morgan saw him the chrysalis of puberty had hardened around him a little more. He couldn't be sure what would emerge once the transition was complete.

He'd always been such an easy child to raise. He'd never needed much in the way of instruction or correction about what was right or wrong. But lately, things had changed. At school, he'd fallen in with some older lads who skulked and smoked and played truant, and in the last week of term he'd been caught loitering in town. His headmaster had quite rightly torn a strip off him and promised that the cane would follow any repeat of the offence, but in a subtly accusatory way he'd laid half the blame at the feet of his parents.

'It can happen, Mr and Mrs Baxter,' he'd said. 'Even good boys can be adversely affected in . . . troubled homes.'

Bobby must have said something to him. Perhaps to get out of receiving six of the best, trying to find some mitigation for his behaviour, he'd let on about his father's absence.

Morgan had told Bobby that he was working away on a building site, but he didn't think that the boy believed him.

He'd surely heard the arguments. He must have listened to his mother crying in the kitchen.

Morgan was certain that Bobby had overheard him sobbing too, on those nights when the war wouldn't leave him alone.

Bobby returned with a bowl of hot water and Morgan worried that having given him a job he would now think himself entitled to stay and watch the play.

'Anything else for me to do, Dad?' he asked. His glasses had steamed up and he removed them to wipe the lenses clean on his scarf. Without them he looked so different: mole-eyed, lumpen in the cheeks, not his bonny Bobby any more but curiously old, his face flickering with the ghostly impressions of the adult he might become. Morgan wondered if they would get along.

'Listen, I want you to stay down here while the show's on,' he said.

'But why?' Bobby replied.

'We've been over this.'

'I know, but . . .'

'Do you need me to go over it again?'

Bobby conceded, but Morgan knew that look in his eyes. He was already devising a more subtle strategy of persuasion.

'Is that Grandad?' he said, pointing to the three photographs on the wall.

'You know it is,' said Morgan.

'Was this his dressing room?'

'Why else would the pictures be here?'

'It was his and now it's yours,' said Bobby. 'So, really, it's ours.'

He had a familial right to be here, was his point.

'It's not anybody's,' said Morgan, although in truth his father had made it his own. A candle-lit junk shop, he recalled, a child's paradise of costumes, masks, wigs, stage swords, musical instruments, dangling marionettes, boxes of magic tricks: the accoutrements of the all-round entertainer.

Good old Bill Baxter. There he was with his head inside a cannon. There he was juggling with fire. In the other photograph he sat at a piano, accompanying some portly tenor in coat-tails one Christmastime that had long since turned to dust.

In his day, in those impossibly distant, seemingly carefree years of the twenties and thirties, folk had flocked to the People's Playhouse night after night to see clowns, comics and crooners, but then the war had come and with the theatre being so close to the docks and in danger of falling into the sights of Heinkel bombers it had been shut down for the duration.

A wise precaution, right enough, though in the end it had suffered nothing more than a strafing of shrapnel across its frontage, a light wound when so many buildings around it had been gutted by incendiaries and parachute mines. Yet there had been no eagerness in the owners to reopen after the Victory. Like everyone else, they'd had more pressing things to deal with. No one had any money, half the town was in ruins, and their star, the great Bill Baxter, had been crushed under the rubble that had once been Inkerman Street. No cowering in a shelter for him, the stubborn sod.

It had taken a committee of local dignitaries to get the theatre up and running again, which they'd done in 1946, predominantly to save one thing: the Old Play.

It had been staged at the Playhouse on New Year's Eve for longer than living memory, a tradition that they didn't want to see forgotten about and lost. And so every December since, the doors had been unlocked and the cast and crew had reassembled to put on an ever more extravagant performance. Each year, the Committee welcomed them all back, and in their first address reminded them what a privilege it was to help preserve this festive institution, how important it was that the story continued to be told. A story of how England once was and how it might be again.

They'd been there at the rehearsals before Christmas, the Committee; all twelve of them sitting in the front row, whispering to one another and making notes – about him, thought Morgan. They seemed to have been singling him out for scrutiny, even though, like the rest of the cast, he knew every line backwards.

But the Committee members were very particular about how the Old Play ought to be performed, and on the night itself they generally had a list of eleventh-hour suggestions to pass on to the actors, the stagehands, Props, Lighting, Sound Effects and Wardrobe.

Well, if they wanted to talk to him, thought Morgan, then let them come. But he'd tell them straight that they were cutting it fine. If they had things to say then they ought to say them at rehearsal, not sit there muttering to each other. They couldn't just snap their fingers and demand that he iron out some imperfection as he was about to step onto the stage.

Yet when there was a knock at the door his pugnaciousness wilted and for a moment he thought about pretending that he wasn't there. But it was only Colin, one of the stagehands, a young lad of eighteen or so who always had the same look on his face, a sort of scathing disdain. He was canny and ambitious, apt to remind the Committee at every opportunity that he was ready to step into any of the parts should they require him to.

'All right, Bob?' he said. He and Bobby had already met, then.

'All right, Col.'

Bobby was in awe of him, of course. He was easily led, just as his headmaster had said.

'What is it?' asked Morgan.

'Message,' said Colin, lingering in the doorway, rolling a cigarette. 'The Committee are on their way.'

'Right.'

Colin licked the edge of the paper and then slipped the fag behind his ear.

'You seen the Minotaur down here yet?' he said to Bobby. He made horns with his fingers and moaned like a bull.

'Don't,' Morgan said. 'You'll give him nightmares.'

Bobby laughed and shook his head and glanced at Colin to make sure he knew that he wasn't *really* frightened. He wasn't a child.

'You do know that it's curtain up in sixteen minutes,' said Colin. 'Well, fifteen now?'

Instinctively, Morgan turned his wrist, but remembered that his watch had gone missing.

'I couldn't get down the high street. They'd closed it off,' he said. 'I had to take a detour.'

'To where?' Colin sniffed and smiled to himself, having picked up the fug of boozy breath in the room.

He shared a conspiratorial smile at the phoniness of grown-ups with Bobby and closed the door.

'It was the weather,' Morgan called after him.

Snotty little bastard. It was true. Well, mostly. Partly. The high street *had* been flooded, the rain had been relentless.

He'd only intended to have one in the Butcher's Arms on his way to the theatre, but without a watch he'd lost track of time and sitting by the fire . . . a second brandy . . . he must have dropped off.

'Hey, why don't I go and help Col?' said Bobby, getting to his feet. 'I could be his assistant.'

'No. Stay put. Read your comic,' said Morgan and nodded him back to the bench at the dressing table.

Bobby did as he was told but Morgan felt the boy's eyes on him as he sat down and took off his cardigan and his shirt to start washing. The water in the bowl had already lost much of its warmth and he felt his skin tightening as he scrubbed at his face and neck and soaked his scalp. His hair, or what was left of it, congealed into short black strings, and with half a dozen passes with the razor they were gone.

'Why do you need to do that?' asked Bobby, gazing at him with fascination. The difference the absence of those few hairs made always startled Morgan too. The face looking back at him in the mirror could have been someone else entirely. A diseased, penniless tramp who'd been shaved for the sake of hygiene.

'I'm supposed to be poor,' he said.

But it wasn't only that. The audience had to despise him. That was the Beggar's function in the Old Play these days. Not like in his father's time. Back then, the Beggar had been a loveable rosy-cheeked scoundrel, an ex-soldier turned puckish folk hero in a bright costume of things he'd bartered for on his travels or found by the roadside. Morgan had stark memories of watching his father pulling on striped pantaloons and mismatched boots, a redcoat jacket and a hat like Robin Hood's.

It was the Committee's opinion that over the decades the Old Play had drifted far from its origins and by the time the war had come the moral of the story had been hopelessly corrupted. But now that they'd taken charge, they'd turned the Old Play back into an edifying fable, and the role of the Beggar had been changed from the common man's martyr to a criminal who fully deserved what was due to him. Morgan couldn't have looked more different from his father. He wore a long linen smock and nothing else, and the greasepaint that he smeared over every inch of exposed flesh from his crown to his toes had been blended to a pale, cadaverous yellow that under the spotlight gave him the pallor of one not long for this world.

As he made a start on colouring his nose and cheeks, a high-pitched grinding sound came from one of the other rooms in the basement.

'Props,' said Morgan, eyeing Bobby in the mirror.

They'd be making last-minute alterations to something at the behest of the Committee.

Bobby seemed to enjoy the power of the noise the way he might have marvelled at the ascending scream of the Spitfire on the cover of his comic. It promised something exciting that he didn't want to miss, and he tried again to find a way around Morgan's misgivings about the play.

'Can't I just stand at the side of the stage? Col said I could help him pull the ropes.'

'I've already told you, no,' Morgan replied.

'But you've not told me why.'

'Bobby, we've had this conversation a dozen times. There are some things that I just don't want you to see.'

That, of course, only made him all the more indignant.

'I'm not a baby.'

'I didn't say you were.'

Outside in the corridor, the children who played the Greenwood Folk, the sprites of the forest, clattered by singing and laughing.

'*They're* my age. Or even younger,' said Bobby. 'And they're *in* the play.'

'I don't care,' said Morgan. 'I want you to stay in this room. All right?'

Bobby sat back glumly, listening to the audience arriving in the auditorium above, and Morgan was glad that the boy was down here. Out of the rumble of feet and conversations, raucous cheers and chants erupted that sounded as if they belonged on the terraces of the football ground across town. Most of the audience was drunk by this time.

They got more boisterous every year, and the Beggar was the hardest part to play. Everyone heckled him, of course, that had become customary under the direction of the Committee, but some – especially the younger men – liked to think that they were as much a part of the entertainment as the actors on the stage and spent the weeks leading up to the performance practising their jibes. And their aim too. For as well as insults, they'd started to throw other things in the last couple of years.

At the end of the trial scene, rotten eggs or black potatoes or mushy crab apples would come hurtling towards Morgan out of the darkness. He didn't want Bobby to witness that any more than he'd want the lad to watch him thrashing about in the throes of a nightmare. He was being cruel to be kind for Bobby's sake. What boy would want to see his father so helpless?

The shrieking of metal in the props department revved up again, so loud this time that Bobby put his hands over his ears as he grinned. For Morgan, with the anaesthetic of the brandy wearing off, the noise was like a blade cutting into his skull and he willed it to stop, which it did after a further minute of grating and squealing. In its place came a vigorous rap at the door.

'The Committee to see you,' he heard Colin say outside.

'Give me a hand, Bobby,' said Morgan and nodded at the costume hanging from a nail.

He stripped down to his underwear, shivering, and pulled on the shroud that Bobby passed him as quick as he could.

Colin knocked again, louder this time, desperate to impress with his officiousness. Morgan opened the door to his habitual sneer and the Committee's grinning, benevolent faces. Their breath smoked in the cold air and stank of sherry.

He let them in, all twelve, the men in dinner jackets and the women in plush evening dresses. One or two were wearing paper hats and looked a little on the gormless side, having had too much to drink. As if they were entering a lift, they shuffled to the edges of the small room, smiling chummily at Bobby, who blinked and gawped.

Beckett, the retired alderman, who'd been one of the principal founders of the Committee, put his hands on Morgan's shoulders and looked him over approvingly.

'Wonderful,' he said. 'Truly wonderful. Your father would be very proud of you. I knew him, you know. A fine actor, Bill Baxter.'

He said the same thing every year.

'And here's the next generation,' he said, ruffling Bobby's hair. 'How marvellous. Come to learn the ropes, have you?'

'What is it you wanted to see me about?' said Morgan.

'Oh, we shan't keep you long,' said Beckett, still with his hand on Bobby's head. Then, with an affected discretion, he added, 'To be honest, old thing, I didn't want to bother you at all. It's the others. They're worried.'

Mrs Laycock, the Chair, glowering as always, brushed the word aside impatiently. There was something haughty and swan-like about her, Morgan thought.

'We just want to be certain that you'll be able to perform at your best tonight,' she said. 'That's all.'

Leaning against the door frame, smoking, Colin grinned to himself. No doubt he'd taken great pleasure in telling the Committee that Morgan had arrived long after everyone else, a little drunk.

'I'm sorry,' said Morgan. 'I've left my watch somewhere. And with the weather too . . .'

Catching his drift, Mrs Laycock shook her head irritably. 'No, no, it's nothing to do with that. It's something that we noticed during rehearsals.'

Here it came.

'Go on,' said Morgan.

Mrs Laycock hitched up her white elbow-length gloves against the cold as she considered what to say.

'Well, we felt that there was something . . . missing,' she said.

'I knew my lines, didn't I?' said Morgan, and the rest of the Committee smiled condescendingly, as though he hadn't quite understood the point.

'Oh, no question of that,' said Beckett. 'You were word-perfect. You always are.'

'It was more the performance itself,' Mrs Laycock said. 'We felt as though you were – how should I put it? – just speaking the lines, rather than being the character. It's merely an observation, of course. I'm no expert.'

'Well, I'm sorry you feel that way,' said Morgan, and he was answered with murmurs of reassurance. There was no need for him to apologise.

He looked around at the circle of genial faces, the dickie bows and the pearls. There being so many of them in the room it felt claustrophobic. The ceiling had started to drip with condensation.

'All we're suggesting,' said Major Broad, the Secretary, 'is that when words sound like words, when an actor *seems* as though they're acting, it can shatter the illusion of reality. And the audience must be able to believe that what they're seeing is real, no?'

Morgan didn't think he'd done anything differently in rehearsal from any other year and he considered himself a decent enough actor to have set aside the problems at home and the trouble Bobby was in at school. He didn't think any of that would have affected his performance.

'We have been wondering,' said the Treasurer, Miss MacLaine, 'if you were getting tired of it all. You've played this part for so long now. Perhaps it's time to think about handing the burden to someone else.'

'It isn't a burden. I'm fine,' said Morgan. 'Look, what is this really about?'

Boldness was unusual for him, and it caused Mrs Laycock to shift uncomfortably.

'I was rather expecting to have this conversation with you alone,' she said, meaning that Bobby was preventing her from speaking her mind.

'Here, why don't I take him?' said Colin, nipping out his fag.

'Well, now that's an idea,' said Beckett, cupping Bobby's cheek. 'Go and join in, young man. Get your feet on the boards. I'm sure there'll be a spare costume.'

Colin nodded and Beckett turned Bobby in the direction of the door.

'Hang on,' said Morgan. 'I'd rather he didn't . . .'

'He'll be all right,' Beckett smiled. 'It's in the blood.'

Colin put his arm around Bobby, who gabbled on excitedly, and led him out into the corridor. Everyone waited until the door had closed and the footsteps had receded.

'We've made some alterations,' said Mrs Laycock.

'Alterations?' Morgan replied distractedly, determined to go and find Bobby as soon as the Committee left and tell him that he wasn't going anywhere near the stage.

'Alterations to the ending of the play,' Mrs Laycock continued. 'Improvements, more accurately.'

'There aren't new lines you're expecting me to learn, are there?'

'No, no,' said Beckett. 'We wouldn't do that to you, old boy. Not at this late stage. Good heavens.'

'Then what?'

'Well, this is it,' said Mrs Laycock. 'Telling you what to expect will rather spoil the effect of the surprise.'

Seeing that Morgan was confused, Beckett put his hands in his pockets and laughed. 'I did warn you that this might only muddy the waters, Dorothy.'

There was a light-hearted tone in his voice, but it only seemed to make Mrs Laycock brusque.

'All we're asking,' she said, 'is that you stay in character, whatever happens. We don't want the ending spoiled by any . . . abnormal reactions. You mustn't leave the stage until everything's over. This is an important night. It'll be a special performance. The Old Play will end exactly as it should.'

'When have I ever broken character?' said Morgan.

'Well, quite,' Beckett agreed.

Mrs Laycock huffed out a white breath of exasperation. 'Just remember that people have paid a great deal of money to be here.'

'He knows that,' said Beckett. 'He's a professional. Like his father.'

Mrs Laycock cast her eyes to the wet, glistening ceiling, which creaked under the weight of the incoming audience.

'We'd better take our seats,' she said, not particularly reassured, it seemed, that anything had been resolved to her satisfaction.

Beckett clasped Morgan's shoulder. 'Well, break a leg,

old son. You'll do us proud, I'm sure. No need to look so worried.'

'When you're on the stage, you *are* the Beggar. Don't forget that,' said Major Broad and shook his hand.

The others offered him similar words of encouragement and filed out one by one, with Beckett and Mrs Laycock engaged in a hushed argument as they went off down the corridor.

It was typical of them to do something like this. Make some modification with minutes to go, or descend to his dressing room talking about important nights and special performances and telling him not to worry.

Once they'd gone, Morgan called for Bobby but there was no answer apart from the echo of his own voice. Either the lad was ignoring him or he'd already gone backstage. Every room Morgan peered into along the corridor was empty. In fact, the whole basement seemed deserted.

But as he went back to his dressing table and finished his make-up, he heard what he thought was an animal. The Committee were keen on using the real thing. The year before they'd procured a donkey for the Beggar to ride onto the stage. Perhaps they had decided that the Magistrate should have a hunting hound that matched his viciousness or that the Tuppenny Hag needed a familiar.

Yet it didn't sound like a cat or a dog. It was hard to say what it was. Or where the noise was coming from, even. Sound carried so erratically down here in this labyrinth of passageways that what seemed close by might be far off and what was faint might have been coming from the room next door.

There. It came again as he stepped out into the corridor and made his way to the stairs. It was Colin, or probably Bobby copying Colin. He was mucking about somewhere, making the sound of the Minotaur, an agitated, mournful lowing of something penned in against its will.

The backstage area bustled with final preparations and Morgan waited for Bobby to appear. But there was no sign of him or Colin, and he asked Rennie if she'd seen them.

'Sorry, no,' she said, too busy to talk, and darted off to hurry the stagehands along.

The others in the cast were there in the wings. Douglas as the Magistrate in a grotesque, Nero-like mask that had been made by some Italian craftsman using real skin and hair. And Judith as the Tuppenny Hag, who crept about hunched like a snail under a heavy brown mantle and secreted pig's blood wherever she went from a bladder hidden inside the folds of her cloak.

He'd have asked them if they'd seen Bobby, but the Committee insisted that once the actors were in costume they were to stay in character until the curtain came down, and so they would only pretend that they'd never heard of him.

It seemed most likely that Colin had got Bobby dressed up like the rest of the children as one of the Greenwood Folk.

They'd been sent out of the way to the wings on the other side of the stage and so Morgan couldn't quite pick the boy out from the crowd of grass-coloured faces.

'Wake up. Get hold of it for fuck's sake.'

Ted from Props handed Morgan a rope which tensed immediately as the Beggar's donkey tried to get away. It was a mangy, temperamental creature from a local farm that pissed and defecated whenever and wherever the urge took hold – which was often enough for Ted's grandson to find gainful employment with a bucket and a shovel.

The donkey gasped and strained against its tether. Perhaps it was this poor thing he'd heard down in the basement, thought Morgan, not Bobby making animal noises at all.

It complained again, louder this time, and Morgan tried to calm it down with a stroke of its neck.

It was no wonder it was jittery, the way the audience was clamouring for the show to start. It wasn't the excitement and expectation he remembered from his father's time but a frustrated impatience. As Mrs Laycock had said, they'd paid a lot to be here.

Nowadays, the audience was entirely composed of those who had bid successfully for a ticket at one of the gala dinners and shooting weekends the Committee held throughout the year. They were heated, even violent affairs, Morgan had heard, especially amongst those who were trying to get a foothold on certain social and professional ladders. To be seen at the People's Playhouse on New Year's Eve meant that you were someone of note.

It was the guarantee of lavish spectacle too that made the competition for tickets so fierce. The promise of *realness*.

On the stage, living silver birches had been brought in to create the English woodland setting. And Enid, who played the Maiden Queen, was being buried under leaves that had been gathered from the parks across town during the autumn.

The chemical broth that was used to create a layer of mist seemed to have been improved since last year as it looked as if real clouds had descended through the theatre roof and settled in the boughs of the trees. At the back of the stage, large mirrors were carefully angled so that, to the audience, the forest looked infinite. They'd been well disguised this time, thought Morgan. He couldn't actually see them at all, only their effect.

He heard the children laughing on the other side of the stage. That had to be Bobby, the one with blond hair. He'd taken off his glasses. That was why he hadn't recognised the boy earlier. Morgan waved, but Bobby was too distracted by everything that was going on, too fascinated by his own transformation as he admired his green-painted hands and his costume.

There would be no chance of persuading him to go back to the dressing room now. No time to get into another quarrel about all this. Morgan resolved to have it out with the boy's mother tomorrow. She knew full well that he didn't want Bobby even to see the play, let alone take part in it.

If it's such a terrible thing to watch, why do you go back every year? she'd ask him.

Was it vanity? Had he simply been taken in by the Committee's flattery? *You must come and perform for us, Morgan. This part has been waiting for you your whole life. Do it for your father.*

Then was it a duty? Albeit one which he could only perform with a couple of stiff drinks inside him. Or a possessiveness? The veiled suggestion from Miss MacLaine that he ought to retire had only made him more intent on staying. The thought of giving away the role of the Beggar to someone else – someone like Colin – seemed the worst betrayal of his father's memory somehow.

No, he came back each December for something more than all that. The Old Play was good for him. For one night, once a year, he could feel properly punished for those cities he'd set alight.

A slow handclap began in the auditorium and Rennie hurried everyone into their places, beckoning Morgan forward and attracting the attention of her assistant in the opposite wing. He shook the hanging birdcages and the wrens, robins and blackbirds inside began to twitter their solemn winter songs out over the stage. Someone from Sound Effects brought up the moaning of a cold wind through the loudspeakers. And overhead, in the gantry, though they were completely obscured in the swirl of fog, the stagehands began to shake down artificial snow that thickened along the branches of the trees just like the real stuff.

The lights went out backstage and the curtain rose to loud, drunken cheering.

Along with the older boys and girls, Bobby had muscled his way to the front of the children in the wings. Morgan could just make him out, well his white teeth at least as he grinned with the anticipation of what was to come.

All the children in town knew the story of the Old Play, even if they'd never seen it. Parents would tell it to them at bedtime. Everyone knew the plot – how the beautiful Maiden Queen was bewitched by the Tuppenny Hag and put to sleep in the faraway wood. How the Tuppenny Hag tempted the Beggar to take the Maiden Queen's golden locket, which he did so as to feed his starving family. How the Greenwood Folk offered to guide him out of the forest but led him to the Magistrate instead, who pronounced upon him a sentence of death.

The audience was growing fractious and, eager to get things started, Rennie lent a hand and heaved Morgan onto the donkey's back. The miserable creature tossed its head and tried to bite and dug in its feet but with a slap across its nose from Ted it complied and plodded out onto the stage, its bony shoulders undulating.

The audience quietened down but not to silence, never to silence. Rather, they simmered. Tonight, there was an added expectancy, the Committee having promised them a special performance, the quintessential version of the Old Play.

On his mark, Morgan dismounted and wound the donkey's rope around one of the branches. But as he tied the knot, he caught sight of something in the hidden mirrors that doubled and redoubled the images of the trees. A face, a small pale face. It was his own, of course, appearing at random somewhere down the chain of reflections.

Now the audience began to laugh, which threw him a little. There was never any laughter when the Beggar came on and he realised that the donkey had emptied its bowels. The reek of the sour dung caught so thickly in his throat that he moved downstage sooner than he should have done.

He could see the Committee on the front row watching him, Mrs Laycock with her arms folded. Beyond them, behind the brilliance of the spotlight, the rest of the auditorium was a cavern of baying, hooting voices. Someone somewhere shouted at him to get on with it.

He duly began but his words were lost, and he waited for an outburst of shushing to subdue the rowdiness. Below him, Beckett motioned for him to quickly start again.

Gazing up into the snow, which really did seem as if it was falling from a cloud, he spoke his opening lines.

'What wood this is, I cannot say. I know not where I be. Ten days have I been travelling and found no charity. My wife grows thin, my children cry, the baby lies abed. I beg no money, meat or wine, but only milk and bread.'

He took a diagonal path through the falling snow, picking up the firewood the stagehands had put out as he went, and produced his best expression of alarm as the Tuppenny Hag cackled offstage.

On she came in her sloping gait, a thick trail of blood seeping from the hem of her skirts.

'Tuppence for a bag of salt, tuppence for a bag of pins. Tuppence for a dead man's hand, tuppence and I'll eat thy sins.' Chain-smoking Woodbines had given Judith the perfect rasping voice. For tonight's performance, she'd made it even more pronounced.

'I am a poor man, mistress,' Morgan said. 'I cannot buy from thee. I am a wounded soldier trying to feed his family.'

'Then I shall lead thee to a lady,' the Tuppenny Hag replied. 'Who'll give thee something gold. She would not want thy kin to starve, nor have thee begging in the cold.'

Judith's face was deep inside the hood, but when she moved and Morgan saw her for a moment her make-up looked odd. Had she been given a new set of rotten teeth to wear? Or had that Italian craftsman made her a mask like Douglas's?

She limped centre stage and Morgan followed her, catching sight of Bobby's enraptured face in the wings.

Standing over the place where Enid, the Maiden Queen, was buried, the Tuppenny Hag made a rolling movement with her hands that Sound Effects complemented with an escalating rumble of thunder. As it intensified, and rattled the timbers of the stage, the leaves covering the Maiden Queen rose from the ground, spiralled and dispersed, and floated down with the snow.

Usually, one of the stagehands was there in the wings to flap a sheet of wood and cause a draught, but they were cunningly concealed this year. The illusion that the Tuppenny Hag really did have some supernatural command of the air made Bobby awestruck and he nudged the children next to him to share his amazement.

He seemed captivated by the Maiden Queen herself in her white silk gown and her wig of pure white hair. Did he think she was attractive, wondered Morgan. Did he find her desirable in a way that he couldn't yet understand?

'Look here, beggar man,' said the Tuppenny Hag, bringing Morgan back to the moment. 'What's this I've found for thee?'

She reached down and rummaged in the snow and the leaves, and pulled out the Maiden Queen's locket. As well as a mask, Judith must have been given false fingernails by Wardrobe too. He didn't remember her hands looking like talons at the rehearsal. And as if he'd been gripped by the claws of a bird, her palms felt scaly and dry when she encased the locket in his hands.

'Here's enough to feed thy kin. Take it, man, and don't look back. She would not know 'twas thee who took it. Put it in thy sack.'

'I am no common crook,' said Morgan, unable to take his eyes off Judith's fingers. 'I would not do such theft. I'll say that I discovered it and win the lady's thankfulness. Returning it might bring reward. My family might live. If she who once possessed this trinket had it in her heart to give.'

The Tuppenny Hag crowed again as she slowly started to make her way off the stage. The blood that emanated from the underside of her cloak steamed slightly, as if it really was oozing out of her body.

'Would ye let thy family die,' she said, 'to prove thou art a saint? I hear thy wife awailing, man. I see thy children growing faint.'

Once the Tuppenny Hag departed, the Beggar's altruism was indeed short-lived. He was required to seal his fate.

Morgan lifted the locket up so that it caught the light, and he made an appreciative face. In the wings, he saw Bobby admiring the piece of jewellery too.

'Yet she must have such things aplenty,' Morgan said. 'For one less toy, she would not weep. A mere bauble for a lady would fill the bellies of the poorest deep.'

As he placed the locket in his sack, the audience began, as usual, to jeer and yell. But then something flashed past overhead and rattled through the branches of the trees behind him, causing the donkey to flinch and pull at its rope. This was new, thought Morgan. They didn't usually start all that so early.

Before someone with more accuracy had a go, he led the donkey off the stage, catching another glimpse of the face – his face – reflected in the fabricated depths of the woods. The fact that it seemed to be moving of its own accord was just an illusion, a quirk of the way the mirrors had been set up. As he edged towards the wings, it disappeared completely.

'Come on, hurry up,' Ted barked, and with the same hostility he might have had for a real beggar he pulled Morgan and the donkey off the stage so that the Greenwood Folk could go on.

From the other side, they streamed out – a dozen of them,

maybe more – little ones and older ones, like Bobby. They were supposed to be creatures half-human, half-vegetation, and wore body stockings onto which dried leaves had been sewn so that when they skipped about the stage the susurration sounded like trees in the wind.

Around the sleeping Maiden Queen they formed a circle, hand in hand, and began to sing,

> We are the Greenwood Folk,
> A-wandering the dell-ee-o.
> All among the leaves we go.
> What we see you never know.

By the third repetition, Bobby had learnt all the words and was belting it out with the rest of them. He was such a natural, so confident on the stage. He'd want to come back and do it again. That was it now. They'd caught him, the Committee.

When the song came to an end he knelt with the others in a ring around the Maiden Queen, who stretched and yawned and then gave a start to see the little green faces staring at her. But they had broken the Tuppenny Hag's spell and she insisted on giving them a token of her gratitude. Though when she found her locket was gone, she began to weep.

It all seemed a touch overdone. Enid wasn't usually quite this melodramatic. Watching her closely, Morgan wasn't sure that it was Enid at all but a young girl. One of her daughters, was it? She looked no older than Bobby.

'We will help you, lady fair,' said the Chieftain of the

Greenwood Folk, lifting his red conical hat. 'We will find your golden locket. For there is one we've spied of late who likely picked your pocket.'

'Apprehend this wicked thief,' said the Maiden Queen. 'Bring him to the Magistrate. I will see thee well rewarded. Rubies on a silver plate.'

The children were supposed to be serious at this point, but Bobby was smiling to himself, no doubt thinking of the admiration he'd receive at school next week when he told everyone that he'd performed in the Old Play.

Still beaming, he got to his feet and skipped off the stage with the rest of the Greenwood Folk into the wings where Morgan was waiting.

Now Douglas strode out as the Magistrate to a great roar of adulation. Here was the Law made flesh. Here was Authority in crow-black robes. He began his long lament about wrong-doing and sedition in the royal forest, flashing his sword about for emphasis, and Morgan sidled through the gang of children to speak to Bobby. He took the boy's hand and led him out of the throng, telling him that he ought to go back down to the dressing room now. He'd had fun. He'd seen enough.

When Bobby tried to pull himself free, Morgan turned to look at him, ready to put his foot down. But the child in his grasp wasn't Bobby, or even a boy at all. He let go and the little girl he'd mistakenly dragged away went back to the other children, who were sniggering amongst themselves and looking over at Morgan with a kind of glee, as though they knew something he didn't.

Distantly, he heard the animal noise again. It was still down in the bowels of the theatre somewhere, or even out in the alleyway perhaps. And someone was shouting too, as if trying to control or corral it.

He realised that Rennie was trying to get him to listen.

'Wake up,' she said. 'Aren't you sober yet? You're on.'

'Where's Bobby?' he asked her again. 'He went off with Colin.' But she dismissed the question tetchily and gestured for him to get back on the donkey.

On stage, the Magistrate had got a fire going and was warming his hands as he delivered the last lines of his monologue.

'The King and Queen have only love and kindness for the lowly. And yet these peasants steal from them with avarice unholy. Woe betide the nation where all deference is forgotten. The poor and their ingratitude will turn this nation rotten.'

Morgan stooped to ask Ted if he'd noticed Bobby or Colin around, but he seemed not to hear him and handed the rope to the little girl with blonde hair. She gave it a yank and Morgan felt the donkey jolt into life beneath him as he was carried out onto the stage with the rest of the Greenwood Folk following.

'Ah, come, weary traveller,' said the Magistrate, taking the rope from the girl. 'Come sit you by the flames. You cannot journey onwards now. The snow lies deep. The daylight wanes.'

'I thank you, sir,' Morgan said, his voice sounding very small suddenly. 'I will not stay. For I have many miles to ride.'

'But kindness,' said the Magistrate, 'should never be denied. Not by one as poor as thee. Take your rest. Give thy sack to me.'

It was hard to believe that Douglas was wearing a mask at all. It was so lifelike. There was a sheen of sweat on the brow from the heat of the fire and the lights.

Morgan realised that Douglas was staring at him, his pupils strangely red, and he quickly gave his next line.

'My wife awaits my swift return,' he said. 'Ten days have I been hither. The children cry, the baby wails, with hunger they will wither.'

'But what hast thou to give them, man? Come, let me fill thy sack with bread. Should you homeward turn with nothing, then they are already dead.'

To signify his guilty conscience, to try to prevent the discovery of what he'd stolen, the Beggar had to be seen to grip the sack tight in his arms and really struggle with the Greenwood Folk who swarmed around him trying to take it. He was to let this go on long enough for the audience to start shouting encouragement, which they did. So much so that the uproar made the donkey buck and twist and shake Morgan to the floor. There were gales of laughter from the audience as the donkey bolted from the stage, kicking its back legs. The children, too, fell about at this unexpected slapstick and Morgan tried to ignore the pain in his back as he got to his feet.

The sack was now in the hands of the Magistrate, who felt around inside, turning out pieces of mouldering food that made the audience groan with increasing revulsion. Eventually, the Maiden Queen's locket was found and the Magistrate held it up so that everyone, including the Greenwood Folk, forgot about the hilarity of seeing the Beggar fall and let loose a volley of invective, booing like children at a pantomime.

'Thou villain,' cried the Magistrate, stepping closer to Morgan. 'Thou wicked man. What hast thou to say?'

Douglas wasn't wearing a mask. How could it be a mask?

Morgan faltered and broke the rhythm of the exchange, and heard the audience muttering with discontent.

'My lord,' Rennie hissed from the wings. 'Wake up.'

'My lord,' Morgan said, recovering himself. 'I saw it in the snow. Dropped by mishap along the way.'

The Magistrate withdrew his sword from its scabbard and aimed the tip at Morgan's heart.

'A liar and a thief, no less, who makes innocents his prey. Good Greenwood Folk, detain this man. He must be made to pay.'

At this point, the Beggar had to try to escape and Morgan made a sideways movement, his legs genuinely weak, his back still smarting from being thrown off the donkey, but the Chieftain was quick and caught him by the arm, calling for the rest of the Greenwood Folk to bind him.

Suddenly, there were dozens of little hands on his body as ropes were lashed around his wrists and ankles much tighter than usual. The little girl with the blonde hair had got up close to him, Morgan noticed, and was digging her fingernails hard into his arm, euphoric at being given licence to inflict real pain. She was squeezed out by two others who pinched and prodded at him as he looked around to see if Bobby was there somewhere in the brawl. But the green faces came and went and none of them were his.

With a little arm locked around his neck, actually making him choke, Morgan went to his knees. This was the cue for the Magistrate to turn to the audience, his sword held high above his head.

'All must be damned for evil and sin, whether nobleman, pauper, stranger or kin. The law is the law. A crime is a crime. If this man is guilty, then all must say aye.'

As usual, the speech was greeted with the loudest and longest cheer of the night. The Greenwood Folk jumped up and down. The Chieftain threw up his red conical hat. But this year, the racket was especially strident. When Douglas tried to deliver his final lines, his voice was barely audible over the mob.

'Out with the old year, in with the new. At the last stroke of midnight must thou pay thy earthly dues. Hark! Do you hear it man, the verdict of thy peers? May God have mercy on your soul when thy horrid executioner appears.'

Returning his sword to its sheath, he exited the stage to rapturous applause. Morgan felt the weight of the children gradually lifted as one by one the Greenwood Folk left too. The little girl had drawn blood where she'd grappled with his arm, but she capered off, laughing with the others, leaving Morgan alone with the audience.

Every year, a few people brought bugles or trumpets with them, and from various points around the auditorium fanfares began that were loud rather than tuneful.

Midnight had come.

Now they mocked him from all sides and called the Beggar every filthy name they could think of as the missiles began to rain down. Something putrid and vinegary hit Morgan in the eye, his chest was spattered with red pulp, his ear rang from the kick of a flying boot. Other things skittered through the leaves or thudded into the trees and shook down the powdery snow. Sound Effects set the thunder rolling again. The birds in the cages were beside themselves, battering at the bars to try to get away. Backstage, the poor donkey brayed and wheezed.

In the front row, the Committee members were standing. Everyone was surely standing now to be able to stamp their feet so hard. The crescendo reared up like a great wave that, at the moment Morgan expected it to fall, grew higher still.

But the play would soon end. The Beggar's execution was never actually *seen*. It was something that the audience had to imagine for themselves. Yet Rennie was allowing them to get into a true frenzy this year, she was really delaying the curtain. When he looked to the wings, no one seemed in any hurry to bring it down. Rather, they all stood there watching him intently.

A pungent pear split against his chin; the snot of a broken egg ran down his forehead.

Was this the change the Committee had made? To prolong the Beggar's mistreatment? To allow him to be abused for a few minutes more until he was truly sorry for what he'd done?

They didn't know what remorse was. They never had to dream of Dresden and Hamburg.

Eventually, the racket started to die down, the projectiles petered out. He'd never heard the theatre so silent. Now the curtain would surely drop. The audience had seen the Old Play as it ought to be. The Committee had got their ending.

He tried to read their faces – Beckett, Mrs Laycock and the rest – but they were looking past him towards the rear of the stage. When he turned, he saw that everyone in the wings was staring in the same direction too. The Maiden Queen, the Tuppenny Hag, the Magistrate and all the little Greenwood Folk jostled to get a good view. But there was still no Bobby. No Colin.

The wood appeared to have a true deepness to it now, as though they'd not used mirrors at all this year. The trees that stretched away into the mist seemed as real as the ones on the stage.

Out of the depths, Morgan heard the animal again. It was coming closer with a stag-like roar.

There was a movement in the gloom, and something started to emerge cautiously, the pale face that he'd seen earlier, obscured by the haze of the fog and the still-falling snow. Was that Colin? Morgan wondered. Had he finally bagged himself a part?

But when this new character advanced a little more, he saw that it was the size of a child, yet made to look old and sinewy, a clay colour to its naked skin. Two little horns budded from its head.

It had to be Bobby. They'd got him up to look like a goblin or a devil or the Minotaur. Though that wasn't quite it. The costume, the make-up, they were astonishing, unlike anything Morgan had seen before. Under the glare of the spotlight the face of this thing was horribly disfigured, like a lump of dough that had been punched in. The eyes, he noticed, were half closed and squinting, as if the thing needed glasses.

It bellowed again in a noise that was too low and gravelly for Bobby to make. Or perhaps not. After all, he was, slowly, becoming a man.

Whatever they'd dressed him as, whatever this creature was supposed to be, it looked at the Beggar, at Morgan, with great interest, like a dog that had cornered a rat and didn't know what to do next.

But at a double clap from Rennie in the wings it moved towards him purposefully, its mouth curling into a version of a smile, as though it had suddenly understood the damage it could do – and the mercy it could deliver – with the axe it carried.

A real one, Morgan realised. Recently sharpened.

A DOUBLE THREAD

Imogen Hermes Gowar

I awaken to the sound of a sewing machine. The back and forth of a treadle, vibrating through the ceiling as rhythmic as a heartbeat. It is coming from the attic above my room: many times I've lain listening to the joists humming with its motion, and been content that somebody up there was working as hard as they ought to be, but for a long time it has been silent. I did not expect to hear it tonight.

Nobody should be in the attic. Nobody should be sewing on the machine. It simply cannot be. And yet it rumbles on. Outside the wind is blundering about the house, and the sea on my horizon is roaring, but still the rattle of the sewing machine penetrates it all, persistent, accusatory, until I press the pillow over my head to block it out, and still the noise comes and comes. Even when I take the laudanum I keep at my bedside the rhythm penetrates its fog: 'It's me,' it seems to purr. 'It's me, it's me, it's me.'

In the morning I will venture upstairs and find all just as it ever was: a single bed neatly made, fashion plates pinned to the walls, measuring tape coiled, shears hanging on their nail. Nora Landry's sewing machine stands as she left it on that final morning, needle engaged, threaded with a reel of blood-red silk.

*

Nora Landry was her name, and she came to me on no sturdier a recommendation than that she was short of work and I was short of a lady's maid.

'I'd vouch for Nora any day of the week,' my aunt told me. 'You'll find her no trouble.'

She said this last part with meaning and the other ladies of her bridge circle nodded, also with meaning. The news of what my Nicholson had done – how she had taken *one look* at our new situation and vanished; how she had left me without help so abruptly only a few days into a planned stay of several months – would sustain them for some time. They had made it their business to find me a replacement: you might say that provincial folk have warmer hearts, but *I* say there is always a certain relish to be had in being peripherally associated with a scandal. And even before Nicholson, mine was quite a scandal.

'What training has she?' I asked.

'She'd very clever parents. Her father was a tailor; her mother was in service with me before she married . . .'

'*Very* talented,' the ladies chimed in. 'Made lace. Took in sewing. Nora's a credit to them both.'

'God rest their souls,' said my aunt. 'What dear people. I miss her mother terribly: I do take a special interest in poor Nora now she's all alone.'

'So she's never been a lady's maid?' I persisted impatiently, since we were straying from the particulars. This got them going.

'She's helped *out*,' one or other of them protested. 'She's stepped *in*!'

'That's how we do things in these parts,' Aunt said. 'One gets to know which young ladies are reliable in a pinch. I'm sure there's not one of us who hasn't had a few days from her here and there.' She tapped her lower lip. 'Our Nora needs something more regular.'

'I think I'll send for someone from London,' I said, just to set them off again.

That Penzance sits at the very edge of the civilised world, perhaps some distance beyond it, is an indisputable fact, and yet these ladies were duty bound to dispute it nevertheless. Provincial folk cannot help but insist that London has nothing that they do not, and besides all my aunt's friends were in a great flutter at the thought of having a lady like me at their Christmas ball in a few months' time. They'd have done anything to prove to me that Penzance was as bustling a metropolis as the one I'd been obliged to leave; that I might find all my accustomed comforts and entertainments here, that I – in short – could be happy in spite of it all.

'You see,' Aunt had already nudged me over dinner, 'we keep as good a wine cellar here as any,' and then, 'you *see*, our assembly rooms will keep you entertained.' And yes, indeed they might, for they advertised a valiant schedule of lectures and recitals, which looked at first like an abundance, until one understood that this was the sole venue for such things. In London the amusements were inexhaustible – always an opening of this or an extended run of that – but in Penzance there was only what there was. Yes, I might see a play, for the three days it was in town. Yes, I might attend a Christmas ball, but it was *the* Christmas ball, and if I missed it there would be no other. And if I were to lose a lady's maid? Well, these good women were determined that I would find the only possible replacement.

'Don't hire some girl sight unseen,' my aunt was saying now. 'You don't want another like your last one. And who would make the journey out here at such short notice?'

'My friends will know of someone,' I said doubtfully. 'I'll write.' I knew, in my heart, that nobody would be inclined to do me any sort of a favour while my husband's trial went on. If there had been anyone in Chelsea whose mercy I judged robust enough to throw myself upon, I would not, after all, have fled to Penzance.

'You'll be back in London before you know,' soothed Aunt. 'It'll all be over by spring. Have Nora tide you over and search for the perfect girl when you're home again.'

I hesitated. 'That's a long time to have nobody who understands my hair.'

'How difficult can it be? Look, she's reliable. Not flighty. Obedient, hard-working, a good learner. I should think dear Nora will do you very well for the time being. Added to that,' she said in a coaxing manner, 'she was apprenticed to a very fine couturier in Truro. She sews like an angel. Makes all our best dresses.'

Well, that piqued my interest. I'd cast an eye over each lady's gown, of course, and had satisfied myself that they were well done. There must be a decent seamstress in town, and this was of particular interest to me since I had with me a bolt of crimson silk waiting to be made up into something magnificent. I looked again at the dresses of the lady bridge players. They were ghastly old-fashioned, all swagged and tasselled and furbelowed, bustles like the back half of a pantomime cow. No use my commissioning a dress if it were to turn out like that. 'Maybe so, Aunt,' I said, 'but what does for you ladies won't do at all for *me*.'

'No indeed! You'll have your own ideas, of course.'

'I always do. And you think this woman's competent?'

'Nora Landry is a marvel,' the ladies told me. 'Whatever you ask, she'll sew it. Just show her a picture. She'll know how. She could have had quite a career had she accompanied her employer to London – had her parents not been ailing by that time. But London's loss is Penzance's gain.'

I was dismayed when this Nora Landry came to me. She was nearly thirty and not pretty – tallish, wide-shouldered, thick black hair with a frizzle of grey through it, and dressed without one hint of fashionable sensibility. She stood on the rug in Aunt's upstairs parlour with her hands clasped and her head down as if she'd been brought in for a scolding.

'Your dress is nice,' I said, to be kind. It wasn't – it was a dark grey wool, overly sober, overly honest about her heavy body – but I saw that it was skilfully constructed, and its small lace collar was beautifully worked. 'I hear you're a seamstress.'

She said nothing. Parted her thick pale lips, looked at the floor, closed them again.

'Do you keep up with the fashions?' I prompted.

She looked at me then, startled, wary. 'I –' she tried, and I heard a little tick-tick as she began to worry at the edge of a nail. She dropped her eyes again, said nothing more, although her fingers squirmed together still.

'It's not a trick question,' I said in my jolliest tone. '*I* like fashion. The styles are hard to come by here, I'm sure.'

She cleared her throat, and when she brought her hand to her mouth I saw she was shaking. 'I keep up with the fashions, madam.' Her voice seemed to fail her, and she finished in a whisper.

'You'll have a great deal to keep on top of if I hire you,' I went on. 'A lady's maid is a position of great responsibility. You will be secretary, hairdresser, seamstress, housewife, all rolled into one. Nicholson knew *everything*. She replaced my gloves before they wore through, she brushed my clothes daily and then she cleaned the brushes, she washed all my delicates herself rather than entrust them to the laundress. She took charge of my correspondence, passing on the delightful letters to me and handling the tiresome ones herself. She kept a notebook devoted entirely to my requirements, right down to the dates of my monthlies. And she did all this with perfect discretion. I'm sure I know only the half of her duties – I suppose I shall find them out soon enough, now they are not being done!'

I laughed lightly, but Nora's expression did not change. 'Do you think you're matched to this task?' I asked.

She nodded. She did not look me in the eye. My

expectations had been low, but I was astonished that this creature was the best Penzance could come up with: she had all the scintillation of a dairy cow. If Nicholson were here she'd have caught my eye and smirked, and afterwards we would have howled with laughter at the pure lumpen idiocy of this Nora Landry. Oh, Nicholson! Most perfidious of servants! Where was she now? Already in London, no doubt, she and her irreproachable record-keeping. Who knew what she might do next, with the press baying for the smallest detail of my family's private life? Perhaps there were advantages to my choosing a stupider candidate for the moment.

'To return to your sewing,' I said. 'I have a commission for you. Come with me.'

I led Nora onto the landing and up the stairs to my room. Aunt's house was built around a large spiral staircase, so wherever one was on it, one heard all the activity from above and below, and because all the doors opened onto it one could always insist one had been innocently passing by (just as Aunt happened to be at that moment) and not eavesdropping at all. My aunt gave us a warm, conspiratorial look which Nora did not return. She followed me as to the gallows: grim-faced, hands clasped, shoes dragging on the thick carpet.

On the second floor, my room had a view all the way down to the beach, which at this time of year was a sorry sight. The stoic, straw-hatted donkeys had been led away for the season, but a herd of padlocked bathing machines huddling in the shelter of the sea wall shared their air of despond. I'd always thought of Penzance as a quaint, sunny town, cottages and churches nestled cheerfully among the palm trees, but it was a good deal surlier than I remembered from my childhood summers, the wind rattling about its crooked streets colder and more forceful. The granite houses had their doors and windows shut tight and the flowers in their gardens were fading.

No matter. I'd brought my silk with me.

When I had Nora's full attention, I took up the parcel and shook it out across the bed. The fabric tumbled forth, more beautiful even than I remembered, for when I'd chosen it in the draper's back in Mayfair it was one of many fine things, and here it was like nothing else. It was a blood-red shot silk, which glowed black in its creases, and as I unfolded it yard by yard it hissed as if it were angry. Nora Landry stood perfectly still, although her lips moved silently as if she were calculating something. Her heavy cow eyes moved across the fabric. I'd expected her to be astounded but she simply looked at it, and asked no questions. I longed to gather it up and press it against myself, to roll myself in it.

'You can touch it,' I said, which I meant as a favour to her but which she seemed to take as an order, and dutifully took it between her thumb and forefinger without looking at me. I saw that her fingertips were bulbous under bitten-down nails, and the skin there was shiny and sore-looking. 'That's enough,' I said.

Nora turned her head questioningly in my direction but still did not quite dare to lay eyes on me.

'I want an evening gown,' I said. 'It's for the wretched Christmas ball. You've a clear two months to work on it.'

Her lips were moving again but she didn't say anything.

'Look,' I said, and brought out the album Nicholson and I had made. For months we'd snipped fashion plates and society portraits from magazines, French women with white arms and narrow waists, whose gowns were draped across their bodies in the Grecian style: I showed Nora that there was almost no bustle; no adornments of fussy lace or silly glass cherries; no detachable bodice or tiered flounces; no hat. It would show my décolletage, my shoulders, my back. 'I want it to look as if it might fall off me at any moment,' I said. 'I want it simple to the point of wickedness.'

Nora flinched. 'Simple takes a lot of work,' she said.

I laughed. It was the first time I'd liked her. 'So you understand,' I said. 'Can you do it?'

She was tracing the lines of the gowns before her with her sore fingers. 'I see how it's done,' she said in that gruff, awkward voice of hers. 'I can make it the way you want.'

'The way a couturier would?' I said. 'I've been all around the world, you know. I've been dressed by Worth, by Pingat, by Laferrière; were I in London I'd go to Liberty and see what they could do for me. That's what I expect.'

She showed no surprise or admiration. Her demeanour changed not at all. 'Of course,' she said.

I'd thought she would be delighted by the opportunity to dress a lady so outside her own sphere, who might introduce her to things she could not hitherto have dreamed of, but she went on as dull as a plank. It made me snappish.

'I'll know if you cut corners,' I warned her.

'Yes, madam.' She stepped forward to examine the fabric once more. 'The draping you want – it's not possible without foundation. I need to know what corset you mean to wear.'

'Quite so,' I said, and brought them all out. This was very pleasant: I explained each one to her – who made it, for what occasion and so on – while she held her stolid silence, chin down, breathing through her mouth. How much she comprehended I don't know, but to narrate my triumphs and my sensations did me a great deal of good, and by the time I was finished I felt entirely invigorated. Something must have penetrated Nora's skull for she touched her thickened fingers briefly to the most prized of all my undergarments: a steam-moulded corset (the patented Izod method), pearl-white, intricately boned like fan-vaulting for the body. It held its shape like a beetle's carapace.

'That is the one,' she said.

I forgot, for a moment, that she was a dullard, or that I was never to give another servant an inch of quarter. She understood my clothes: she would make me a dress. We grinned at each other.

No sooner had Nora let the smile escape, she seemed to cram it back in again. Her face reddened; she dropped her eyes. She looked away with a stupid air of appeal, as dogs do when they know they have done wrong but cannot puzzle out how.

'The position's yours,' I said. I turned to the corsets scattered across the bed, the creased silk heaped just as I had left it, black and red as embers, hissing to itself. 'Clear these things away.'

As coincidence would have it, Aunt was on the landing again when I left my room.

'You seem happy,' she said. 'How did you find Nora?'

'I hired her,' I rejoined.

She beamed. 'How wonderful! Dear old Nora, it's a weight off my mind to know that she'll be employed all winter – and we've room for her here. I'd like to have her in the house.'

She had not responded to *my* coming to live in her home with anything like this enthusiasm.

'You might have warned me she was an idiot, dear Aunt,' I said cheerfully.

'Excuse me?'

She had dropped her voice to a whisper.

'I don't believe there's a single thought in her head,' I went on loudly. 'I never met anyone with so little to say for themselves.'

'Oh,' said Aunt. 'Well, no, she's not much of a talker . . .'

'That she isn't,' I said, and did my best Nora Landry impression, stooping my head and goggling my eyes, making my lips move in silence. My aunt's face grew hawkish and I knew at once that I had made things complicated for myself.

'She's *shy*,' Aunt said severely. 'Shy and terribly nervous!

Perhaps that's why she seemed stiff to you. But she has a good heart and we who know her well think very highly of her.'

'Sorry, Aunt,' I said.

'Can you be kind to her?' she demanded.

My face was hot. I glared at my feet, brimming with rage. 'Consider your station,' she went on. 'Consider your good fortune.'

I would have protested then, and opened my mouth, but she cut me off: 'Your good fortune *compared to those around you*. You've fallen on hard times – I cannot imagine your distress – and so I forgive you a great deal. But never let me see you mock someone less fortunate than you. Never let me regret introducing you to Nora.'

It would be a long winter indeed if I could not placate her. I rolled my eyes and sighed, 'I didn't think.' Then, because she was still waiting, 'I was wrong.'

'Please,' she said. 'Nora's all alone in this world and her life has been a sad one. I know that you'd rather be in London, or Paris, or wherever it is you go . . .'

'I have my sights on New York,' I said.

'. . . but for now, you are in Penzance. And you must find the grace to like it.'

The weeks passed, and in Penzance the weather flew. Cloudbanks fat as plums might suddenly rend open to spill sunbeams across the sea and the town; the sky might clear to a guileless blue while the cold numbed fingers and toes and the wind became a bully. Autumn was gone and still I could not warm to Nora Landry. Every morning I loathed her irresolute knock on my door, the shuffling way she carried in my tea. I loathed the feel of her breath when she stood behind me at the dressing table, the frowning doughy face she wore as she attempted to puzzle out how to fasten the clasp of my necklace, the nervous squeak of air in her throat as she pressed her panic down.

How silent and rigid she was, how hesitantly her hands moved across my body when she dressed me, how the words seemed to die in her mouth when I asked her opinion: if I asked her again, louder, she grew quieter still. How *slow* she was, how lacking in spirit! I simply could not credit why my own family tolerated her – were kind to her! Whenever he met her on the stairs, Uncle would say, 'Miss Landry, my dear. What a pleasure,' and what's more said it warmly, spreading his arms in surprise and welcome. She, of course, merely ducked her head and let him squeeze her hand.

I had kept Nicholson about me constantly, for one never knows when one might need a fresh glass of water, or a lozenge, or simply wish to exchange some amusing private observation on the appearance of another person in the party. When I asked Nora Landry to sit by me she did so in a rigid, poised, quivering manner, and when I asked her to read to me she would stammer and stumble until tears came to her stupid eyes. So I released her into the house. She'd my gown to sew, of course, and the cold had compelled me to have her make up new flannel underclothes, the most provincial of garments, so I was content that she was busy in the attic sewing room Aunt had prepared for her. But sometimes I went onto the landing and listened to the sounds of the house. Sometimes when the door to the basement stood open, so that up came the sound of clattering pans and women's laughter, I knew – I simply *knew* – that she was down there among them.

Aunt had that jovial sensibility typical of well-born countrywomen who have known their servants all their lives, and their servants' mothers too: she was often below stairs, not only with her own staff but any local who dropped in (and well they might, for she kept a pound cake ready to cut from at any moment, and the tea caddy stood open all day). Never once had I been visited by the impulse to invite the butcher's lad in to swing his legs and tell me about his mother – indeed, on Cheyne Walk such a thing would have been quite impossible – but for Aunt it was a mania. This particular morning I heard the below-stairs conversation wander from jam puffs to how dear eggs had become lately; then whether to curry the rest of the duck; and on to who had taken up the lease on the shop by the Market Building, and whether Mrs So-and-so had had her baby yet. I did not hear Nora's voice but I was certain she was down there. Their conversation twined about her presence: I felt the shape of her implied in its spaces. I leaned on the banister and glared down at the chequerboard flags below, listening. But if Nora spoke, her voice was not substantial enough to make its way to me.

Presently, Aunt came up the narrow basement stairs,

humming to herself, and started up the great staircase. By the time she saw me she was almost upon me, and she started. 'My dear! I didn't expect anyone to be . . .' She eyed me. '. . . to be lingering here.'

'Is Landry downstairs?'

'Why, yes, changing the water for your flowers.' She smiled. 'I do like to have dear Nora about the place.'

'Call her Landry, please. While she works for me she ought to be addressed properly.'

Aunt laughed. 'Goodness, I shall struggle with that. But' – she straightened her face, noticing, I suppose, my annoyance – 'I'll try.'

'Not that she deserves to be treated as a lady's maid,' I sniffed, 'being such a sorry one.'

'Join us in the kitchen,' said Aunt, seeming not to hear my complaint. 'You'd be most welcome.'

'Pooh! Not me!'

She smiled. 'Perhaps it's not your way, to mingle with those who serve you, but I do find it pays to be attentive to them. I'm only fetching my old mittens for Jenny to mend. Here, come down with me.'

Against my better judgement, I did. The stairs to the kitchen were narrow and steep, with a treacherous turn halfway. 'Like descending into a burrow,' I laughed to Aunt, who did not reply. Below was a cavernous room, whose high, small windows kept it in semi-gloom. The housemaid sat by the hearth with a pile of boots before her and a brush in her hand; Cook was rolling out pastry; the ostler was leaning back in his chair with a newspaper spread before him; and Nora Landry held her cup in both hands, blowing a dimple onto the surface of her tea.

She struck me as different. She held herself more loosely – shoulders less rigid, and her hands did not roam or scrabble once she laid her cup down, but rested lightly on the table as if she gave them no thought at all. She was not quite smiling, but she had turned her eyes trustingly to the ostler as he read out some item of news, and looked upon him as if she were not afraid at all.

Imagine my irritation. So she did not need to be so awkward; so her stammering and stumbling was not after all the best she was capable of; so she could, if she chose, do me the courtesy of decent conversation. I took a seat at the table with a smile, and Nora at once seemed to fold into herself, her head stooped and her shoulders hunched, her face grew stupid. I saw her lips move in perfunctory greeting but her voice seemed stopped in her throat.

'A bad do,' said the ostler, waving the front page at the room, 'this trial. It's plain as day that this gent burned the mill down for the insurance.'

'James,' said Aunt softly. *I* was beyond speech.

'But with workers inside it! *That*, I cannot fathom. And when so many of his cronies in government saw fit to conceal the facts of it, you have to wonder what he was doing for them in return. The man's a crook. The man's a toad. It makes a mockery of everything.'

'Can we . . .'

'Well, he won't get away with it,' the ostler went on. 'They'll find him guilty, as they ought.'

I sat still. Aunt stared at me, and the maid sat buffing away assiduously, although the shoe in her lap shone: it was as if by continuing in that rhythmic motion she might hold time at bay and suspend us in the moment before disharmony descended.

At last I said, 'You surprise me. I thought gossip travelled faster in these little towns.'

'Beg your pardon?'

'My dear,' Aunt began to gabble, 'we have done our very best to be discreet about it. We have tried to protect you.'

'That's my husband,' I said, gesturing to the front page. 'That's *his* mill.'

Oh, how he scrambled to apologise! How he crushed the paper in his hands, how he flapped its sheets this way and that in his anxiety. 'I meant nothing by it. I never thought—'

'I daresay you didn't,' I said drily.

'Well, it's hardly a wife's fault what her husband does,' Aunt chimed in. 'Our guest may have had no idea at all . . .'

She looked at me kindly, but her words inflamed me. 'What newspaper is that you're reading?' I snapped, taking a glance. 'I see. Barely worthy of the name. Swill for the masses is all they print – they are always prejudiced against the well-born, the leaders, the achievers.'

'It's dreadful what he's done,' said James stoutly. 'You can't deny it. He's a crook. He's a murderer.'

'Sheer sensationalism!' I cried. 'Lurid, ghoulish, cheap.

How many mills and factories does my husband own that have never suffered so much as *one* fire (of any significance)? How many thousands of people has he employed over the years who have *never* suffered injury or death in their place of work? Strange that the press is entirely *incurious* on that subject. Hard-working men and women and dear little children put food on the table thanks to the employment he offers them, but as soon as something goes wrong – *that's* what the papers pick up.'

'Can you really excuse what has gone on?' the ostler demanded.

'Considering this country's absolute dependence on cotton, I certainly can. If you hate it so much, why don't you stop buying it? Besides, I would think that any patriotic man would be very sorry indeed to see my husband's work – which adds so much to the economy here and abroad – forced to cease. Imagine how a trial like this could damage him! Nobody thinks of *his* welfare in all of this, although he contributes a thousand times more than any menial he employs.'

Nora was tracing her sore red fingertips across the surface of the table, following its whorls and lingering on its dents and scars. Her eyes were resolutely lowered. She breathed through her mouth. She was, once more, an idiot.

'Landry,' I said to her, so that she jumped and emitted a strange gasp of surprise. 'Bring me my flowers. Sew me my clothes. That's what you're here for, isn't it? Not to sit around gossiping.'

*

What I loathed most about Nora Landry was how skilled she was at her work. Her attic room was neat and orderly, lit by a dormer window which looked – as my own, larger window did – to the churning sea at the foot of the town, flint-coloured now and speckled with foam. When I came up she showed me red flannel petticoats with hands that were actually shaking, but when I took them to the window for a better look I saw that they were perfect. I turned them inside and out, inspecting the seams: the nap was thick and soft under my fingers, the length generous, and everything so beautifully stitched and decorated with stripes of black wool pieced in. They were simple garments, but made with such care and good sense: I'd been expecting – rather hoping for – some sloppiness that might betray her stupidity, but there was no evidence of it at all. Nora lingered, breathing shallowly. A sudden gust of rain clattered against the window like gravel, and the wind got up a quavering song.

'I wonder what work you've neglected, that you might spend so much time on these,' I said.

She froze where she stood, like an automaton when its penny has run out, and then lurched back into life, saying in her low voice, 'Well I . . .' and dithered on, her voice dipping in and out of audibility, her hands clasping and releasing and reclasping one another. 'It's a deal of work but I went as fast as I could – with the petticoats, and the drawers, and the shifts – everything you wanted.'

'I suppose the muslin for my gown is delayed, then.'

She cleared her throat and blinked hard. 'No, madam. I have it ready for a fitting.'

She had a dress form tucked away in the corner and I had thought it empty, but when she brought it out I saw that upon it was my dress, the very dress I had dreamed of, wasp-waisted, draped in the Grecian style, and, more than that, Grecian in colour too: a crisp parchment-white calico. I circled it. It stood there proud and bleached, the ghost version of itself.

'That's splendid,' I said before I could stop myself.

'There are one or two more things I might—'

'No, no. Do nothing to it. I want to try it on immediately.'

I fetched my intended corset and she dressed me. It felt strange to stand on the boards of her attic in my stockinged feet while she pinned the bone-white gown into place above my spine. It was just as I'd hoped it would be. I turned this way and that in front of her mirror, looking over my shoulder to see how my bare back looked, saw myself a white-shouldered caryatid, the humble calico transformed. It fitted me perfectly, and it lay so casually across my body as if nothing held it up at all, as if it would slip off at a moment's notice.

'Think how it will be in red!' I said. I could imagine myself arriving at the assembly rooms, peeling off my furs to reveal my naked arms, my high bosom, all those folds of smouldering crimson, the only one of my sort in Penzance.

Nora smiled, shy as a child singled out for praise. She bent about me, straightening the skirt, adding another pin, and her hands as they passed my waist and calf and shoulder were all at once deft and purposeful, and her downturned eyes were clever, and she assessed me as a craftswoman should.

'I'll start to cut the silk for the gown itself, if you have no objection,' she said, and she even sounded different: authoritative, as if she were certain of her value to me. 'I can start this evening. Remember, madam, it'll take me a little longer with the lining and the finish.'

'Oh, take the time you need! I can wait!'

She took the muslin off me and dressed me again in my ordinary clothes, and while we didn't speak we were enclosed in a shared halo of satisfaction and excitement. I remember her swift hands removing the pins in one direction, fastening my buttons in another, as she hummed lightly under her breath, a Nora transformed. *Nora is a marvel*, Aunt's friends had said, and now I understood. But I said nothing to her of it. I simply stood still and let her buzz around me in her happiness.

By December, I was in very poor temper. The trial was not going as much in my husband's favour as his lawyers had assured him it would. There is a ghoulish public appetite for such incidents – which seasoned industrialists all know cannot be helped – which couples unfortunate words like 'scandal' and 'tragedy' to family names. Add to this, Nicholson had of course reappeared in London and had begun to betray my confidences in the gutter press at the slightest provocation. None of it was permissible in court, so the joke was on her since all she betrayed was her own classlessness. It didn't bother *me* in the slightest, but it made it troublesome to socialise. Penzance was preparing for Christmas, and all the bridge ladies had 'at homes' with twinkling candles and heaped sugarplums and so forth. I did my duty in attending them, but the conversation seemed to evaporate around me. In I would glide, beneath the milky-berried mistletoe and the red-berried holly, and the knots of people came apart for me, the circles of conversation re-forming a few steps away. If I went to the buffet table there was never a crowd; if I took myself out for air everybody else went in. I never joined the dancing.

'No matter,' I said to myself. 'The Christmas ball is coming. My gown is almost ready. And I will be the most splendid person there and then they'll see – then they'll see!'

The gown was more often than not to be found beneath the needle of Nora Landry's sewing machine, and if not there then across her knee as she saw to its more intricate details. She sat in her attic with the gown slumped across her lap like a tamed dragon, seething gently as she moved her hands over it, turned it, brought it to her face. Late at night when I lay in bed I heard the treadle of her machine through the ceiling like a heartbeat. Sometimes when Nora was busy elsewhere I went up to her room and stared at the gown on its form, half-become. Each time I was almost surprised to find it waiting in the shadows, a blot of deep crimson, headless, limbless, and yet its own entity. How often I stared at it, as if it were a woman I envied but whose friendship I longed for.

And how I resented Nora for being its keeper, blank-faced, lumbering Nora who had no finer sensibility whatever, no spark of art, but upon whom I was nevertheless dependent for my great moment's delivery.

Of course, two days before the ball the dress was not done. This I was alerted to when the maid-of-all-work brought up my morning tea, a dark and thickly filmed brew made from the leaves in the common caddy, I could tell at once, not the special blend I had brought with me and which Nora was under strict instruction to keep apart from whatever Aunt drank.

'Where's Landry?' I asked, sitting up in bed. She stared at me, so I had to prompt her: 'My maid?'

'Oh, Nora? Why, she's upstairs working on the gown. I've brung your breakfast things up myself, to save time.'

'On whose authority?' I demanded, and rose from the bed. 'Fetch me my kimono. Fetch me my slippers. I'll deal with this.'

Nora was in her attic, head bent over the offending item, stitching furiously with those raw fingers of hers. The sky at the window was purplish, not yet light, and she relied on the light of a candle, which made crisp, dark mountains of the gown's folds. She looked up when I stalked in in my silk kimono wrap, and lost her composure immediately, fumbling with her needle and dropping her thimble as if it had become slippery.

'I ask so little of you, Landry!' I cried. 'The scantest duties, and yet you cannot fulfil them.'

'I'm sorry. Madam,' she faltered, 'I am trying – I endeavour to . . .' She gestured to the gown. 'I thought it would do no harm for Jenny to bring you your tea this once, given the urgency—'

'Nobody is to bring me tea but you,' I said. 'Nobody is to fulfil any of your duties but *you*. If they exceed your capabilities there's an obvious solution.'

She said nothing.

'Why isn't the gown finished?' I demanded.

'Madam, I'm sorry,' she said. 'I tried. I'm trying. It will be done, it *will*. It's only the hem left. It's only the buttons to put on. It's very difficult to—'

'It's none of my concern, what is *difficult* for you. I simply don't care. I care only that my needs are attended to.'

'What's going on up here?' said Aunt, who had appeared in the doorway in her own wrap. 'Nora, are you still at it? Have you slept?'

'Landry is behind with my gown,' I said, and stamped my foot. 'I'll have no time to try it on before the ball!'

'Goodness but she's worked so hard,' said Aunt, inspecting the gown in Nora's lap and squeezing her shoulder as she did so. 'Nora, it's beautiful. The finest thing you ever made. And see, my dear, there is almost nothing else to be done to it – the very smallest finishes. You'll have it in time.'

'She's ruined everything,' I said.

Nora looked at Aunt with the weariest of eyes, and I was filled with hatred for the communion they shared. 'Not so,' said Aunt mildly. 'She's done wonderfully, considering the labour of this thing – and the skill. On top of everything else she's tasked with, she's pulled off a miracle. Really, Nora, you could make a name for yourself – there are few seamstresses with talent like yours.'

'Would you stop?' I cried. 'You'd never say a ploughed field was the work of the yoked oxen. You'd never credit roast beef to the turnspit. Never! Landry's no different, you know: she has merely been trained to complete a necessary set of actions. That's what she's good for. Stop buttering her up: she ought to know her station.'

Aunt stared at me in stupefaction. 'I try so hard to think well of you,' she said.

I had no time for her recriminations. Before I knew what I did, I had snatched the dress from Nora's lap and crushed it to my chest, its fabric rough and smooth at the same time, cool and hot. 'I will find someone else to finish it,' I said, 'someone who'll be glad of the work.'

Nora sprang up and followed me across the attic. 'Madam, please,' she said. 'There's nothing to it. Let me.'

I headed for the stairs. 'You had your chance.'

'Please,' she repeated. 'I have brought it this far, all my own work. Let me do the finishing. I know it best.'

We were standing at the top of the stairs, as close as when she dressed me, with her fingers and mine both clutching at the dress, which in the half-light was a deep soft black, all ash and no ember. How clearly I recall her face at that moment, for it was only inches from mine, that unlovely, inelegant, tremble-lipped visage with its eyes very wild and dark. 'I can't wait to never think of you again,' I spat. Our hands were still tight against one another. The gown flopped sideways, showing all its insides, the boning channels edged with tiny stitches, for although the dress looked light as a cloud it was full of steel. Sewn into the lining I noticed something that had not been there before: a pale rectangle, embroidered with the words

LANDRY
PENZANCE

'I'll tell you again,' I said. 'This is *not your work*.'

She was tugging on the dress still, her knuckles white, afraid to do it damage but determined nevertheless to take hold of it again. 'Please,' she said.

'It was my idea,' I went on, 'my creation, and I will wear it. *I* am its finishing touch. What are you to it but a mechanical?'

I felt Nora's grip tighten at the very moment mine loosened. We were at the top of the stairs – she pulled back, hard, and met with no resistance from me – she tumbled all of her own accord, without so much as a shove. I'd swear any oath that this is the truth. And it was such a large staircase, you will recall, and so steep. There was nothing to be done at all.

A dreadful time, it was. Not that I remember much, for the doctor gave me a draught as soon as he arrived, so that

Christmas left only a few strange impressions upon my memory: spilled port spreading across a white napkin; the swell and ebb of candle flames inside ruby glass fairy-lamps; amaryllis and poinsettia unfurling grand plush petals. There cannot have been much merrymaking. Aunt wore black. What they did with Nora Landry I don't know: there must have been a family plot somewhere, to reunite her with those who loved her, but I never asked and Aunt never said.

The wind got itself up into a frenzy and stayed that way as the year turned. I lay in bed while it battered at the windowpane with its bare hands. It sighed and keened out there and, indoors, I did the same, plucking at the hem of my red flannel petticoats for comfort. Something peculiar had come upon me – a sense of hovering presence, as if I had heard an irresolute footstep outside my door, as if I expected at any moment for familiar hands to lay my pearls upon my throat or add pins to my hair. One day I ventured onto the landing, and stood there listening for the sounds of the house, the kitchenful of chatter that I had become so accustomed to. I heard nothing. There was nobody laughing or gossiping, neither upstairs nor down. The housemaid passed me in silence, so that a breeze stirred my skirt and touched the nape of my neck. I leaned upon the banister, looking down the spiral of the stairs and then up, until I could bear to look no more.

'Are you all right, my dear?' Aunt asked when she found me there. So deep in reverie had I been that I jumped, and heard a gasp of surprise that was at once of me and not. I gripped the handrail.

'Now,' she said, steering me back into my room, 'we must discuss what comes next. When it might suit you to leave.'

A shaky breath passed through me. 'I'm not ready,' I told her.

'I understand.' She helped me into my chair and opened the curtains wide so I could see the sea all ruffled, lying in the bay as if it were a pool of crumpled silk. 'But I think *we* are ready. I don't mean to distress you, but the house . . . my staff . . . it would be better for them . . .'

That pricked me. 'Better for *them*?' I asked. 'What about *me*? You'd wash your hands of me, for them?'

She was turning a garnet ring round and round her finger, and twisting her face into an approximation of contrition. 'Forgive me,' she said, 'but I have discharged my duty towards you. I am easy on that account.'

'So you'd cast me to the wolves! How like you,' I growled. I'd have put up more of a fight except that something very queer had overcome me, such that it was as if hands were upon me, deft sure hands moving across my body to unhook buttons and pull tapes loose; hands smoothing my bodice and tucking my collar, hands fastening brooches and gathering pins. Aunt was talking on: 'Now you needn't go immediately – perhaps in a week or so – and perhaps your husband – perhaps his people – they might find you somewhere secluded to recuperate . . .' but all the while I was barely listening, rooted as I was to the chair while the hands of a servant crossed over me, and a little exhalation of worry sounded in my ear.

I sprang to my feet. 'As you wish!' I cried. 'But leave me now; leave me for now.'

She protested a little but allowed herself to be ushered from the room. I slammed the door behind her and sat down on the bed, trembling. What on earth to make of it all? I felt those busy hands on me yet, the familiar feeling of being tended to which now began to frighten me. I rose, but the movement was attended by a sigh at my shoulder; I crossed the room but I felt a jostle at my skirts, a hastiness of breathing following me about. 'It's the wind,' I said to myself. 'Old houses have draughts,' and the presence sighed in acquiescence.

I was not quite right in myself – I knew this – and I got under the bedcovers, and wrapped my arms about myself, and tried to shut it out.

And now the sewing machine. Each night after the last of the house has gone to bed, I hear it begin to whirr, and I lie here irritated by its persistence, the dogged unerring drone that reminds me too much of Nora: stolid, expressionless, bent over her work for hours without any apparent desire for novelty. I have begun to believe that it must be one of the maids taking advantage of the situation. Girls like them are never displeased to have a sewing machine in the house, for they are always in want of some new little garment or other. How ghoulish to use a dead woman's machine! Surely even Aunt, who forgives her servants everything, could not forgive that. I decide that tonight I will set this opportunist straight.

I rise from the bed and, taking a candle, tiptoe in my red flannel nightgown onto the landing. Now the sound is unmistakable: the whirr of the needle, the here-and-there of the treadle, and every now and again the clunk of a seamstress halting her work to end a seam or change direction. It comes from above, the last flight of stairs to the attic room, whose door – I see as I lean out over the banister and peer upward – stands ajar although no light escapes from it. I creep up the stairs, barefoot, candle aloft. My heart feels too large for my chest, bruised by my ribs as it beats against them, although I know that this disturbance is only the work of some upstart servant, and add confidence to my step. Into Nora Landry's room I go, and find it as dark as it had seemed from the stairs, full of the rattle of the machine. I am confounded, look about, think the room at first quite empty, until I behold the awful sight of a figure upon the floorboards, tall and imperious, turned towards me, as if in expectation, as if in judgement.

I scream. I fall to my knees with gibberish falling from my lips; I clasp my hands and beg that I be spared, that I be forgiven. I am still screaming when Aunt and the maids rush to see what the commotion is, bringing more lights with them, so that when they haul me by my armpits from the floorboards and I reach a trembling finger to point at what scared me so, what we see before us is only my poor gown, rescued from the cold clutching fingers of Nora Landry and hung back on its dummy, headless and limbless and blameless in the candlelight.

'Who would hang it up so?' asks Aunt.

'I did, ma'am,' said the youngest of her maids. 'I thought, to keep it nice . . . Nora would want . . .' and to my shock she pressed a handkerchief to her eyes.

'You did as you thought right,' said Aunt, putting an arm about her shoulders. 'But really, Jenny, to arrange it so – of course our poor guest was frightened.'

'It's nothing,' I say crossly. 'I was not really afraid.' My eye is called back to the gown on its mannequin, standing so frankly there, inscrutable and yet perfectly alert to me. The sensation is something akin to catching a glimpse of oneself in a mirror one did not realise was there: recognition mingled with the uncanny, a person known intimately and yet not at all. *Is that what I look like*, I wonder, staring at that haughty faceless figure. And at the same moment those disembodied hands return, running along the hem of my nightgown and tweaking one-two-three-four as if somebody is crouched before me, pinning my skirts to just the right length. I hear a husky voice faltering into silence, something more than a sigh and less than speech, but when I look down I see nothing amiss, just my bare feet and above them Nora Landry's even stitches on the red flannel.

All this took place a year ago, and I can laugh at it now. I have put an entire ocean's distance between myself and Penzance, and I feel all the better for it. In New York nobody cares about petty old-world gossip, and can't see what all the fuss over my husband's trial was ever about: he was found not guilty, after all.

I stand in my dressing room, hair up, diamonds on. I've a new maid, Williams, who knows what she's about: she brings out a puff of pure white rabbit fur and I close my eyes as she pats it all over my body, catching me up in a soft and violet-scented cloud, gathering me into the wings of doves. She dusts my throat and shoulders and bosom with rice powder, the nape of my neck, the insides of my elbows, until I am not so much woman as pearl; a lady as shining as the moon.

Downstairs, somebody is already taking a turn on the grand piano, little flights of notes meeting and dispersing in the air. Laughter; chinking glasses; they are waiting for me to make my grand entrance, but I will let them anticipate me just a few minutes more.

Williams laces me in: the Izod corset, as Nora Landry intended. It's tight, but then it must be, because the dress is as simple as simplicity itself. When it goes over my head I am enveloped in dark, rushing silk, as if it had swallowed me up, the red shifting into black as it hisses about my ears. And then it is upon me, and I see in the full-length mirror a woman transformed – myself and yet more than myself, a woman with long white limbs and a narrow waist, bare-shouldered, swan-necked, draped in a dress so entirely without adornment it is almost frightening, shot silk dancing from stormy to electric.

Yes. This is how I always imagined it would be. For a long time after Penzance I thought I'd never wear the gown – my mind was so unsettled, my understanding clouded – but as Christmas came around again, I found myself thinking, *Why not?* It ought to be admired. *I* ought to be admired. Amusing to think that anything of Nora Landry might shine in Manhattan, but I will remain coy as to the identity of my couturier: there is nothing more glamorous than exclusivity.

The hands of the maid are still on my waist; she sighs almost in my ear. 'Get away,' I say, and Williams steps back in surprise.

I leave my dressing room and make my way to the top of the stairs, and the gown is alive with me, breathing against me. I take handfuls of its fabric and feel it resist me, heavy and chafing and delicious.

Down the first flight of stairs, alone, my steps slow and careful. I can hear the murmur of my guests washing around the marble walls of the atrium where I will descend. My husband will be there, my dear husband who has endured such trouble this year and who at last can celebrate. And here I will be at the top of the stairs, this triumphant wife of his, for everyone to see.

A sound, in my ear, as if a breeze passed by. I pause. I am as yet out of sight of the party. I have not yet reached the last flight of stairs, the great sweep that will make me visible to the crowd waiting for me below. I take the banister in my hand and steady myself. The dress is splendid, I remind myself. *I* am splendid.

It comes again. Not a sigh but a swift gasp, as if someone had been taken by surprise, as if something had made their heart pound in their chest. *My* heart is pounding. My palms are damp. And this feeling is rising within me – this sick hot tremulous sensation – and my breath quickens and I must stop to quieten it, to smooth my skirt, to press my hands, cold from the banister, against my brow. Then I propel myself out to the top of the stairs where I can be seen, and the crowd waiting below all give vent to their admiration – their awe – and raise their coupes de champagne to me, me, me, that pale-shouldered woman clothed in boiling, undulating silk. I raise my chin high and smile.

It's then I feel her hand on the small of my back – it's then that I am sure. She is tweaking the drape of my gown so it's just so, straightening one of the tiny buttons she sat up covering in self silk the last night she lived. I can feel her breath on the nape of my bare neck.

'Oh, madam,' says a wisp of a voice in my ear, before she gives me one deft push and I tumble forward.

THE SALT MIRACLES

Natasha Pulley

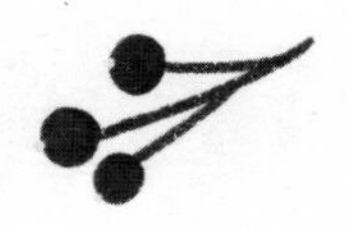

Mhairi had never once gone to St Hilda on purpose. Sometimes the storms washed you there, and you sat in the eerie little harbour below the ruined village and felt that tightness in your lungs – it appeared like clockwork within a nautical mile of the island – until the weather broke. She didn't know what was wrong with the place, but something was. This was the first time she had steered deliberately into the mist.

She wouldn't have done it now, either, if the bishop hadn't been paying so well; and if his reason for going hadn't been so interesting.

'I have a priest out there, the warden of the island,' he had said, looking lost when she found him outside the harbour-master's office in Glasgow. Everyone else was ignoring him. 'But I should never have sent him. I've just had – terrible dreams. I have to go and fetch him back.'

Dreams were an extraordinary reason to spend a hundred pounds, but then she supposed that sort of thing was to be encouraged if you were a bishop.

As she took the boat up to the wharf, the bishop was already springing out and climbing the ancient iron ladder there before she'd even cast up the mooring line.

'Hey!' she snapped. Land people did all kinds of stupid things at sea, but she'd never expected an old man to do that. 'You could get crushed, don't—'

'There's someone up there!' he shouted back. 'Look!'

There was. A man was running down from the deep caves further along the shore. Not just running in the brisk cheery way of someone who liked exercise. Running like the Devil was behind him. It was impossible to make out his face in the mist, but Mhairi didn't need to. He was clearly terrified.

'Flint?' the bishop shouted hoarsely into the fog. 'Is that you?'

THREE WEEKS EARLIER

Flint had never been so glad to arrive anywhere. It took three days to reach the island. You needed a good weather window, and by the time they did manage to land, they had tried four times and turned back three. The sea had never liked him, but the water around this little archipelago seemed to have a personal grudge. This was the first time he had been upright all week.

The ship sounded its fog bell. It had to ring every ninety seconds, lonely in the empty harbour.

There was so much mist that all he could see was the jetty, even once the boat coasted in on the current towards the barnacle-distorted steps. The ship was invisible now. Even its skeleton was lost in the fog.

And just like everyone had promised, the water around the island was pink. Not just a vague rusty colour, but brilliant flamingo pink. Fascinated, he leaned against the side and touched his fingertips to the surface. They came away feeling, of all the odd things, much too dry.

'It's salt,' the second mate told him, surfacing from a stream of general swearing about how unsafe this was. Every so often, the second mate remembered what Flint did for a living and asked him unconvincingly to pardon his French before reeling off a lot more French.

'Salt?' Flint ventured, feeling like he might be poking a dragon.

'Water's far saltier than the sea usually is. It's algae, the pink stuff. Right. There you go, Father.' They bumped the jetty. The second mate gave Flint a look that said he was glad it wasn't him staying on the island, and slung a mooring line over a rusted iron bollard.

Flint edged out, and then *land* came up through the jetty. Instantly, the seasickness was gone. He'd known he felt bad for the last few days, but it was only now that it was gone that he realised how much of his mind it had taken up. He could think again. He was noticing the way the seaweed coiled, and how the fog tasted clean, and how *warm* it was, even two inches from the pink water. Bliss.

'Back for you in February, then. Cast me off,' the second mate said.

'Hang on,' Flint said, holding the mooring line. 'I've been wanting to ask, but I've been, you know, head-first in a bucket the whole way. What do *you* think is going on here? What happened to the people who've gone missing?'

The second mate shrugged. 'People go a bit funny here. A whole Christmas selection, this lot.' He jerked his head up to the little lights that shone through the mist, presumably from the pilgrims' camp.

'A whole . . . Christmas selection?'

'Nuts,' said the second mate.

When the original islanders had disappeared a hundred years ago, they didn't take their sheep; instead, they left them to walk wild here. And wild they stayed. The jetty led up to a path that was nothing but stepping stones in the mossy grass, and on the verges, looking at him with some scepticism, were the sheep. They didn't look like ordinary sheep. They weren't white or fluffy, but brown, their coats matted in uneven elflocks.

He took a photograph with his new Kodak. He wasn't very good with it yet – it was a lovely thing, all mahogany and brass and a special concertina section that moved the lens in and out, but it was a bit technical if most of your education had hinged on Biblical Greek – so he had to pause to fiddle with the focus, and as he did, he turned it the wrong way. The sheep blurred to a brown splodge and way behind it, somewhere on another path, the lens showed him a tall figure standing in a thinner band of fog. For a strange split second he thought the figure had antlers. But then he turned the lens the wrong way again and he lost it, and by the time he thought to take the camera away from his face, whatever it was had gone. He blinked twice, trying to make it make sense. It wouldn't. Well. Fog was funny that way.

The only buildings on the island were: three cottages, one of which would be his; the church, with its grim tower; and beyond that, uphill, ghosts of stone shapes that looked like beehives, or cairns. The old village had been ruined long ago.

Tents dotted the sheltered grassy space near the harbour. There were five. Until recently, there had been five pilgrims. Now there were only three.

'The captain of the post ship wrote to me,' the bishop had told him at the briefing. 'He said something along the lines of "one is unfortunate, two looks like carelessness". He's worried about the conditions on the island. It's been owned by the Church for a thousand years, so it's our problem.' He sighed. 'Beats me why anyone goes out there. St Hilda isn't a very exciting saint, and the place is desolate. Three days at sea – honestly. It would be easier to get yourself over to the Vatican.'

'But maybe not cheaper,' Flint pointed out, in his unofficial capacity as the bishop's shoulder-angel.

The bishop gruffled into his wine. 'Anyway, if you can make it out there without being shipwrecked or eaten by sea monsters, just have a poke at the pilgrims and make sure they're not – you know. In imminent danger of doing something silly. I suppose we should really have had a permanent warden on the island as soon as people started going again. I just didn't dislike anyone enough to sentence them to it.'

'About that,' Flint said. 'There are some newspaper reports about someone being cured out there. Just locals, it's the *Stornoway Chronicle* or something, but the news is getting around. What's behind that?'

'Is that why you volunteered?' the bishop said. He didn't have to say what he thought about basing one's opinions on articles in the *Stornoway Chronicle.*

'Partly.'

'It was one veteran with a limp last year. He was working on a trawler that stopped there in a storm. Stranded for a while. After: cured. Probably psychosomatic.' A few years ago, the bishop had got heavily into the new Sherlock Holmes stories and learned about deduction, and Flint sometimes seriously considered sending Mr Conan Doyle a curse in the post, because now the bishop didn't believe in miracles.

The bishop sighed and topped up Flint's wine. 'But Flint, are you sure you're happy to go at Christmas? If there's one thing I'm certain about, it's that there are no miracles on St Hilda.'

'What? Endless time to talk to interesting people and maybe prove you wrong—'

'I just don't want you to be disappointed when—'

'I'll be Eve in a cider factory,' Flint told him firmly.

*

Someone nearly as wild-looking as the sheep was out with a camping stove and a kettle. Flint raised his hand. The man waved back, only just more than a shadow in the fog. Up close, he was bedraggled, and he smelled of damp leather coat. It seemed odd to camp out in all this wet and horribleness when there were spare cottages which could have been rented out, but maybe that wasn't in the spirit of pilgrimage.

'So you'll be Father Kang?' the man said. His two front teeth were gold, which made Flint think of pirates. 'I'm Kerryn. Welcome to St Hilda! Was it a good journey?'

'Hell. I'm so happy to be off that ship. Let's fetch the others. Come to the cottage, we'll all have some tea.'

The cottage was unlocked, like the bishop had promised. When Flint opened the door, a glorious wave of heat riptided him in. Some blessed hero had lit the fire. The grate was big enough to stand in, a kettle steamed on the black stove, and everywhere there was a wonderful oil smell from the constellation of lanterns in the rafters. There was even an Advent candle, burned carefully down to today's date; the eighteenth.

Flint filled up with happiness. A few hours ago he had thought he would never want to stand up again, but now he was so full of energy it seemed odd that he wasn't glowing.

There was an enormous, well-stocked pantry, so Flint made sandwiches and tea and kept having to bat off all three pilgrims who wanted to do it for him.

There were two men and one woman. Kerryn was older,

with a puff of mad hair and a magnificent beard. The room soon started to smell of his wax jacket, so Flint stoked up the fire and took all their coats so that it wouldn't seem like he was being sniffy. The lady was the kind of person who looked like she did a sea swim on New Year's Day *and enjoyed it*, all windswept and steadfast; and the younger man was the nervy-seeming type who would have done well as a student at an especially strict seminary.

'Aren't you young?' the lady exclaimed, peering into Flint's face. The two of them were having a small fight about who should carry the tray.

'No,' laughed Flint, and stamped on the need to explain that there were places in the world where humans had not subsisted for generations in sub-Arctic conditions on a diet more usually suited to horses. It would have been smug. 'But that's very kind.'

'It's all right, she can't see,' Kerryn put in warmly.

'Only the one good eye,' the lady agreed, and it was true; one of her eyes was pale from a cataract, and the other was going the same way. 'But Kerryn's already been cured, so it's my turn next!'

'Kerryn's already been what, sorry?' said Flint, trying to tell if it was a joke. He handed out plates for the sandwiches and together they all arranged themselves on the sofa and the armchair. Everything was upholstered in brilliant yellow corduroy.

Kerryn looked shyly pleased. 'Nerve damage, couldn't stand up straight. Now; well.' He was bolt upright. 'Just waiting now for passage home. I'm booked to go on the second, after New Year.'

'Nerve damage,' Flint repeated, trying hard not to sound like every single atom in him wanted that to be true. He looked Kerryn up and down, hunting for any sign that this was a conman who might have some deal with the local boats to get more pilgrims to come here. A story of a cure would be superb for business.

Or; *or.*

'Fell off a gantry at the shipyard,' Kerryn explained. 'Doctor said it was hopeless.'

Flint struggled to keep his voice level. 'I'll need to interview you later, if you won't mind, for the Church?'

Kerryn beamed. 'I was going to ask you to. Want to get it verified properly, you know? She takes a little while, the saint, but once she gets going, she knows her stuff!'

Flint had a vivid flash of a future where he chased down the medical records and a solemn doctor who admitted to being entirely bewildered because the injury had severed important nerves, here was the X-ray, look at that dreadful crack, you'll never stand upright again with that, and yes, of course the next step would be to testify to the investigation committee at the Vatican, no question about it.

'A little while?' was what he said instead. 'How long?'

'Been here since early September,' Kerryn said. 'Rosemary's been here nearly as long, haven't you, Rosie?'

'Two weeks less than you,' she agreed.

'The first man who was cured,' said the younger man,

who hadn't spoken so far. 'He was stranded for most of the winter.' He was English, and he spoke in such a precise way that Flint suspected him of being the sort of person who would have said *amusing* rather than *funny*, and maybe even of being called Timothy. 'We've tallied it up and we think it takes roughly forty days to be cured.'

'I'm on thirty-eight,' Rosemary said gleefully.

Flint looked between them all. Forty days; holy things did work in circuits of forty days. Christ in the desert for forty days. Noah in the Ark. But then, they would know very well how to sell it to him, if this was a hoax.

'But Father,' Rosemary said earnestly, 'you'll be wanting to hear about the ones who disappeared?'

'Yes. I do. Is there anything you can tell me?'

Rosemary cast another uneasy look around the cottage, as if the fire and proper food might ruin her chances of getting her sight back. 'Will you not open up the church, Father? It's official church business, after all.'

'Open it up? Has it not *been* open?'

'No,' the English man explained. 'Locked. We've never found a key and we didn't want to damage anything.' He held his hand out suddenly. 'I'm Bruce,' he added.

Flint wouldn't laugh. He would not. You couldn't go around laughing at natural Timothies for being accidentally called Bruce. He coughed. 'Right. I'll find a way in.'

The church was locked and there was indeed no key. The lock, though, was enormous and ancient, and so Flint meant to just unscrew the whole thing. There were tools in the cottage's shed. He was surprised when he was partway through taking off the handle and something clanked on the other side, sounding a lot like a key. When he slid some ancient newspaper underneath the door and whatever had fallen, and pulled it back out, it was. A heavy brass key. Locked from the inside. There must have been another door, round by the vestry.

When he pushed open the door, the air inside was cold, and it smelled like new cement; sharp and salty. There was a hole in the roof high up, and bats in the rafters, and a beautiful owl asleep on the lectern. He stepped inside slowly, still waiting for his eyes to get used to the gloom, and paused when something crackled under his boots.

Salt; it was all over the floor, chunks of it. He couldn't see where it might have come from. It creaked like snow as he walked down the nave to the low vestry door.

The vestry looked as though the last priest had left a few hours earlier, even though it had been more than a hundred years since those original islanders had disappeared. There was a washing line with someone's socks on it across the fireplace, vestments on a rack, and a glass on a side table – empty now, with a reddish residue that said it had been half full of wine. It didn't seem like the room of someone who had packed up and gone elsewhere.

'Nobody knows where they went,' the bishop had said. 'The post boat came one week and they just weren't there any more. Hard life, though. I suppose there's only so long you can live off sheep and gannets; and the priest, well, he was odd. Had them praying six hours a day. Can you imagine?'

What Flint wanted to know was, what had made a whole village of working shepherds think there was a *need* to pray for six hours a day? Something must have been happening. He looked through the desk, but there were no convenient diaries. Only an open Bible, alongside some sermon notes. Flint tilted it to see, in case there was something useful there, but then frowned. It was based on a passage from Ezekiel.

Ezekiel didn't usually come up much in modern sermons, because most priests now had a clear opinion about him, and it was that he had smoked an awful lot of something upsetting and come out with what even the kindest diplomat would have to call an enormous bunch of bananas.

Ezekiel had seen angels, which seemed like promising sermon material until you heard how he described them.

Each one had four faces – a person, a lion, an ox, an eagle – and six wings; and there were topaz wheels with them, rimmed with eyes.

It was a strange choice. Usually, passages like that just confused people. Flint read through the notes, trying to find anything that might show why the priest had chosen it, but they were feverish and strange, and he couldn't understand.

It was only as he was leaving that he realised he had found something out after all. There was no back door. The priest had locked himself in and then vanished.

Knowing what that probably meant, Flint searched the whole church, even the tower, but found nothing; no noose, no bones, no sign of violence. He couldn't decide if that made him feel more or less uneasy.

The crunch of his steps on the salt was louder than ever.

It wasn't normal salt, not the kind you found on a table. It was mottled and lumpy, bright white in places, brown in others, stuck together with the damp, more like rocks sometimes. The only reason he'd known it was salt straight away was that he had seen it like this before. There were pillars of it around the Dead Sea; hence the old story about Lot's wife. Maybe that strange priest had brought it in here, a hundred years ago. Salt was for purification.

Well. He could make the place nice again at least. The pilgrims needed that.

There were still candles and brooms in a cupboard. He lit the candles on the altar, moving quietly to keep from bothering the owl, and then started to sweep a path through the salt. It would be useful when the snow came, and the snow was coming soon; the clouds were turning that pearly way they did before the first fall of the winter.

The three pilgrims were appreciative about the church and the candle; too appreciative really. Flint didn't often think ill of the bishop, but it did strike him as bad that no one had been sent out before now. If the two missing people had committed suicide, he would be profoundly unsurprised. He had known the island was a long way from anywhere, but he hadn't really understood how difficult it would be to live for weeks and weeks in tents. Even Kerryn looked tired and stale. Bruce had a terrible, consumptive cough.

'So,' Flint said. 'What do you think happened to the people who disappeared?'

'The original islanders, or the two lately?' Kerryn asked.

'The two lately.'

'Same as whatever happened to the originals, for my money,' he said seriously. 'Perhaps they were Taken.' He nodded upward.

Flint did believe that things like that could happen, but he also believed that a) the Almighty had invented physics for a reason, and b) the Almighty had forgotten about the United Kingdom. 'Did anyone talk to them, before?'

'Kept to themselves,' Rosemary said apologetically. 'But they were cured, Father, they'd not have done violence to themselves.'

'Cured of what, was it?'

'Deafness and cancer,' Bruce provided.

'Right! Deaf as a post he was when he came, the lad,' Rosemary put in. 'And she showed me that tumour. It was like a tennis ball to start with. But after a couple of months . . . nothing. She was going to report the miracle to the Church upon her return. Have it investigated and everything.'

'Deafness,' Flint echoed. 'So – did you hear him talk, after he was . . .?'

'Oh yes,' Kerryn said. 'Spoke beautifully, even though he was mute before.'

Flint found himself clasping his hands against his heart, which must have looked silly, but he was trying to cradle the silvery wisp of hope that was starting to flutter there, so that it wouldn't be stolen. The bishop's voice in his head told him sternly to be logical.

Flint had a serious moral problem with *logical.* If you used enough logic, you could explain anything; just like how cameras made everything look black and white. But what it didn't account for was that away from that greyscale picture, there was also colour. And the worst thing about it, the very worst, was that even though seeing things in colour or in black and white was nothing but a choice, *logical* came with a chilly pontificating sense that if you chose not to use the black and white filter, you were wrong.

'And – has anyone been through their things? Found anything that might shed some light on this?'

'We looked in, of course,' Bruce said. 'But there were no notes, if that's what you're asking, Father. Just their clothes and things. Not packed up. We left the tents up so you could see if you liked.'

The tents were so cold now that frost sparkled inside as well as out. Neither of the vanished pilgrims had kept a diary. There were no cameras. The lady had been in the painstaking process of drawing her own postcards; she had done beautiful sketches of the cliffs, the ruined village, the gannets. On one, there was a figure with antlers standing up on the clifftop. He paused over that, because it looked just like what he'd seen through his camera, but he still couldn't think what it could be.

The bishop would say it was the Brocken spectre of a rearing stag, or something else nerve-blastingly ordinary.

In the man's tent, the only unusual thing was opiates. The deafness must have been caused by something nasty. The date on the bottle was September and the man had gone missing in November, though, and when Flint counted out the pills inside, what was clear that some time toward the end of October, the man had stopped taking them.

So maybe he had been feeling better. Or maybe he had realised he was becoming addicted to them. Impossible to say.

He would need to get in touch with the man's physician, once he was back on the mainland. As he made his way back to the cottage, he had to clench his hands, which were shaking with hope.

The cottage was talkative at night; its thatch clicked and settled as the cold gripped the island, embers popped in the grate, and gannets called to each other on the roof. There was a tiny bedroom up a steep set of stairs, but he was cold and hunched up on the couch near the living room fire.

He had the one book he'd been able to find about the island, a rough history that covered its discovery and then the arrival of St Hilda herself. She wasn't one of the fun saints. These days she wouldn't have been saint material at all. She had come here because of some rumours of a demon on the island, and her one miracle was that she had vanished some sheep who had been cluttering up the site upon which the church was being built. It was in the days when the Church had press-ganged saints wherever they could find any.

He was almost asleep when he saw the light in the fog, way up on the cliff on the far side of the island, right in the top corner of his window frame. It was nowhere near the pilgrims' camp, but pilgrims did all kinds of things. They went to pray in strange places and at strange times. Usually he would never have worried. But at night, in the fog, on an island with no real roads, when two of the three pilgrims were very ill – he had to go up and look.

It was a silvery night. The fog was luminous, and in some places he even had a shadow. He took a lamp anyway, the steel handle squeaking where it hinged into the lantern top. The noise was enormous in the quiet.

Even though he knew the island was only a mile across, it felt like much more after the steep climb through the ruined village and the old cairns where they had stored gannet carcasses. St Hilda was basin-shaped, its cliffs high around the rim. The sea roiled white three hundred feet below on his right and the cold was gnawing now.

As his lamp swayed, the shadows leapt. He kept feeling certain that someone was walking not far from him, parallel, though whenever he shone the light full that way, there was nothing. Grass and rocks.

His chest was going tight with sourceless anxiety.

St Hilda had thought there was a demon here. Flint

believed in demons very much, but he didn't believe that they were things that walked and spoke and made themselves irksome to passing saints. They were phenomena. When you saw a surge of murders in a city full of unrest and rage; that was a demon. When a hateful little man decided to starve thousands of people in camps in South Africa, it wasn't human nature.

He wasn't sure what someone like St Hilda would have meant by a demon. For those early missionaries, it was a broad term; demons were foreign gods or the elves in the hills, or the undying huntsman who warded the forest.

Along the way, dotting the grass like boulders, were hunks of salt, some about waist high, some nearly as tall as a person. Because the rain partially dissolved them, they formed wicked points and harrows. That rain ran in rivulets to the cliff edge, so briny that it killed the moss and the grass along the way, so that the land was criss-crossed with dead veins.

At the far side of the island, the side that stared into the Atlantic, there was a mighty tower of rock, and around it, thousands and thousands of gannets. Even from a good distance, it smelled of salt and feather-oil. Up its length were alcoves in the rock, and way up close to the top, almost lost in the fog, a tiny, impossibly perched hut.

With a light inside.

Climbing up to look would have been idiotic. He'd fall and die, or worse, he'd fall and not die.

'Hello?' he called up over the noise of the sea, trying to

not sound too indignant. 'I'd really like it if you came down. It's not safe. If anything happens to you – I don't even know how I'd get help.'

There was no reply.

Rosemary couldn't see, Bruce could hardly breathe; the only person it could be was Kerryn.

'Kerryn, is that you?'

Nothing.

Well; he could ask everyone in the morning and, naming no names and being very tactful, ask that people didn't risk breaking their necks to spend a night in an insane gannet-colony hut.

As he turned to go, he fell over something. He went down hard on both hands, and though the lantern handle stayed around his wrist, it shrieked as the steel ground against a rock, and the flame almost went out. For a second he thought he'd just caught a funny-shaped boulder, but as he sat back, annoyed with himself, he saw that it wasn't. It was a big lump of salt, but this time, it had a very clear shape. It was a gannet. Perfect, with folded wings and a powerful beak.

He brushed the salt feathers. Hard-packed and sticky; not like table salt at all.

'How did you get out here?' he asked it, confused, and charmed. It was lovely.

As though seeing one had trained his eyes, he saw the others. All around him, scattered about the grass and the rocks, glittering in his insufficient lamplight, there were more salt gannets. Some sitting, some frozen about to fly, some asleep. Thousands.

The pilgrims were around a fire and singing Christmas carols when he got back. After the eerie mist walk and the salt birds, it was a disconcerting contrast to get a little cheer from them and a hip flask thrown at his head. He caught it and laughed a laugh that became less strained as it unspooled.

'Ah, there's himself!' Kerryn exclaimed. 'We hoped you'd come out if we sang loud enough.'

'Yes, listen, I – um . . .' Flint trailed off. They were all here. 'There's someone up in the gannet colony.'

'Of course,' said Rosemary. 'That's the saint.'

Flint looked back the way he'd come, to where that lonely light was still there on the gannet tower. The saint; or a fourth pilgrim. In the morning, he'd take up some supplies. Whoever was up there – they had to be living off gannets, and God knew where they were getting their water.

When the first violet line of the dawn cracked the horizon at close to ten o'clock, Flint made the climb again with a box of food and a note, set it on a rock where he hoped it was easily visible, and stood looking up at the hut high on the gannets' spar, wondering what he should do now. He still didn't think he could make that climb, but even if he did, whoever was up there might not interpret it as concern. A person did not decide to live on a rock tower in a gannet colony if they enjoyed other human beings.

All around him, the new sun glittered in the salt birds on the ground, tinting them mauve and gold. They looked incredible, but they were unearthly too, and the longer he stood there, the deeper he felt how he sometimes did around gigantic machinery – this wasn't a place meant for human beings.

He was about to turn away when a sad cheep stopped him.

There was a gannet, still with its baby fledging, sitting right by his foot. He knelt down, but it didn't even try to shuffle away. It didn't look very well. He hesitated, worried about scaring it, then picked it up and wrapped it in his coat. Half-heartedly it tried to peck him, but then settled. At least he could keep it warm at home.

And then – well. He'd checked the tents, asked the remaining pilgrims, looked through the church. He didn't have any answers about the missing pilgrims. He would just have to get on with the business of trying to look after who was left.

By the time he reached the garden gate, Bruce was banging on the cottage door.

'Bruce?'

'You have to come and see,' Bruce shouted, pulling his arm. He looked wild, all his pedantic precision vanished. 'You have to – it's Rosemary!'

Flint thought about saying hang on, I need to do something with this bird, but he was having visions of accidents, of Rosemary drowned in the sea, or broken at the base of the cliff, or hypothermic after trudging around trying to find a saint.

Rosemary was fine.

Rosemary bounced out of her tent and shook his shoulders and yelled at him and he didn't understand, and then he did.

Both of her eyes were bright brown again.

'Come on!' Kerryn shouted, herding them all towards the church. 'Let's go, come on, come on! Rosie, get the whisky!'

They lit the candles on the altar, laughing, and when he thought they would turn serious and kneel, they cracked open the whisky. Startled at all the noise, the bats flapped out through the hole in the roof. Kerryn had brought in a tin whistle, and just like that, the old church was full of shrill bright music and merry tipsy laughter.

'I just woke up and it was better!' Rosemary exclaimed for the twelfth time. She kept touching her eyelashes.

Flint laughed too and had to take about twelve photographs before he could catch her standing still enough to focus properly, much hindered by how Kerryn kept trying to take the camera off him and replace it with a glass.

He did drink the whisky in the end, so happy he felt like he might fizz away. If there had just been a telegraph here, he could message straight back to Edinburgh to tell the bishop he'd found him a miracle, a *real* miracle; the world could have colour again.

'What's that in your coat?' Bruce asked him; the whisky was making him much friendlier than normal.

He'd forgotten about the gannet. Worrying that it might have got squashed, he unfolded his coat. 'I found him up on the cliff, I don't think he's very . . .'

He stopped, because what he had tucked into his coat wasn't a baby gannet any more. It was a perfect salt bird. Particles of salt rubbed off when he touched it.

He had picked up a living bird. Flint dropped it and found himself backing away.

His boots crunched in the salt on the floor, and against something else, something harder. It was a gold ring. With the feverish thought that maybe one of the others had lost it, he picked it up, but stooping brought more salt into view, some of the stuff he'd brushed up against the wall when he was tidying.

More rings winked in it. Rings, and steel buttons, and a key.

His lungs tried to get behind his backbone.

'You look like you've seen a ghost,' Bruce remarked.

Flint forced himself to smile. 'I look sad when I think,' he explained, and slammed an internal door on the need to shout: the islanders didn't leave a hundred years ago. We're walking in them.

There were no telegraph lines. The first boat wouldn't come until after New Year. He had a box of flares, but he hadn't seen any ships since arriving; most of them would have gone back to the mainland for Christmas. There was no way, at all, to get help.

He scrubbed his hands raw in the sink, not even knowing why he wanted to, except that he had been carrying around something dead.

He couldn't think. He was worse for the whisky.

Something flickered off to his left, out in the garden. He looked, not sure if it was a sheep or his eyes making shapes in the mist-rain. As soon as he looked away, he saw it again. He stopped, because he felt panicky for no reason. It was sudden and entire – like altitude sickness. It didn't feel like it was coming from inside him, but something – *wrong* – from outside. Thin air, even though the air was the best he'd had all year.

Slowly, he turned his head away, but not all the way, and pretended to be looking at the stove. The flicker in the garden came back. He thought there was a flash of red cloth, and then something wooden and rounded, like a cartwheel, then horns, and perhaps wings, huge, like a gannet's, but when he swung back again, there was no cart and no cloth, no wings. There was nothing in the garden except old roses and holly, and the rickety gate.

Annoyed, he pulled open the front door to try to make his mind see the same thing as his eyes, which started to water immediately in the cold. The little gate. The rose bush. The holly. At the church, the pilgrims still sang, their voices echoing. *Glad tidings of great joy I bring . . .*

And right in the middle of the garden was the ghost of a

form in the mist, someone tall, crowned with a haze of shapes that looked, at least in the snatch of a second he had to make any sense of it, like antlers.

Flint fell over backwards.

Then it was gone.

Where it had been, there was the box he had taken up the cliff with the supplies. On the box sat a beautifully made holly wreath.

He stared around, trying to calm down, but he had been hit by an overpowering sense that taking the box up to the gannet tower had been very, very stupid. However modern the Church was now, whatever the bishop's thoughts about logic and Sherlock Holmes, there was still old knowledge unforgotten. There remained things in the world that you should never invite in. Horned things that walked in the deepest dark of the year.

Cold to the marrow, he built up the fire and sat almost in it. Once his hands were hands again and not ice claws, he pressed them over his eyes and tried to pull his thinking into a straight line.

What he knew was: something on the island was turning living matter into salt. Someone – *something* – was up on the gannet tower. They had left him a holly wreath.

And: a hundred years ago, the salt had killed the original islanders. Lately, two more people had gone missing.

Kerryn said he had been cured. Rosemary *had* been cured. Flint had seen those cataracts.

The people who disappeared were also supposed to have been cured.

St Hilda had thought there was a demon here.

'Father?' Rosemary said, leaning around the door.

Flint jumped so hard he twanged the nerve down the back of his skull.

'Sorry,' she said. She wasn't at all as merry as she had been before. She looked worried. 'Sorry to disturb, Father, but we can't find Kerryn. He popped out to bring in some water and never came back.'

Part of Flint knew already what he was looking for. Not even very far from the old faucet where the pilgrims got their water, in plain view, he found it. It had been out in the rain for what must have been an hour now, the features that would have made it immediately recognisable lost, but he knew it hadn't been there before. A man-sized hunk of salt.

He prodded at the top of it and salt chipped away, falling in glittering uneven lumps. His insides twisted when he thought of what he was actually doing – digging at human remains – but he kept going. He wanted to be sure. It was hard, because everything was going blurry. He couldn't understand why until he pulled his hand over his eyes and realised he was crying.

There were two gold teeth, sitting upright, only about a quarter inch into the salt.

*

He ran back inside to scrub his hands again. From somewhere over on the other side of the camp, more towards the harbour, Bruce and Rosemary were still calling. Braced against the sink, he stared at his own reflection as if it could help. It looked as bad as he felt. Dishevelled, pale, sheened with panic-sweat.

'You have to get the others off the island,' he said to it, to hear a human voice.

Flares. He would have to try the flares, on the off chance a ship was passing. Sometimes – ha, God – there were miracles.

The tin box looked like it used to have someone's lunch in it. Inside, though, there was a flare gun, and heavy cartridges marked in orange.

Rosemary and Bruce were coming down the garden path as he was going up.

'We can't find him—'

'Keep looking,' he said. He couldn't think of anything else to say. 'I'm going to the top of the cliff, see if I can make anyone see a flare. There must still be trawlers out.'

Rosemary brushed her hand across her face to wipe away the rain, and Flint stopped dead, because once she had, there was a strange pale residue left in her hair.

'Rosie,' he said quietly. 'Have you got something on your hands?'

She looked. 'So I have. I wonder where that . . .'

It was her fingernails. They were crumbling. The whites were already salt.

Rosemary looked confused, but Bruce didn't. He met

Flint's eyes past her shoulder and there was horror written across his face. Flint stared back, trying to beg him to stay calm.

In a voice so strained it was cracking, Bruce said, 'Give me the pistol, Father. You stay here with Rosie: I'll go up.'

'Can you go all the way to the top?' Flint asked, worried about Bruce's lungs.

'I'll manage,' Bruce said. 'She needs you.' He didn't say, *for the last rites.*

'Oh, but I'm all right,' Rosemary said, puzzled.

'Let's just sit down for a bit,' Flint said softly. 'I'm tired, I think I'm coming down with something.'

Bruce ducked his head and went back out into the rain and the dark, and Flint sat down on the yellow corduroy sofa with Rosemary, and gave her a cup of tea, working harder than he had ever worked in his life not to cry again, and watched her turn quite quickly and without noticing at all, into salt.

He stayed kneeling on the floor long after he had finished the prayer. The tears were beginning to freeze in his eyelashes. He had let the fire go out.

Miracles and salt, and a thing outside with no real shape, or dozens; it was nagging at him that this was familiar in a strange, ancient way. The more he saw, the less he was surprised – it was answering to some story in his head that had been graven there for a long time.

'Like Lot's wife,' he whispered pointlessly to what had been Rosemary.

The story was that she had looked back at the fall of Sodom and Gomorrah when she had been told not to. It was a strange story. Lot was still supposed to be a virtuous man even after he'd hurled one of his daughters to a baying mob; but his poor wife was blasted to sodium chloride just for seeing the destruction of the kingdom she was running away from. It didn't make sense, if it was supposed to be a morality tale.

Flint didn't think it was meant to be moral. It was just a way to explain why there were huge salt pillars all around the Dead Sea. Oh, there was a lady once, she annoyed the archangels while they were doing for the Cities of the Plain.

But Rosemary hadn't looked at anything strange, and there were no falling cities here. And as Bruce had said, it took time. Forty days; and first, you were cured.

Miracle, then salt. It was like they were part of the same process. First it tipped in your favour, and then it went too far.

It was slowly that he realised Bruce should have been back by now. He stood up painfully – his knees hurt – and leaned out of the front door, trying to see if there was a lamp coming down the cliff path in the freezing drizzle, but there was just darkness.

He might have collapsed up there. Flint pulled his coat back on.

On the dark path up the cliff, shining the lamp to either side to try and see if Bruce was crumpled somewhere just off the path, Flint realised he had a carol stuck in his head. It kept playing around and around, like a skipping phonograph.

Fear not said he, for mighty dread had seized their troubled minds . . .

Like before, his heart was sprinting, and some of his panic didn't feel connected to the situation. It was a quality of the air. He could taste it – something electric.

'Bruce?' he shouted up the path, hoping, but not much.

Up on its spar where the gannet colony whirled, there was a light in that tiny hut again.

All glory be to God on high . . .

Whoever was up there, if he couldn't find Bruce he needed to talk to them now. Maybe they could help. And maybe – Jesus Christ, maybe all this was why they were up in the hut. Not because they were hostile to other people, not because it was a more punishing sort of pilgrimage, but to get away from whatever was turning people to salt.

He ran the rest of the way and still there was no Bruce.

'Hello!' he yelled into the dark and the rain. 'Please, I need some help! People are – people are dying! Do you know what's happening, do you – *Please* come down!'

The door didn't open. Flint turned around, still hunting for Bruce in the insufficient lamplight, his hand frozen to the lantern loop and his insides clenching with the horrible thought that maybe Bruce had fallen off the cliff.

Dread burst across the back of his head. He went still, and tried hard to breathe normally past the unassailable certainty that there was something right behind him. Not someone.

Something. His whole mind roared with the memory of what he had seen before, the thing with antlers, the mess of weird images in the garden, the cloak, the wheel, the wings, and, like minds sometimes did when they were under exactly the right strain, his hurled a new thought at him.

Ezekiel.

Four faces – a person, a lion, an ox, an eagle – and six wings; and there were topaz wheels with them, rimmed with eyes.

It wasn't nonsense. What he *meant* was, it had been impossible to get a grasp on what he was seeing, because it wasn't one thing, but a churning of different ideas all competing for atoms.

The angel of the Lord came down and glory shone around;
Fear not, said he . . .

'Don't be afraid,' someone said, or not some *one;* it was many voices all saying the same thing.

Flint fell onto his knees and didn't look. Lot's wife had looked, and what if Rosemary had too, what if Kerryn had, and God, where was Bruce—

'It's safe for a little while,' the voices said, narrowing into fewer than before. 'Even in proximity.' Hands, human-seeming hands, took his arms very gently and half helped, half lifted him onto his feet. 'Let me take you home.'

In the light in the little cottage, the thing seemed like a man, although if he looked at it sideways it was wrong. He caught snatches of other shapes, some that he knew – antlers, a wing – and some too strange to make sense of. But seen straight on, he was tall, with hair as black as Flint's, and dressed far too thinly for the wolf winter; his sleeves only reached his elbows, and the cotton was thin and soaked. Up close, he smelled of burning. He put Flint close to the fire and built it up again, his fingertips soon dark from old ash.

Flint felt dislocated from everything. His wrists hurt. Where the thing had touched him, he was burned. Not badly, but like he'd scalded himself with hot water.

'What is happening?' Flint whispered.

'I stayed up there because the further I am from you, the longer it takes.' The thing glanced at him with amber eyes that weren't human. 'The salt.'

'Oh,' Flint breathed.

'Sitting here this near to me – you would have two hours or so. I'll go before that.'

'I'm going to die in *two h—*'

'No,' the thing said, quite gently, 'you would, if I stayed. But I won't stay.'

'The miracles,' Flint said. 'You . . .?'

'You'll know if the salt is coming. There are miracles first.'

'Why?'

The thing shook its head a fraction, looking troubled not to be able to explain well. 'We are like lodestones, but what we pull is not iron. It's . . . all that makes you, and all that makes the world. First, it makes miracles. Later; salt.'

Flint had both of his hands against his own throat, trying

to warm the feeling back into them, and trying to calm down. 'How – how did you come to be here?'

'I disobeyed.' He didn't elaborate, but in a way that looked involuntary he did flicker; the shape of him was lost, and instead there was a shudder of images – broken tree chariot sword red cloak – and then he was man-shaped again, clenching his hands. Those were things to do with war, Flint thought; long-ago wars.

'What . . . what's the – range? How far from you do we need to be, to be safe?'

'A mile or so. At the very edge of the island, the effect is weaker. The sheep know.'

'Why haven't you— why not warn people? Why no fences, or no . . .?'

The thing looked puzzled. Flint might as well have asked why it hadn't tried talking to the birds.

'Why did you come for me?' he asked instead.

'You have been very kind. You tried to help.' It flickered again, but it was a different sort of flicker, calmer, softer, and Flint realised that this was what it looked like when the thing smiled. 'You would only have climbed up if I hadn't come down. So.'

'My name is Flint,' Flint said at last.

The thing said many words at once, all the voices fracturing. Some were words Flint knew and some were other languages, and it was so much all at once that he felt as though the thing had dropped his whole brain in freezing water.

AGELLOS DAIMON SERAPH
DEMON LILITH DEVIL FIRE
holy condemned fallen αγγελος
神
מַלְאָךְ
ANGEL messenger

He had to press his fist against his heart. He wanted to scream and run away and hide all at the same time, but he couldn't do any of it. Dread was pulsing off the thing, as traceably as the draught was coming from the badly fitting windows.

The thing seemed to see that Flint couldn't do very much with that, or with any of it. 'I'm going. Don't try to see me again.' It looked Flint over with something close to concern. 'You must get away from this island as soon as you can.'

'There are no ships until after New Year,' Flint managed. 'Nine days at least. Is that too long?'

It thought. 'I don't know,' it said, and then it was gone.

Now

Mhairi switched the engine off and swung onto the wharfside ladder to follow the bishop. For an elderly gentleman, he was quick, and he had already covered most of the ground between them and the running man. Once the wharf ran out, it was treacherous going. St Hilda's beach was all rock and pebble, ankle-twisting and skull-cracking. She followed fast, worried that he would fall. It took three days to sail home. Three days with a broken anything was probably enough to die of it.

'Thank God!' the man was crying. He was English. Mhairi tried not to be sceptical. In theory she did see that sometimes English people could have a genuine emergency, but in her experience, an English 'emergency' was not getting the kind of cake you wanted. 'We have to go! We have to go *now*, you can't be here, no one should be here!'

The bishop looked terrible. 'Son, slow down, what's your name?'

'Bruce, it's Bruce, I've been hiding . . .'

'Where's Father Kang? Where are the other pilgrims?'

Bruce was shaking his head, mute. 'We have to go—'

'No!' the bishop shouted over him. 'Mhairi, there's supposed to be a priest and two other pilgrims here—'

Bruce was weeping. 'You can't go up there! It's not – you'll die. You'll die! I'm only alive because I stayed in the caves – the sheep know, you have to stay on *this side of the—*'

'Calm down,' Mhairi told him, not wanting a panicking

Englishman on her boat as well as the dreaming bishop. 'We're going up there to look, all right? You can sit on the boat if you want, but the sea has laws. If there's people in distress, I have to help. Now tell me where they are.'

'They're dead! We have to—'

'All right, on the boat,' she cut him off, to save time.

Amazingly, Bruce did calm down. 'I'll wait on the boat,' he said in a small voice.

Mhairi and the bishop walked up the beach. Winter mooring was different from summer mooring, which was shallower and further along, but the two paths met just before the village. There was something at the fork of the road, though, a standing stone – or, no. It was another of those creepy pillars of salt that studded the island.

This one looked nearly like a person, weathered but recognisable. Around its neck there was a wooden sign on a string.

I FOUND YOU A REAL MIRACLE
—FLINT

The bishop choked. He touched the salt, and as he did, steel buttons fell away from it, all in a line, like they were from a waistcoat.

'No!' Mhairi yelled, because beyond the bishop's shoulder, she had just seen that bastard Englishman steering her boat out and away from the harbour. She ran back towards the wharf, shouting and waving, but she could see him in the cabin. He didn't even look back. He was heading straight out to sea.

The bishop had seen too, but if he cared he wasn't showing it. He was standing with his hand on the side of the salt pillar as if he were touching a real person, and now his eyes were lifted up, towards the cliff.

'There's a light,' he said, sounding strange. 'Someone's here.'

He was right. It was tiny, way up on the cliff, above the fog.

Mhairi tried hard to pull herself around to the new facts, which were that neither of them would get off this island for days now. 'Let's go and see who it is.'

BANISHED

Elizabeth Macneal

Based on a true story.
Edinburgh, 1754

I was caked in snow by the time I arrived at Preston House, my nose dripping, my fingers gnarled with cold. It was a blessed sight that greeted me: fires blazing in the hearths, a plate of steaming mince pies, so hot that I scalded my mouth. Garlands were slung from the picture rails, in great big bushels – holly and ivy for eternal life, the berries for Jesus' shed blood – and the air was thick with the scent of ground cloves and ginger.

The master wanted to see me at once, the maid said, leading me through the hall, then outside again. We bent our heads in the sleet, trudged towards a library pavilion, its windows lit like a gingerbread house, brightening the snow around it. Just before the maid raised her hand to knock, she turned to me and whispered, 'Is it true?'

'Is what true?'

'That you can speak to spirits, banish them. That you are a sort of witch.'

I smarted a little at this. 'I am no witch.'

I thought of the tales my grandmother had told me – the Castle esplanade, half a century past: ash falling like snow on the High Street, a charred scent like burned pig in the air. She'd seen it all: the witches rolled down the hills in barrels and ducked in the Nor Loch, shivering and writhing like pale grubs.

'But you will rid us of her spirit,' she said, biting her fingernails. 'She's a tawpie, with the temper of a devil. She will kill us all in our beds, one of these days.'

'I will do what I can.' But still I found my hands were trembling; trembling at what was ahead of me.

The door opened, and there he was, James Erskine, Lord Grange: spotless, pristine, his shoes and fob gleaming, no lint speckling his shoulders. His portrait flickered in the candlelight: the hint of a smile, long red robes. I wondered what I was supposed to say to a man such as this, a man who commanded the laws of the city. I clasped and unclasped my hands, fidgeting in the chair he allotted me.

'I will explain myself briefly,' James Erskine said, petting a small white dog that nuzzled his fingers. 'I find myself tormented by the spirit – by the spectre – of my late wife. She will kill me, I swear it. She rages and storms. She poisons my food. She—' He cowered, rubbed his nose. 'She has made my very life fearful, a misery.' He lowered his head, wiped underneath his eyes. I felt a stirring in my chest, almost maternal.

'And how, if I may ask, did she die? I often find the hauntings are related to the nature of the spirit's death.'

'It was unexpected. She – she was staying with a friend on

Niddry's Wynd. I had her buried a Christian in Greyfriars Kirkyard. She was not young. She was nigh on fifty years of age.'

'And that was recently?'

'No, no. That was fifteen years ago.'

I stared. 'It is unusual, sir, for a spirit to lie dormant for all that time. To rear up so suddenly.'

He pulled on a curl of his wig. It was cold in the room, I realised, despite the fire. The yule log seemed to putter out, the sea wind whining against the casements like a dog at the door.

'In order for me to banish her spirit, I must understand the cut of her,' I continued. 'What was she like?'

He shook his head. 'It is – difficult to express the – the pain that she caused me and my family. Her father was hanged as a murderer, and I suspect she inherited a little of that bad blood. She would sleep with a blade under her pillow and said it was a reminder of whose daughter she was. She had a maniac, drunken violence – she would barrack me in the street, beat our children, and threatened to do a mischief to herself, to run through the streets naked to humiliate me.' He paused. 'It is difficult to confess these things, to speak them aloud. To admit that this was the lady I married.'

'And why did you?'

'Because I got her with child, and I could not dishonour her.' He stared out the window, wide-eyed.

'It must have been difficult for you, sir. To be yoked to a person when there was no love or affection.'

He nodded. 'These were matters which could not be redressed in a court of justice, and we had not then a madhouse. And now I fear that, having failed to kill me in life, she will do so in death.'

He started, fell back in his chair. The candle flame flattened, pinched itself out. There was a high whining and it was only after a moment that I realised it was the dog, cowering under the table, ears flattened. It began to lick its leg, the flesh red and bloody where it had nibbled off the fur. The windows quaked in their frames; the fire snuffed out as though doused with a bucket of water. I let out a small cry, my fingers working the skin of my wrist like cloth. A sawing sound, like a surgeon at work on a bone, and it cut through me, seemed to slip and needle under my scalp, as though I was being pricked with a thousand pins. She was angry, aye; furious: I had scarcely seen the like. I covered my face, cried out,

'Lady Grange—'

An echo, a sound like the wind skipping over the waves.

And then, suddenly, the room fell silent. The dog was still snarling, snapping, whimpering, its tail between its legs. I found my voice, thumped my chest, and it came out as thin as a reed. 'It is my experience—' *Cough.* I cleared my throat. 'It is my experience that the spirits who require my care are those who have an injustice to address.'

'An injustice?' he scoffed. 'Oh, how I wish a body as clean, as logical, as my own profession, as the law, might intervene and determine what is *just*. But we are past that now.' He turned to me, concern on his face. 'I should warn you that she torments every inhabitant of this house. That you might find yourself unsafe here. You may leave now, if you wish. I am loath to endanger your life too.'

Then I felt it again; that creep across my skin as though I had dipped my hand into the sea, and there was the dog again, growling, its hackles up. Lord Grange stood suddenly, staring wildly around him, reaching for the poker that sat in the bucket outside the hearth.

'Begone,' he shouted. 'Spare me, Rachel, I beg you!'

I cried out, noticing the glowing poker before he did, and he dropped the fire iron with a shriek, clasping his hand. He plunged his fist into his claret, panting hard.

'You see what she has done!' he wept.

'Sir,' I said, reaching for his hand, calming his quick breaths. His wrist quivered beneath my fingers. The flesh of his palm was raw and livid, the skin singed clean away. I would apply a poultice of herbs. I had a full arsenal with me. Ground peppermint for sleeplessness; nightshade against the rats; marigold ointment for wounds; ground crab eyes and claws for heartburn. And as I reached for my snow-crusted bag, I knew it with a certainty. That Rachel Erskine, Lady Grange, was ferocious, vengeful, and that my own life was in danger.

❧

For dinner, the maid brought out slivers of cold goose and potatoes, left over from Christmas Day. It was only now that I saw that the greenery on the walls was beginning to wilt. The flagstones were littered with red berries like little drops of blood.

'You said your mistress had the temper of a devil,' I said.

'Aye,' she replied. 'As ferocious as her spirit that now haunts us all.' She shuddered, gripping her arms. 'She had me beaten for locking a door against her. She would rail at her children. She was a drunk, with a maniac violence, a most unnatural mother.'

The story was so similar to Lord Grange's that I nodded, certain of this woman's character. But how was I to banish her? How was I to confront this spirit, attempt to understand her? I had never been hired by a man as powerful, as famous, as a Lord Justice Clerk, a man who commanded and controlled the most influential men in the city. If I succeeded – I narrowed my eyes. I *would* succeed. I had never failed before. I needed the small pay I would receive. I thought of my mother, wasting at home, how soon I would be able to bring her beef for her broth.

The night wore on and I was afraid to go to bed, afraid to be alone in this house. I drank more than I ought to have done, the claret rich and silken, hail battering the casements. The twelfth cake was dry, full of hard little currants, but still I ate until my stomach ached. And all the while, the red-haired maid chattered, questions heaped on questions.

'How did you learn you had a gift? Were you born with it? Who was the first spirit?'

And I began to talk. Usually, when I was spirit-banishing, I was the one who stayed silent, who asked the questions, but she was so sweet, so wide-eyed that I could not resist. I told her about my childhood on Cramond, how my sister and I would gather mussels on the rocks. And how, one afternoon when I was scarcely six, I'd looked around me and seen that the sea had sneaked up on me and cut me off, that even then it was inching up the rocks I stood on. The shores were empty and I quickly learned what a helpless thing it is to cry out and know that no mortal ears will hear you, that your shouts are as empty and useless as the wind.

The minutes ticked past and the water licked at my ankles, slapped my thighs, tugged at my armpits, as cold as a knifing. And then, suddenly, a great wave came and swept me out, and I felt that frozen tongue roving all over me, the icy hand at my mouth, clawing at my hair. I flailed and kicked, my dress heavy, my boots leaden, and then it closed over me, my body heaved this way and that, something sharp scoring my wrist, the harsh butt of a wave against my chest. I fought it, furious, but it was no good: the sea was in my mouth, and my lips opened and closed, desperate for a small flash of air, and I knew then, as the currents tumbled me about, as the last small bubbles rose from my mouth, that it was all lost.

Poor lamb, they'd say, six years old, gone and drowned a day before Christmas, eaten up by the sea, a tale to frighten other weans who might pick mussels on the shore and not heed the tide. I thought of my little sister, Lib, counting cockle shells on the sand, up to her ears in wool; I thought of the click of my grandmother's needles as I drifted off to sleep each night, the smell of peat smoking in the hearth. I could see it then: the light of the candle flickering like sunrise, a split of brightness cracking across me.

But what does it mean to die and be brought back to life? I did not breathe for a full five minutes, the fisherman said, after he'd hauled me out by the arm like a particularly heavy catch. I lay on the wooden floor of his boat, surrounded by the silverish flip of mackerel and his bucket of lugworm bait. I was dead, he was sure of it. My lips were blue and my eyes were blank and staring. A dead child is a sore sight for anyone. He hit me about the cheeks, shook me, and then when he turned for shore I reared up, warm sea liquid pouring from my mouth, my back bent in a fit of coughing. I was back, alive again, with the grey sky arcing overhead, my lungs panting like bellows, but I could still see that shard of light in the corner of my eye – a small, lit candle.

'And then what?' the maid asked, leaning forwards. 'Was that your gift?'

I only realised it later, I told her, when I'd been carried back to the cottage. There, sitting in his chair in the corner, was my grandfather, a man we had buried in St Dunstan's churchyard two summers before.

'Grandfather?' I wept. 'Is't you?'

'Delirium,' the fisherman said.

The maid gasped.

'I knew it was not madness,' I continued. 'I knew, as I

touched his coat and he smiled at me, that a small door had opened between me and the spirit world. And that night, as I lay on my truckle bed, and my grandfather told me a story about the clam folk who dwelled in the sea, I knew what it was to have an ear listen out for me, to have someone hear my call and save me.'

The maid sat back. 'Well,' she said. 'Well. What a way to make a living.'

She yawned, as wide and unabashed as a cat. And I realised how late it was, how tired I was from the talking. So when she offered to bring me to my chamber, I agreed, but each step I took was heavy and plodding. I tried to remember the hallways we walked down, the turns and staircases we took, in case I was pursued. In case I should need to flee.

❧

The room was small with no hangings on the bed, a small window that overlooked Lord Grange's library. It was still candlelit, and I wondered if he slept there, why he had not come in.

'Here is some whisky and comfits,' the maid said, placing them on my table.

As she crossed the room, it was an effort not to turn to her, not to beg, *don't leave me.* But I steeled myself and thanked her, sat on the bed with its creaking springs. Better to busy myself with unpacking my small bag, laying each trinket carefully on the desk by the window. Small tin bells I would use to soothe Rachel. The sack of pine needles I would throw into the fire to catch the edges of her.

No fire had been laid and I wished I had brought my cloak with me. It was worse to lie in bed too cold to sleep, so I paced the room, hands tucked into my armpits for warmth. I had a job to do, I reminded myself: I must focus on my task.

'Rachel Erskine?' I called. 'Rachel Erskine? Lady Grange? Show yourself.'

I knew she would come in her own time. They always did. The hour ticked on. I rearranged my bells, my pine needles. I could see Lord Grange's library in its pavilion, its windows glowing. How small he looked, little more than a doll! He let in a couple of men, and they talked, and I wondered who they were, and why they'd tramped along the sea-front, and not come in through the house.

The black of night deepened. The snow began again. I would save the rest of my whisky for when I was properly cold. My candle was soon melted down and I thought that I might creep down to the scullery for a fresh wick or a hot drink. The boards creaked, my hands fumbling for the door. Locked; I rattled the wood and it would not give. Who would shut me in here? I felt the worry in my chest, tightening like yarn. But I knew the answer with a sureness.

'Rachel Erskine,' I cried out. 'Rachel Erskine, show yourself.'

And I knew, as I heaved uselessly at the door, splinters piercing my hands, that Rachel Erskine would not be won over as easily as the other spirits. She would not simply be coaxed away. She wanted something; I knew it. I could feel her fury, licking through the house. I had felt it earlier in the library, seen the livid glow of the poker. And what was I to do? I was there to oust her spirit, not run from it: I traded on my reputation. What would Lord Grange say if I howled the house awake, if I screamed until a maid came with a spare key? No; there was nothing for me to do but endure it. I stalked up and down that small chamber, blowing into my hands to warm them. I tried to think soft thoughts: the church at Christmas with its scent of pine and old stone; the shops on the High Street stacked with sugar-coated plum cakes.

'Rachel Erskine, Lady Grange,' I muttered again and again. 'Rachel Erskine, show yourself.'

But when I heard the crash of the window, I am ashamed to say I let out a cry of fear. I leaned against the frame with all my strength but found myself flung backwards, that icy sea wind hurling itself inside until the room was as cold as a charnel house. I saw my pot rocking on its edge and lunged for it, but too late, my piss seeping all over the floor, slipping between the cracks.

'Rachel Erskine,' I cried again. 'Tell me the truth! Tell me what happened!'

In my ears, Lord Grange's words echoed.

Maniac –

Drunken violence –

Her father was hanged as a murderer –

You might find yourself unsafe –

With shaking hands I took a sip of whisky – retched. Stale, stagnant, putrid, as sour as the liquid a surgeon might pickle a limb in. How curious when I had drunk a pleasant sip only an hour before. I gagged, spat the mouthful across the room, wetting my already cold bed. My bells tinkled and rang. The pine needles pattered across the floor. If I squinted, I could just see the blue edge of her, dancing in a fury, whirling with her hands out, breathing her spite against the walls. The plaster bubbled and split.

I had my faculties, I told myself; I had logic, reason. I needed to talk to her, not run from her. But still, every sinew in me longed to shout, *Begone, Rachel Erskine*, to fear her like a child fears a big, slavering dog. I could bear it no longer. I threw myself on my bed, flimsy blanket pulled tight over my head. I was close to begging, close to weeping. My limbs shook violently as though in a fit of ague, my knees tight under my chin. But as, at last, I drifted off to sleep, it was the beat of a woman's laugh I heard, as if this were nothing more than a game.

When I woke, my mouth was dry and the glass of whisky was gone.

❧

'You see, I think, the nature of the spirit I must contend with.'

I could feel the prickle of Lord Grange's eyes as they took me in: the heavy lines under my eyes, my creased clothes, the quiver in my hands that I did my best to still.

'You see, perhaps, the suffering and torment I endured as her husband.'

It was no surprise that the maid had blabbed to him about the state she had found me in. Just after dawn, she'd heard me pounding the door. She had unlocked it, pursing her lips as she surveyed the blistered walls, the upended pot, the pine needles scattered across the floor. 'I had – had a terror in the night. A dream,' I had told her, and she'd given me a look that said, *Aye, right.*

'Please help me,' he said, a desperate edge to his voice. 'She has made my life a torment, unendurable.'

I noted the dregs of claret in his glass, though it was scarcely midday, the way he kneaded his brow, pulling at the soft flesh. And I saw clearly how I might summon Rachel: she would come when black-mouthed, his accusations whipping her into a fury. I had to try to make her speak. I had to understand her, though I knew, too, how risky it was. Someone as vengeful as her – she might punish me for making her vulnerable. I touched my throat, felt the thrum of my pulse as though to remind myself I was still alive.

I took a breath. 'You say she caused you pain. That she had a maniac violence. In what way?'

It was not difficult to let him run free, like a wind-up toy suddenly released. He leaned forwards, his eyes darting, a quiver to his lips, and truly I pitied him. 'She made threats against me, against my life. She would have had me exiled, murdered.'

'And how?'

There was something about this that did not make sense to me, something that I could not puzzle out. Why her spirit had been quiet fifteen years after her death, and only reared up recently; how she, as a lone woman, could wield such power against a man such as him. There was something missing, something that caught like a hangnail.

'How did she die?' I asked.

'In her sleep,' he said. He looked exasperated. 'I told you yesterday. In 1732 in the house in Niddry's—'

I saw at once that it had worked. The dog's ears flattened, and I could make out her shape more clearly now – the blue tinge of her knotted hair, her hands that carved the air in a ferocious scything movement. She was older than I expected, more haggard. She could not, surely, have been a woman of fifty. She looked older, perhaps by two decades. I rapped my skull as though to make sense of it.

Liar –

The word, shallow and hissed, sounding like little more than the wind. Only I caught it, only I heard its edges.

'Tell me why you are here, Rachel!' I implored. 'Tell me your story. I want to hear it. The truth of it.'

Lord Grange looked wildly about him. 'Truth?' he demanded, his voice thick with dread. 'You surely cannot commune with – with the creature? She cannot torment me yet with her lies—'

And I saw something ugly in him: something that was not fear at all. No; it was fury that pulsed through him, fury that puckered his brow, and if Rachel had been standing here, alive, he might have strangled her.

He thought her dead and silenced; he thought he was the only one with a voice, that a spirit could not speak. I glimpsed her, vengeful and cackling, saw her long fingers knock the edge of his inkpot, the liquid glugging out across his correspondence. He let out a cry, righting the pot, clasping his hand where it had grazed hers. I saw a blood blister forming beneath the surface of the skin, and he sucked on it, hard.

'Rachel, tell me the truth!' I begged again, as she whipped across the room.

Dead in my sleep, she spat. *Hands, fists pulling me from the bed, thrown upon the floor, a rag stuffed in my mouth – the cargo, the cargo –*

The cargo? It came to me, as clear as a bell. She had not died as he claimed. Then how did it happen? What had her husband done to her?

His words on the first day came back to me. *These were matters which could not be redressed in a court of justice, and we had not then a madhouse –*

What *justice* had he meted out instead?

My heart beat wildly. And why? She must have endangered his life somehow, his reputation.

She would have had me exiled, murdered.

Everything about his person spotless, gleaming. Shoes, fob, waistcoat. As though he would not allow the slightest taint upon his person.

An hour ago, I would have voiced this, interrogated Lord Grange. I would have watched his expression carefully. But I noticed a cruelty that pulsed through him in a way I had not before. He had spoken so clearly the afternoon before, steepling his fingers. *You might find yourself unsafe here.* My mind ticked. I realised, suddenly, where the danger lay. Not with Rachel, but with him, Lord Grange, who was now standing to his full height, hurling a decanter at the wall. Red claret spattered the plaster.

'Begone!' he bellowed. 'Devil!' He turned to me, a fire in his cheeks. 'You will not speak to her? You will not commune with her? Swear it!'

He put his face close to mine. I thought of the coach that had brought me here, the thick snow; I thought of my flimsy shoes, and the flat grey sea. A vein beat in his temple, his breath hot and meaty, spittle flecking my cheek. 'You will stay until she is gone. But you are not to exchange a word with her.'

I nodded, the lie already thickening in my mouth. My voice quavered only a little. 'No, sir. Those are not my methods.'

Because I knew that I had her then: I knew that if I dared to stay, Rachel Erskine would talk to me that night.

༄

That evening, I sat at the small table in my chamber. The maid brought me a dish of mince pies, but some small rodent had already been at them, the pastry nibbled, raisins spilling out. I did not touch them. I began to think outlandish things: of poison, of hemlock and nightshade.

When the maid left, I stayed sitting at the table, listened. There it was. The scratch of a key in a lock. So it had been the maid who had imprisoned me here, under Lord Grange's orders no doubt; not Rachel at all. He didn't want me roaming the house, escaping. There were things that he didn't want me to find.

I watched him through the window again, seated on his velvet throne. Again I watched a few men arrive and leave, and later the red-haired maid came to the door and he let her in. I watched for a little while as they fucked, her plump pink body rising against his.

Ah, I thought; of course. How that girl must gobble up anything he told her! How closely her words had echoed his, *a drunk with a maniac violence. A drunken maniac violence.* He must have known my window looked on to his pavilion; he might have drawn the curtains. I wondered who else had looked out of the window and seen a similar thing. His children, understanding where their father's allegiances lay? Rachel, heavy with her ninth child, parting the curtains, seeing a young maid's body grasped in her husband's arms, rising and falling, her narrow throat thrown back in ecstasy, in rapture?

'Rachel Erskine?' I called, but my voice sounded muffled, timid. Again I was possessed by the urge to run, to pack my small linen bag and break down the door; to escape from the window if I had to. To take these small lanes by lantern alone, until I came across a house or an inn. But I thought about the coins, dropping into my purse; and more than that, I thought of that cackling spirit, the fire in her, the way she'd breathed *liar* across the room. I had heard from Lord Grange, and now I wanted to know her side of matters. I wanted to know the truth.

'Rachel Erskine, show yourself,' I whispered, shaking the small bells. I held a single pine needle over the candle, watched as it glowed and cracked. The room cooled, as though plunged into water, and there she was, sitting opposite me, her hands clasped in her lap. She was clearer now, through the pine smoke: the girlish line of her mouth, her grey eyes that stared into mine. A heaviness under her eyes, almost seventy. Gone were her tricks, her antics, her cackle. She sat there, stilled.

'Rachel,' I said.

She licked her lips as though about to speak.

'Your husband speaks calumnies about you. Will you remain silent? Will you tell me the truth of it?'

There was one question, thick in my mind – and what then? The other spirits had disburdened themselves, found themselves lighter by having spoken the truth, and then it had been easy to coax them away. But Rachel Erskine? I knew enough of her to grasp that she was like a dog with a stick: she would not leave a wrong unrevenged.

'Tell me the truth, Rachel,' I murmured, casting a look at the door. There were other servants in this house; other maids whom Rachel had not chased away. The keyhole glinted, shining like a mouse's eye, and I took a scrap of linen, plugged it. I would have to talk quietly, because if he discovered me – I swallowed. Could I? Dare I?

I thought of another time, how the fisherman had said, 'I heard her calling and I thought I was too late,' and how my voice had seemed empty, cut out, resounding flatly against the waves. I thought what it meant to be heard.

'Tell me how it all began,' I said. 'I am not afraid of you.'

I felt Rachel lean towards me, felt the coolness spread through my arm, up my back. I angled myself closer to her, waited for that low whisper of words, waited to catch the edge of them. I reached instinctively for my quill and paper, began to scratch down the words that she spoke.

When we were newly married, I wrote, and my scribbles on the page grew and grew.

❧

When we were newly married, I would sit in my husband's library helping him with his entreaties about his brother, the 6th Earl of Mar, in exile for Jacobite sympathies.

'Take care,' he would say, 'as this letter could be a noose about my throat.'

We knew well how the slightest powder would catch. But I was proud to help him, to be the factor on his estate, and in charge of his affairs. Not to be, as he put it one afternoon, 'a silly, mindless wife, with a wit as sharp as—'

He flailed about for the right analogy.

'This letter-opening knife,' I finished for him. 'That could not even gut a fish.'

He laughed and cast his pen aside and pulled me on to his lap. His hands were on my hips, my belly, his kisses on my throat. I laughed, too, until I felt the baby flickering in my belly, and from outside I could smell the flowers I had planted in the garden. Lavender and hedges of common elder. He called me naughtie and a devil and I felt his ribs shake with merriment. Naughtie, was I? I picked up that old blade and ran it against his thumb. It would not cut the skin but left an imprint and he cried out with delight at my daring, pulling me closer, unbuttoning his trousers.

'But I thought I was a devil, and now you commune with me,' I said, pretending to pull away, but I knew he held me fast. 'Remember I am a murtherer's daughter,' I whispered, 'and should sleep with this blade under my pillow so you do not forget it.'

How easy to forget, to craft something new in face of what followed. And was I easy? I was not. I was hungry for life, for responsibility; I was ravenous for it.

And how many children were enough? Seven, eight, nine? Each blunted me, shifted me away from myself. A decade of my life I spent as a sow, a whelping bitch, vomiting and wrung out and ungainly. And then the babes!

Their gasping fish mouths and clutching little hands, my breasts aching and dripping milk, tightly bound; a few months until it began again. Perhaps I ought to say I loved those children, but I did not. The ones I loved were the ones I lost because they had not yet grown teeth and claws, had not bawled their pink rage at me.

The ones I loved bled away in a pan. And through it all: James drifting in and out, unencumbered, free as a tomcat. His body, unleaking, whole, entirely his own. I paced the halls of our house, waiting for the clip of his horses, for his return from London, for scraps he might cast of this other life he led, in town or at the Bench or in the taverns, until I might have cut my wrist on my anger, until my fury was blistering and I barked at my children and barked at the maids, and my body filled with yet another child as though it meant to eat me up.

The library key was gone; I pressed on the wood. Locked, hard against me.

It washed over me: all those evenings we had spent by candlelight, working through his correspondence. When had I lost him? When had he tired of me? My body grown undesirable, the skin on my belly puckered. My resentment at him seeping out in anger, in sharp words. I pushed the wood, harder, cried out.

I let out a scream, clawed at the wood, barged and pushed, and all while my son and daughter and maid watched with cold, shut faces, little imprints of their father, turned against me.

'Fie,' I shrieked. 'Fie!'

And I would have beaten them too if I had not been wrestled to the floor and pinned in place there, my mouth filling with blood. As I lay there, bucking like a fish fresh caught, I knew at last that my grip had faltered; knew that I was shut out, entrusted with nothing; and I knew my fists might as well have pummelled air because where was he but in London, far away from me, and he had not even had the courage to lock me out himself.

He did not reply to my letters but wrote endlessly to my sons, and I knew they complained of me, that their missives were full of schemes against me. The power that men have to wield and withhold! But as I reared up from the floor, a burning certainty filled me: that as God was my witness, I would fight him. I would not make myself small and meek and box myself away, as he would have me.

What is it to be cut off, isolated, left alone? I confess in those days it was a mere foretaste of things to come. He separated himself from me, gave me no money, shut his doors against me. I became nothing to him.

Sometimes I would touch my throat just to hear the vibration of my voice, to know that it still made a sound. I began to feel like a ghost, like a thing unseen slipping between the walls.

When I came across him in the street with my son one afternoon, all my fury burst out. A crowd formed and I saw his hard, sealed face as he hurried himself away, as he scurried into an inn and shut the door against me.

Mad, he would say, mad.

Two hours I waited, my hands cold and white, my breath icy, until my anger cooled and was replaced by something harder, emptier, like a stone in the belly. I saw, standing there, that I was losing control; that this scene had cost me. He had presented himself as a man to be pitied, while he had cut me off without a penny. I did not have enough money for bread. I saw how men on the Bench like him, men of influence, nudged each other and turned away from me; I saw how whispers spread, and I knew it was he who was spreading them. What a thing it was to have a circle of powerful male friends, to carry influence. I began to hear stories of myself, whispered back: that I had forced him to be my wife down a pistol's barrel, that I slept with a knife under my pillow to remind him whose daughter I was.

The soft reminiscences of our early days were chewed and spat out: those nights by the fire, how he drew me to him, the things I had said in jest or softness sharpened against me. Everything was written over or magnified; my outbursts murderous rampages; my dislike of my children a devilish disposition; a few drinks a vicious drunkenness. I was made into something new, terrible, and as I stood in that street I could feel myself becoming it: I could feel the bite of desperation, the need to make myself heard at whatever cost.

I thought of my father and how his heart curdled with the need for revenge, how he had stalked that magistrate in the streets, to his house, to church. I thought of how he had stood in Hope's Close with his shotgun pressed into Lord Lockhart's back.

And how, when his finger pulled the trigger, there was no undoing it.

A gun, once discharged, cannot have the bullet packed in.

I thought of his hanging on St Giles, his hand cut off, the bloody stump which I saw later when they cut down his body and brought it home and buried him under the flagstones.

Because I knew, as I sat alone in my room and fidgeted with my hair and burned with the desire to have my husband hear me, the one thing I had left in my artillery. The letters we had written, his brother imprisoned even now. The men I saw him let into his library at night and the conversations and correspondence

I had once been privy to. A coterie of powerful men, all of whom were secret supporters of the Jacobite cause, who met in the pavilion at Preston House. It was sedition, enough to incur the gibbet or the axe.

That finger, twitching the trigger.

I would write him a letter, setting out what I planned to make known.

And I thought only of the echo of that bullet, the moment of impact: I thought of the instant he would hear me, when he would know my power; but I was blind, then, to the wider reverberations, how I was, in effect, turning the pistol on myself.

A little after midnight, I was woken abruptly. Hands on me; men's voices, shouts, a fist in my mouth. Ripped from the bed, flung to the floor, unable to catch a breath. I tore the rag free.

'MURTHER!' I cried. 'MURTHER!'

Pain all over; its dull thud. Teeth spat on to the floor, the taste of iron in my throat, the rip of my hair. I thought they would kill me; I thought I was already dead. The ricochet of my skull, beaten against something – wood, a fist, the floor? – hands grasping at me, a group of them, all men, and me, bundled downstairs as still as a corpse, head knocked against the banister, my whole body aching, the gag tight and sour against my face, the sharp throb of my mouth where my teeth were missing.

All of this, arranged from London, as easily as a man clicks his fingers for a drink.

But I did die that day, I realise now. An empty coffin lowered into a grave in Greyfriars Kirkyard, mourned, gone, fifteen years before I breathed my last.

The cargo; I hated to be called that, even more than 'damned bitch', because to them I was nothing but baggage. 'The cargo,' they laughed as they lugged me from place to place, as they locked me in dungeon holes and cattle byres and sheilings and half-ruined buildings, moving me after nightfall on horseback, my arms lashed to my sides. Some nights they would simply lie me down on the cold, damp grass to sleep. Every place was unfamiliar, every scene new and foreign to me.

Three days and nights of rowing, and nothing about us but the grey waves. No land, no sight of anything.

My wrists and feet were bound, a noose around my neck that was tied to a great stone, for they said they would throw me overboard if I made a fuss. I began to quiver and shake, thinking what would happen if the waves knocked and tipped our little boat and how I would sink, dragged by my throat, helpless against it.

There at last was a small flash of land: tall, ragged cliffs, not a tree in sight. We docked beside some rocks. Where was I? Truly it felt to me like it was the end of the world.

St Kilda, I was told at last, and I had not heard of it. Such a vile, nasty, stinking isle! Scarcely a soul spoke my language and I spoke not theirs. My cell was a cleit, little wider than a pantry, with a turf roof.

The years melted into each other; I ate little but puffins and fulmars and their eggs, or sooty oatcakes. I had no shoes or stockings.

Sometimes I would think of my husband and it was more than I could bear: his warm bed and the women who warmed it; his decanter of fine claret, dinners of fresh whiting and samphire.

But this was not the worst of it. What a thing it was to be denied paper to write on. Nowhere to record my plight.

I scratched letters on leather with coal, on rocks with stones, my name, endlessly: I am Rachel Chiesley, Lady Grange!

Most days I would walk the cliffs and scream at the sea, cast my voice into the wind, into nothing, and bawl about my life, what had happened to me. It did not matter. Soon, I was moved again. More men and a boat to bring me to more caves by the sea, reeking of smoked fish, until, at last, I felt the ice lodge so firmly in my bones that my spirit drifted on and away, and I was finally erased, and I knew he had got what he wanted in the end.

∽

When Lady Grange had finished speaking, she drifted out the window and was gone. My candle guttered and spat and I stared at the paper in front of me, the words I had written. A shuffling at the door; I seized the paper, crumpled it down my dress, breathing hard. The linen was still stuffed in the lock, but what of the creak of my nib against the paper, the slow dip of the ink? What would Lord Grange do if he knew what I possessed? Knowledge was powerful, destructive. This was a man, after all, who had had his wife exiled, half-murdered.

The paper was hot against my skin, scratching. I should burn it; I should tear it into shreds. But I did not move.

Had a maid heard us talking?

And when my room was unlocked, I took a breakfast of bannock cake and the letter was still in my dress. And when Lord Grange summoned me to his library, it was still there, and I wondered if the ink had left an imprint on my skin, if her story was bored into me, like the tattoos on the sailors in Portobello.

The terrier yapped; his books glinted. I bound my hands under my thighs. He was Lord Justice Clerk. I felt weighed, assessed, my guilt written all over my face. I distracted myself by reading the titles lining his shelves, taking them in for the first time.

Daemonology, I read. *The Discoverie of Witches. A Most Certain, Strange Discovery of a VVITCH.*

It all began to make sense: Lord Grange believed in witchcraft.

There, surrounding me, were volumes and volumes of words that black-hearted men had scratched down, silencing woman after woman. I thought of the city, filled with smoke and screaming; I thought of my grandmother, adding pine branches to the pyre so the smoke might kill the women before the flames; I thought of the laws and the hunts that this man – fingers linked across his belly, his portrait shining behind him – would bring back if he could.

And a previous suspicion began to solidify into hard fact: that he would have had his wife hunted and burned if she had lived half a century ago, if laws had not been drawn against it. I thought of how he had poured poison about his wife into the ears of powerful men. *She would murther me* – I saw how he had detached himself from her, cut her off, how he had goaded her, and then – the community against her – how he had spurred his circle into action. Had her taken out, banished, ostracised, all while he pulled the strings from London, three hundred miles away. How cleverly he had had his witch hunted and caught.

'And you did not speak to her?' he asked, through narrowed eyes. He speared a piece of venison, chewed it slowly.

'No.' I kept my face level, calm.

'Clarry said she heard you speaking in the night.'

'I – I – have terrors. My mother often complains I chatter through the night.'

Another mouthful. Fear spread up my arms, hot and prickling. I raised my chin. 'Would you have her gone at any cost, sir?'

He stared at me. 'I have brought you here with one purpose. Can you misunderstand it?'

I shook my head, adjusted how I sat. The letter seemed to rustle against me.

I glanced at the house. There was my attic window. I saw shapes moving across it, ransacking it, checking what I knew. How long until he had me searched, intent as a witch-finder looking for devil's teats? How long until he pulled the letter from my stays, learned everything I knew?

He ate on, his knife scraping the plate, the flesh brown and glistening. His whiskers trembled, each swallow hard and violent, the meat practically unchewed. I noted the pinkness in his throat, like uncooked meat, the twitch in his temple.

'This meat is rancid,' he announced suddenly, casting it away from him with an abrupt violence. 'It has been – it has been poisoned by—' He looked about him and I knew what he was thinking, what he called her. *The Creature.*

And I saw too how he blamed her for everything, how the meat was probably thirteen days old and first served on Christmas Day, the maid simply thoughtless or lazy; and how he had blamed Rachel for every one of his misfortunes in life, too, whether alive or dead.

The terrier was at the door, keening for a piss.

'Let it out,' he commanded, but when I opened the door and a sheaf of snow fell on to the threshold, the dog would not go. It whined and yapped and, finally, wet the floor. Lord Grange cursed, and stormed across the room, and was about to grind the dog's face into its own mess when I saw its ears prick, its tail lie flat. Lord Grange drew his hand back as though the dog had bitten it; he cried out, 'You were meant to rid me of her!'

He thought she was here, I realised, but in truth she was not; it was the cold of the open door nipping at him, his dog cowering because he bore down on it, as it growled and cowered and hissed until, at last, backed into a corner, it lunged forwards and bit his leg.

It was as though a gun had been fired, the change in him. He reached for the animal, pale and white and small, and beat its head against his desk. I let out a cry and lunged for him, but he flung me back, and he beat it and beat it and beat it, like the arm of an anvil might slice up and down.

❧

At last he stopped and sank back into his chair. I did not look at the small bundle in the corner, motionless and bleeding. He kneaded his brow between his fingers, panting hard, his leg stretched before him. I could see where the dog's teeth had pierced the skin, six puncture marks that were now weeping blood.

'Help me,' he said, gesturing at the hand I had bandaged on the day I arrived. 'With your – your herbs.'

I bowed my head, instructed the maid to bring me my linen bag. The contents were all disordered, a few vials missing, but I said nothing. I took out a glass bottle, carefully labelled. He winced as I wetted a cloth and passed it over the wound.

'Her spirit – her spirit was in the dog,' he muttered. 'I know it.'

I stared at him, did not argue. His voice slurred, thick with wine, and I wrapped up a handkerchief of peppermint and told him to boil it in water, to drink it when he was troubled and sleep escaped him.

'Drink a little,' I told him, nudging the claret towards him. 'It will ease your pain.'

I waited until he was insensible with drink, until he slouched back against his chair with red-rimmed eyes. I stood, alert as a hare. I knew what I must do: I had two hours, perhaps three, until he came to his senses and began to search for me. I left along the quiet path that his Jacobite kinsmen had taken, legs firing like pistons, glancing behind me, for a horse, for anyone who might be there to chase me down. The sea howled, the waves crashing against the shore.

I held the note tight against me, held it as I ran, as, at last, I bent over with exhaustion, spat on the sand. I knew that I could not leave Rachel's words unspoken, no matter what axe swung down on to my own neck: I knew that the letter must be read, distributed, her truth known. I would write copies, circulate it through the coffee houses and taverns and tea tables of the city. I would have her story told.

He had given his permission tacitly in his answer to my careful question. *Would you have her gone at any cost?* If her story was heard, she would vanish; she would trouble him no more.

As I raced along the shore, stumbling on loose stones, I thought what it was to humiliate a man, to have him fear he might lose his standing in this world. A Lord Justice Clerk in red velvet, setting the law, meting out his punishment.

In the coming week, the streets were lit with scandal, the story recited to those who could not read. *Have you heard; have you heard; have you heard?* The story reverberated down closes and alleys, through tenements and town houses. Humiliation: that was the only punishment that would ever be handed out to a man of his standing.

I waited for the knock on the door. I waited for the sound of hooves, the men pounding up the stairs. I dared not hope it was as I suspected. And yet – nothing. It was a few weeks later that I heard the news from London. 'Wasn't that the man you'd helped with the spirit?' my mother asked me. 'Lord Grange, found dead?'

I bit my tongue and busied myself with scrubbing the sheets.

'Perhaps it was,' I said. 'God rest his soul.'

I recalled the day I had returned from Preston House. In in the bright light of morning, I had noticed that the labels of my herbs were muddled. I had raised a hand to my brow, cursed. I was meticulous, careful. Of course, I thought, *of course*. The shadows at the window; could it have been *her*?

I thought of the drink he might have made, not steeped peppermint but nightshade, the fits that would have gripped hold of him, the poison rooted in his heart.

I smiled; wrung out a cloth. Before he died, he would have seen the truth outed, his reputation in tatters. I thought of Lady Grange on that distant, lonely island, howling her fury into the sea, and the story that she was, at last, able to tell.

AUTHOR'S NOTE

This is a fictionalised account of the true story of Lady Grange's kidnap and banishment to St Kilda in 1732. In James Boswell's *Journal of a Tour to the Hebrides* (1785), he wrote: *After dinner to-day, we talked of the extraordinary fact of Lady Grange's being sent to St Kilda, and confined there for several years, without any means of relief. Dr Johnson said, if M'Leod would let it be known that he had such a place for naughty ladies, he might make it a very profitable island.*

Almost all of the details surrounding Lady Grange's life and that of Lord Grange are accurate, and I have even used some of Lady Grange's own words in the italicised sections. However, I have taken three major liberties. The first is the nature of the letter. Lady Grange managed to convince a minister on St Kilda to write and disseminate a letter describing her kidnap, which was circulated in Edinburgh when she was still alive. While it meant that her narrative and account was heard, this letter had little impact on her immediate situation as Lord Grange swiftly arranged for her removal to Skye, where she soon died. The remaining liberties are on the nature of Lord Grange's death, and, of course, the idea that he was haunted by his wife – which I put down to wishful thinking.

THE GARGOYLE

Bridget Collins

It was a steep climb from the railway station, especially with a suitcase in either hand. By the time Ash reached the great stone gate that led to the Old Town she was sweating, in spite of the freezing salt wind at her back. When she set out she had thought that she was travelling light, apart from her portable typewriter, but now her arms felt stretched and raw with fatigue. She gazed out at the glinting grey landscape below, longing to pitch all her luggage over the parapet and have done with it. Grim, practical common sense made her draw a long breath, flex her aching fingers, and pick both cases up again. It would not be far now.

She had not been to Lye since she was a child. In her memory it was a blue, summer-sparkling, miraculous place, full of mysterious cul-de-sacs and twisting streets, a bewitching maze of sunlight and shadows. She had run with Isabel – her true love, even then – up Watchbell Street, giggling and slipping on the cobbles, lurching into the shocked arms of fusty old gentlemen, light-headed with the heat and the taste of the distant sea. Later, in the long evening, they had wandered hand in hand – lagging twenty paces behind her uncle and aunt – past the King's House and the old apothecary's and the red-brick Grammar School; past enclosed squares of garden, past window-boxes foaming with lobelia, past old houses, houses with many-paned windows, houses with coats of arms, sagging roofs and skewed chimneys, with too many doors or none . . . It had been an enchanted day, a rare moment of respite from her father's drunkenness and her mother's scandals, a day of stone mermaids and strawberry ice and Isabel's hot fingers in hers. Ever since, whenever she read 'Lye', or caught sight of a map of the Sussex coast, she had felt a pulse of warmth, and smiled as though it had been a hundred years ago, not twenty. That had been why – oh Lord, had it really been for so flimsy a reason? – she had let Edwin talk her into this absurd excursion, and why she was here, now, chilled and aching, lugging her suitcases up East Street along a pavement so narrow it threatened at every moment to shrug her off into the road. Because she had been sentimental, and stupid: she had not considered, for example, that in December there might not be the same largesse of sunshine and roses, she had simply heard him say 'a little place in Lye—' and been overwhelmed by yearning and nostalgia.

No. It had been that; but not only that. By then, she had been desperate to nod, and agree, and get out of his office; if he had proposed Timbuktu she would have waved her hand in exactly the same way, feigning ease through a fog of humiliation. No doubt he had seen through her pretence, but with characteristic tact he had removed his glasses and polished them on his handkerchief, blinking. 'A little time away,' he said, 'that's all. Time alone, to concentrate. Time to woo your muse.' He replaced them on his nose. 'Come on, ducky, don't look like that. I am not a bit surprised that your second novel should give you trouble. And this draft has great promise. I only feel— Well.' He held his hands over the pile of painfully typed pages like a pianist about to launch into the funeral march. 'I am quite certain that this book will be just as good as your first, eventually. It only needs work. A few days of solitude will be just the ticket.'

She had bowed her head and reached for a cigarette. If she were a man, she had thought, she would grab his lapels and haul him to the window; she would suspend him above the grinding London traffic, and while he wriggled and pleaded she would ask him how the bloody hell she was supposed to rewrite an entire novel in three months, when he could not even tell her what exactly was wrong with it. The fantasy was so strong that she felt her legs tense, as though she were taking his weight. She said, with an effort, 'And if it doesn't . . .? If I can't—'

'Don't be silly, my dear. You have an enormous talent. You must trust that. No,' and he held up a finger, 'I won't hear it. The author of *Felicity* has a duty to her public. Go to Lye, mull things over, and come back ready for a big push.' He slid the manuscript towards her. 'And don't glare. I know as well as you do that your Christmas is always dreary, and that damn cousin of yours leads you a merry dance.'

'Isabel is going to St Moritz.'

'Then there's no reason to object, is there?'

'I wasn't objecting. All right.' She ground out her hardly smoked cigarette, gathered the dog-eared pages into her arms and stood up.

'It's a quaint little place,' he said, 'looks out on the churchyard – and the town is very artistic – all sorts of writers have lived there—'

But finally her feelings got the better of her: she slammed the door on him so hard that the plaque that said *Edwin Guddle, Literary Agent* slipped and stuck at a drunken angle, and she did not nudge it back into place.

She had thought, then, that at least the worst was over – but oh, what a fool she had been! Since that day in Edwin's office her helpless humiliation had only grown more intense, and now the thought of being face to face with her book, without distractions, made her cringe. She should never have come. Better to be anywhere else – pretending to enjoy sweaty parties in London, or enduring suspicious looks at her stepfather's dinner table, or even sitting in silence with her aunt in Norfolk, without Isabel . . .

She halted, letting her cases rest on the ground, and shook off the grasp of self-pity. She had come to the church. There, on the other side of the graveyard, was an irregular terrace of half-timbered cottages, their black and white muted in the winter afternoon. 'Next to Fishgut Alley,' Edwin had said; so it must be – ah yes, that one, with its single gable and medieval overhang. Her heart lifted to see a line of coppery firelight between the curtains, and she sped up, sliding a little on the slick cobbles. The key in her pocket bumped against her hip. Then, at last, she pushed open the heavy door, found herself in a warm low room, full of the glow and scent of a good wood fire, and shut out the freezing dusk.

For a moment she did nothing but stand and breathe the scents of old smoke and furniture polish. It was, in fact, a quaint little place. The soft light glimmered on the table and chairs, and drew answering gleams from a silver candlestick here and a ship in a bottle there. The rug in front of the hearth was well-worn, and the chesterfield beside it was cracking a little with age – indeed, nothing was new or pristine – but the shabbiness was comforting, like the worn covers of a favourite book. The lamp beside the window murmured faintly in a draught, and shone a little brighter, as though to greet her. Beside the fireplace there was another low door, which she supposed led to the pantry; on the other side a narrow staircase led upwards and out of sight. But it was only when a log fell in the grate, collapsing with a huff of sparks, that she blinked and started forward to explore.

She had guessed right: behind the door was a little pantry-cum-kitchen. The range was lit, and hot; set out on the counter was a covered pot of stew and potatoes, and a dust-encrusted bottle of wine. Beside them a spotless white tea-towel covered a plump sultana cake. In a low cupboard – as she had requested, being determined to fend for herself and keep her own hours – were ranks of tins. It would not be a varied diet, but it would suffice. As she stood up again, a bronze-gold gleam by the back door caught her eye. She peered closer, and laughed. Half a dozen bottles of whisky, with a note. *Work well, my dear. E.* Clearly Edwin had forgiven her for her curtness.

She searched for a glass and poured herself a generous measure. Then, with the glass in her hand, she ascended the stairs, her mouth tingling, welcome heat spreading down her throat and deep into her belly. Here there were more low beams, and a floor that rose and fell in a wooden wave. The bedroom was narrow, with a small square window at either end, and simply furnished; the patchwork quilt on the bed was faded and coming apart at one corner, but the mattress was firm, and the sheets scrupulously clean. Next door was a larger room with a wall of bookshelves and a desk in front of a tall window. She leant over the desk to twitch aside the curtain, and saw the church silhouetted against the charcoal-clouded sky. She was about to let it drop when a clot of darkness darted across her field of vision, and she recoiled; but a moment later she saw that it was only a last clinging tuft of leaves on the topmost branch of the beech tree in the churchyard, tossing in a gust of wind. The same gust rattled the window pane and enveloped her in a sudden chill. It was the sort of picture that she might have revelled in – the sort that could be incorporated into a moment of Gothic drama, full of shadows and mystery: she could imagine Edwin's pencil underlining her descriptions of bare-fingered trees in the dense winter dusk, the gangrenous, fat-bellied clouds above the church roof, the hunched gargoyles looking out over the graves, and adding *Perfect!* in the margin. Or – even better – if Isabel were here to shiver and take her hand, and say, with that breathy hitch in her voice, 'Oh! How too, too sinister!' But tonight, being disinclined to think about writing, or Isabel, she let the curtain fall and turned away.

She cast a cursory glance over the bathroom, which was newly fitted and not shabby at all, Edwin having an unmanly penchant for luxury and hot water, and descended the stairs. The lamp gave another friendly flicker at her approach and she sank onto the chesterfield, abruptly so weary she could have fallen asleep then and there. The fire would need another log soon, but not yet. She tipped up her glass and found, to her vague surprise, that it was empty. That gave her just enough impetus to get to her feet again. More whisky, and dinner. Well, if she could call it dinner, it was not yet five o'clock – but she did not care, she was hungry and hazy-headed, and there was no one to raise an eyebrow if she ate at this hour. She would unpack tomorrow; set out her manuscript and notes and faithful Remington Portable tomorrow; begin work, tomorrow . . .

She did not dwell on that. She was already lifting the pot of stew on to the range, a little clumsily, so that gravy slopped and hissed, fragrant and savoury; and the rush of saliva into her mouth, and the growl of her stomach, drove everything but the thought of supper from her mind.

It was still early when she climbed the stairs to go to bed. The effect of her excellent dinner, accompanied by half a bottle of wine, was compounded by the fatigue of the journey so that she could hardly keep her eyes open. She had often struggled to sleep in an unfamiliar place, but when her cheek met the pillow she had only time to notice a faint scent of laundry soap and close her eyes before she was unconscious.

She slept deeply, dreamlessly, for a little while, until the urge to empty her bladder tugged her uncomfortably back into wakefulness. She fumbled for her bedside lamp, forgetting for a moment where she was; then the matchbox slipped to the floor with a rattle and abruptly she remembered that she was not at home, and there was no electric light. Never mind. Carefully she slid out of bed, groped her way through the blackness to the bathroom, relieved herself, and padded back along the landing. But at the doorway to the study she paused: earlier that evening she had not quite pulled the curtains into place, and there was a patch of thinner darkness where they did not meet. Through that narrow gap she could just make out the bony branches of the tree beyond the window, and beyond that, the thick turret that stood gloating at the corner of the church roof. She was about to turn away, shivering, when her attention was caught by something – some niggle of curiosity, or confusion, something that she could not put her finger on, enough to make her pause, squinting through the darkness. As though the church were different – as if some small, but significant aspect of it had changed—

There was a scratching sound overhead. She froze, forgetting everything else.

Mice. No. Rats.

She took a deep breath. She did not like rats very much.

If Isabel had been here, she could have mustered enough bravado to laugh, and pretend to be fearless; but as it was, she stood quite still, her fists clenched, wishing she could run out of the house and away. There was a cold, creeping feeling on the back of her neck. A pause, filled with the thumping of her heart – and then the noise began again, a thick, ponderous scrape like a sharp stone being dragged across the tiles. *Was* it a rat? It was too singular, too heavy, too – she squeezed her eyes shut – too deliberate. It might be something larger. A squirrel? A cat? But there was something reptilian in that dry slither; and at the same time, absurdly, she imagined a mind as quick and strategic as her own, calculating, advancing . . .

It stopped, again, too suddenly; it was still there, directly above her, and in spite of herself she could not shake the sense that it knew of her presence, and was waiting. She waited too, every nerve strained, until she thought her lungs would burst. At last the sound came again, not, after all, remotely human: a slow hoarse scuttling, a scrooping pounce—

Now it was hanging under the eaves, above the window. She heard the osseous flick of something against the glass. For a few seconds she stood still, hesitating; then, just as she brought herself to move towards it, the animal scrattled sideways, and was gone.

There was no need to open the curtains, after all. She leant on the back of the chair, weak-kneed with relief. Oh, how foolish she was! It had been a rat, of course it had been a rat, she would write and tell Edwin to put down poison, but only a rat, how absurd to have been unnerved by a mere rat! Good God, she was going soft.

She shut the study door and fumbled her way back to bed. For some minutes she could not quite relax, in case the scuttling sounds should recommence; but she heard nothing more. She nestled deeper into the bedclothes, and after a while a quiet rain began to patter on the window panes, and lulled her back to sleep.

The next morning she discovered that there was no coffee. She brewed a furiously strong pot of tea instead, cursing Edwin, and in her bleary resentment almost knocked the teapot off the counter. She dawdled over her second cup, watching the sleet blow into Fishgut Alley, to put off the moment when she would have to begin work. At last, because she knew she would despise herself if she delayed any longer, she stumped up the stairs, drew her battered manuscript out of her suitcase, and settled at the desk to study it.

Some time later she sat back, massaging her aching neck, sick at heart. It was only now that she admitted that she had harboured a last insidious hope that perhaps, after all, it was not so bad as all that – that a few well-placed descriptions, an elision here, an addition there, might solve the problem in a few days. But in the grey, miserable light of the winter morning she had no illusions left. Was her insipid, lifeless heroine really based on Isabel, whose slightest gesture could make her choke with desire? How could she have failed to see that the other characters were wooden, the dialogue stilted, the very conceit of the whole endeavour entirely barren? She had read epitaphs with more vigour. There was no solution that would not require the redrafting of every page – and worse still, the precise nature of any such solution eluded her entirely. No spark jumped, no electricity hummed, the entire novel was as flat as the paper she had typed it on. Poor Edwin had been kinder than he had any need to be when he had said it showed promise.

The church clock struck noon. She put her head in her hands. She was glad the fire in the hearth downstairs had burnt out, because she could hardly have resisted the urge to shovel the fat bundle of pages into it and have done.

Damn it. She shoved herself backwards, nearly toppling the chair. She would not sit here and mope, descending deeper and deeper into a morass of self-pity. Fresh air and exercise, that was the thing. When she had been writing *Felicity*, a brisk afternoon constitutional had invariably unblocked her creative waterworks and brought her back to her desk with renewed momentum. A little self-discipline, a little determination, and an absolute refusal to indulge her own weakness: *that* was the best prescription for art, as it was for life. She hurried down the stairs, pulling on her jacket, and stepped out into the winter day before she had time to change her mind.

The sleet had stopped, which was something. She set off at a swift pace, her head lowered against the bitter wind, turning along the left side of the churchyard and off down West Street; but she could not keep up that pace for long, and she paused at the corner to catch her breath. Here the walls on either side created a pocket of stillness, although the chill in the air seemed to intensify. In front of her an eighteenth-century house stood facing the church. She remembered her Uncle Anthony pointing it out to them, that long-ago summer day: 'Here,' he had said grandly, 'there lives the famous author, S. L. Amies.' Naturally, neither she nor Isabel had heard of Amies; but they peered enthusiastically into the windows, and shrieked and giggled when a greying lace curtain was twitched by a crooked hand. Amies was long dead now – with not much loss, she thought, to the world of literature. She did not care for his particular brand of ha'penny horror; as far as she was concerned, any writer whose plots necessitated a denial of the laws of reality was hardly worthy of the name. But a sting of unaccustomed humility followed hard upon the thought: who was she, after all, to pronounce on other authors? She moved on down Mermaid Street, grimacing.

She was tempted, passing the old inn, to warm herself with a hot toddy beside the fire – but no, she must not give in, she would make herself fit for nothing, and she hurried down the hill over the greasy cobbles before turning left again. Finally, making a loop, she came up through the stone gatehouse to the High Street. By now her face was stinging with cold and her shoulders ached from hunching against the wind. When she passed the bookshop she ducked without thinking through its little doorway.

She had only meant to stop inside for a second, long enough

for a few lungfuls of warm air, but she caught the curious eye of the shopgirl and hurried into the nearest alcove to cover her embarrassment. And there, unexpectedly, she came face to face with the long-dead owner of that gnarled spasmodic hand: between the bookcases there hung a portrait of S. L. Amies himself, and below it was displayed a handsome biography in black cloth with gilt edges. Apparently there were those who found not only amusement but significance in puerile fantasies of ghosts and hauntings. She glared at the old man in the painting, resenting his success, his reputation, and his sex. She would wager that no one had called him *over-ambitious* or *unwomanly* or *perverse* . . . And yet, as she met the painted gaze, her resentment died. It was impossible to envy a man with such eyes: impossible to feel anything but pity and repulsion, so strong was the light of despair that shone through the inert brushstrokes. She clenched her jaw, wishing she could stare him down; but at last, of course, she was defeated. Instead her glance slid down and sideways, to where Amies's bony fingers rested on a pile of books: *Tales of the Macabre*, *The Shadow of the Tower* and – half turned away, only just legible – *Dr Faustus*. How arrogant, to put his own work in the same pile as Christopher Marlowe! But it was not arrogance in his face; it was horror, and misery, and regret. The shop door rattled in a gust of wind, and she shivered.

'Can I help you, sir— I mean, madam?'

'No,' she said with a jump. 'No, thank you, no . . .' And she shoved past the shopgirl, back the way she had come. There was a copy of *Felicity* beside the counter, which ordinarily would have made her linger to admire it, secretly hoping that someone might look at her and murmur, 'I say – aren't *you* Miss Ashwell Scott?' But she did not pause. In spite of the freezing winter weather, it was a relief to stumble out into the High Street, away from that disconcerting picture.

She strode up to Church Square with a rather forced energy, swinging her arms like a gym mistress. But as she drew closer to the little house her reluctance to return to work grew. She hesitated by the north door of the church; but she was not welcomed by the Church of England, she had known that for longer than she cared to remember. Instead she shoved her hands into her pockets and took the path across the graveyard, squinting at the headstones. Most were mossy and illegible, especially in the dimming light; even though it was still early afternoon, the clouds hung low and heavy, and the bleak winter colours were slowly draining into grey. She shivered again, harder. She had come past the west door, to where the corner of the church roof was decorated by a blunt turret like a chimney. She stopped beside a holly tree, pulling her jacket even tighter. It was made of stout woollen tweed, but suddenly it seemed as thin as a silk handkerchief. Too cold. She should go inside. Back to work—

She caught her foot on something, twisted her ankle, hopped, staggered, swore and reached out to steady herself. Her hand met dank stone. A gravestone; well, of course, what else would she expect to find in a churchyard? She bent to look, and a swinging tendril of spiky leaves tugged at her shoulder. *Septimus Louis Amies, 1870–1919.*

A part of her was pleased that she did not recoil. She only stepped back, wiping her gritty hand on her trousers. It was hardly a coincidence. Where else would Amies have been buried but here, a few yards from his house? But surely the dates were wrong – she had thought the man in the picture seventy, at least . . . She crouched to look closer, in case she had misread them. No. Neither was there anything else on the headstone, nor to mark the grave, except that – she wrinkled her nose – some animal had apparently got into the habit of relieving itself just beside her feet, leaving a bare patch in the grass. She thought of Isabel's nasty little poodle – the sort of dog that would deliberately choose a grave to piss on, if it could – and how Isabel's eyes would brim with tears if anyone criticised it. One day someone would wring its neck, and good riddance. She glanced round. Or perhaps this particular place was simply too shaded, too bleak, to allow anything much to grow. Certainly it seemed colder here than it had on the other side of the church; and, looking up, she saw that it would be perpetually overshadowed by that ridiculous stumpy turret, which was crowned by an irregular lump of stone. She squinted. A gargoyle. It was bending forwards, clutching some implement, and after a moment she realised that it held an age-eaten quill in its stone claws. Not a recording angel, but a scribbling demon . . .

'Ye'd better not stand there gawping.'

She swung round. There was an old man, well-muffled, his eyes bright in a weather-ruddy face, on the path.

'I have every right to stand where I choose,' she said, with as much dignity as she could muster. It had no effect on the old man, who regarded her unsympathetically.

'Ha,' he said without rancour, 'and ye've a right to stand under a tree in a storm.' He shuffled past, knocking her aside when she put out a tentative hand to help him. When he reached the place where the paths diverged, he glanced back and jerked his chin upwards. 'Don't draw his attention,' he said. 'The longer ye stand and stare, on an afternoon like this . . . Looking for new blood, he is, been looking for years . . .'

'I have no idea what—' she began, but he had already shrugged and moved away, leaving an after-whiff of wet wool. She bit her lip. How stupid, to care what some insalubrious grandfather said! She did not even understand what his warning meant – she had been too bewildered to take it in – already she could not, exactly, recall his words, only that he had said she should not stand under the holly tree. She looked up: she could well believe there was snow on the way, with the clouds sagging low over the roofs. But even in a blizzard she would be able to stumble across the churchyard to her front door, it was only a matter of a few yards. Oh, for heaven's sake, how melodramatic! There was no sign of a single drifting snowflake, nor of a gale strong enough to blow tiles from the roof of the church, nor of any other calamity, lightning or earthquake or fiery rain.

But, after all, she had had enough of exercise and fresh air. She told herself that it was merely the inclement weather which made her want to go back inside. Even so it took an effort to walk along the path to the gap in the churchyard wall, and thence to the little low door beside Fishgut Alley, without once looking over her shoulder.

She worked until the church clock struck six – that is, if you could call it that; if staring at the paper, and making lists of new names for her characters, and pacing, and swearing, could be described with that kindly word. She worked until her eyes stung, and her head ached, and she was more convinced than ever that she could not make any headway at all. At last she shoved her chair back so hard it nearly toppled, and she had to catch herself with a jerk. 'Damn,' she said, 'damn, damn, *damn* . . .' and heard her voice crack.

She dragged her hands through her hair, trying to ease the pain over her temples. It was time for a drink before dinner, and a few pages of a book pulled at random from the shelves, and maybe a bath. Time to think about something – anything! – else. She might even compose a letter to Isabel— No. Not that. Not until she could report that her novel was progressing, and that she hoped the skiing was divine, and she might make time to see Isabel after she returned, if she were not too busy . . . Well, anyway. Whisky, that was the first thing. Something to warm her blood and chase away the numbness that still clung to her skin.

In short, she resolved to pass a pleasant evening if it killed her; and she did, although she was conscious that it took determination to read, and bathe, and even to lift her glass.

After her bath she came downstairs in her robe, damp-haired and light-headed, and set the table for her dinner. There was a portion of stew left – she realised now she had not had lunch – and she followed it with two enormous slices of the sultana cake, the remainder of the bottle of wine, and a boiling cup of sweetened tea with another slug of whisky. At the end of the meal she felt more solid, and after another hour of reading *A Duchess in Distress*, stretched out on the sofa, she was a little consoled; if she failed entirely as a literary novelist, at least she might earn a living churning out the terrible yellow-backs that Edwin was so unaccountably fond of. But what nonsense! Tomorrow she would make a breakthrough – tomorrow, or the day after. It was only a question of time. One way or another . . .

The church clock chimed ten. She let the book fall to the floor, not bothering to keep her place. She was tired, and shivery, and a good night's sleep would do her good. But for some reason she did not feel inclined to mount the stairs, settle down in that clean, comfortable bed, and shut her eyes. In daylight she had pushed the thought of last night's rat-noises to the back of her mind; but now she knew she could not lie in the dark, wondering if the scratching might begin again. She shuddered, and a raw frisson ran down her spine. How her head hurt! She could not stay on the sofa. She already had a crick in her neck, and the fire she had painstakingly built in the hearth was dying, only half consumed. Damn it, she was not a child, pleading with Nanny not to go to bed without a nightlight. She refused to let an infestation of rodents keep her from sleep. She got up; and then, with a defiant tilt of her chin, she strode into the kitchen, filled a glass with whisky and gulped at it. She could not quite manage to finish it – she put it down, still a quarter full – but already she was giddy, and her eyes were heavy. She lit a candle and carried it unsteadily up to the bedroom; and then, by the light of the wavering golden flame, she fell asleep.

She did not know what time it was when she awoke. It was dark; the candle had burnt out; she could not have moved or spoken, so strong was the panic that had taken hold of her. She lay frozen, her muscles thrumming. Was it scratching that had awoken her, or some other noise, or none? Yes, there it was. A slow, mineral-clawed rasp, the hiss of scales across— No. No, nothing. Or was it? She could not hear past the roar in her ears, the grinding pulse of her own blood. The air around her was icy. Slowly she curled her fingers into her palms, and her skin crackled as though it were covered in frost. Above her, to one side, a greyish light outlined the edge of the curtains. She had forgotten to close them, and the moon threw a square of pewtery light on the floor, criss-crossed by the lattice of lead. There must have been clouds blowing across the sky, for the shadows grew dull and dissolved, and the room sank deeper into darkness.

Someone was watching her.

Not a rat. Something more, something malign and knowing – something that was human enough, at least, to wish her ill . . . It was impossible. She had seen in that moonlit glimpse that the room was empty. And yet she knew with every nerve that it was true. She was like a small animal, conscious of a predator: the instinct was so strong it overrode every rational thought. But, she thought helplessly, there was no one here, there was no one—

The moon came out again, swift as the kindling of a cold white flame outside the window. And there, looming against the net of diamond-shadow, was a shape – a dense, deformed hump of darkness, an indistinct, malign, *wrong* thing—

She would have cried out, if she could; but there was no one to call, no one who could help. Everyone she loved was far away. She shut her eyes, stupidly, as if she could render herself invisible; but not to see anything was worse. With a reckless effort she pulled herself up against the bars of the bedstead and turned to look at the window. If there was something outside . . .

Nothing. She saw only the church and the churchyard with its holly and beech trees, and the moon half smothered in cloud. And now – she blinked – the shadows that fell upon the floorboards made a perfect mathematical drawing, every dim rhombus complete and unblotted.

She shifted, staring, to make certain – heard a soft noise from beside her – felt the light touch of something by her leg – and with a convulsive scrabble found her hand closing on the matchbox. It must have fallen into the drawn-back sheets when she put the candlestick down – so the noise had only been a horrid, half-awake dream-version of the matches rattling as she turned over . . .

She gave a little gasping laugh. There was nothing to be

afraid of. Her limbs still tingled with the aftermath of fear; but gradually her heartbeat quietened, and her breathing steadied. A night terror, that was all. She had suffered badly from them when she was small. She had not had anything so vivid for years – but what did she expect, sleeping in a rat-infested house, next to a draughty window, after dosing herself with whisky? She exhaled, slowly. The warmth was spreading back into her hands and feet, and the air did not seem so perishingly glacial. She dragged the bedclothes into a more nestling shape, and shut her eyes.

But she could not clear her mind. To calm herself she deliberately summoned image after image: Isabel's face in an illustrated paper, the portico of the British Museum, the boats on the river at the foot of the hill . . . But try as she might, every one melted inexorably into Lye church under racing moonlit clouds. It was not, however, the view from her window. For some reason, in her mind's eye she was standing on Amies's grave, looking up; and, every time, that tableau brought with it a spasm of dread that jerked her back into wakefulness. She told herself that this, too, was the after-effect of too much alcohol. But it was a long time before a merciful veil fell over that lingering picture and allowed her to drift off.

It was late morning and the room was full of daylight when she awoke. She felt bruised all over, and exhausted; in her dreams she had been running, calling to Isabel, who would not or could not hear. She hauled herself out of bed, and the world tilted and spun. If she had not been so ferociously thirsty she would have lain down again and drawn the covers over her head. Her joints hurt, and the soles of her feet prickled as she walked over the cold floorboards and down the stairs.

She drank a large glass of water, which was so cold it eased the roughness in her throat; then she made a pot of tea, and with dogged persistence and liberal use of newspaper managed to relight the fire in the hearth. She had no appetite, but at last the room grew warm around her, and the strong tea cleared her head. There was an envelope on the doormat, and she hauled herself from her nest on the sofa to pick it up. She had assumed it was for Edwin, but as she turned it over she saw her own name, in Edwin's handwriting. She opened it, and rolled her eyes: it was a Christmas card, or a parody of one, an obscene pen-and-ink sketch with a frame of holly and ivy. *My dear Ash, hope you are getting on splendidly! The publishers are most eager to read it. Keep your lovely nose to the grindstone. E. x*

She stared down at it. She wanted to cast it into the fire and go back to bed. If only she could sink into oblivion, and forget about the book entirely . . . Instead, with a groan, she put the smutty little card on the mantelpiece, and went upstairs to wash, dress and get to work.

She could not concentrate. The pages in front of her were as dull and uninspired as they had been the last time she read them; and every few minutes she found that she had raised her head to stare at the sleet sliding down the window panes. In her sleep-deprived state, her vision played tricks; when her eyes were drawn, as they always were, past the melting flecks of ice to focus on the church beyond, she had the impression that she had missed something, some movement or change in the fabric of the building . . . But nothing had changed at all; even the sleet went on and on, as though it would fall for ever. Several times she got up to pace, slapping her hands together to warm them, jumping from foot to foot to increase the flow of blood to her brain, even breaking into hectoring speech as though she might break the impasse by giving herself orders. Lunchtime came and went, but she was not hungry.

She wrote ten different opening lines, all of them laboured and embarrassing. She drew a diagram of the plot. She drew a family tree of the characters, shut her eyes and drew lines at random between the names. When that did not produce any new ideas, she tried to draw Isabel's face from memory; tried to remember the first lines of *Paradise Lost*; tried to calculate how she might live, if she were to give back the advance from the publishers and retire into obscurity. A weight grew in her breast. The leaden afternoon darkened, and the room grew colder and colder. Once she thought she heard the harsh slow crawl of claws over the roof, but when she jerked upright, her heart pounding, it transformed into the creak of branches in the wind and the rattle of sleet on the tiles.

At last, through a fog of hopelessness, she heard the church clock strike six. Dinner. That was what she needed; yes, dinner, in the company of strangers, in a warm, well-lit, bustling little room, where there would be cheerful voices and festoons of tinsel and greenery. She did not want to talk, merely to be in the presence of ordinary, jolly people with uncomplicated lives and loves. She imagined Edwin raising an eyebrow – 'Ducky, what a terrible snob you are!' – but he would be wrong, it was not snobbery but envy, a deep, childish desire to be merry and thoughtless and good-hearted. She ran down the stairs, plucked the key from the dining table and strode out into the square. She had flung on her overcoat in such haste that it was flapping open, and she stopped under a streetlamp to button it and light a cigarette.

There was a light in the church, gleaming through the stained-glass windows in a blur of jewel-colours. It wavered as someone crossed in front of it. Then the organ rumbled the beginning of 'I Saw Three Ships', paused, repeated a phrase, and stumbled on, the unseen player so disarmingly inexpert that she felt her eyes prickle. As a child she had loved Christmas: the carols and bells, the blown-glass-and-candlelight blaze of the decorated tree, the hopeful hoarding of gifts until the moment on the day itself when she would pass them over, her heart thudding. She still remembered walking to church – she must have been seven or eight – holding her mother's hand, and Isabel turning to smile as they went through the lych-gate. She had not imagined, then, that when she grew up she would not be welcome in the congregation. If only she were still as innocent – if only she could look up at those glowing windows and feel the old trust, the old happiness and belief that she was loved!

If only, if only. Oh, it was absurd – surely she was coming down with something – to be so affected by nostalgia and loneliness. But still, if only . . . What would she not give, to know she was not alone? *Ask and it shall be given unto you.* She tried to swallow the pain in her throat. Once, in a dark, golden Venetian church, Isabel had scribbled a prayer request, looked up, shrugged and said, 'Honestly, Ash, darling, I need all the help I can get – if my dress isn't ready by next week . . .' Superstition, she had thought then, and laughed indulgently. But now – if *only* . . .

She looked upwards. The sleet blew stinging into her face and she shut her eyes, but she kept her face tilted towards the church, and the heavens above it. 'Help me,' she said. 'Please. Help me—'

But some other impulse cut her off, mid-plea. What was she doing? She opened her eyes hurriedly and looked around. The square was empty. No one had seen her. No one had heard her. She drew her coat more tightly round her shoulders and spun away, puffing on her cigarette.

She hurried along the edge of the churchyard and down West Street, giving a wide berth to a house with an improbably leaning chimney as though it might crash down onto the cobbles. Sleet drove down her collar and through her hair. As she came to the corner the wind died. Another phrase of music rang out, but now it was discordant, charmless. She slowed to a halt; and then, in spite of herself, she turned to look back the way she had come. There was the corner of the road, where she had been standing a moment ago; there was the church, its windows dim, the roof gleaming wet, under the louring heavens . . .

Only she saw now, with a jolt, that it was not the heavens to which her prayer had been directed. When she clenched her eyes shut against the sleet, she had not realised that her face was tilted towards the stumpy pinnacle at the south-west corner; so that anyone walking by might have thought she addressed the gargoyle that crouched on top of it. Not that anyone *had* been walking by. She glanced round, trying to master the sudden irrational discomfort that had taken hold of her, as though she had betrayed herself to a mocking gaze – no, worse, as though she had taken a wrong turning and did not know yet where it would lead. She had already satisfied herself that no one had seen or heard her; so why was she gripped by this creeping – but it was not horror, that was too strong a word, no, this unease . . .? She jumped as her cigarette burnt her knuckles and flung it aside with an oath. For a moment she thought someone behind her chuckled, but the windows of the eighteenth-century house were blind and shuttered, and the street was empty. What difference did it make, where she had directed that grotesque plea?

None, she thought. For God's sake, none. And with a furious shrug she set off again, hissing through her teeth as the sleet ran down her cheeks in freezing tears.

The Mermaid was full, and noisy, brimming with cheer like a tankard of mulled ale. Although the barman looked her up and down, taking in her short hair and mannish clothes, he did not refuse to serve her; and when she had eaten her fill of jugged hare and apple pudding she sat in front of the vast inglenook fireplace, lulled by the hum of voices and warmed by the fire, until her eyes were heavy and her limbs felt like softening wax. It was a shock to force herself out again into the cold. The sleet had stopped, but the clouds had not cleared; she had overheard someone say that there would be snow before morning.

Although it was late, she took the long way back, down the hill and up again via Watchbell Street; she told herself that she wanted to clear her head. All too soon she came to the corner of Church Square, where the north wind caught her off guard and made her gasp and huddle into her coat. She put her head down and strode towards the door of the little house, fumbling for her key.

Something moved in the corner of her eye. She turned and stared, blood pounding in her temples, her stomach tight. It was the same scuttling swoop of dark-in-the-dark that she had seen from her window, the night she had arrived – but now she could see it was not the tree swaying in the wind but a skitter of blackness along the graveyard wall, a feral, almost-human movement that made her catch her breath. The air that she drew in was tainted by a whiff of rot that was both earth and corpse, stone and putrid meat. She clenched her jaw, trying to make out what the thing was. An animal. Too large for a rat, too humpbacked for a cat. She could not think of any species it might be; certainly not anything native to Sussex. Something venomous, something vile . . .

She was afraid. The cold moisture that made her shirt cling to her had not soaked through her coat but sprang from her skin. There was a shudder beginning at the base of her spine; any moment it would rip through her, uncontrollable. It took all her strength to put one foot in front of the other. Only a few yards before she could open the door, and slam it behind her . . . In spite of herself she looked again to the side, not wanting to pass too close to the— the *thing* – and saw that it was not there. Her heart jumped into her mouth, choking her. Where had it gone? Had she imagined—?

But the fear did not recede. It had slipped out of sight, that was all; every instinct told her it was still close, and watching. She had to concentrate to fit the key into the lock of the little low door, and for a queasy second she could not get it to turn. Then, at last, she collapsed across the threshold. The room was dark, full of dense black shapes that crouched and loomed. She groped for the table where she had left the lamp, felt it under her fingers, grabbed, and heard the glass chimney smash. There was a gurgle and a sharp smell of oil. She swore. Her pulse was thundering in her ears.

Something moved through the doorway. Through her roaring blood she heard the door creak as it swung gently on its hinges – felt a sudden drop in temperature – caught her breath—

Only the wind. Only—

But she could not hold her nerve. She blundered forward, knocking against the edge of the table, and flung herself towards the stairs. Behind her the door crashed shut, making the stairs quake as she dragged herself upwards. She did not dare to pause, or to listen; if something was pursuing her, she would rather be blind and deaf than risk hearing it – *that*—

She wrenched the bedroom door open, staggered inside, and slammed it shut. She leant her back against the old wood, bracing with all her might. Stars whirled and burst in the corners of her vision. A minute passed, and then another. In the faint light from the window she could distinguish the burnt-out candle beside the bed. She sprang towards it, and with shaking hands she struck a match, jabbing and prodding until a tremulous flame took root in the stub of wax. Then, in the guttering light, she knelt down and drew her suitcase out from underneath the bed. She had not unpacked entirely; it was only a question of gathering her pyjamas and dirty underwear and closing the lid. She could stay at the Mermaid tonight, and go home to London tomorrow.

When she stood up, her head spun. She picked up her suitcase and swayed; she had to rest her hand against the wall to steady herself. Her skin felt flayed and tender. But she could not pause to coddle herself; she must get out, get away ...

She drew a breath and stepped out on to the landing. Christ, it was cold. Was there a window open somewhere? The study door was ajar; she could feel a wave of icy air emanating from the gap.

Her typewriter. Her novel.

She drew a juddering breath, torn between pride and cowardice – for she knew it was nothing but cowardice, this fierce animal instinct that told her to flee, now, *now* . . . But she could not, would not, leave her novel behind. She flung open the study door.

On the desk, where there should have been nothing but a pale pile of paper, was a sickening, gleeful clot of darkness, the size of a human infant. It was bloated, appallingly misshaped, like a thing long dead or unborn; it had teeth, and festering eyes, and in its taloned hand it held a stone pen, eroded by centuries of wind and rain.

It was the gargoyle. It could not be, but it was. It was hunched over her manuscript; and with a sound like acid eating through rock, its pen moved, scribbling and scribbling.

She was woken by the peal of bells. She opened her eyes to the clear depthless light of a snowfall reflecting on the sloping ceiling, and gradually it came to her where she was, and that it must be Christmas Day. She remembered a long night of pain and diabolical dreams, interspersed with freezing, swirling periods of daylight: no doubt she had been feverish for a long time. But now her head, although light, no longer ached; and her hands, when she lifted them from the patchwork quilt, were steady. Whatever illness had thrown her into that state of febrile terror, it had passed.

She got to her feet and shuffled carefully to the door. Then, wrapped in her robe, shivering, she ventured out on to the landing. The window in the study was open, and the bells were so loud the sound made her teeth vibrate. She padded to the desk to draw the casement shut, and as she fastened the latch her eyes fell on her manuscript. A drift of sparkling snow lay on the top page, whiter than the paper, as white as the world outside; but it was not that which had attracted her attention.

She brushed it aside. Underneath, the page was full of writing: writing which was not hers.

She did not consciously read what was written there. It leapt into her mind, as if unmediated by her eyes and brain. It was a new plot for her novel, set out in a scheme of chapters and scenes, with here and there a phrase of description so vivid it made her blink.

She drew out the chair and sat down. For a long time she did nothing but sit, staring unseeing at the snow-covered church.

It was a good plot; a perfect plot. The novel that she could write . . .! Why had she not considered before that she might kill off her heroine? That she might turn her pathetic portrait of Isabel into a cruel, blistering satire, culminating in violence? It would shock the world and make her name – trump *Felicity* ten times over – and the critics would applaud her daring, her wit, her clear-sightedness. Edwin would blench, at first, but his disapproval would soften when it dawned upon him that he had another triumph on his books; and as for Isabel, who might recognise herself, well, it was no more than fair, after the torments of the last years.

And perhaps, she thought, that writing was her own, after all. It was cramped, odd-looking, with a touch of the gravestone about it – but still, it might be hers, scrawled in a fever-dream so deep she did not remember it. She could not let superstition get in the way of artistic ambition; she had every right to seize ideas, no matter where they came from.

Her gaze lingered on the turret opposite, where the gargoyle crouched, its pen poised, its face comic and harmless under a soft cap of snow. There was nothing to be afraid of there; nor below, where Amies's grave lay under that kind white quilt – where surely, in the spring, new grass would cover the bare earth.

The congregation began to emerge into the churchyard, their faces bright against their dark coats and hats, the children's voices shrill and sweet. She sat unmoving, the first sentence of her new draft beginning to take shape, and the bells rang and rang until the air trembled.

THE MASTER OF THE HOUSE

Stuart Turton

I

If you have found this letter, then I should tell you that I never meant the boy harm, and, thus, could not have predicted what was to come.

My dear wife Lucy died after twelve years of marriage, leaving behind an eight-year-old son I had no patience to raise. We named him Thomas, for my father, but he was, in every other way, Lucy's child. I had gladly granted her dream of motherhood on the understanding that he would never become my burden.

In the seven months that followed her death, I made do as best I could, bringing in a governess to fill the emotional void in his life. They were close, after a fashion, though it was clear Thomas craved my attention above all else.

I could not give it to him. I ran a successful law practice in the City, which accounted for every spare second of my day and many more I could not find. We did, however, breakfast together each morning, and that's where the argument occurred.

He'd slept badly the night prior, complaining of a ragged voice curling out of the darkness. He'd cried out, waking the governess. She could not soothe him, and, breaking the habit of our household, she'd fetched me.

There was – I will say it here – a vein of malice in the governess. She was the new type, young and affectionate, and convinced that a child's well-being was best served by constant attention. Thomas was to be played with, and coddled, and told he was special. He was, in short, to have his father's presence whenever he desired his father's presence.

It was cold that night, full of winter. We had our hearths piled high, embers glinting among the coals as snow fell outside. Our Christmas decorations were strung about the place, and we had a large tree that had already started to drop its needles.

Thomas's room was along the corridor and I made my way there in my nightgown and cap, yawning and slow, my anger building with every step, for nobody likes to be forced out of their bed.

The governess obviously knew she'd done wrong for she slunk ahead wordlessly, hugging the shadows.

Upon seeing me Thomas leapt out of bed and stood up straight, a shameful glance drawing my attention to the wet patch upon his nightgown.

I shook him by the shoulders. 'What's all this nonsense?' I demanded angrily. 'To have me out of my bed when I have important work to do tomorrow. And to shame yourself by wetting the bed, no less.'

I turned my fury on the governess.

'He shall sleep in his soiled sheets tonight, with every candle snuffed. I'll not hear a word from either of you. Tomorrow, at breakfast, we shall see what you've learned.'

And upon such solid foundations of fatherhood I returned to my bed.

2

Thomas was already at his breakfast when I arrived in the dining room, a solitary electric light lurid on the ceiling.

Besides his plate were his tin trains, which accompanied him everywhere. He had a fascination with all things mechanical, especially steam engines. He'd once expressed an interest in becoming a train driver, or an engineer, but I'd reproached him for these meagre dreams.

I took my seat on the opposite side of the table as usual. Underneath my calm exterior, I was ashamed of how I'd treated him last night. I had inherited my father's temper, and my mother's loathing of it.

I would have apologised immediately, except it's impossible to raise a child on the back foot. All I could do was try to find virtue in the mistake and make up for it quietly at a later date.

I waited for him to greet me, as was proper, but he continued to roll his sausages around with his fork, ignoring my presence.

'Thomas,' I barked, causing him to jump. It was then I realised he'd been daydreaming – another vexing habit of his.

'Morning, Father,' he said sullenly.

I shook my head, annoyed to find this fresh day already souring beneath me.

In an attempt to redress my mood, I stared at the window beyond him. Snow had been falling for the better part of the week, churned into black slush by the hansom cabs and omnibuses that had become such a feature of the city.

Soot wriggled out of a thousand chimneys, while traders hung plucked geese from their stalls. Christmas trees were held fast by their ropes, as if awaiting ransom, while chestnuts blackened in braziers and a few exotic oranges shivered in their nets.

Many in my profession thought living near a market to be uncouth, preferring the generic sophistication of Kensington and Mayfair, but I found it invigorating. A man needs fear to get ahead in this world. He must understand the gravity of poverty, which is always trying to pull him down.

My own father taught me that. He never taught me anything else, so must have reckoned this one lesson sufficient.

I never knew what he did, except to say it was never enough. My enduring memory is of grey whiskers and watering eyes, of breath thick with alcohol. Whatever he earned, he drank away, distilling rum into bitterness until, finally, he was killed by a cutpurse for five shillings and the boots on his feet.

I tell you this not for sympathy, but only to make you understand why I considered myself a good father in comparison. Thomas may have struggled for my affection, but he would have an education, a fine position in my company, and a fortune to inherit. He was to be given the world, and the resources to make of it what he wished. What more could be asked of me?

Such were my thoughts as I unfolded my newspaper at the table that morning and waited for the cook to bring me breakfast. A salted egg, as ever, on toast.

'Last night you wept and wailed fearing demons,' I said. 'And yet, this morning, here you sit unharmed. What say you to these facts?'

'He says he'll take me from you on Christmas Eve,' replied Thomas, his voice so low I didn't initially catch it.

'You're mumbling,' I replied, lowering my paper to gaze across the table at his face. It was stricken, yet strangely defiant. He was a pale boy, with his mother's freckles and brown, oval eyes. He would be handsome one day. For whatever that was worth.

'The Master of the House says he'll take me from you in two weeks,' replied Thomas, glaring. 'At midnight on Christmas Eve.'

Was it the nature of the proclamation that deceived me? For it was delivered with hate, rather than fear. The boy was challenging me.

I raised my paper again, putting him behind the Sudan War and the grain tax. I did not understand this game, and would not tolerate it.

'I plan to let the governess go,' I said. 'She has put ideas in your head. She has made you fanciful and impertinent, and I will not have it.'

He mewled, like an animal caught in a trap.

'Please, Father, no!'

'I will hear no more on it,' I snapped, refusing to meet his eyes. It brought me no joy to cause him pain, but he had to understand that lies would buy nothing from me.

He didn't speak for a few seconds, leaving us to the crackle of the fire and the buzzing of the electric bulb.

His voice – when it came – was small, and stinging.

'I hate you.'

'That is the natural state of all fathers and sons,' I replied coldly, from behind my newspaper. 'You'll grow used to it in time.'

3

Dismissing the governess was a mistake. That much became apparent immediately. I had taken her influence for malign, and judged her harshly for giving the boy too much sway, but without her presence Thomas became wild.

We kept a wooden Advent calendar, with carved nativity scenes counting down the days until Christmas. Every morning I opened a fresh panel to find the picture burnt, or defaced in some dreadful way.

Thomas denied any involvement, angrily blaming the Master of the House for the desecration.

After a week of lies I hired a governess who had a reputation for hammering wayward boys straight. The esteemed

Mrs Hunch lasted until the morning of Christmas Eve, clutching her Bible as she fled down the steps into the first blush of wintry daylight.

I'd tried to coax her back inside, to air her grievances in the parlour, as was proper, but she railed against such a course, refusing to set a solitary foot in my house.

Standing on the street – in sight of God and all our neighbours – she proclaimed that Beelzebub himself stalked our corridors. She told me she'd heard Thomas talking to somebody in the dead of night, and had left her bed to investigate, only to find his door fastened shut.

'Impossible,' I'd argued, trying to claw back a little of the dignity I'd already lost. 'There is no lock on his bedroom. A young boy has no need of privacy, nor right to it.'

'It was held fast!' she repeated hysterically.

Calling out to Thomas, she'd been roughly told to leave the house by a voice that sounded like the breeze through a tattered banner.

'It was the voice of the Devil,' she'd wailed, pressing her Bible to her breast. 'I felt his malignancy in my heart.'

Heavy steps had chased her into her bedroom, where she'd locked herself in and prayed until morning.

Unfortunately, her invocations hadn't stopped a dreadful face from trying to force its way through her mirror; they hadn't silenced the pounding on the door, or the rattling of the handle.

She'd found the courage to demand an explanation for what was happening, only for Thomas to reply from the corridor.

'Thomas?' I repeated, surprised.

'He told me that he was being protected by the Master of the House,' she said, pale as the snow gathering on her shoulders. 'And that any sin I visited upon him would be returned a thousandfold.'

'A fancy!' I'd protested. 'Thomas brought me the same story. It's a young boy's imagination. A trifle.'

'The Devil himself has laid claim to your son,' she said, shivering. 'You need a priest not a governess.'

I would have argued further, but she swept off into the swirling snow, leaving me alone on my doorstep, among the whispers of market traders and passers-by.

I confronted Thomas immediately, taking him roughly by the arm and accusing him outright of tricking Mrs Hunch. He tried to wriggle away and, in my anger, I acted as a father ought not, striking him across the cheek with the back of my hand, bloodying his lip.

Immediately I felt my father's hand across my own face.

I had never hit Thomas before, and believed myself above such acts. My shame only made me angrier, for none of this was my fault.

'The Master of the House will take me away tonight,' said Thomas, trembling slightly, his arms held stiff at his sides. 'If you wish to keep me—'

'Stop this,' I cried, shaking him by the elbow.

'If you wish to keep me,' he continued, ignoring my entreaties, 'you need to be in my bedroom at midnight to confront him.'

I pushed him roughly backwards, unnerved by the flatness of his manner. He had driven a Christian governess out of our house, blotted our family name, lied to his father, and now he pressed forward with this ridiculous tale.

'The Master of the House said I'll have to stay here if you come for me,' he said defiantly. 'But I hope you don't. I hope I never see you again.'

Shaking with rage, he fled into the depths of the house.

4

It was nearing midnight on Christmas Eve, a time of families and festivity, laughter and excess.

I had sent the servants home and was drinking brandy in the sitting room alone. I was in my favourite chair by a guttering hearth, staring at our Christmas tree. In years gone by, my wife had spent many happy hours decorating our trees with candles and baubles, gingerbread men and paper chains. I played the piano and served mulled wine, while Thomas handed her decorations and became tangled in the tinsel, much to her delight.

Since her death, I had not the heart for any of it.

This year I'd left the tree for the servants, who'd decorated it haphazardly and in evident haste; a few bows scattered among its needles, the star listing drunkenly at its summit. There weren't even presents for Thomas, as I'd quite forgotten to buy any.

The grandfather clock chimed midnight, each dong rocking the house like a blow from an outraged god.

Stumbling backwards, I watched in horror as the windows shook and the coving fell from the ceiling. The chandelier swayed dangerously overhead as ornaments shattered and paintings abandoned their grip on the walls.

A voice crept out of the darkness.

'The boy has accepted my offer.'

I spun around, searching for its source, but it was everywhere, thick and thin, sharp and flat. The shadows had simply opened their mouth.

'Who goes there?' I demanded.

'The Master of the House.' The voice scuttled across my skin, bringing goosebumps after it.

'I'll not fall for these parlour tricks.' My voice trembled, unable to believe that Thomas had been telling the truth.

'Then we shall both enjoy this Christmas, for I have my gift and you have yours. Thomas will burden you no longer.'

'No!' I was surprised at my own vehemence, for I did consider the boy a burden. But he was *my* burden. That was the fact of it. Whether I enjoyed it or not, my duty was clear.

'I wish to keep him,' I stammered.

'You had only to be in his room at midnight to prevent me from claiming him, yet you could not rouse yourself to such a simple effort.'

'He's my son,' I protested.

The house quivered, the chandelier shaking.

'He'll be waiting for you in my garden,' replied the voice, coiling around me. 'Hold out your hand.'

'Why?'

'Every house requires a key.'

Something terribly cold brushed past me in the darkness, turning my stomach. A flower landed heavily in my palm. It had eight purple petals and a blood red stigma. Thorns rose along its black stem, each one hooked and sharp. To my disgust, it was wiggling like a millipede.

'Clutch it,' demanded the Master of the House.

I did as I was asked, the thorns burrowing into my skin, warm blood dripping between my fingers. In a matter of seconds, it had attached itself quite firmly to my palm.

'You have until the last petal falls to turn back,' warned the voice. 'Once the flower is bare, you and your son belong to me.'

As quickly as the assault began, it ended. The voice evaporated, leaving the sitting room still once again.

Sprinting into the entrance hall, I took the stairs two at a time. An impossibly bright light spilled from Thomas's bedroom.

Skidding inside I found a door open where no door had previously been, a brilliant white glare pouring through. Thomas was being led inside by a long-fingered hand that shone like starlight. This was all I could see of his abductor.

'Thomas!' I cried desperately.

My son glanced over his shoulder at me, his face afraid but his eyes defiant. My presence did not arrest him. If anything, it set him more firmly on his path.

Staring straight ahead, he walked through the door.

I'll confess I did not immediately follow him, for I was too stunned by what I was seeing. I was a man of rational mind, who adhered steadfastly to a series of iron principles. I worked hard, was reliable and sober, and accepted with good grace that the rest of the world would likely not follow my fine example.

I saw no sense in the occult, or superstition. I did not believe that spirits rattled tables, or fairies played at the bottom of gardens. I feared God, but I did not trust Him with my best interests.

But tonight, all of my beliefs were for naught. Something evil had invaded my home.

It was only as the door started to swing closed that I was finally roused to my plight.

Squaring my shoulders, I dashed into the light, following the son who'd chosen to flee with the Devil.

5

I was in a grand entrance hall of the sort commonly found in those huge, draughty country piles favoured by the aristocracy.

Dust lay thick on busts of Roman emperors, while damp consumed oil paintings of sun-dappled olive groves and ruined coliseums. Above me hung a ragged chandelier, half shrouded by a moth-eaten white cloth.

A great marble staircase climbed wearily towards the first floor, and a huge pair of studded doors led outside. Windows revealed snowy grounds and a forest beyond, made silver by moonlight.

I turned on the spot, astonished.

By any logical assessment, a door in a wall should lead to whatever was on the other side of that wall, but this was clearly not my neighbour's home.

'Thomas!' I called out, seeing no sign of my son.

My voice ran around the hall and up and down the stairs, but returned to me with empty hands.

It occurred to me that I might follow his footsteps in the dust, but there were none to be found. It made no sense. Thomas could not have passed through this hall without leaving some mark, yet that seemed to be the truth of it.

I stared at the odious flower dug into my palm, discovering it had already lost a petal.

The Master of the House had instructed me to deliver it to the garden, which, at least, suggested a direction to follow.

I rattled the handles of the front doors, hoping to get outside, but they were locked tight.

There were four other doors in the hall, presumably leading deeper into the house. I had clients who owned homes like this, and I had a passing understanding of their layout. The garden would be out through the kitchen.

I chose the door I thought most likely to take me there, finding a message hastily carved into the wood.

The Master of the House is always behind you. Do not tarry. He hungers.

My heart racing, I took hold of the doorknob and was thrown into immediate darkness. Squinting, I could just make out flickering stars above and below.

No, not stars.

Stars didn't notice you. Their light didn't turn towards you, scratching your skin. Stars didn't drag themselves closer.

The world snapped back.

I was standing in a modest living room, a roaring fire in the grate and a stubby Christmas tree beside it. There were presents underneath, wrapped in brown paper and red bows.

Shallow, desperate breaths escaped me as I tried to make sense of what had happened.

What on earth had I just seen? And where had I been delivered, for this was not the stately home I'd left. The ceilings were lower, the brickwork modern. It smelt of roasting potatoes, rather than ancient decay. An oil lamp burned on hand-me-down furniture, next to a steaming cup of tea.

Through the leaded windows I saw a busy street, somewhere in the north of England, judging by the factory smokestacks rising above the terraced houses opposite.

'How did I . . .'

I did not finish my sentence. I was afraid of my own voice. It was the instrument of my profession, placing forth facts and battling across courtrooms. It was never cowed, and it never wavered, but, in that moment, it was riddled with uncertainty. It was the crack before a child fell through the ice.

I went to the window, outside which two young boys were chasing a hoop with a stick through the swirling snow. I wanted to open it up and ask them where I was, and what day it was, and whether they were part of what was happening to me, but the latch wouldn't budge.

A gentleman with a cane and a bowler hat strode purposefully by. I banged on the glass with my fists hoping to gain his attention, but he simply adjusted his cuffs and moved along.

A young woman and her friend came past with a perambulator. They were chatting and laughing, bundled up in their coats.

Picking up a paperweight from the sideboard, I struck the glass with every ounce of my strength. It didn't even leave a mark.

The young women passed by the window without a single glance in my direction. This was beyond ignorance. They could not see me, or hear me. I was certain of it.

Defeated, I collapsed onto a green sofa.

I squeezed my eyes shut and took a deep breath, trying to right myself. Desperation was quicksand. If you gave yourself to it, it would swallow you completely.

Another breath. Then one more.

I opened my eyes and held up my hand, gratified to find it steady, and dismayed to discover the flower had lost another petal. I had lost one in each room, leaving me with six.

I cast my gaze around, trying to make sense of this puzzle.

I could still see the stately home through the door I'd just walked through, its dimensions unsettling to say the least.

What was the purpose of all this? Why would the Master of the House bring Thomas here?

On the cushion beside me, I spied legal documents bound in expensive twine. Untying the knot revealed them to be adoption papers.

In practised motions, my fingers traced the lines of prevarication and obfuscation, until I found the name of the child being adopted.

Thomas Carrow

That was my son's name. He was to be adopted by Jonathan and Henrietta Digby. I searched for the reason.

'Parents . . . deceased,' I read in disgust.

These Digbys had my child, but where did the Master of the House fit into this? Was Jonathan Digby the true name of the Master of the House? I gazed at the secondhand furnishings, knowing that I'd missed my mark. Devils had no need of thrift.

Shaking my head, I finished reading the papers. The only other useful fragment of information was the date: 24th December 1907.

It was a strange error to find on a legal document, for while the day was correct it was actually 1901.

I might have left it at that, except a feeling of unease

persisted. Behind the last two doors I'd found rooms with seemingly no relation to each other. Was it possible for time to be equally unmoored?

Reaching for a scrunched-up newspaper on a nearby armchair, I confirmed the date as being the 24th December 1907.

A great nausea overcame me. How long had I spent among those stars? I had a busy practice. Impatient clients. Did they think I'd absconded? Were the police looking for me? Either way, my reputation would be in ruins.

Something tickled my forearm.

Glancing down, I saw a spider scurrying towards my elbow. I brushed it away, then noticed another on my trouser leg. I squashed it, but two more took its place.

Ten more.

A dozen.

I leapt up from the sofa, swiping them off my body. Spiders were spilling out from between every cushion in their hundreds. They piled across one another in a great seething mass, submerging the couch and spreading across the carpet.

Shivering in revulsion I leapt for the nearest door.

6

Upon touching the handle, I was once more cast into darkness and surrounded by those hungry stars. They were closer now, like rats crowding a corpse.

Blood was thudding in my ears, each beat driving a spike

through my chest. Buckling in pain, I looked down to find my heart writhing furiously in a nest of gore and broken bones, pumping black blood through veins which I suddenly wore on the outside of my body, such that they tangled and trapped me.

I screamed, and was still screaming when a new room appeared around me.

7

Staggering across uneven floorboards, I frantically examined my body, finding everything, mercifully, back where it ought to be.

I let out a breath of relief but couldn't shake the sense that something was missing. There was an emptiness inside, a sense of having left part of myself in that darkness to be gnawed upon.

Shivering in my thin shirt, I examined my new surroundings.

I was in a bedroom, simply furnished with a neatly made single bed, and a wardrobe propped up on one side with a block of wood. There was a crucifix on the wall, and a picture of George, Prince of Wales in the King's regalia, with a plaque informing me he'd taken the throne in May 1910.

1910!

I'd lost nearly a decade in three doors.

I buried my head in my hands. Kings were dying. Empires

shifting. Somehow, the world was turning, and history proceeding. Had I no bearing on any of it?

I was a successful man, influential in all the ways society allowed me to be. Could I be so easily plucked from the world? Had I no destiny to interrupt?

And then the darker thoughts. Ten years gone by: had anybody missed me?

I had no parents alive. No wife. No aunts and uncles. Ours was a family tree stripped of every branch. My clients would have found new representation. The servants new employers. My home a new owner, my fortune gone to my next of kin, wherever they may have been. Everything had been for Thomas, and Thomas had fled.

Anger surged through me. My son had led me into this torment. Why had I followed him, when he'd gone so willingly? Did he even deserve all I'd done for him?

Fresh air was what I needed, but the window was closed fast.

It was a prettier view than it had been in the last place. There was a mill on the other side of a cobbled street, a huge waterwheel being turned by a fast-flowing river. Beyond that were rooftops, and mountains in the distance.

Snow was falling, suggesting it was winter. Some half-wrapped socks had been thrown on the nightstand, alongside a bottle of cheap perfume. Was this another Christmas Eve?

I stared back at the door I'd come through, at the sitting room on the other side. The spiders were gone, the hearth still burning cheerily. I could go back, I realised! Back to my

Christmas Eve, and the life I'd painstakingly built. I could retrace my steps, unwind the years. Nothing was lost, except the son who'd brought this upon himself.

I made for the door, only to be arrested by a shelf filled with a boy's imagination; books by Rudyard Kipling and Jules Verne; a tin model of a green automobile. I'd seen such things at shows, and even taken a ride in a client's Ford once. I'd been shaken so hard my kidneys had knocked together.

I picked the model car up and spun the wheels, reminded of Thomas's toy trains. He counted Isambard Kingdom Brunel among his heroes, and we'd spent entire weekends travelling across the country on the GWR, wandering Brunel's canals and peering up at the viaducts, astounded by the great man's ingenuity.

I put the car down, surprised by my own fondness for these memories.

My son was a curious fellow, concerned with matters of engineering and architecture. To my shame, I'd been short with his questions and visibly annoyed at his slow-footed wonder and boyish silliness.

'Thomas!' yelled a woman from somewhere in the house.

'Yes, Mama?'

My heart froze. That was my son's voice on the other side of the door, though aged considerably. There was none of the child's reediness. The voice had bulked out, stretched to fit his throat. The coronation picture suggested it was 1910 at least, making him seventeen. A young man.

I reached out towards the door instinctively, only to

stop at the last moment. To touch that knob was to be transported.

'Thomas!' I cried, pounding on the wood in frustration. 'Please. I'm here.'

'Yes, Mama!' he yelled down the stairs.

'I've ironed your dad's suit for you to wear,' came the reply.

'I don't need dad's suit.'

'Eliza will like to see you in a suit.'

'We're only going to the pictures.'

'You'll not take a nice girl like that out wearing those oil-soaked rags. Come and put it on, or I'll be after you with my spoon.'

'That suit isn't very much better than rags,' he grumbled, going downstairs.

'Thomas,' I howled again, knowing it was futile. Nobody I'd come across so far had been able to see or hear me. Why would he?

I banged the door once more in frustration.

He should have been studying to go up to Oxford at this age, not frittering his time away with some girl.

I laid my cheek to the wood, burning with curiosity. I wished to see his face; to know whether he'd grown tall like me. Did he still have his mother's freckles?

Would I even recognise him?

A thud drew my attention towards the window. Then another, and another. Snowflakes were hitting the glass with the force of thrown stones.

I went closer, my nose almost touching the cold pane.

Each flake had four scrambling legs, and a mosquito's proboscis. They were scratching at the window, trying to get in.

The thuds were coming more and more rapidly, the glass shaking under the assault. The snow wasn't falling any more; it was flocking. A great swarm had gathered in the air and was driving straight towards the fragile glass.

Evidently the Master of the House didn't want me lingering here.

The bedroom had two doors to flee through. One was closed, the other slightly open, leading back into the sitting room. I could return to safety, or continue this reckless chase.

I had five petals remaining on the flower.

I stared hard at the open door, willing myself to be rational. Thomas had sounded healthy and loved. Why would I pursue him, when it would only lead to further ruination? How would it benefit either of us?

And yet, hearing his voice had stirred something. It's true that I had no patience for the boy, but I'd harboured dreams for the man.

If the pattern held, behind that closed door I would find another chapter in his life. How could I resist the chance to see who he'd become? I had petals enough to risk one more room. I could always turn back after that.

Against all reason, I put my hand on the doorknob and felt the world fall away.

8

I did not my open my eyes this time. I had many faults, but an inability to learn was not one of them. I knew the stars were waiting, restless and malignant. They had their own games to play with me, but I would not indulge them.

Screams shattered my smugness.

Hundreds of them. Millions, perhaps. Cries of agony and suffering. Men and women pleading to be spared.

I pressed my hands to my ears, but they pierced my soul.

I was listening to the last seconds of a million lives, knowing they'd all died in this place. Amongst the laments one desperate voice rose louder than the others, querulous and afraid.

It was my own.

'No, no, please,' I was sobbing, like a child. 'Please, mercy.'

I prayed, then. Prayers I hadn't recited since my mother took me to church. The words were fumbled, clawed from memory. Splinters of a broken shield.

They wouldn't save me.

9

Wedding bells pealed, their jauntiness baffling.

I blinked my eyes open to discover I was in a church's vestry, a priest's robes laid out on a table, the flaking white walls adorned with a simple crucifix.

Heads in hats bobbed by a small Gothic window. Through it I could see a graveyard, and beyond that a newly married couple making their way through a crowd of people throwing rice.

Their backs were to me, but the husband wore a military uniform and walked with a limp, leaning heavily on a cane. The wife was a narrow thing wrapped in clouds.

The fashions had changed. The clothes more embroidered, looser and more colourful. To my eyes, they were mermaid scales, devoid of decorum. What was this world becoming?

'Announcing Thomas and Eliza Digby,' called out somebody in the crowd jubilantly.

He took their surname, I thought bitterly.

Given everything else, it felt ridiculous to care for a name. After all, my father never had. He'd soaked ours in alcohol and scandal. Growing up, I'd hoped to dry it out; to burnish it and pass it on. I'd hoped Thomas might one day carry it with pride. I never imagined he would drop it so easily, and his father with it.

'This is my doing,' I murmured.

I hadn't given him anything to love, or honour. I'd sought to provide for his future, caring nothing for his present.

A petal detached itself from the flower, floating gently to the ground. Only four remained, but I finally understood my purpose here.

My son was loved, yes. But to what end? A simple bedroom in a modest house. A second-hand suit to court in. A tiny church, and a humble wedding to a girl like every other.

There was no wealth here. No education. This was a life devoid of ambition, at the mercy of whatever the world did to him.

Could I change it?

The Master of the House had told me that Thomas would be waiting for me in the garden. If he was walking a room ahead of me, did that mean he'd seen this life as I had? Perhaps this was a warning to both of us.

Noticing movement from the corner of my eye, I turned to see a thick velvet curtain snaking towards me, its material become the pink flesh of a human tongue.

It coiled beneath the table, leaving thick mucus across the stone floor.

I backed away in horror, then darted around the reaching tip of the tongue and put my hand on the doorknob.

10

The stars were so close they blinded me, their light slicing my skin. They ripped open my thoughts and emptied out the contents of my black heart for inspection. Under their scrutiny I was dissected, every shame laid bare.

I saw Thomas at his mother's funeral, weeping and alone, desperate for comfort. I saw myself by his side, heartbroken and oblivious to his reaching hand.

I heard the sobs from his bedroom, and saw myself walk by without pause.

I saw myself upbraid the governess angrily because Thomas had come running through the house, laughing for the first time in months. His joy had felt like an insult to Lucy's memory. I had wanted him to be crushed under the same grief I was.

Furniture materialised, walls and a floor. I could not see any of it through the blur of my tears.

II

Falling to my knees, I vomited onto ancient floorboards.

I'd been ransacked.

There was no warmth in me, no happiness left. I'd been shown every crack in my character. The comforting lies I'd built around my weaknesses had been torn away, leaving only the raw nerves of my regrets.

Wiping the vomit from my mouth with a sleeve, I noticed my hand trembling uncontrollably. I wasn't sure how much more of this I could endure.

'Courage,' I said out loud, dredging up what little strength remained to me. 'Courage,' I repeated, more firmly. 'A few more rooms and I'll be with Thomas.'

I had entered a long medieval gallery, a gale blowing snow through an open window. I shivered, but it wasn't the wind that chilled me.

The gallery was narrow and endless, the floor, walls and even the ceiling covered in dried blood. It was lined on both sides with thousands of paintings, each one showing somebody screaming in terror in this very room.

Their clothes went back centuries, and their names, births and deaths were recorded beneath. Only one canvas was blank, but it had my name etched on a brass plaque.

Henry Carrow born February 4th, 1861. Deceased, January 24th, 1925.

I shook my head, backing away from this wretched proclamation as another petal deserted me. I had three left, but there were no doors to escape through.

Thudding footsteps sounded in the vestry, drawing close behind me. The world became thin, stars shining in everything. Here, at last, came the Master of the House.

I glanced at my portrait, seeing my face twisted by the terror I felt.

It was a trap, I realised. I'd been chased into this corner like a hunted fox. Any minute now, the Master of the House was going to add me to his collection.

I howled in frustration, sobs gathering in my throat. I understood now the mistakes I'd made with Thomas, but I'd never get the chance to apologise for them. I'd never be able to set them right, as a father should. I could not imagine a crueller fate.

The wind whipped through the window, sharp and cold. We were high up among mountain peaks, clouds below and swirling snow all around.

Squaring my shoulders, I clambered onto the casement as the gallery shook under his steps.

I could feel the Master of the House behind me. The air had become heavy, clutching, trying to drag me back to him.

'You'll not have me,' I declared.

Keeping my eyes forward, I extended a leg into nothingness.

12

I hit the stone floor as if I'd fallen out of a chair, letting out of an *oomph* of surprise, followed by a roar of triumph.

The ferocity of my relief surprised even myself, for it had been a long time since I'd met any incident in my life with such feeling.

Getting to my feet, I smoothed my shirt and trousers, recovering myself.

I was in a large country kitchen, the air humid and steamy, and filled with the heartening smell of roasting meat. Pans bubbled on stoves as liquid slopped over the sides to sizzle in the flame. Sturdy wooden counters were piled high with dishes for Christmas dinner. There were five baked turkeys and ten fat geese. Piles of stuffed hams, platters of oyster soup and trays of roasted potatoes, sprouts, cabbages, parsnips and carrots.

This was a place of abundance and opulence, but it made me uneasy. A kitchen such as this should have been a bustling place, boisterous with servants. This emptiness made it sinister.

I wondered if that was the result of the automata. White porcelain boxes abounded, humming and shivering, intent upon their unknown purpose. I did not know how far into the future I had come, but I had not anticipated how swiftly the world would change in my absence, or how easily it would abandon elegance for convenience. From fashion to technology, the advance of years struck me as entirely wretched.

Through the latticework of a high window, I saw snow-covered grounds and a solitary child throwing snowballs at the boughs of a tree.

My heart leapt. Could that be Thomas?

I pressed my face to the window, trying to see better. The child was bundled up and impossible to identify, but the Master of the House had told me he'd be waiting in the garden.

Was I truly only a door away from him?

I opened my palm, staring at the flower. Two petals remained, but there were four doors to choose from. I couldn't risk ending up in a boot room or a coal shed. This was my last chance to retrieve my son and escape this place, but how was I to know which door led outside?

Above the cacophony of flame and bubbling water, I heard a strange noise.

I tensed, expecting steps, but it was more desperate than that.

Following the noise across the kitchen I arrived at

the pantry and slid back the screen, stumbling backwards in shock.

A man was bound and gagged, his body cocooned and dangling from the ceiling. He was screaming through his gag, wriggling madly, trying to free himself.

'Get me down,' he cried as I uncovered his mouth. 'Hurry, before the Master of the House comes back.'

I was too overcome to move, surprised by the euphoria I felt at seeing another person after all this time.

'Find a knife, damn you,' he screamed, trying to kick me. 'We don't have time for you to gawp.'

I flew into the kitchen, yanking drawers open one after another. I didn't know where they were kept. I hadn't set foot in a kitchen since letting go of my mother's skirts.

'I need to get into the garden,' I said over my shoulder. 'Which door will take me there?'

'Get me down and I'll answer your questions,' he said. 'Hurry, he'll be—'

Steps shook the windows, a pan rattling off the stove and onto the floor.

Our glances met, his expression flickering from fright to despair, then acceptance.

'Hide,' he whispered urgently. 'And whatever you do, don't look at him.'

'What about my son?' I hissed under my breath.

'The final door on your left, but burn the flower before you go. It isn't a key, it's a noose.' Plaster dust fell from the ceiling as the steps drew closer. 'Hide,' he urged.

'What about you?'

'Your chance at nobility will come,' he replied grimly. 'Just as mine did.'

The door groaned open, forcing me to leap out of sight behind a giant porcelain box that felt like it was quivering in excitement.

Steps thudded across the kitchen, my bound friend praying.

I heard the scraping sound of a knife being drawn from its block, then a scream of agony.

Vomit rose in my throat.

There was a tearing noise, the screams cutting off abruptly.

For a second, silence reigned, only to be replaced with slurping.

I pressed my fingers into my ears, but it wasn't enough. There was a wet thud as something hit the floor.

More tearing followed, more slurping, and sounds of relish. Bones cracked, muscle ripped.

The Master of the House was enjoying his Christmas lunch, but I passed out long before he finished it.

13

How long did I slumber? I'll never know. The kitchen was much as I left it when I crept from behind the strange porcelain box. The same pans bubbled, the same meat roasted, and it was still snowing outside.

My poor friend was dismembered on the table, his blood

dripping into pools on the floor. I briefly caught sight of his cracked bones, tatters of flesh still hanging from them, but my disgust and anger were on the far side of a window, knocking for my attention.

I thought only of Thomas.

I dreamed of straightening his bow tie, before he went to meet a girl. I dreamed of standing by him when he wed and greeting my grandchildren when they were born.

A pan of potatoes was bubbling on the stove. I dragged it to one side, revealing the flame beneath.

The flower dug itself even tighter into my palm, the pain almost unbearable. It seemed we both understood the cost of second chances.

Turning my head, I lowered my hand to the heat, keeping it there even as my flesh bubbled and my throat became raw with screaming.

Finally, the flower released its grip, falling into the flame to be consumed.

There were no stars when I left the kitchen. No torments. No tortures. I walked through the door and out into the family graveyard, snowflakes stinging my exposed skin.

'Thomas!' I yelled, stumbling forward through the graves, hugging myself. 'Thomas!'

Huge holes had been dug and filled with human bones. Weeds twisted up through eye sockets and poppies grew through fingers, hundreds of ravens plucking at loose flesh.

'Dreadful beasts, aren't they?' said a voice at my ear.

I spun around to find an elderly woman at my elbow. She

was shorter than me, her face creased but cheerful. She was dressed in a charlady's shirt and apron.

'Are you the Master of the House?' I said in a shaking voice.

She regarded me solemnly, as if deciding whether to mock the question.

'Yes,' she replied simply. 'Though not this one. Don't worry, he won't disturb us. I've locked the door after you.'

She lifted my hand, tutting at the burnt flesh and the gouges made by the flower's thorns.

'You've been in the wars, haven't you?' she said. 'Let's see if we can't get that fixed up.' She tugged me gently.

'Where's my son?' I demanded. 'The Master of the House said—'

'He lied,' she interrupted, though not unkindly. 'That's his way. Thomas was lost to you the second he left his bedroom. He's lived his life. The Master of the House even showed you some of it.'

'No,' I said, shaking my head vehemently. 'I can change it. It was a warning.'

'It was seed,' she declared. 'The Master of the House feeds on regret, and he fattened you up by showing you what you'd missed.'

She blew out a long sorrow-filled breath. 'Parents and their children. He'll never go hungry.'

'But I saw him!' I pointed past the graveyard. 'He was throwing snowballs at the boughs of a tree.'

'That was your grandson,' she said. 'Thomas's family lived on this estate for a number of years, after . . . well, best you see for yourself.' She tugged me by the hand again. This time I was too bewildered to resist.

She led me through the graves to one that was upright and well-maintained, fresh flowers laid in front of it.

Thomas Digby
Husband, father and loyal friend.
1893–1931

'He only was thirty-eight years old,' I said, struggling to comprehend it.

A few hours ago, he'd been a boy. *My* boy. I'd heard his voice as a young man, so full of promise. I'd seen him married.

'He went to war,' she said. 'Not all of him came back. He did the best he could, for as long as he could.'

She offered me a tatty photograph dated 24th December 1931. I had seen a few of these in my life, but this one was in colour, and was startling in its clarity. It was an informal picture of the house staff. My son was in the second row, still leaning on his cane. He was in his late thirties here, and grown tall. His oil-stained overalls suggested he'd become a mechanic.

'This was the last picture taken of him,' said the elderly lady kindly.

'He was handsome, as I'd predicted. And there was his mother, shining through his face, like the two images had somehow been overlaid.

I touched his cheek, a lump forming in my throat.

He had his arm around a young woman's waist, two young boys sitting cross-legged by their feet.

My head was spinning. The charlady helped me down to the snow-covered ground before I fell.

'You did well to get here,' she said, holding my hands in both of her own. 'The Master of the House has lured thousands of people to this place over the years. Not many have the fortitude to get this far.'

Her blue eyes shone and were merry, but there were depths I had not the courage to plumb. I found myself looking away, a great humility come upon me.

'Who are you?' I asked.

'A caretaker would probably be the best description.'

'What does this place need with a caretaker?'

'Everybody needs somebody to take care of them,' she replied shortly, as if the question was foolish. 'I'm responsible for the message you saw on the door. Well, my friend Ethan did the actual carving. He died recently.'

'Ethan? Was he . . . in the kitchen?'

'Yes,' she said sadly. 'Poor Ethan.'

I felt a gentle warmth flow into my hands. Peering down, I saw them bathed in golden light, my wounds knitting back together.

I gazed at her in amazement, earning a ghost of a smile.

'The Master of the House has no use for the children once he's lured them into his web,' she explained. 'They're useful bait for the parents, but they don't have sorrows enough to sate him. A long time back, that's all this place was: room after room of parents chasing the screams of their lost children, growing steadily riper on guilt.'

She sniffed disdainfully. 'It was a little Old Testament for my taste. Me and the Master of the House have a long history, so I struck a bargain with him. Any child that made it safely though his maze to this garden could go free. That's where we come in.'

'We?'

She grinned at me toothily, a little flush coming into her cheeks. 'Do you know the strange thing about this place?'

'Everything,' I replied.

'Oh, you're quick, that'll be nice.' She paused, considering me. 'The labyrinth is different for every person who enters it, but it doesn't change once you're here. Now you've found your way to this garden you can make your way back to the entrance hall. You're free of the flower and you know where all the traps are. You even know how to hide from the Master of the House.'

'And what use is any of that now?' I said, dejected. 'My son is already gone. It was all too late.'

'There are always more children.'

Her gaze lingered on mine. There were lives in there. Endless lives.

'I tricked the Master of the House, you see. He made the bargain thinking the children would never be able to find their way through the maze alone, but "alone" was never part of our agreement. For a little while now I've been recruiting resourceful people like yourself to guide the children safely to me. I can show them the way out. I can find them new families, as I did for Thomas.'

The warmth went out of my hands, the glow diminishing. They were healed completely.

'There you go,' she said cheerfully. 'Good as new.'

I was staring at the piles of bones suspiciously. For all her outward geniality, I couldn't help but wonder whether this was just another trick. I'd never seen the Master of the House in the flesh, and his torments, thus far, had come in every conceivable guise. It would suit him to sharpen kindness, and slit my throat with charity.

'If you don't trust me, I'll not attempt to convince you,' she said, answering my unspoken thought. 'Except to say the Master of the House is already whispering to an unhappy little girl in Liverpool. In an hour or so, she's going to turn up at the entrance hall with nobody to meet her.'

I sucked in a cold breath, staring at the snow gathering on my hands. It was Christmas Eve, I remembered vaguely.

'What if I say no?' I replied.

'I'll show you the way out,' she said, shrugging. 'This isn't a punishment, Mr Carrow. You don't need to be redeemed. You weren't an evil parent, just a poor one. It's a hard job, and it doesn't suit everybody. There'll be plenty worse who don't end up here. Sometimes, bad luck finds you because you're standing in its way.'

My thoughts flashed across the monuments of my life, from my law practice to my house on Finchley Road. Thomas and my late wife. The only things of value to me were the things I'd offered the least care; the things I'd lost.

Then I thought of a little girl, terrified in her bed as a

voice curled out of the darkness. How could I go back to my life knowing I'd abandoned her to this? The old woman was right. I wasn't a good father, but I could, at least, try to be a better man.

'I'm scared,' I admitted.

'That'll never stop,' she responded, tapping the back of my hand companionably. 'There's no hope in this, Mr Carrow. No reward. This is just a job as needs doing, but, eventually, the Master of the House will catch you, and you know what happens then.'

We spoke for a little longer, but what we said doesn't really matter any more. Not for you, or me.

I've written all this down and left it in the entrance hall, where I hope you'll find it.

I've guided hundreds of children through the house since the conversation in the graveyard, but I can feel my time growing short. The Master of the House never tires, but I have. I've grown old in here, his steps getting a little closer each time through.

I need somebody to take my place.

You see, this isn't our story. This isn't a morality tale, or a judgement. We weren't chosen by the universe to be redeemed. We're here because we're not special. We're here because there are so many of us, and we're all so ripe with regret.

If you find my benefactor, thank her for me. Tell her I'm going to see my son, and I'm grateful to her for making me finally worthy of him.

ADA LARK

Jess Kidd

Ada Lark (orphan, eightish, waifish) has been in the employ of Madam Bellerose (formerly Betty 'The Knife' Rigg, fifties, will stand in a storm) for as long as she can remember. Of the orphanage that reared her previously, Ada recalls nothing. Only perhaps cold, of a biting, numbing kind, raggedy hems and little blue hands and feet (not necessarily her own). Liberated at a tottering age, Ada happily bears no lasting marks of institutional life apart from a terrible fear of rats and a missing toe. But now neither cold nor vermin plague her, for Madam Bellerose's house in Pimlico is plush with luxury and warmth. The principal rooms boast all-day candlelight, heavy drapes and thick-pile rugs, providing unrivalled comfort and discretion for Madam Bellerose's patrons, living and dead. This twilight environment is not only best suited to discourses of the Otherworldly kind, it is flattering to Madam Bellerose's mature beauty. Lit by candlelight, her bosom is alabaster and her complexion dewy. Her dark eyes twinkle as she receives her supplicants in the reception room. The glossy black coils of her hair shine and the rich embellishments of coiffure and gown, throat and wrist, catch marvellously the firelight. Ada knows that Madam Bellerose's true magic is worked in her own transformation. An hour ago, the old lag was sitting wigless at her dressing table with a face like a crumpled bedsheet, scowling against pipe smoke and an unkind slant of winter sun. But truly, it is in the séance room that Madam Bellerose comes into her full power. In the dim, with all but a few candles extinguished, her eyes burn with psychic sight (or, as she is buffeted by supernatural forces, close, startle open and roll about in her head). Her changing expressions are riveting to watch; a frown of pain on her milky brow, a sudden pang of death-guilt, the final euphoric release. There can be no doubt that she is truly the mouthpiece of the dead; at every performance her body (sturdy as it is) gives voice to a chorus. From the dredged-up moan of a lost sea-captain, all brine and grinding shingle, to the sweetest whisper from the lips of an ill-fated debutante as her broken heart flutters its last. It would strain the strongest of nerves. A maid stands by with smelling salts and there is fortified wine to be had. Madam Bellerose offers the perfect union of edification and diversion. Through her occult ability the bereaved are reassured, true heirs identified, slanders corrected and wisdoms imparted by the dearly deceased. Her success is attested by the avalanche of letters that arrive at her writing-bureau. Outside the daily performances (and twice-weekly matinees) Madam Bellerose grants private sittings for those whose status or circumstances require enhanced privacy.

Ada dreads the private sittings which lengthen further

a day that already starts hours before her employer rises to tamp her pipe. Ada's tasks are many: carting slop-pails and filling coal-scuttles, decanting sherry and steaming puddings, turning down beds and polishing shoes. Ada the practical can undertake any of the thousand mundane chores incurred in the running of a handsome townhouse with a staff of only one grizzled maid-of-all-work and a gnarly cook. For Madam Bellerose requires strict confidentiality regarding the happenings under her roof and servants that don't tattle, earwig and bleat are as rare as hen's teeth.

There is one task that is Ada's alone.

Madam Bellerose, when in her cups, delights in recounting how she searched all the orphanages in London for one small enough and puny enough, steady enough and quiet enough to fulfil a remarkable destiny. Being: to assist the foremost psychic of the age as she rose like a comet in London society. Growing misty-eyed, she recalls how she snatched Ada from the jaws of poverty, fed and clothed her, blessed her with a cheerful name and bestowed upon her a profound esoteric secret.

This secret, indeed the premium secret of Madam Bellerose's success, aside from handsome eyes and a repertoire of voices, is a modified mahogany table. She got the idea more than a decade ago from some clever-arsed contraption or other at the Great Exhibition. Her first husband was a cabinet-maker and her second a showman, so it was natural that her widow's profession would combine the two. Madam Bellerose's Psychical Table is round, accommodates four to six punters holding hands and is waxed and buffed to a lovely lustre.

Where this table differs from every other table in London, grand or humble, is the concealed compartment in its pedestal. Once inside, a small, thin child will find above their head levers, hammers and a magnet, all of ingenious design. The operation of the magnet will move a planchette on the table's surface to spell out messages from beyond the grave. The levers and hammers will unleash a volley of scrapes and taps, perfectly replicating the fingers of the dead. The table also has the capacity to rock and tilt, a feature used only for the most emphatic of spectres, for Madam Bellerose considers it showy.

Innovation can be hard won. The prototype was plagued with jamming hammers and inadequate magnets and clanked and twanged like a dying piano. When building an operating compartment slim enough to sustain inspection by an unbeliever, Madam Bellerose forgot to add ventilation. This resulted in the unfortunate demise of an undernourished crossing-sweeper. But by the time Ada Lark was procured, deloused and toddled into a dimly lit drawing room in Pimlico, the table was in full working order.

It is Madam Bellerose's greatest misfortune that she is unable to share the genius of her invention; she would certainly patent it otherwise. It is Ada's greatest fortune that she has grown hardly at all and remains slight enough to squeeze into the dreaded table and manifest a whole haunt of ghosts nightly. Ada has no doubt that her employer is of a ruthless bent. She only has to look out at the small grassy mound in the garden where the bones of Billy the Broom moulder.

The means of ventilation, from which Billy did not benefit, is a finger-width strip of latticework. The operator sits knees to ears, arms stretched above the head. The table must be played by touch, for if the séance room is dark, the compartment is darker still. Despite the regularity of being enclosed in a space no bigger than an umbrella stand (twice daily on a matinee), Ada has never got used to the heart-thumping dread of it, the darkness and suffocating heat that builds. Worst of all is the sound of the lock Madam Bellerose turns once she closes the compartment door. Ada must breathe against the panic. She must listen for the arrival of the sitters, the swish of satin skirts, the creak as they take their chairs. She must bite her lip against the cramping of her limbs. She must force down sneezes and stifle coughs. She must ride the waves of Madam Bellerose's inspiration, taking care not to misspell a name or tap a tardy reply. But the sound cues are muffled and the script often changes. Once the room is empty and the takings have been counted, Ada hears the turn of the lock and is born gasping from the compartment. A good performance is rewarded with a grunt. A bad incurs a night with the rats in the cellar.

For all this, it has never occurred to Ada to question her place, or to seek help, from the cook, the maid, or the callers. There is space in the garden for another little grave-mound and Madam Bellerose has demonstrated that the lattice can be closed as well as opened.

Right now, the lattice is open. Ada dozes with her nostrils against it. The matinee is over, the private session is to come.

A kick to the table's pedestal jolts her awake.

'Stow the snoring, gentleman calling.' Madam Bellerose is hoarse. Today she has given voice to three deceased consumptives and a murdered cattle auctioneer and interpreted a legion of scribbling and banging dead. As Madam Bellerose tells her punters, the key to her unrivalled success is her ability to summon spirits both within and without. Sometimes they speak *through* her, sometimes they speak *to* her.

Ada watches through the lattice as the room brightens. Madam Bellerose has candles lit and the decanter brought in. She takes the low couch in the corner while she waits. A gentleman arrives presently. That he is a gentleman is attested by his appearance: upright bearing, gracious gestures, whiskers resplendent. He is dressed in full fig and beautifully spoken, with high-born vowels as rich as plum pudding.

'Madam.' He gives a chivalrous bow and reaches for her hand. 'Cecil Woodgate. A pleasure to finally meet you.'

Madam Bellerose dignifies his presence with her best curtsey, before addressing the stranger in tones raucous and familiar. 'Cecil Woodgate, my arse!'

Ada is gripped. Madam Bellerose's pipe is lit and her wig lies discarded on the hearthrug, the decanter is empty and they have sent for champagne and offal. The familiar stranger is elaborating on a plan. The plan is simple and cannot fail, it will set them both up for life, in ridiculous luxury, all the needful and don't they bloody deserve it? Madam Bellerose listens while sucking jelly from a pig's trotter.

'Bring your wealthy widow here,' she says.

'Betty, cop an ear! She won't leave the house on account of her dead daughter, won't take a piss without asking her first. The whole household in thrall to a ghost!'

Madam Bellerose hesitates. 'You believe in it?'

Woodgate snorts. 'Whispers on the wind, footsteps in the nursery, what do you bleeding think?'

Madam Bellerose holds out her glass. He opens another bottle.

'All the little ghost needs to do,' he murmurs, 'is convince her mama to remarry.'

'The dashing Mr Woodgate, I presume?'

They clink glasses.

'Except I don't make house calls.'

'You've a fine set-up here, ain't you?' Woodgate takes in the comfortable room with a swill of his glass.

Madam Bellerose looks at him closely. 'What of it?'

Woodgate smiles. 'You've done well, girl. But there are other mediums on the up. And who's to say someone won't reveal your methods, expose your tricks?'

She narrows her eyes. 'You'd do that, tulip?'

Woodgate feigns offence. 'You hurt me, Betty. For every grieving believer there's a detractor. Peering and prying, nit-picking, working out how you pull the strings—'

'There are no strings: I have the gift.'

'Course you do, ducks.' He smiles indulgently. 'All I'm

saying is, you do this one job and you'll want for nothing. Whether you decide to carry on with the old table-tapping is down to you.'

Madam Bellerose stands, trotter in hand, and crosses the room. She opens the curtains and points out the window. Ada sees, illuminated by the street-lamp, a flurry of falling snow.

Woodgate is unruffled. 'The roads are passable and it must be Christmas Eve.' He lowers his voice in mock-sorrow. 'The dead always mark their anniversaries.'

Madam Bellerose sniffs. 'So, how much?'

Woodgate walks over to her, dips his head, whispers in her ear. Madam Bellerose starts pleasantly. He catches the greasy trotter she drops.

'Double it.' Madam Bellerose glances across the room. 'And my table comes too.'

Woodgate nods, takes a bite of her trotter and bares his teeth in a grin.

Madam Bellerose's household makes hasty preparations to decamp. Travelling clothes are aired. Fine gowns are readied. She personally dismantles and packs her table, pipe clamped between her teeth. All sittings are cancelled for the foreseeable future, much to the dismay of her patrons. Instructions are given to the servants to close up the house indefinitely. Following her visit to the country Madam will be seeking warmer climes. Indignation loosens the tongues of the gnarly cook and grizzled maid; they share a fig pudding in the kitchen, a concession to the season, before they are turned out, with new positions to find, at their dizzy age.

Ada listens to their uncustomary chatter as she washes the scullery floor.

'What about her that's turning us out: there will be no luck there?' ventures the maid.

'Calamity and ruin. Madam will meet her death on the icy road. Overturned carriage,' replies the sage old cook.

'What of the orphan?' asks the maid.

Ada puts down the mop, pushes open the door a crack.

'Is that one still around?' The cook glances towards the scullery. 'I barely see her.'

'There's not much to see, thin little thing.'

'It will be the workhouse.' The cook folds her arms high on her bosom. 'Or else out on the streets when Madam has finished with her.'

'Christmas or no Christmas.'

The cook nods contentedly.

The maid tuts. 'Shocking.'

'Isn't it?'

The morning of departure, two days before Christmas, Ada brings Madam Bellerose's breakfast tray to the dressing room. The cook left early with a carpet bag rattling with stolen cutlery so Ada prepared the tray herself, placing carefully the cocoa, buttered bun and dish of pickled eggs. Ada's knock at the door goes unanswered. She enters the room to find Madam Bellerose sitting by the window, staring out into the garden in the direction of the small grassy mound with a lost expression. Glancing up at Ada, she appears to regain herself.

'Ada Lark, you've been happy here.' It is not a question.

Ada gives a bob and sets the tray down.

Madam Bellerose rises, takes Ada by the hand and leads her before the looking-glass. 'Do you see what I see?'

Ada peers. She sees the odd glassy brightness in her employer's eyes, a face crumpled in the daylight—

'Don't look at me, look at yourself, girl.'

Ada regards her own unremarkable self: the plain bonnet and drab dress, the slight frame and sharp elbows, the searching eyes and the pinched face. A thought strikes her: she looks like a ghost of a girl, lost and faded.

'Don't you ever eat?'

'Yes,' lies Ada.

'But you never grow.'

Before she can stop herself, Ada glances out of the window, to the garden and the small grassy mound.

Madam Bellerose lets go of Ada's hand, regains her seat at the dressing-table and takes up her cup of cocoa. 'You will accompany me to the big house in the country where I will give a private session for nobility.' She puts on her la-di-da voice. 'Hadlow Hall, Lady Bentham, if you must ask.'

Ada feels a surge of excitement.

'Don't get too excited. You're to travel by trunk. It'll be cramped, but no more than you're used to.'

Ada is aghast. 'By trunk?'

'I can't afford anyone seeing you – ain't you the helpful dead?' Madam Bellerose selects a pickled egg, avoiding Ada's gaze. 'Work the table one last time and you're free to go.'

'Where would I go?'

Madam Bellerose waves her away and sinks the egg in one mouthful.

The trunk is surprisingly spacious after the Psychical Table. As she lies inside, Ada feels hot and cold and a variety of jolting, from rhythmically bearable to teeth-rattling. She can discern sounds and scents through the keyhole and the cracks in the ill-fitting lid. The shouts of station guards and the smoke from train engines. The topple of boxes and the mustiness of the parcel carriage. The snort of waiting carriage horses and clean country air. She has been furnished with gingerbread and a stoppered bottle of milk for the journey and wrapped in old shawls.

Lulled to sleep by carriage sway up the two-mile drive to Hadlow Hall, Ada is bumped awake, step by step, up the servants' staircase. The footman deposits the trunk, none too gently, in the guest room.

Ada lies very still. Hearing only the sound of her own breathing. Smelling only milk-soaked wool and broken gingerbread. Otherwise, she feels only a sharp pain to her head, no doubt acquired during the final stage of transit.

She waits, quietly moves her numb limbs, waits again.

Then she hears it: a soft tapping on the lid of the trunk.

*

Ada, breath held, listens. The tapping, after a while, becomes playful and suggestive of a jolly tune.

Ada summons up courage and whispers, 'Is anyone there?'

The tapping stops and is replaced by a scrabbling and scratching that seems to be spreading all over the exterior of the trunk.

Ada screws her eyes closed and tries to imagine something pleasant, seasonal even; carollers with bright lanterns, decorated shop windows, a family around the table, roast goose and parsnips, oranges and chestnuts, teeth and worm-tails, beady eyes and claws—

The scrabbling is now concentrated at the front of the trunk, around the lock. Ada feels a huff of freezing air through the crack in the lid. The lock clicks and the trunk is thrown open. Ada gingerly opens her eyes. She stands up and looks around. She is all alone in a beautiful room.

A room far finer than Madam Bellerose's parlour even. The only sign of that person is a travelling cape slung over a chair. A lively fire burns in the grate and paintings of mild-eyed ladies gaze down from gilt frames. Tall windows give onto expansive grounds; a terrace and the bones of a formal garden lie under snowdrifts, untouched but for the feet of birds and squirrels. In the distance, the sky turns the colour of new bruises with the snow yet to fall. This, and the shadows already forming in the corner of the room, attest to the dying of the day. The lamps have been lit in readiness and their light is as soft as the rugs and the sheen on the silk brocade walls. A four-poster bed with pale blue coverlet, a comfortable armchair, a variety of cabinets and vases, all polished and dusted and cared for by unseen hands, complete the bright and comfortable picture.

Grubby and bewildered, Ada is entirely out of place.

Noticing she is trailing gingerbread crumbs and milk she goes to the washstand. She stands in her shift to clean her dress. Thus occupied, she feels a draught behind her. A heavy fog hangs over the trunk. It spreads, curling past the fireplace; the merry flames diminish and die. The fog circles a table-lamp, which burns blue and gutters. It ruffles the curtains and mists the windowpanes. It is like no fog Ada has ever seen, even in London. The fog gathers itself to the size of a well-fed eight-year-old, wavers for a moment and then rushes to the door, threading out through the keyhole with a shrill whistle. Ada puts her eye to the keyhole. Beyond is an empty corridor. Her view of a marble console table begins to cloud. Ada jumps back from the door, certain that the fog is *looking back at her*. Then – and Ada's heart skips sideways to see it – the handle turns and the door opens. Outside, in the hallway, the fog is gone. Ada hesitates, casts a glance back at the empty room and the opened trunk, closes the door and begins to walk.

The fog catches up with her at the end of the corridor, on the turn onto a landing. Ada doesn't need to look behind to know it is there. She feels its dank presence behind her. She speeds up, blood rushing in her ears. The fog follows. She quickens her pace. The fog speeds up. Ada looks back, the fog seems to be gathering momentum, growing in height, filling the corridor, thickening. Ada passes a hall window, so does the fog, the window instantly clouds. Ice forms on door handles as they pass. Ada breaks into a run, the fog sinks into a tight grey ball, it ricochets off walls, sometimes disappearing through them, always coming back. The fog waits for her round corners, she runs through it and is drenched with cold. Ada and the fog tear down hallways and duck into empty rooms. They pass servants, maids in white caps and aprons, who flatten themselves against doorways and stare down at their shoes. Ada has no breath to cry out to them. But then suddenly the fog stops short and dissipates. Ahead, framed by the light from an open doorway, stands a grave and lovely angel.

'Are you dead?' the angel asks.

'I don't know,' replies Ada.

The angel's name is Lady Bentham. She is less luminous than on first appearance but no less marvellous. On further inspection, her beauty is clearly mortal. Her face may be grave, but it is not unkind. Her fair hair is shot with silver strands and the lines on her face attest to long years of grieving. She wears mourning black with purple trim. Lady Bentham also revises her first opinion of Ada, deciding that she is not dead. Ada is thankful of this as she sits on a chair by the hearth with a blanket around her shoulders. A tea tray has been set between them and the fire crackles steadily. The fog has taken itself off to skulk behind the curtains.

'It was the shift, you see,' says Lady Bentham apologetically. 'I thought it was a shroud. You do look frightfully peaky. Do you ever eat?'

'Not much, your ladyship,' Ada admits.

'Will you try?'

Ada assents. The lady pours tea and cuts a wedge of cake.

'How did you come to be at Hadlow Hall?'

'I can't remember, your ladyship.'

Lady Bentham looks at her kindly. 'Memory is a tricky thing, isn't it? Slips happen to the best of us. Perhaps you had better stay until you recollect.'

The curtains undulate, a jubilant rush of cold air rushes past Ada's knees, the fire sputters and goes out. Lady Bentham blithely eyes the chimneybreast.

A soft knock; a lady's maid stands in the doorway. She is dressed in a version of Lady Bentham's attire, only plainer, if possible. Her russet hair is neat and her expression is one of patient forbearance. She holds an armful of gowns, struggling under their limp weight. The fog pours out of the grate onto the hearthrug and creeps away, behind dainty tables and embroidered fire-screens, to slink through the open door. Ada could be mistaken, but the maid appears to keep the door open a little longer than necessary.

'You have found the gowns! Bring them, do!' Lady Bentham frowns. 'A moment – did I hear the carriage?'

'Yes, ma'am. Mr Woodgate and his London medium arrived earlier. You had them sent into the library.'

Lady Bentham smiles. 'Dear Woodgate, he always has some jolly plot or other in hand, doesn't he?'

The maid looks sceptical. 'Yes, ma'am.'

'And Reverend Toop?'

'He's taking a turn around the maze, ma'am, to regulate his magnetic equilibrium.'

'Of course. Well, they must wait a trifle longer. First, we must attend to our mysterious little visitor here – let's dress her up, she'll be such a delight!'

The maid throws a doubtful look in Ada's direction.

A gown is chosen from the musty selection and Ada is dressed in a plum velvet two decades out of fashion, if she knew about such things. It hangs from her, making her already pale face look ghastly. But her wearing of it seems to please Lady Bentham in a tragic sort of way. The maid tightens the sash and brushes Ada's hair into something resembling order.

Lady Bentham blinks back her tears. 'Charming! You must join us for dinner!'

Her maid gives a polite cough.

'Yes?'

'Begging your pardon, ma'am, might the company below be a bit ... *unsettling* for a child?' the maid finishes with a kind glance in Ada's direction.

'Would it? I hadn't thought. How old are you, child?'

'Possibly eight, your ladyship.'

'Practically grown. Are you afraid of ghosts?'

'No, your ladyship. At least, not that I know of. Are there any in Hadlow Hall?'

Lady Bentham touches Ada's cheek. 'Let's hope so.'

*

Lady Bentham looks every part the grave angel as she enters the library with the regal posture born of good breeding, her stature accentuated by black silk crêpe. The effect is not lost on the three waiting guests, who rise in unison. Woodgate bows gallantly, Reverend Toop adjusts his pince-nez and Madam Bellerose simpers.

The library has been made festive, with green leaf and red berry decorating mantelpiece and bookcase. Comfortable chairs have been ranged and the firelight gives a warming glow. With the lamps turned low it takes a moment for Ada to see – standing ready-assembled in a shadowy corner – Madam Bellerose's Psychical Table. Although somewhat diminished by the proportions of the room, the sight of it fills Ada with dread. The confining compartment, the suffocating darkness, the contortion of body and mind required to manifest whole armies of ghosts! And all the while, the threat of the lattice closing. At this last thought Ada is struck by the awful certainty that her fate at the hands of Madam Bellerose will be neither the workhouse nor the street.

'Let me introduce your fellow house guest.' Lady Bentham holds her hand out to Ada.

Madam Bellerose's eyes fall upon her charge. Her smile is extinguished.

'I found her drifting along the corridor with no recollection of how she came to be here. Imagine! Of all the strange happenings in this strange house.' Lady Bentham turns to Madam Bellerose. 'As an expert on hauntings, can you shed any light on this mystery, madam?'

Madam Bellerose shuffles and reddens. 'Indeed, I cannot, your ladyship. My business is with the mysteries of the spirit world, not the world of the living.'

'Of course.' Lady Bentham smiles her sad smile. 'On that note, I'm afraid the charming Mr Woodgate brought you here on false pretences. You see, I'm not entirely sure we need a medium to interrogate our dead – they are given perfect licence at Hadlow Hall.'

Madam Bellerose smiles back. 'You misunderstand, your ladyship. I am simply here to act as an instrument.'

Ada steals a glance at her employer. After a shaky start she seems to have regained her footing.

'A go-between.' Resplendent in midnight blue, Madam Bellerose has regained her air of mystical authority. 'To channel your questions.'

'I do have questions,' replies Lady Bentham.

'Following my sessions, the dear departed often find peace and disappear entirely. For instance, when a spirit is finally able to communicate a long-held message—'

'I do not want my dear departed to go,' says Lady Bentham quietly.

There is an awkward silence. Reverend Toop takes off his pince-nez and puts it on again. He squints myopically around him.

'It is rather fascinating, is it not, that Madam Bellerose has identified one of the primary functions of spirit-haunting, namely, that a ghost must always have a *purpose.* Whether this be predictive, as regards the demise of a family member, or practical – the locating of a lost object of importance – or malicious, in the creation of general mayhem. Several remarkable cases in recent history involved a spectre setting right quite terrible wrongs. The pointing of the dead finger, if you like. Such cases, however perceptive, *accurate* even, can generally be debunked as claptrap. All that is required is an objective mind—'

'Thank you, Reverend.' Lady Bentham addresses the rest of the company apologetically. 'Reverend Toop prides himself on his objective mind.'

Woodgate smiles. 'I, too, had reserved judgement on this matter, Reverend, until I was astonished by unquestionable evidence – of a personal nature – that Madam Bellerose had the ear, nay the voice, of my dear deceased father. Now I am a firm believer. I challenge you, sir, to draw any other conclusion.'

The vicar looks peevish. 'I am certain Madam Bellerose's performance will be an edification for us all.'

'Well, the stage has been set for Christmas Eve.'

Lady Bentham shivers. 'Let us talk no more about that occasion, Mr Woodgate, tomorrow will be upon us soon enough. In the meantime, I invite my guests to be at liberty.'

Reverend Toop raises a finger and throws a marked look to his host.

'I am forgetting,' she says wearily. 'Reverend Toop has invited us to an informal lecture here in the library. The theme escapes me.'

Reverend Toop, all gratitude, adjusts his pince-nez. '"A Treatise on Otherworldly Communication (Hitherto Unproven by Men of Science and Letters)". If I can, in fact, summarise my work—'

Lady Bentham taps his arm. 'Perhaps you can enlighten us after dinner, Reverend? Shall we?'

The dining table is vast; even Madam Bellerose seems daunted by the array of cutlery and tiny silver pots and swags of poinsettias and candied fruits. A forest of tapered candles burns with steady flames, happily untouched by the chill air prowling under the table. Ada wonders if she's the only one who notices the flapping of the linen cloth and the ruffling of the carpet fringes. Liveried servants stand by, as inert as the marble busts that bookend the heaped dishes on the sideboard. Haughty portraits adorn the walls; Lady Bentham's ancestors wear powdered wigs and buckled shoes. Arch ladies in fancy gowns wield elaborate fans. Game gentlemen strike poses with swords. Dogs, hunting and lap, look down the slopes of their noses.

Ada glances round at her fellow diners. Lady Bentham is laughing at Woodgate, who is re-enacting a seemingly hilarious anecdote with a rakish grin. Reverend Toop is polishing his pince-nez, which the butler helpfully retrieved from the soup tureen. Madam Bellerose is waving her empty wine glass at the footman. Her eyes meet Ada's. She takes up her butter knife and draws it across her throat in a terrifying gesture.

Ada lowers her eyes to her first course and notices that letters have been traced in her pea soup.

N E L L A

'Nella,' reads Ada.

Lady Bentham stops laughing and stares at her. 'What did you say?'

'Nella. In my soup.'

Lady Bentham lets out a sob, halfway between terrified and jubilant.

Woodgate is all action. Ada's hands are inspected and found to be relatively clean and certainly soup-free. The cook is sent for and the butler questioned. Both can attest that there were no letters written in the soup when it was served. Lady Bentham professes herself too agitated to eat but rather sits gazing at Ada's soup-plate as if upon the face of a beloved. Madam Bellerose empties the best part of a decanter with a mutinous look. Reverend Toop has gone to find his magnifying glass.

'She's here,' says Lady Bentham to Ada. 'She has given so many signs, but this—'

Woodgate lays a gentle hand on her arm. 'Your ladyship, the child is overwhelmed: see how pale her countenance is? Permit me to take her to some fresh air.'

Lady Bentham barely raises her eyes from Ada's soup-plate. 'Of course, dear Woodgate, do.'

Ada can tell from the grip of Woodgate's fingers on her shoulder that he means her no good. He trots her to the French windows and opens them. The night air on her face is not colder than that collecting around her ankles.

'Here's a trick for you,' he hisses. 'Disappear into that bloody table tomorrow, else you won't be *playing* the ghost. Understand?'

The lady's maid, whose name is Kitty, is to accompany Ada to her room. The cook will send up something more fitting for a child than haunted soup. Downstairs dinner limps on. Lady Bentham is distracted and Madam Bellerose a little worse for wear. Woodgate and the Reverend are explaining difficult things to one another with the aid of tabletop alignments of silver cruets and broken crackers.

As they climb the grand staircase Ada notices a sprig of holly pinned under the pleat of Kitty's gown.

The maid notices Ada looking. 'To ward off spirits, miss. Irish old wives' tale.'

'Are there spirits here?'

'I couldn't say, miss.'

Which means *yes*.

Ada notices that the fog, which had been following them, has lagged behind. It curls up on the bottom step.

'Who is Nella?' she asks.

The maid frowns. 'It's not my place, miss.'

'Please.'

The maid nods. 'Come this way, miss.'

At the end of the corridor there is a large ebony-framed painting.

Kitty raises her lantern. 'Eleanor Bentham, her ladyship's only child.'

A life-sized portrait of a fair-haired girl in too-tight plum velvet stares belligerently down at them. Clutched tight in her chubby hands, a golden ball.

Ada catches the maid's quick movement as Kitty crosses herself.

Behind the painted girl the grounds of Hadlow Hall have been perfectly rendered. The formal garden shrouded in snow. The sweep of the lawn down to the old stone wall. But the gate in the wall is open. Glimpsed beyond is a dreary landscape, a marsh perhaps. The sky shows its last fire, burnishing the child's hair. A sleek raven eyes her ominously from a nearby ornamental urn.

'What happened to Eleanor Bentham?'

Kitty flinches and looks around her. Ada can sense her growing unease. 'That's a story for daylight hours, miss.'

Ada drops her voice to a whisper. 'The fog—'

'*Daylight*, miss.'

Ada nods.

Kitty opens the door to the nursery and glances at Ada anxiously. 'We have better accommodation at Hadlow Hall, but Lady Bentham asked for you to sleep here.'

The room is so cold Ada can see her breath.

Two chambermaids battle the cobwebs, a third hastily coaxes a fire alight. The furniture is heavy and the windows are barred. An attempt has been made to soften the room with floral wallpaper, which blooms with peonies and mould. There are shelves for legions of china dolls with spiteful faces and picture-books that sag with damp. A dapple-grey rocking horse pulls its lip back in a sneer, its mane and tail hang knotted and tatty. Mice seem to have gnawed a passage through a blank-windowed doll's house.

The chambermaids complete their tasks and rush out of the room shivering.

Kitty puts the lamp on the nightstand, turning up the flame as high as it will go. She draws the heavy curtains and turns back the counterpane. The sheets may be freshly laundered but the bed looks sour and lumpy. Ada could even wish herself back on her cot by the kitchen range at Madam Bellerose's.

Kitty unpins the holly sprig from her dress and slips it under Ada's pillow.

'Leave the lamp burning and don't get out of the bed,' she whispers. 'No harm will come to you.'

Ada lies down under sheets as cold and dank as opened ground.

'Just think, miss, tomorrow is Christmas Eve.' Kitty's smile falters; she frowns.

Perhaps she, too, sees the shadows deepen in the corners, or the glint in the dolls' eyes, or the rocking horse move but very slightly.

'Good night, miss.'

Ada catches the words Kitty says under her breath as she leaves the room: *God bless.*

It is unimaginable that Ada can sleep in such a place but sleep she does. Perhaps Kitty's blessing works a protective magic, or perhaps the holly sprig weaves a shielding spell. Or perhaps the events of the day have finally exhausted her.

Ada's sleep isn't peaceful.

In her dreams she roams the corridors of Hadlow Hall. Only now there is no grave angel to save her. There are no servants or guests either. She is completely alone in the big house. She tries every door – library – dining room – nursery – guest room. As she heads down the main staircase the front door opens to reveal a dazzling world of sunlit snow.

She steps outside, feeling the crunch of snow underfoot, and walks down the terrace past the icy outlines of the formal garden.

And now, in her hand – why, a golden ball!

A perfect globe for her to throw again and again into the sky. Dazzle of blue, sparkle of gold. But when she misses a catch the ball rolls away. Down the ball rolls, over the vast lawn. The ball rolls lightly, leaving only a faint trace in the hard frozen snow. She gives chase, all the way to the old stone wall where the frosted skeletons of espaliered trees wait for summer.

In the wall, the gate is open.

Beyond she glimpses a vast flat landscape of half-melted pools and low hillocks and dead reeds. The ball rolls out of the gate and she must follow.

Ada wakes late to the sound of a chambermaid with a clanking breakfast tray; she quickly sets it down and is gone. Ada dresses in the plum velvet and goes to the window. Outside lies the scene of her dream, only now the snow has started to thaw and the gate to the marshes is locked and boarded up. Voices drift up from the terrace. Ada opens the window and peers out, recognising Madam Bellerose's best bonnet from above. At her side, Woodgate lopes, gallant, conducting her around ice patches. Perhaps sensing they are being watched, he looks up. Ada ducks back but fancies it is too late, for when she peeps out again Madam Bellerose is staring up, scowling. A little way after them walks Reverend Toop, swinging his walking stick and holding forth. Lady Bentham looks to be in her own reverie: from time to time she glances at the gate or picks at the dead flowerhead she carries.

Behind Lady Bentham: a gathering fog.

Kitty finds Ada a pair of stout shoes, a too-big cape and an old bonnet and they go walking in the grounds. Ada notices that Kitty has a fresh sprig of holly pinned to her gown.

Ada insists on a turn along the terrace.

She points out past the sweeping lawn to the gate in the wall. 'I dreamt last night that I went out there. Is the gate ever open?'

Kitty shakes her head. 'Lady Bentham says the marshes beyond are dangerous.'

'You promised to tell me what happened to Eleanor.'

'I did.'

They walk in silence. Ada feels a chill that has nothing to do with the weather.

'Kitty, what is that fog? You've seen it, surely?'

'The fog comes in from the marshes, that's all, miss.'

'Kitty, it threads through keyholes and turns corners.'

Kitty bites her lip. 'Some people see it, some don't.'

'But you see it?'

'I feel it more.'

They round the house and walk out onto the gravel drive. Hadlow Hall is lovely with its stonework honeyed in the winter sun. Stone steps rise to a front door decorated with a glossy holly wreath. Through the ground-floor windows they catch a glimpse of the spruce tree that stands in the grand entrance hall, decorated with glass baubles and beads, candles and paper chains. They head out of the grounds and along the lane to a chapel.

The chapel is squat and mossy. Lying low in a field of sheep who pay the visitors no mind. Kitty pushes open the heavy wooden door and latches it behind them. It is dim inside after the sun. The chapel has been swept clean and decorated too. Jars of cut branches decorate the altar and there is a small bunch of holly and ivy at the end of every pew.

Kitty leads Ada to a marble plaque under a stained-glass window. In a dapple of coloured light, Ada reads the inscription.

Eleanor Elizabeth Bentham

24th December 1835–24th December 1843

Cherished Daughter of Charlotte, Lady Bentham

In the Arms of Her Dear Papa

'They are a tragic family,' says Kitty. 'Lord Bentham died when Eleanor was only days old; his horse bolted. Lady Bentham raised the child alone and she doted on the girl, seeing no wrong in her. Eleanor grew up to be headstrong and a little unruly by all accounts.'

'She died twenty years ago today.'

Kitty nods. 'On her birthday, miss.'

'How did she die?'

'She strayed out onto the marshes while she was playing and never came back. She certainly perished there, likely losing her footing as the light died, only her body was never found.'

Ada touches the carved marble, a cherub face with blank eyes. She thinks about all the different things death might mean for a person.

'People say that's why her spirit is restless. Eleanor is blamed for many of the mishaps up at Hadlow Hall. Some say she plays tricks.'

'What tricks?'

'Oh, slamming doors, toppling coals out of the fire, tripping the housemaids and rattling the bottles in the cellar. Some servants won't stay.'

'And then there's the fog?'

'Yes. That's often worse.'

Ada looks at the memorial and wonders what it would be like to be Eleanor. Would she, too, become a cold patch on a landing? Or letters spelt out on a medium's table, a faint voice from beyond? Who would want to ask a question of her? Not Madam Bellerose, that's for sure.

The living must look out for the dead or how else can there be a haunting? Ada thinks of the small mound in Madam Bellerose's garden and the crossing-sweeper sleeping under it. Who is listening for his voice? His words and taps?

'They say that her ladyship's heart was broken when her husband died but lost entirely with her child.'

'So sad.'

Kitty nods. 'She refused every suitor, all down the years, staying alone. Although there are still contenders.' She throws Ada a sly glance. 'Mr Woodgate has been on the prowl for a while now.'

'He's not who he seems,' says Ada, surprising herself.

'I don't suppose he is. Every peacock puffs out his feathers,' replies Kitty. 'But would it be so awful for her to have some company? Do you know, I think that's why he brought that medium here, to lay the dead to rest to make room for the living.'

They walk back to the house, Ada reflective now. Kitty glances at her from time to time.

'What is it, miss?'

Ada considers telling her the truth, about Madam Bellerose and Woodgate's plan. If they have their way, she'll be playing the ghost of Hadlow Hall later. But surely Kitty would think less of her? All the people that she, too, has tricked?

'Have you any more holly, just in case Nella doesn't go quietly?'

Kitty smiles. 'I'll go and cut a rake of it.'

*

On parting, Kitty gives Ada a gift. It's a thing of wonder; an orange, girdled about with golden ribbon and studded with cloves. The wonder of it is that Kitty made it for her. She calls it a *pomander*, Ada calls Kitty *fancy*. Kitty laughs and Ada does too.

Wanting to look at her gift uninterrupted, Ada takes it to the nursery. The room remains dank and cobwebby, but it is no longer freezing. The china dolls are still sly and the rocking horse still sneers, but the room does not unsettle Ada as much now. The bed has been made and the fire lit, although it burns woefully, as if the flames are lying low.

Ada takes the pomander to the window and opens the casement to give the cobwebs an airing. She turns the fruit in her hands, closes her eyes and inhales citrus and clove, which, she thinks, will forever be the scent of happiness.

If Ada was paying attention, she might have heard the door to the room softly open, she might have glanced behind her and seen the approaching figure—

A blow is struck.

Ada falls.

The orange falls too. While Ada collapses on the dusty rug, the fruit, dropped from her hand, topples out through the casement window. The orange lies stunned on the hard-packed snow a moment, then begins to dither along the terrace. At some point it turns and, gathering speed, sets off across the wide white sweep of the lawn.

*

Ada wakes to darkness and the familiar smell of beeswax. At first, she thinks she might be dead, tucked up tight in a coffin. But if so, there is something wrong with the positioning of her arms; held straight up, not by her side, palms together.

'Wakey-wakey.'

She smells stale breath, tobacco and port wine. At the lattice is Woodgate's eye.

'Right, now. Séance is about to start. Nella is going to tell Mama she is happy in the otherworld and that Mama ought to marry Mr Woodgate, who is a good egg. Got it?'

The eye disappears, to be replaced by Madam Bellerose's mouth. 'You'll use the planchette this time, not your bloody soup. Mind your spelling.'

'You don't understand,' says Ada weakly. 'There is a real ghost here in the house.'

The mouth purses and then disappears.

There is a brief discussion outside the table, the two voices low and hissy.

The mouth is replaced by the eye.

'What do you mean?'

'I didn't write in the soup, the ghost did.'

Woodgate's eye widens and disappears.

The voices again. Madam Bellerose's has an edge of panic, Woodgate's a tone of gruff reassurance.

His voice, loud and near. 'Is this some kind of funny business?'

'No! I never lie!'

'If there's funny business,' spits Woodgate, '*this* happens.'

The lattice slides shut. The darkness is crushing. After what seems like the longest time the lattice slides open again. Ada pushes her nose to it, greedily inhaling.

Beyond the table, frantic mutterings, then the two voices are silenced by the opening of the door. Ada waits. Her ears sharpen. She hears the small clank that is Madam Bellerose taking a nip from her hipflask. The slight scrabble that is Madam Bellerose placing the planchette with its pencil ready on the table top. The hushed shuffling as the others take their seats. The faint hiss as the candles are snuffed.

Ada peers out at their legs, recognising despite the dim: Lady Bentham's black gown, Reverend Toop's scrawny calves, Woodgate's knee, hopping with impatience, and the stubborn bulk of Madam Bellerose, feet planted.

Madam Bellerose will be smiling at each of the sitters in turn.

Now Ada hears her voice, muffled but still audible. The mysterious voice she reserves for speaking about the dead. Not the voice she uses to harangue Ada, order up trotters, or carouse with her fellow lags. Madam Bellerose begins by imparting the sitters' duties. They are to stay seated and holding hands, refrain from shouting out or breaking the circle. They may ask the spirits questions when prompted by herself and only then. The spirits, via Madam Bellerose, have multiple means with which to communicate with the living: tapping, tilting and writing. Madam Bellerose cordially draws the sitters' attention to the planchette, an ingenious apparatus which allows the dead to scribe for themselves. Madam Bellerose will accept no responsibility for any disturbances, breakages or damage to persons or property. Following a sitting, she warns, there may be either an increase or decrease in supernatural activity.

'Shall we begin?'

Silence. For ages.

Madam Bellerose is letting the tension grow. She takes a deep breath and lets it out slowly. Soon she will enter the trance state, her eyes open just a sliver, barely breathing.

She calls upon the spirits to make contact.

Madam Bellerose is jaunting along marvellously. She has started with lesser spirits: a hooded monk who haunts the rhododendron dell, a heartbroken soldier and a nameless old lady who frequents the fireside chair in the drawing room. Lady Bentham identifies her as Dear Grandmama. Suggestions for the efficient running of the estate are shared, a recipe for fruit cobbler is imparted. The sitters pay all this no mind; everyone is waiting for Eleanor.

Madam Bellerose falls silent, and then, 'There is someone else here, they are coming through from the realm beyond. I can't quite see you, dear. Come forward into the light, that's right. Who have we here? A little one?'

A gasp from the direction of Lady Bentham.

'Yes, dear?' Madam Bellerose is listening carefully to the dead. 'You want to give us a name? Five letters? A five-lettered name. Can you spell it out, dear? In your own time, poppet.'

Above, four pairs of eyes are fixed upon the planchette.

A fog has drifted into the library almost imperceptibly. It draws in around the table and the circle of people holding hands. Ada, looking out, realises that she can no longer see the shapes of the sitters' legs. The pedestal, and therefore her compartment, is engulfed. What's more, the fog seems to be glowing, as if by moonlight. Ada watches, enthralled, as a wisp comes curling in through the lattice. It winds gently around her outstretched arms and brushes along her fingers as they rest on the mechanism that controls the planchette. Ada, unable to run from the fog, succumbs.

A laughing girl holds a charming toy. A magical ball as from a fairy tale, as round as an orange, as perfect as the sun – as golden as her hair in the sun. The sun that might thaw the snow, but it is nearly Christmas and there must be snow. It is her birthday and there should be snow. She throws the ball higher and higher. It spins and sparkles. She dances with it out across the lawn, down the slope, loving the cold air on her face and the crunch underfoot. Only her footprints in this bright frozen world. She misses a catch and the ball rolls down the path and under the gate. The girl gives chase. Ignoring the calls of the nanny, the gardener, she bolts through the gate and out into the wide-open space of the marshland, benign under the sun-dazzled sky. A place of wading birds, waving reeds, low hillocks, rushes rustling, greedy pools, sucking earth, the closing of the day, hot panic, missed footing, the winter moon, dead calm.

Madam Bellerose asks again, 'Can you spell it out?'

The fog considers, Ada smiles in the dark, the planchette moves.

BILLY

Later Ada will overhear the footman talking, for wasn't he standing at his post just outside the library door? As far as he gathered, after the ghost wrote, the few candles that remained lit blew out and the planchette took flight, clobbering two of the party senseless and knocking a third's spectacles to kingdom come until all three ran from the library. A lamp was lit and with trepidation the butler went in. There, sitting at the table, happy as you like, were Lady Bentham and Miss Ada, holding hands.

The doctor was called. The London medium lost her front teeth and Mr Woodgate had a broken nose for his trouble. The language from him wasn't that of a gentleman. The language from her wasn't that of a lady or a gentleman. The pair were asked to leave sharpish.

On Christmas morning, when a fresh fall of snow has made the world pristine again and the sun dazzles in the bluest of skies, Ada and Lady Bentham walk down the terrace. They take a turn through the ornamental garden and cross the lawn to the gate in the wall. The old gardener follows. Ada doesn't have to ask if he's the same gardener who called out to headstrong Nella as she ran after her golden ball. He nods to Ada with a strange air of recognition.

Lady Bentham gives the order and the gardener opens the gate.

Her ladyship shivers to see the frozen marshland before her but Ada takes her hand. Even with the new drift Ada can make out the track marks that lead under the gate and onwards.

The object they are looking for is surprisingly far from the wall. Lady Bentham credits Ada with supernaturally keen eyes to have seen it from the nursery window. Ada mumbles something about the glint of gold ribbon. The pomander is returned to her and its whereabouts carefully marked. The sexton and the stoutest-hearted servants will stand by for the first sign of thaw.

In the great hallway eight candles are lit on the spruce tree, one for each year of Eleanor.

⁂

Ada and Lady Bentham work in companionable silence in the library. There is much to do. Ada has been practising with the planchette at the Psychical Table. Adjustments have been made for her: there is no longer a secret compartment.

Lady Bentham is at her desk. She is writing a treatise on otherworldly communication to rival Reverend Toop's.

A soft knock and Kitty is standing in the doorway. She still wears a holly sprig; although they all know it doesn't dissuade the spirits, Kitty says she feels the better for it.

'The sexton has arrived, your ladyship.'

Lady Bentham puts down her pen and rises stiffly; she has got older waiting for the spring. She holds out her hand to Ada, who comes to her side. 'She might leave us.'

'She might.'

Lady Bentham nods. 'Then I am ready. What of you, Ada Lark? Will you haunt awhile?'

Ada smiles.

Kitty is sure to hold the door open behind them, although in truth, it's been a clear morning up at Hadlow Hall.

JENKIN

Catriona Ward

I named him that when I was small. Where the name came from, I don't know. Perhaps we had a cat or a yard man called Jenkin at the time. I'm not like Vera, who loved our gardeners and remembered each one. I don't know what Jenkin is or where he came from or anything about him except that he has followed me all my life. I see him in the corner of my eye, slipping around baseboards and through gaps in drapes. In my childhood he would weave through the railings of the school yard. Now he scurries between the bar stools of the Bagatelle in the Village, avoiding dancers' legs with ease. His paws make no sound on the cracked floor.

The particular thing about Jenkin was this: he only appeared when I told a lie, or was otherwise behaving in a deceitful manner. Now, was it Jenkin who caused me to be untruthful? Or was he drawn by the untruth itself – attracted to its scent, like a hungry child outside a bakery on a cold morning? Mama always said that lying was the worst sin. Vera has never lied in her life, I think, but I can't seem to help it.

He is roughly the size of a house cat, but his body is more like that of a river otter, long and sinuous yet somehow thick, too. At the top of his neck, however, is a likeness of a human head – though crudely rendered in brown fur. Sometimes the Jenkin-face has whiskers and a snout, sometimes it is very human-looking with a small pert nose not unlike mine.

It might sound strange, but for most of my life I never thought too much about Jenkin, unless he was actually visible. We don't tend to question what we have grown up with.

My mother died in the November of 1948. So at the cold, linty, pocket-end of the year Vera and I found ourselves packing up the house where we had lived all our lives. If there's anything sadder than putting the affairs of the dead to rights on a cold November afternoon in Poughkeepsie, I don't know about it. There was no time to spare – the house was already sold, being in a nice location for the downtown stores and so on, and with a smooth green lawn which had been my mother's pride and joy, and a cherry tree that spilled out a white veil of blossom like a bride each spring. Even in the cold, dead part of the year you could tell it was a happy place. The only thing that ever marred the peace here were the fights between me and Vera. It's difficult to be a sister. My mother despaired of us. She used to say, 'One day I'll be dead, and you'll only have each other.' It didn't seem possible at the time that this would ever come to pass. But here we were.

We tried to remember that we had had our turn, and now it was time for another family to have theirs, for children to run in the halls again. Our mother's illness had been long. Maybe the house itself wanted a new life.

Vera and I clung to Mother's dresses and wept. All that first day we could do nothing at all but cry and hold one another. 'I don't want to put her away,' said Vera, stroking her cranberry-coloured winter wool.

'Neither do I,' I said, 'but it's time.'

'What will happen to us, Maggie?' Vera, at nineteen, was two years younger than me. She had always been dreamy and looked to me for decisions.

'We've talked about this,' I said with more confidence than I felt. 'We will have the money from the house. We will go to New York and be secretaries. We are young and ready to work hard, and there is a great demand for businessmen to have personal secretaries.

'But we do not type or know how to file things.'

'We will learn. I have booked us two places at Miss Alperton's school on Madison Avenue. We can stay with Cousin Charlotte. After three months we will be efficient and organised and employable. Won't it be fun, maybe?'

Mama had been so old-fashioned. She moved through the house to the slight creak of her corsets. The house had always felt like a place out of time, and I wanted to be part of it all. Even in my sadness I felt such longing in the pit of me – for brilliant lights and Broadway musicals, and Perry Como concerts and walking in Central Park. These things felt like a cord on my bellybutton drawing me towards the city, sometimes painfully.

Vera whispered, 'Cousin Charlotte always raps me over the knuckles with her soup spoon.'

'We only need stay with her until we're settled,' I said. 'Then we'll get a place of our own. Two city girls!'

'I want to stay here, at home.'

'Well, we can't, as I have explained a hundred times.' I was overwrought and exasperated, and she shrank from me, her eyes big and scared, as though she thought I would hit her. Vera feels too much human contact like an injury, whereas I am just the opposite.

After Papa's death we found that he had plunged all the money into exciting ventures – dentures for dogs was one, as I recall. Another was a project to bury armaments in holes all over the country in case of another civil war. Mama was already ill by then, so she never really knew the extent of it. We didn't want to trouble her and there was always the thought in my mind that something would turn up when the time came. In the end I had been forced to make it turn up, and I still wasn't sure I had done right. It was difficult, I was discovering, to be the head of the family, to make decisions for others. Though looking at Vera's pale face, I could see it was just as hard to have decisions made for you. I felt sorry and hugged my sister. After a little hesitation she hugged me back.

'Can I go to the cherry tree?' she whispered into my ear.

'All right,' I said, as gently as I could. 'But no climbing, Vera.'

The cherry tree leaned over the fence from the neighbours' yard. When we were children, my mother was angry about it because the branches spread shadows over the south-west corner of the lawn in the summer, which made the grass scant and poor. She was always trying to get the neighbours to cut it down. But then Vera struck up a friendship with their son, Alec, which turned to being sweethearts, and Mother had to leave it be. Getting her daughter married was more important than good grass, I guess.

Now Vera smiled her most secret smile. 'Mother won't know if I climb,' she said. 'Come on, Maggie. Just once. I loved climbing that tree. I don't know why you decided I couldn't, all of a sudden.'

'That tree's not safe,' I snapped. 'You know that. Why must you be so exhausting?'

I tried to ignore the dark stirring from the corner. Jenkin looked at me from the shadows with my face. My eyes were as yellow as buttercups in his dark fur.

Vera's face collapsed like a pushed peach and I felt awful again.

That night Vera and I slept in Mama's bed, curled up in one another like cats, breathing the last of her perfume from the sheets. Well, Vera slept. I lay awake and stared at the ceiling, watching all the choices that had brought us here run across the ceiling like a map of fire.

Alec and Vera were the kind of sweethearts who Mama never worried about leaving alone together, because all they'd do was giggle and blush. Alec was a sunny kind of boy. But then he went to war. He said he'd be back for Vera. But when he did come back, he was all hollowed out inside. He didn't talk much any more but he'd stare.

Not at people, but at objects – a passing bus or the sugar bowl. I asked him once what he was doing and he told me, 'Counting things.' It was how he kept the thoughts of death at bay, he said. He counted the sugar cubes, clouds in the sky, buttons on my dress. He spent a lot of time on those buttons.

It was me who found him, hanging from a branch of the cherry tree. On our side, too, feet dangling above Mother's spoiled lawn. It was spring and the blossom was just out. Translucent petals were pasted to his still face. I thank God every day that Vera was away on a visit to a friend and not due back until the next day. They had cut him down and taken him away by then.

We told Vera that Alec had died in an accident. She cried for weeks. But I felt relief, and saw it mirrored in my mother's face. Alec hadn't been himself since the war. That sunny boy had been gone for a long time.

I saw Alec's protruding purple tongue every time I looked at the cherry tree. I smelled the mess he made in his pants. I was glad Vera didn't have to know all that too. But we never let her climb the cherry tree, after it happened. And *that's all folks*, as they say on *Looney Tunes*. Sometimes I say it out loud to myself, if I am frightened. *That's all folks!*

I wish we had a television. I love the television. There was a big set in the window of Marshalls on Main Street. I would stand in front of it for hours, that last, sweltering hot summer before Mother's death, watching Betty Crocker or *The Kate Smith Hour*. Maybe we could afford to rent a little set of our own, I thought, once we got settled in New York. I looked forward to it with an almost carnal pleasure.

The next day was a little better; at least Vera and I felt able to get on with the actual business of packing. In the morning we cleaned out the vast pantry, threw away all Mama's stores of preserves and pickles. The new owners wanted the place empty.

In the afternoon we folded china tenderly in newspaper. It was all to be sold separately. I love china, and always feel it is something like a person in its nature, being so brave and breakable. We were wrapping my favourite set, the rosebud set, when I saw that Vera had stopped and was staring at the newspaper in her hand.

'Vera,' I said gently, 'let's not dawdle.'

'But Maggie,' she said. 'Look at this.' She held up a handwritten letter which had been concealed in the folds of the *Poughkeepsie Argus.*

The writing looked familiar. *Sandrine*, I thought, my breath frozen in my throat. I lunged and tore the pages from Vera's hands.

'Maggie! What are you doing?'

When I looked at the letter my heart slowed its hammer blows. It was not what I had feared. It was not from her after all. And I could see that it had been caught between the pages of a knitting pattern – Mother always loved those. She must have folded up the paper absent-mindedly when called away by some task or visitor and the letter sat there, concealed, until Vera took up the newspaper to wrap the china.

The letter was dated some six months before.

Dear cousin,

I know there was disagreement between you and me, but I would like to extend the hand of friendliness. I have heard that you are not well, and I know that your daughters will have nowhere to go when you are gone. Forgive my bluntness. There is no point trying to talk around such matters. The point is, that I will offer Vera, at least, a home. I await your reply.

Your cousin
Eliza Ellis

There was only a mailbox at the top of the letter. 'Post Office, Box 6264, Cary, Maine.'

'Don't you see?' Vera said. 'It's Mama, looking after us.'

'I don't think—'

'How did I come to take up that piece of newspaper, among all the others? And look at the numbers, Maggie! She was sixty-four when she died. And six was her favourite number, and there are two of us!'

'Oh Vera . . .' It was useless to argue with her when she began focusing on the numbers. It was a habit she had picked up from Alec in those late days.

'Don't say I am being silly. Don't.' Her petal-like mouth crumpled. 'We aren't meant to be secretaries, Maggie. Family is more important.'

I leant forward and took her hand. 'All right. Let's at least write to her.' I thought there would be no chance of getting a reply before we were due to take up our rooms on 59th Street and start the secretarial course in two weeks' time. Probably having received no reply, this cousin would have changed her mind, or moved or something. So it was only a three-cent stamp and it would come to nothing.

When Vera was eating her lunch I flipped through the rest of the pile of newspapers we had set aside for packing. But there were no other letters hidden in the pages, from Sandrine or anyone else, and I could not quite tell whether that made me happy or not.

Of course, part of my desire to go to the city was Sandrine. I knew she had gone there, after it all happened. I also knew how unlikely it was I would find her. She was probably married by now. Or dead, maybe.

Ten days later, as the removal men were taking away the piano and the rest of the drawing room furniture, I stood in a cloud of dust and surprise, reading the letter from Cousin Eliza.

I had not expected that you would both come. However, I understand that Vera cannot really travel alone. So I will wire the money for the train.

I put the letter into the pocket of my overalls and decided not to say anything about it to Vera. What was the good, after all? The plans were already made, we weren't about to go off to Maine at a moment's notice, for goodness' sake.

'Shut up,' I said to Jenkin, who was slipping in and out of the packing cases, making a sound like a kettle.

Jenkin looked at me and hissed, and I suddenly realised I had never heard him make a sound before.

I woke in the night with a hand about my throat. I gasped and thrashed. Each finger pressed on my windpipe like a vice.

'You weren't going to tell me,' Vera said in my ear, 'about the reply from Cousin Eliza.'

I wheezed; I could see stars and red flame on the air. 'Let me go,' I mouthed. 'Let me go.' Darkness clouded about me and I felt myself sinking, before the small, strong hand released its grip.

Vera got up from the mattress where we slept (the beds had been taken yesterday) and went to stand by the curtainless window. She was a black shape against the stars. I stood and came to her slowly.

'Do you – do you go through my things?' I asked. A peculiar buzzing had begun in my head. 'Have you gone mad? You snoop. What gave you the right to do *that*?' I pushed her hard in the chest, and she gasped and fell, hitting the boards hard with a crack.

'Vera,' I said, anxious. 'Oh goodness, Vera, I'm so sorry. I didn't mean it.'

Vera got up, rubbing the back of her neck. 'Why must you always lie? To get people to do what you want them to do?' She came close. 'I'm sorry I hurt you. But you hurt me first. It's not like it was, Maggie. There's no Mama to keep the peace between us. All we have now is one another.' She poked me in the collarbone with a sharp nail. 'You have made sure of that. And here's the thing: if we don't go to Maine, I'll never speak to you again. I'll live with you, sure. I'll eat with you and go to that awful secretary course, and in front of other people I'll talk. But at home when it's just the two of us, you'll just live in silence, long silence, for ever, until you go mad *just like me.*'

I took a deep breath. 'All right. Compromise?' I tried to make my voice like Mother's. It always used to calm Vera down when she used that word.

Vera nodded sullenly and I felt a whistle of relief inside me.

'We'll go to Maine,' I said. 'For the winter only, all right? Save some money. Then in the spring we'll come back to the city.' I looked for Jenkin but he was nowhere to be found, so I realised that I must be telling the truth.

She looked at me, dark eyes resentful, and I held my breath.

'All right,' she said. 'That's a fair compromise.'

I felt the umbilical cord that bound me to the city draw tight and burning, and then snap. *I'll be with you*, I promised New York. I won't let the north country take me. Because I knew, of course, that this might be Vera's intention – once we were up there, there could be a hundred obstacles preventing our return.

'I hate the city.' Vera began to cry. 'I can't stand it, everyone all pressed in together like corned beef.'

'Oh,' I said, shaken. 'Don't cry, don't. Come and cuddle up. It's cold.'

She crawled underneath my blanket, grateful and shivering.

Penn Station was a haze of steam and shouting. We found our seats and unpacked our sandwiches. Cousin Eliza had wired enough for the tickets, no more, and we couldn't afford the restaurant car. I touched the newspaper-wrapped package I had stowed in my purse for luck. I thought I deserved at least a small memento of our old life, and by the time the new owners noticed that the rosebud tea set was missing a cup, we would be well away.

The train wound north from New York City. Vera sat very still and upright, watching the land pass by. I knew her feelings were deep. It was a week until Christmas: it would be our first away from home – our first without a home.

'Maggie,' Vera said as we sped through New Hampshire, 'I have never asked you exactly how Alec died. But actually, I would like you to tell me.'

I looked at her in surprise.

'With Mama gone,' Vera said, 'we're the grown-ups now. So I'm going to act like one. And that means looking things in the face.'

'It doesn't matter how, V,' I said softly, taking her hand to soften the blow. 'I'm sorry. It was the war. It took so many, even after it was over. But you are being very grown up.'

I felt a tug on my skirt. A soft brown paw had reached out

from beneath my seat. All five claws were hooked into my woollen skirt. But that was not what alarmed me. I could see the dirty boards of the train carriage under my foot. I could see it *through* my shoe, through my foot, as though for a moment I was transparent as glass.

I screamed and shook myself loose. The paw vanished.

'What is it, Maggie?' Vera cried.

'I caught my skirt on a nail,' I said and bent over. Jenkin was crouched beneath my seat, eyes burning like sulphur.

Not all lies are bad, I hissed at him under the noise of the train.

At a tiny station after Portland we stopped, and everyone got out on the platform and walked, their breath white gauze in the freezing air. The land around was all rushes and lakes and the sea creeping inland with long fingers. It would be beautiful in the summer, no doubt, but it seemed a cursed place now, a place from which all life and light were banished, under a grey strangling cloud.

Then the sun came out from behind a cloud and the snow gleamed white as a bridal veil and the setting sun gleamed red on the water and it seemed the most beautiful place I'd ever seen, for a moment, just a moment – before the world was plunged back under a mantle of cloud.

Vera and I made our way to the washrooms at the end of the platform. A woman stood at the entrance to the ladies', hands on her hips as though to make herself bigger. She wore wool pants and a long coat, and I had a vague memory of having seen her on the train. A porter lounged nearby – uncomfortably near this location, I thought.

'They're being cleaned,' the woman in the wool pants said, though she had to tell us twice, her accent was so strange.

'Oh,' Vera said, uncomfortable. 'Well, we can wait.'

Then the woman said, 'They're out of order, being fixed.'

'I thought they were being cleaned?' I said sharply.

'Out of order.'

At that moment a scream, the like of which I have never heard, pierced the air. It was ragged, high, a needle to the ear, barely human. It came from inside the washroom. The fierce woman threw herself against the door, pounding on it. 'Oh darling,' she cried. 'Let me in. Let me help!' The scream rose in pitch and fury until I thought my skull would crack. 'Billy' – she turned to the porter – 'break it down!' Suddenly the porter sprang into action and hurled himself at the door. It felt like we were at that part of a play where people who had previously seemed strangers are shown to know one another.

I took Vera's arm and hurried her away, back onto the train. The high, unearthly wailing followed us through the cold dusk, punctuated by the cracking of wood as the door gave way. It felt too dangerous to look back.

The car that met us at Augusta Union Station was a Studebaker, a car I happen to admire very much. The woman who jumped out to help with our bags was a little younger than Mama had been – strong, grey-haired, wearing pants – it seemed to be the fashion around here. 'I'm your cousin Ellis,' she said, friendly. 'Eliza's such a fussy name. You girls cold? There are rugs in the back.'

She whistled as she put our bags in the trunk, and I couldn't help feeling smug because I had had her pegged for a whistler the moment I saw her.

The seats were white and red leather, and the radio was tuned to something jaunty and new. Ellis drove very fast along the icy roads. 'Got to get there before the snow,' she said when I protested, and went back to whistling along to the radio. As we went further from town we lost the station and it turned to static. Ellis turned it off, and it felt very quiet with just us three and the engine, as we sped along the shore, the sun a bare rim of gold over the sea to the west.

Cary sits at the inmost tip of one of the deep, narrow bays that cut the edges of the Maine coastline into ragged fronds, like a pea on the point of a knife. Some windows were lit, as we drove through the town, but these were soon lost in the dark behind.

We turned off the road between two gateposts, up a gravel drive, to be met with a blaze of light. The house was large and it seemed like every window was afire. There was an evergreen wreath on the door. Inside the warm hall, by a curving staircase, was a Christmas tree. Vera made a small sound of delight in her throat.

'You'll be tired,' Ellis said. 'I'll show you up to your rooms.'

'We want to share,' Vera said. 'We're used to it.'

'Surely not. You will need your own space, two young ladies like you.'

'We will share,' I said firmly.

'Sixteen stairs,' Vera whispered to me as we followed Ellis up. 'That's a very lucky number, Maggie!'

Our room was wallpapered with a pattern of cheerful yellow flowers, and the twin beds were made up with yellow and cream linen. The drapes were heavy, rich and thick, made of gold brocade. Vera and I hovered uncertainly. Everything matched everything else and we felt out of place.

After Ellis had said goodnight I unwrapped the rosebud teacup and put it on the dresser. It sat there, pretty and loving like Mother, a reminder of her and of home. Then Vera and I crept into one of the single beds and, clinging together, fell into an uneasy sleep.

I was locked in the privy with Sandrine, and when I looked down I saw that the floor was rising slowly, slowly towards the ceiling. The door was locked and no one would come, despite our screaming. Soon there was not enough room to stand upright and we were forced to tip our heads to the side. Then we were bent double, crouched and folded up like jackknives, and then the ceiling and the floor closed together and we were being crushed. I heard the crack of Sandrine's bones breaking.

I awoke to the sound of someone screaming very loud and near, and it was me. Vera was shaking me. Sun streamed in at the windows. 'It's all right,' Vera said over and over. I stretched cautiously, my limbs exploring their freedom with relief.

That morning Cary House was full of that northern sea-light you get up in those parts. In the daylight, we could see that the house sat on a promontory and that the ocean surrounded it on three sides. There was no beach and only one lonely deep-water mooring, the rock dropping away abruptly into the lashing waves.

Eventually we found the breakfast table and Ellis in a sunlit parlour. She seemed to have made a good start without us. Her plate was covered in crumbs and dark smears of blueberry jelly.

She gestured to our places and we sat tentatively. It is intimate, eating with someone for the first time, and breakfast in particular can be so awkward, everyone half awake and not knowing who needs the cream.

Ellis handed me a newspaper and mindlessly I riffled through the pages.

'Why do you always do that, Maggie?' Vera asked suddenly.

'What?'

'Flick all through the paper like that before you read it.'

'I'm eccentric, I suppose.'

'I find talk at breakfast an obstacle to digestion,' Cousin Ellis said, and I lapsed gratefully into silence. For a time there was no sound but the munching of English muffins.

When Vera had finished her last bite Cousin Ellis nodded, as if at a signal.

'You will want to work,' she said, certain. 'There is wood to be chopped – can you do that?'

We shook our heads, miserable.

'You should learn. Hearty young women like you! Theo can teach you. What about mending?'

Vera brightened and nodded. 'I'm good with a needle,' she said.

I looked at my hand – for a terrible moment, I could have sworn I could see the butter dish through it, and the brightly coloured tablecloth. 'I'm disappearing,' I said stupidly.

'What?' Ellis's glance was sudden and sharp.

'I will learn to split logs,' I said.

An amiable red-cheeked boy of about twenty poked his head into the room. 'Shall I clear?'

'Yes please, Theo,' said Ellis. 'And take Maggie here with you. She needs to learn outdoor tasks.'

Theo was actually a fairly good teacher, as these things go.

'Don't aim for the top of the log,' he advised. 'Aim for the base. Like the axe has already split it in two, get it?'

'Thanks,' I said. 'What's Ellis like?'

'The boss, you mean? She's all right. Fair.'

I gave up. Men never know how to describe people properly. You need a woman for that.

The axe cleft the log with a crack, showing the vulnerable white flesh within. 'That's all, folks!' I yelled.

*

I took the logs to the store, pleased with my efforts. My hair was a bird's nest and I was perspiring freely, but I felt better than I had done in months. Perhaps Vera had been right. This would be good for us.

I threw my armful onto the pile and was turning to go when I was stopped by an eerie sound. The log store held some of the heating pipes that ran throughout the house – I could hear voices. Metallic and hollow though they sounded, I realised I could hear Ellis and Vera talking in the living room upstairs.

I moved quietly closer to the pipes.

'I miss her,' Vera was saying. 'And Maggie will never talk about it, because she thinks *she* is my mother now. But she is *not*.'

'I'm sorry,' Ellis said, sounding sad. 'When my own mother died I felt it like a wound in my side.'

'We used to be friends, but all Maggie does is this, now, like this, like this, this . . .' I could tell Vera was making that face I hated, which was supposed to mimic my expression. I caught her doing it behind my back sometimes.

Ellis was laughing. 'Oh come, now. Surely she has friends.'

'None to speak of,' Vera replied. 'She had some kind of trouble at school, some kind of reputation, I'm not sure what exactly. She never formed any lasting bonds. Or had a beau. Not like me.'

'You're a fine-looking girl,' Ellis said. There was quiet for a time and I suppose they were stitching.

'The thing is, Vera,' Ellis said in a rush, 'you must not

rely on Maggie too heavily, or take her as an example. Do you understand?'

'Why?'

'She is unnatural. Did your mother ever speak of a woman named Sandrine?'

'No.'

'Oh,' said Ellis, flustered. 'Well, never mind. It was something your mother once said . . . but maybe I misunderstood.' There was a lurch of dread in my heart. It's true that sneaks never hear any good of themselves, but this was worse. Ellis knew about me.

I strained closer, but Ellis and Vera seemed to have moved into another room or maybe didn't feel like talking, for there was only quiet after that.

I heard a scratching noise, and a long, mean, thin brown tail raised itself from within the log pile. It formed the shape of a question mark.

'Oh shut up,' I said. 'I was eavesdropping, that's not the same as lying.'

Jenkin smiled and I saw his fangs gleam white below his yellow eyes in the dim. And I saw that my hand, where I steadied myself on a log, was for a moment transparent – the ghostly outline of a hand. A chill ran through me.

'What is happening to me?' I said quietly. I had no expectation of an answer.

'You're doing it to yourself, Maggie.' The voice seemed to come from the air, from all about. It was gentle, elderly, like a kind grandpa. I wondered wildly where in this log store there could possibly be an older gentleman concealed, when I saw with horror that Jenkin's little snout was moving with the speech. He was not speaking, precisely – the voice was from everywhere – but they were his words.

I gasped and backed away a step or two. 'I didn't know you could talk,' I said at last.

'I couldn't, before.' The kindly voice filled me, the spaces within me. It was horrible. 'But I get stronger with each of your deceptions. And you get thinner and thinner. Soon there will be nothing of you left.'

'And what will happen then?'

'I take your place,' Jenkin said. He licked a paw and drew it over his ear like a cat.

I saw then that, beneath the fur, Jenkin's face had changed. His chin had narrowed, and he had a new dark patch on his jaw, just like the mole on my chin.

I screamed and ran, my feet slipping on the icy ground.

Christmas Day dawned dark and stormy. Vera gave Ellis some gloves she had knitted. Ellis gave us each an embroidery frame. I had nothing to give, not being a knitter.

The tree was rich with ribbons and gold baubles. We had never had such a display at home; Mama had preferred homely ways of celebrating, like figgy pudding.

Theo proved to be a very good cook: the goose was done well, there was some sage and orange sauce, very good also, as was the wine. No one spoke to me, but I couldn't have paid attention if they had. My mind worked feverishly on

Jenkin and what he had said. I kept thinking I saw his dark ears peeping around a doorway, or from behind the couch.

'Are you all right, Maggie?' Ellis asked distantly, the third time I grabbed my own knee to make sure I was still there.

He could not possibly really replace me, could he? But then – a talking otter with my face couldn't really appear every time I told a lie, could it? My best hope was that I had some kind of madness or was in the midst of a breakdown. I had never really worried about the problem of Jenkin's existence until now. Because I never spoke about him, it hadn't mattered whether he was real or not. He was as real as my thoughts of Sandrine late on a summer night, for example, and just as implausible.

I longed, not for the first time, for Mama to materialise and solve my problems. Then I remembered what she had told Ellis about me and I felt, for an instant, so furiously angry with my dead mother that I thought I might faint.

The day seemed to last for ever, in that particular way Christmas often does. In the early evening Theo said goodnight and went, gratefully no doubt, to his own celebrations. We sang one or two dreary carols, Vera picking daintily at the baby grand. At about eight o'clock I thought it would be acceptable to make my way to bed. Vera and Ellis were whispering on the couch opposite. Through the window the lights of Cary could be seen twinkling in the distance, over the water.

'Yes, all right,' Ellis said, without looking at me. 'I have always wanted a daughter to leave all this to,' I heard her tell Vera in a low voice.

I went upstairs. In our room, however, there were only Vera's things. My clothes and hairbrush and books were gone.

I went back downstairs.

'Oh, yes,' Ellis said. 'I thought it would be best for you to each have your own room. I am sure you could do with the space. You're in the blue bedroom now, Maggie.'

'But I don't want to be without Vera,' I said.

'You and Vera need to be separated,' Ellis said gently. 'Perhaps this excessive closeness is partly why you've turned out as you have, Maggie. Either way, you are a poison to your little sister. So Vera will stay here, and you will leave.'

'But where would I go?' I asked, stupid. Things were happening fast and my insides were unsteady, like the time I took the tilt-a-whirl at the fair.

'That's not my concern,' Ellis said.

'Wait,' Vera said. Her eyes burned with some feeling. 'You will send Maggie away?'

'It's for the best,' Ellis told her. 'If your sister fights me on this I will be forced to inform authorities about her nature.'

'We'll both stay,' I said desperately.

'You're not welcome, Maggie,' Ellis said. 'Theo will drive you to Augusta tomorrow.'

'I won't go,' I said. 'I won't leave Vera.'

'You'd better go, Maggie,' said Vera, her face closed to me. 'All you do is lie anyway. I can always tell.'

'Vera, don't do this!' I felt the pull of loss, followed by anger.

'Why shouldn't I?' Vera yelled.

'All I've ever done is try to protect you!' Out of habit my

eyes scanned the room for Jenkin, but he was not there. 'Can we talk?' I asked. 'Alone?'

'No,' said Vera. I felt a crown of shame hot around my head. Fighting in front of people is almost as intimate as breakfast.

I seized Vera's arm and pulled her behind me, out of the living room.

'What are you doing?' cried Ellis, running after us, but I slammed the door in her face and turned the key in the lock.

Vera snarled at me, but I kept a tight hold on her. 'I have to talk to you,' I said. Ellis was beating on the living room door and shrieking our names. I could hardly hear myself think. 'Come outside.'

The sound of the sea on the rocks was deafening. The wind was up along the shore and it was set to be a wild night. Out on the tip of the promontory I could hear the bare branches of the silver birches whip the air. Even in the lee of the house, the ground was frozen solid as iron underfoot, and our breath made white plumes in the air.

Vera wrested her arm free. 'Say what you need to say.'

But I just stood there, dumb.

'That's what I thought,' Vera said. 'You are all mysterious hints and secrets, but you have nothing real to give. Do you know that I am in Ellis's will? You're not, though.'

I have sometimes wondered whether Vera has her own version of Jenkin. It has always seemed too private a thing to ask, somehow, even between sisters. If she does, I think it shows her other people's truths, instead of her own lies. Vera doesn't lie.

Vera said, 'Ellis loves me. Why would you try to take that away from me, Maggie? You have hardly spoken to me since Mama died. We used to be such good friends. But you shut yourself away from me – no, even before Mama died. Ever since Alec left me you have been distant, not like my sister at all.'

'I – V, I . . .' But I could not go on. I stared at her, helpless.

'Fine,' hissed Vera. 'I don't want to see you again. And I am keeping the rosebud teacup.'

I don't recall moving towards her, only that a moment later my teeth were in her arm. Vera beat me about the head and screamed. We tore at one another's clothing, at each other's hair. She bloodied my nose and I bent her little finger back until she wept. We rolled around on the icy ground, hitting and snarling like fighting dogs.

Eventually we rolled apart, panting and exhausted.

'Who is Sandrine?' Vera's voice was flinty hard.

'I don't know what you mean.' In the lit window of the hall, I saw Jenkin's face appear. It looked like he was laughing. He had my teeth, one slightly overlapping the other at the front. 'All right,' I said savagely. 'I'll tell you.'

I got up from the hard ground and offered Vera a hand. After a moment of suspicion she took it.

'I'm cold,' she said.

'I know somewhere we can go.'

*

Vera looked dubiously around at the log store but took a seat on a roundel of larch.

'Sandrine is the girl who used to deliver our milk and newspapers,' I said. 'I was eighteen, you sixteen. Alec had just come back from the war.'

'I remember that girl, she had black hair,' Vera said confidently. 'I didn't know her name.'

'Yes. She was a refugee from France.' I took a deep breath. 'She and I used to write to one another, in secret. We hid our letters in the newspapers she delivered.'

'Why did you hide them?'

'For fun.' A large yellow eye peered out from a crack in the log pile. Jenkin blinked. 'No. Not for fun. We – liked – each other but we were afraid Mama would not approve.'

Vera's eyes were unblinking as a snake's. 'Unnatural,' she whispered. 'Like Cousin Ellis said.'

'That's what Alec called it too,' I said, feeling my insides squeezed in a vice. 'He found one of our letters. He said he wouldn't tell anyone if Sandrine and I met him under the cherry tree that night.'

'What did he want, Maggie? Why did he want to meet you at night? Even I never met him at night.'

I closed my eyes. I felt Alec's hands once more on my buttons, counting. I thought I wouldn't be able to say it, but I got the words out somehow. 'He wanted to hurt us, V.'

'I don't understand.' Vera's mouth collapsed and I saw she did understand – the sense of it, anyhow.

'He brought rope with him,' I said. 'A noose. But I got free. And then—'

I felt it all again: the rope creaking against the tree branch as Sandrine shoved the noose over his head and pulled it taut, the writhing weight of him as he rose into the air. I ran to add my strength to hers. The hemp burned our palms, Sandrine and I panted as we fought to keep him aloft. The sounds he made, the like of which I never wish to hear again. Cherry blossom falling in drifts through the air, under the light of the half-moon.

'I couldn't let him hurt Sandrine,' I said to Vera. 'I couldn't let him marry you. He would have hurt you too. He was different when he came back from the war, you know he was, V, something went wrong with him.'

'Oh Maggie, what have you done?' Vera whispered. I saw that she was afraid of me. Then something else flickered in her eyes.

I started to turn but it was too late. The last thing I glimpsed was Ellis silhouetted in the doorway, arms raised, before the blow landed and everything winked out in a rain of stars.

When I awoke I thought I was back there again, under the tree, for I was tied. My breath came hard and fast but my scream was no more than a whisper. Then I saw that I was in the larder, at Cary House, and there were no trees, no cherry blossom, no Alec.

'You're awake.'

'Where's Vera?'

'Sleeping. She's had a terrible shock.' Ellis strode into the larder past the rows of beans. She pulled my eyelid up to inspect my pupils. 'You're all right. No concussion. You'll last the night in here.'

'In here?'

'Until I can get into Cary tomorrow morning and have the police called. You're going to prison.' She stilled my protest with a hand. 'No, don't. There's a particular trick of the pipes between the living room and the log store. They act almost like a telephone. I heard it all.'

After everything we had been through, it was this that made me burst into tears. It was such a stupid way to be caught – I should have realised that sound would travel both ways through the pipes.

'I hate you,' I said thickly.

'You killed a man,' Ellis said, 'and you're going to pay for it.'

I couldn't argue with this, because it was true. I cried all the harder, but not for him or what I had done. I cried because I was missing Vera and I was scared of spending the night locked in the larder.

Ellis regarded me, hand on hip. 'Bawl all you want,' she said. 'You are safer locked up. You won't corrupt your sister, or any other law-abiding citizen.'

The door closed gently, shutting out the light. I heard the key turn in the lock. Ellis's footsteps retreated. I beat on the door and cried for Vera. No one answered. I screamed and screamed into the silence. Behind me I heard spiders scuttling startled through the dark, and I felt almost grateful to them, for being alive and here.

Time moved in fits and starts. I was frightened and longed for company, any company. I was screaming, locked in the lavatory at a train station, only no one was trying to break down the door to get to me.

I took a deep shuddering breath. 'Calm, Maggie,' I told myself firmly. 'You'll get nowhere with hysterics.' A thought came to me. 'I am not afraid,' I whispered. 'I am not scared at all!'

Something bigger than a spider moved behind the bags of flour and cans of prunes.

'Jenkin,' I whispered.

'Hello, Maggie.' He came out of the darkness into the thin beam of light admitted through the keyhole. He squinted up at me. His face was flat like a plate now, nothing like mine – or like any living being's. He said sourly, 'You told your secret.'

'I did. I got the better of you.' And even in the midst of everything, my spirits rose.

'Ah well,' he said. 'You'll start lying to those you love again. Humans always do. I'll get you in the end.'

I leant very close to his inhuman face, close enough to kiss. 'Never,' I said and spat in his eye. 'I'm free.'

He yowled and swore and twisted in the narrow light.

'Quiet in there,' said Ellis through the door. A light switch clicked in the kitchen. Darkness fell. I wondered what prison would be like. I felt sorry for myself, that I had thrown off Jenkin's hold only to spend the rest of my life in another kind of cage.

I heard strange sounds in the night, like rushing water and a gagging, choking noise. '*That's all folks!*' I whispered to myself. At last I drifted into an uneasy sleep and those strange sounds filled my dreams, which were of cherry blossom and rope.

I was woken by blinding light. A giant stood in a blazing portal. Then Vera stepped forward and put her arms around me and helped me up. I was so stiff and cold from the floor. I heard a clicking and it took me a moment to realise it was my own teeth chattering.

'Come out now, Maggie,' Vera said.

'Vera,' I said. 'Oh, Vera.' I held her tightly and she wrapped me in her arms. It was like being held by Mother again.

'Where is Ellis?' I said, terrified.

'Hush, don't worry about that. Come and get warm.'

I was distraught to see that the rosebud teacup sat on the kitchen table, broken into three large shards with wicked points.

Vera said, 'Sorry, Maggie. I know you loved it.' She paused and said again, 'I'm sorry.'

'I know. Me too.' We held each other for a moment. 'Where is she?' I asked. Vera made a little high noise in her throat but did not answer.

I picked up the pieces of the rosebud teacup. It was awful

that it was broken. I wondered if I could mend it with glue – but I saw that there was a peculiar rusty stain along one of its sharp edges, which would make an ugly brown seam. I brought it to my nose and breathed the tinny, fleshy scent of old blood.

'Let's throw it into the sea,' Vera said, watching me.

I stood in the balance of the moment, feeling all the decisions I could take stretching away from me into the future. 'Vera,' I said. 'What did you do?'

'She was going to have you locked up, Maggie.' Vera said, putting her arms around me again. Her breath was warm in my ear. 'It was my turn to protect you.'

We stood together in the morning light and threw the shards of china into the cold water.

There was whistling behind us. Theo strode out of the silver birches, a brace of rabbits in his hand. 'Morning,' he called, cheerful. 'Where's Ellis?'

'Gone swimming,' Vera called gaily. I realised, with a thud of sadness, that it was the first lie I had ever heard her tell.

As we made our way back to the house I pretended not to see what followed us, slipping between the bare trunks of the silver birch trees. Vera stopped and clutched my arm. 'There's something stalking us, Maggie,' she said, frightened. 'A creature. A wolf or a fox maybe. Will it attack us?'

'No,' I said, soothing. 'All will be well.' But my voice shook. I tore my eyes from that terrible thing in the trees and hurried her on, trying not to look back. But I had already seen it. Half of Jenkin's face was now mine, and half of it was Vera's. One blue eye, one muddy brown. I felt his mis-matched gaze on us all the way home.

I closed the front door behind us with shaking hands. 'We need to leave this place. Go upstairs and pack.'

Vera shook her head. 'Why? I like it here. Don't worry so, Maggie. Look.' She picked up a note from the hall table. 'Aren't I clever?' It was a note in Ellis's elegant script, saying she had gone for a swim.

'How did you get her to—' I stopped, because I did not want to know.

'Oh, what does it matter?' Vera said gaily. 'No one will ask questions.' I looked at her face, so dear to me, which shone with pride and happiness, and I felt the plummet of despair.

Late that night when she was safely asleep, I went downstairs to the kitchen and sat at the table. I knew he would join me sooner or later. I didn't know what Jenkin was, but I was sure he wouldn't be above gloating.

Sure enough Jenkin faded out of the shadows, melting into being. His eyes were yellow buttercups. The left side of his mouth was formed of Vera's pretty lips, the right of my thin ones.

'Don't follow Vera,' I said to him, pleading. 'She doesn't deserve it.'

'Doesn't she?' His gentle, refined voice. 'You spat in my face, Maggie. Why would I do you a favour?'

'Please,' I said. 'Just you and me, like it's always been. Leave Vera alone.'

'You want to take on all of the lie?' he said. 'Are you sure? Do you know what the price will be if you do that?'

'I can guess.' I closed my eyes so that I couldn't look down to see my knees flickering in and out of existence. 'If you agree, I'll make sure I'm the most interesting person you could ever be. I'll make a life worth living for you, full of experiences and love and danger and joy. You'll love my life; you won't need anything else.'

'Fine,' Jenkin said, shrugging. 'I could enjoy that. I'm fond of you, to be honest. Vera was never as interesting.'

Once the will was proved, Vera inherited everything. I went to New York and she stayed in Maine. Ellis hadn't been entirely wrong – it does us good to have our own space.

Vera and I see each other once or twice a year. Cary has accepted her as Ellis's heir. She lives quietly by the sea, which she loves, and no one crowds her with their presence.

That was all nearly ten years ago – another life, really. I live in an apartment in Greenwich Village. My neighbours are poets, singers and artists. My dreams of Perry Como seem dreadfully suburban now. I love my apartment – it's cosy, with a view over the trees of Christopher Street. Sandrine has the other bedroom for her studio.

We found each other again on my third day as a New Yorker. I went into the Bagatelle, and there she was, sitting at the bar, dreaming with her chin in her hands, legs crossed, one shoe falling off her toe. I touched her lightly on the shoulder and she shivered, all the way through, like she had been rocked by some seismic force. We just looked at one another like that for a time, grinning and kind of stupid.

I suppose it's not so strange that we should both have found ourselves in that establishment, which is for our kind of girl. But it felt like a miracle.

Sandrine sells oddly expensive clay bowls to hotels and millionaires. I am a typist during the day and at night I try to write poetry. Sandrine and I are as good to each other as we know how. Life is new each moment. We are constantly learning to live it. When I sit by the open window on a warm New York evening and listen to the summer crowds below, as Sandrine's wheel hums in the adjoining room, I am filled with a golden light. Sometimes Sandrine helps me with my hair in the mornings, muttering 'Stay still, Marguerite, you bloody impossible woman,' while holding the pins tightly between her lips and I think, *How lucky I am.* And I think of that locked ladies' room at that station in Maine, and how screaming to get out never did anyone any good. You have to fight.

Jenkin has not left my side since Ellis disappeared. His face gets clearer and clearer, his form more human – a gangling version of myself that walks on all fours, which sits in the corners of the apartment, watching me with those yellow eyes which are set in my own face, covered in spiny brown fur. But the eyes grow less and less yellow, and the fur more scant each year – he looks so like me now that sometimes I am quite startled.

As for me, I carry the secret, the lie, for both of us. I grow fainter and fainter, my edges less sure. Some days when I look at my hand, my arm, my bare feet – they are almost completely transparent.

The day will come when Jenkin is my mirror image, and I have faded completely away. *That's all folks!* Jenkin will replace me then – he will slip into my place in the world, he will laugh with Sandrine, eat my dinner, sleep in our bed – and I am afraid, so mortally afraid that no one will be able to tell the difference.

WIDOW'S WALK

Susan Stokes-Chapman

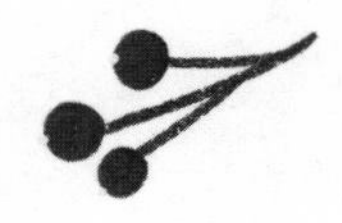

{The Fan} stands as a screen before the
secret whisper of malicious scandal;
expresses the caprices of the heart.

EXTRACT FROM *The Grand Magazine,*
London, November 1760

For Honoria Joseph, proprietress of a prosperous fan shop in a small but affluent town located in the mid-counties of England, the festive period was always a busy time of year. From St Nicholas Day the orders came thick and fast, and Honoria's small band of workers toiled hard to fill them in time for Lord Whiting's annual Yuletide ball on Christmas Eve. Many of her customers had commissioned fans of painted silk, delicate florals or theatre scenes mounted on tortoiseshell and mother-of-pearl, easy enough for Honoria's well-trained girls to create with time to spare; the sticks and guards had been ordered in from the tabletiers, and all they need do was paint the leaves and affix the pleated material to the costly frames. Some orders, however, were of a different persuasion. One such was taking far longer than usual for it was a most special undertaking, and fans of those kind Honoria preferred to create herself.

Honoria closed the heavy shop door against its tinkling bell and locked it tight. Returning the key to her reticule she made her way across the crowded square, its cobbles disguised by a slippery dusting of frost. Though it was only just past four, night had already fallen, and candles flickered brightly in their towering lanterns. Across the way Mrs Moore's confectioner's remained open, as did the milliner Miss Cleeve, their windows adorned with evergreens. Honoria could see the boughs of ivy and spruce through the frosted panes, red ribbons tied prettily to their full and fragrant branches. They hung in Berryman's toy shop too, and as she passed Honoria watched a little girl clutch a curly-haired doll dressed in periwinkle satin, her mother handing a coin to the toymaker over the counter in payment. A vendor selling hot chestnuts near the town hall had drawn an eager crowd, and in the distance the lights of Larkshood Manor twinkled on the hill. It was a charming scene, one that would not have looked out of place on a seasonal print of the sort found in any fashionable stationer, a scene that should by rights lift the heart of many at such a joyous time of year; Honoria, though, took little enjoyment from it, for her mood of late had been troubling dark.

'Good evening, Mrs Joseph,' called the elderly Miss Peters as she tottered across the icy cobbles, leaning heavily on her cane.

'And to you,' Honoria replied and she paused by the well, rested a gloved hand on its stone wall. 'Do you need help getting home? You look awfully unsteady.'

'Just my old bones, pet,' the old woman replied stoutly. 'I'm stronger than I look, though everything takes me twice as long!' Miss Peters peered into Honoria's pale face, licked lips like crushed crêpe. 'Do *you* need help, my dear? You have such a way to walk home, and without your . . .' She trailed off, seemed then by her expression to regret speaking, for Honoria had swallowed hard and clenched her fingers into the cold stone of the well.

'I shall be perfectly all right.'

She had spoken so quietly that in pity Miss Peters reached out, patted Honoria's hand, the icy kid-leather of her glove.

'You're very brave,' the woman said gently, 'very brave indeed. I don't know how I would have coped under the circumstances. So cruel. So cruel . . .'

She trailed off again, and the unspoken words sat heavy between them. Honoria forced an insincere smile.

'I have no qualms about walking alone,' she said, raising her voice a little. 'The distance is not so very far after all, and the solitude gives me time to collect my thoughts.'

Miss Peters bowed her head. 'Of course, my dear, of course. Such a brave woman! May God bless you.'

With one last pat of her hand the old woman resumed her slow course across the square. Not wanting to chance anyone else speaking to her, Honoria rushed in the opposite direction, toward the wrought-iron gate that separated town square and lane, and stepped into the darkness of Widow's Walk.

The hedgerows either side of the path towered over her.

No lanterns guided the way here and Honoria had only the light of the evening sky to see by, the gleam of the waxing moon. She had walked this narrow road many times before, of course, for there was no other way to reach the small and elegant townhouse she called home, but despite her assurances to Miss Peters, Honoria never liked it in winter when it felt so strange and quiet, and it unnerved her to walk that way at night knowing how the lane came by its name.

Widow's Walk. The townsfolk called it this on account of the churchyard on the other side of the hedge, where, buried in a line spanning the length of it, were the graves of unfortunate women who had lost their lives in some unhappy way, each and every one of them a widow. There was Emmeline Shaw who slipped and fell into the river and drowned; Charlotte Grosvenor who took a tincture of hemlock to (as the note she left explained) end her suffering and join her 'dearest Fred'. It was sweet Mary Hampton who succumbed to consumption, and pitiable Tilly Eaves simply lost the will to live after her husband and little child were killed in a carriage accident. Yes, the thought of them unnerved Honoria most dreadfully, their bodies being but a hair's breadth away with only that hedge between them, yet despite her unease she always offered up a little prayer to each and every one.

Those poor wretches! She knew their pain, the torture of heartbreak. To lose one's husband was a trial to any woman. And what tragic ends they made, Honoria thought as she continued down Widow's Walk, the heels of her boots a dull clomp on the earth, mud hardened with ice. Love does funny things to people, when it serves to harm and not heal. It makes fools of the most rational of men, and the kindest of women cruel. It makes one think most strangely. It changes a person. Was she herself not plagued with curious imaginings at night on account of her nerves? No wonder the townsfolk pitied her. No wonder they looked at her with such sympathy.

Honoria sighed deeply. She used to be so carefree, so happy! Benjamin had been such a refreshing change from all those foppish French suitors when she met him in Dieppe, a dancing master to one of her clients. So besotted had she been with the handsome Englishman that she left her beloved France and all she held so very dear to make her home in a country which had done its level best to make her people suffer. And now what had she to show for it? Honoria sniffed, lifted the latch of the gate at the end of the lane. Nothing, she thought, clenching her fists.

Nothing except her fans.

Picking up pace she crossed the bridge, eager to continue work on that most special of commissions, her only remaining pleasure.

There was a skill to whittling bone.

It took many years to master, but Honoria was lucky enough to have been trained by the finest *artistes* in Dieppe, the heart of ivory carving in all of France. Her thorough education meant that she acquired the Freedom of the City almost as soon as Benjamin brought her to England, and it was Honoria's unsurpassed skill that made her so popular. To own a creation by Honoria Joseph, the acclaimed fan-maker who had once produced an ivory brisé for the French queen, was truly a thing to boast of.

Honoria twisted her riffler into a tiny hole to widen it, frowning at the rough *scrape scrape scrape* made by the metal blade. Ivory was expensive, difficult to procure nowadays, so Honoria had been forced to find another material that most closely resembled it, making the task that little bit harder. Still, by the time Honoria was finished Miss Whiting would never know the difference – she could carry it about her wrist the whole night of her father's Yuletide ball without a second thought. Certainly, in the candlelight one could easily be mistaken in thinking what Honoria held in her hand now *was* ivory; the little filigree pattern she was carving within the sanded guard was as fine as any she had created in Dieppe. Of course, bone was lighter than ivory, could be brittle; Honoria would have to ensure it was strengthened by securing the sticks with something appropriate to make up the folding leaves. Chicken skin was usually just the thing, but she did not have the vellum to hand. Instead Honoria had something else, something more than suitable.

Just one day more to dry out, and it would be ready.

Shivering – for the bedroom was frightfully chilly despite the fire burning in its grate – Honoria swept the powdered bone to the floorboards, the candle flame guttering with the arc of her arm. She would prefer to work by daylight, of course; working in such dim conditions made the task of carving all the more difficult and hurt her eyes, but under the circumstances it could not be helped. With a sigh Honoria placed the riffler down, considered how much work still needed to be done. It would take a few more hours yet to finish the guard and she had no time to waste, for the commission must be complete in time for the ball. The first guard was finished some days before, and it lay prettily in the satin tray at the far end of the table, together with the central sticks etched with lace-like stems and thorns. Honoria regarded with satisfaction her work on the guard in front of her, the curve of finely carved petals. She had chosen a series of roses as the central pattern, one that would be continued on to the painted leaves in an elegant yellow display . . .

Behind her, something moved.

Senses sharp as scissors, Honoria twisted in her seat to face the bed, that large four-poster which until recently had accommodated both her and Benjamin so very comfortably. She was not truly expecting to see anyone behind her and indeed nobody *was* there, only Honoria in the chamber, perfectly alone.

Yet.

Honoria pulled the shawl she wore tighter over her shoulders, attempting to ward off the cold. These past weeks she had been almost sure of a presence there in the bedroom, watching her work on Amelia Whiting's fan. It was never anything she could put her finger on, only ever a strange sensation. Now it was there again: an odd pressure in her chest, a full-bodied thrum in her ears that could almost be a sound but could not possibly be one either, for she did not hear it so much as *feel* it. Quiet, but somehow . . . not. A word popped then into her mind and Honoria nodded at it, as if it were the answer, the precise thing.

'Unquiet,' she said to the room. The bedroom felt *unquiet.*

Honoria sat perfectly still, ever so slightly tilted her chin in the direction of the window. Through the thin panes of dimpled glass she could hear the river outside, half-frozen with ice, its watery course sluggish in the frosted bracken mounting the bank. She strained to hear anything else but that strange unquiet stretched out until, at length, it *was* quiet, and Honoria forced out a laugh. Perhaps it was merely her darkling thoughts that evoked in the room a sense of foreboding, for what a silly thing to fancy! This was only her frayed nerves, the trial of heartbreak, compounded by her own tiredness. Nothing more. But . . . Honoria frowned, the shadowed coverlet having caught her eye. Why was it crumpled on the side Benjamin used to sleep, as if he had rested there only the night before? Had Clara not been in here today?

It took a minute or so for the maid to respond to the bell pull, and when she appeared at the door Honoria shook her head in disappointment.

'Honestly, Clara, did you not make up the bed today?'

Clara looked at her mistress, brow creased.

'But I did, Mrs Joseph. After you left for the shop this morning.'

'Then why is it creased?'

'I don't know, ma'am.'

Honoria stared at the maid. It was not like Clara to lie.

'Well,' she said, unsure now. 'Make it up again.'

With a look of concern the maid turned to the bed, straightening the coverlet with sharp efficiency, and all the while Honoria peered into the darkness of the curtain folds that surrounded the bed. Was that a shape now in the darkness, the hint of a human form? But then Clara pushed the curtain aside to tuck the sheet a little more tightly across the mattress, and Honoria shook her head to clear the disturbing thought.

It was her imagination. *Just her imagination.*

'Will there be anything else, ma'am?' Clara asked, quiet, tentative.

Honoria clutched at her shawl. 'Would . . . would you build up the fire? It's dreadfully chilly in here.'

The maid frowned. 'Is it? It feels warm to me.'

Honoria said nothing, looked again to the bed curtain that now, after all that, appeared perfectly normal. Clara bit her lip, stepped forward.

'Are you feeling quite well, Mrs Joseph? You look so pale, so tired! Trapped up here night after night working on that fan, barely eating. It's no wonder you're cold.'

Clara trailed off as Honoria levelled her with a stare, unwilling to be drawn.

'Please do as I say, Clara.'

Biting her lip the maid glanced toward the grate and its

fat flames, then to the empty basket which until recently had always been kept so full at its side.

She said, 'There's scarce room to build it up, Mrs Joseph, but if you insist I'll need more firewood to do it. We've no more upstairs. The rest, it's in the cellar.'

There came then such an odd prickling at her back that Honoria twisted in the chair to look behind her, but nothing was there. When she turned around once more Clara was looking at her as if she had gone quite mad.

'Never mind the fire, then,' Honoria sighed. 'I shall cope for tonight.'

The maid shifted from foot to foot.

'If you give me the key, ma'am, I don't mind fetching some.'

Honoria sucked in her breath. 'That won't be necessary.'

For a long moment Clara held Honoria's gaze.

'Very good, Mrs Joseph,' she said quietly, and with a small shake of the head the maid shut the door.

Honoria slept little. The bedroom seemed to shift and creak in the night, and as a consequence she had tossed and turned for hours before finally drifting off somewhere close to dawn. There had been too the strangest smell in the room which came and went every hour, a putrid stench of rot that made her distinctly uneasy, so when she arrived at the fan shop later that morning she found herself feeling ill with fatigue. She looked ill, too, if the surreptitious glances her girls darted at her every now and then were anything to go by. All her girls were carefully selected from the local orphanage; they understood keenly what loneliness meant. They were kind girls. Decent girls. Honoria knew they felt sorry for her, stepping about their mistress as if they walked on broken china, not quite willing to meet her eye. Instead they would wordlessly bring Honoria cups of black tea and plates of ratafias as she perched behind the counter, trying her best to pretend she did not mind. But Honoria did mind. She did not like people feeling sorry for her.

There really was no need.

It was easier to pretend and keep a smile on her face with the shop so blessedly full; Lord Whiting's ball ensured Honoria had a steady stream of customers. Already that morning she had sold five of her celebrated silk and cut steel fans, one of ostrich feathers, and three of the imported range made of Italian lace she had procured through the East India Company at an extortionate price. It was just as she was wrapping a floral silk fan in tissue paper a little after midday (a pretty purchase made by the mayor's sister) that the bell chimed and in came Lord Whiting himself, his daughter trailing behind, bringing with them a small flurry of snow.

The shop fell into a respectful hush.

It was not often the lord of Larkshood Manor visited The Golden Fan. Certainly, to have two of the three illustrious Whitings deign step through Honoria's door was – so many would think – an honour.

'Good afternoon,' she said as the Whitings approached the counter. 'How might I help you today?'

'Mrs Joseph.' Lord Whiting's smile stretched across his crooked teeth. 'We have come on behalf of my wife.'

Honoria bowed her head. 'How might I be of assistance, your lordship?'

He gestured to his daughter, who was at that moment brushing snowflakes off her sleeves.

'What with you making Amelia a fan, my wife now desires one of her own.'

Honoria paused. 'Of ivory?'

She had not planned to make another. The fan she was creating was special, *very* special, and though Honoria had some materials left over they were meant only for Amelia Whiting. Besides, she thought, there was no possible way she could make another before Christmas Eve, and very politely she told him so.

'No, no,' his lordship replied, 'my wife has no interest in ivory. Forgive me, but she thought the notion of it quite distasteful. No, Lady Whiting hoped you might recommend one that would match her purple taffeta. She would come herself, but is most keen to avoid the cold. It would be awfully inconvenient if she were to catch a chill before the ball.'

'Of course,' Honoria said with relief. 'Perhaps,' she added, reaching beneath the counter for one of her more recent (and terribly costly) creations, 'she might favour this brisé?'

It was truly lovely and well worth the price; a fan of lace dyed plum with cochineal, stitched within a set of gleaming nacre sticks and guards.

'Oh yes!' Lord Whiting exclaimed. 'Just the thing, I'd say. Wouldn't you agree, Amelia?'

That daughter – so pretty and fresh-faced, strawberry-blonde curls bobbing beneath her bonnet – turned her head, lowered her blue eyes to the fan Honoria held between her hands, its radiant rainbow shell.

'How pretty,' Miss Whiting said. Soft, insipid almost. 'It will match her dress perfectly. Yes, Mama will be delighted with it, I'm sure.'

Honoria inclined her head. 'Shall I wrap it then, my lord?'

'Please do, Mrs Joseph.'

And so she wrapped the fan carefully in tissue paper tied with purple ribbon, placed it in a velvet-lined box. When she told his lordship the price he did not bat an eyelid. Perhaps he too felt sympathy for her plight, an odd sort of obligation, or perhaps he was simply too rich to care. Their eyes met across the counter, and it was as he slipped the box into his coat pocket that he leant forward, lowered his voice.

'Still no sign of Mr Joseph, then?'

Next to Lord Whiting Amelia went almost imperceptibly still. Honoria felt the familiar clamp of hurt and anger. With effort, she cleared her throat.

'He's quite gone, your lordship.'

'Ah.'

That pitying look shared by her girls (and indeed those still in the shop who had taken the opportunity to eavesdrop), a sad, sage shake of the head.

It had been a shock, of course, for him to discover the

dancing master's true character, for it had all come out after Benjamin vanished, the rumours spreading like quicksilver: *ran off with a paramour from the next town*, some said; *absconded to London, left in the night with all his wife's money*, said others.

'Good riddance, I say,' Lord Whiting opined. 'You are far better off without him, Mrs Joseph, and I'm most pleased to see you are in a financial position as not to miss him.' He sucked his lower lip. 'I must admit, however, it is a pity, for there are no suitable dancing masters for miles and my Amelia really could do with additional lessons. Her quadrille is damned poor, despite all the weeks your husband spent teaching her. Still trips over her own feet, do you not, pigeon?'

Amelia blushed, trilled a soft and lilting laugh.

'*La*, Papa, you are quite mean!' she cried and her father chuckled in turn, waved his daughter off. As he moved away to converse with another customer who was loitering at his elbow Miss Whiting leant conspiratorially over the counter, pressed her gloved hands on the glass.

'I truly am looking forward to seeing my fan, Mrs Joseph,' she whispered, blue eyes shining. 'I shall be the only woman in town with one made of ivory. Will it be ready soon?'

Honoria gave a nod. 'It shall be ready by Christmas Eve,' she said, soft as feathers. 'I think you shall be very pleased with the result.'

Miss Whiting tapped her hands on the glass with glee, sending an oyster shell tumbling and ruining Honoria's under-counter display.

'May I see it? What you've done so far?'

'Oh no, miss. It is a special piece. Very special. I keep it at home.'

'At home?'

'Where I can work on it in private,' Honoria said. 'It really is a *very* special fan, you see.'

Amelia Whiting's round cheeks flushed with pleasure. 'How lovely of you to give my commission such special attention,' she gushed. 'You really are *so* kind!'

The girl turned back to her doting father then, and with shaking fingers Honoria bent beneath the counter to rearrange the oyster shell against a string of freshwater pearls.

❧

Throughout the day the snow had fallen slowly but steadily, creating a thick white blanket on the ground which made Honoria's lonesome journey down Widow's Walk all the more difficult. Since the Whitings' visit to the shop Honoria had felt listless, irritable, and to calm herself she recited her prayers out loud for those poor widows on the other side of the hedge. She had just finished them when the noise came – so faint it was at first that she barely gave it any mind but when it sounded again, an odd crunching sound, Honoria stopped stone dead in her tracks.

The sound stopped with her.

Next to her the hedge shivered, its frosted tips

glistening in the moonlight. Through the thick boughs of holly Honoria could not see if someone was on the other side and so she called:

'Hello?'

No answer came. Honoria stood quite still a moment, but when the other side of the hedge remained quiet she started up her journey once more, her footsteps a little brisker than they had been before . . .

. . . and the strange crunching came again.

'Is anybody there?' she whispered.

This time there came a sigh, a long expel of air. Honoria's chest tightened with cold, though on account of the weather or some other feeling, she could not be sure.

Honoria Joseph had always considered herself to be a sensible woman. It is true that she had not been herself of late, that the loss of Benjamin affected her more than she thought it would, all matters considered. What, for instance, of her strange imaginings the night before, of all those nights before that? But this she had *not* imagined, and as if to prove it the sigh came once more, together with that sickening crunch. It sounded like the crackle and break of wintered foliage, leaves covered with hoarfrost, the snap of broken ice crystals. Footsteps, then. Someone walked with her on the other side of the hedgerow. But who? Surely the churchwarden did not maintain the grounds at this hour in winter?

'Hello?' she called again. 'Mr Samuels? Is that you?'

No answer, and Mr Samuels most certainly would have

answered if it were him. Uneasy now, Honoria walked faster down the lane, but whoever it was did not let up.

Crunch, crunch. Crunch, crunch.

It was a difficult pace to keep. Her skirts dragged. The sky had clouded over, obstructing the light of the moon. All Honoria had to see by was the snow itself gleaming almost blue; the holly either side of her held within its leaves little flurried mounds of it. Under other circumstances Honoria would have thought it beautiful, would have felt a sense of being safely cocooned within the lane, but now she felt claustrophobic and the unease that had taken over her shifted into the first flutterings of fear.

'Who are you?' Honoria cried out. 'Why do you follow me?'

The footsteps stopped a moment, then started up again.

Crunch, crunch. Crunch, crunch.

She drew back, wondering if she should return to town. But Honoria had closed late that day, so late that Miss Cleeves, Mrs Moore and Mr Berryman had already shut their own shops and gone home – she would only be returning to an empty square. Not even kindly Miss Peters would be out at this hour. Besides, she was more than halfway down the lane; it would make more sense to continue on, to reach the iron gate at the far end as fast as possible.

Crunch, crunch. Crunch, crunch.

Tears sprung to her eyes. The cold air made her sockets sting.

Again she picked up speed. Again the footsteps followed. Honoria clutched at her heavy skirts, tried her best to keep moving through the snow, but her lungs felt tight with the effort of it and all of a sudden she was overcome with an unholy suspicion.

What if it was not a person? What if whatever followed her was not a living creature at all?

All those bodies, she thought, stifling a sob. All those poor unhappy widows! Did they mean to tell her something? Did they mean to warn her?

Crunch, crunch. Crunch, crunch.

'Who are you?' Honoria cried again, breathless with fright. 'What is it you want?'

No answer, not even that dreadful sigh. She looked ahead of her, squinting into the dark, and almost choked with relief when she perceived the glistening outline of the gate.

Honoria ran.

Unthinkable that those awful footsteps should pick up speed and run with her, but they did, that dreadful crunching of snow on the opposite side of the hedgerow a terrifying taunt. Within moments Honoria reached the gate and with trembling fingers she unhooked the latch. She flew through it, leaving the gate to clang noisily against its frame as she ran full pelt across the bridge on the other side, the gurgling of the river drowning out everything except the sound of blood pounding in her ears.

It took Honoria a long while to settle. She ate Clara's white soup and mumbled hare without much enjoyment, but by the time Honoria had set out her gouache paints on a palette she was feeling a lot calmer. Whoever it was in Widow's Walk would not get the better of her; to be sure it was ridiculous to let herself become as frightened as she had, and the next time she walked down the lane Honoria would keep a straight head on her shoulders. Decided, she dipped the paintbrush into bright canary yellow.

It was a delicate operation. The material had been painstakingly soaked in a solution of lime and water and scraped with a pumice, then stretched onto the curved wooden frame. Now it was dry and ready to be painted, Honoria needed to be careful, for the new canvas was extremely thin and the smallest slip could produce a tear. Once she had secured it onto the guards and sticks, however, it would be as flexible and durable as any fan to be found in the finest of palaces.

And despite its origins, the fan had turned into something rather beautiful. In the candlelight the carved bones glowed warmly in their satin tray, and Honoria could picture perfectly how they would look sewn onto the new leaf. She twisted the brush between her forefinger and thumb to achieve a small, elegant flick, then leaned back in her chair to admire. Surrounded by full green leaves and twining stems, was a yellow rose . . .

Honoria clutched the paintbrush tight. Her fingers began to tremble. She shut her eyes.

Once the festive season was over she would be able to think of better things. Perhaps she would move away, take her establishment and orphan girls elsewhere to begin a new life, a place the townsfolk would not send her pitying looks. But until then she must concentrate, not let her dark thoughts interfere with the task at hand. Taking a deep breath Honoria opened her eyes again, committed to painting that second important rose. Only when she had finished did she retreat to her bed.

How long she slept Honoria did not know, but something in the room woke her and, bleary-eyed, she blinked into the semi-dark.

Through the window – in full view, for she had forgotten to shut the curtains – the moon shone milky and fat, and flurries of snow gently fluttered past the panes. Honoria was so captivated by the sight she almost did not notice the shadow at the desk until it moved; then she *did* notice, her insides twisted into a painful knot, and that strange thrum from the night before hummed inside her head.

'No . . .' she whispered, for a dark indistinct shape loomed before the desk, as if it were looking down at the painted husk stretched tight across its wooden frame.

Honoria could not explain how she knew this, how she felt instinctively that the shape was looking at the fan, but it was, *it was*! Her body grew heavy like lead, powerless to move as she watched. The shape did not appear to possess any colour except black despite the cold light of the moon shining into the bedchamber, and a putrid smell came to her nostrils then, the same one she had marked the night before.

The thrum grew louder. As if the dark shape had heard her innermost thoughts it shifted, seemed to turn and stare.

Honoria screamed.

Within moments Clara rushed through the door, her candle trembling dangerously in its holder.

'What is it, Mrs Joseph?' she cried, looking wildly about the room. 'What is it?'

'There! With eyes like devils!'

Honoria pointed at the desk with a shaking finger. Clara turned to look, approached it with small cautious steps.

'Oh, Clara,' Honoria cried, 'be careful!'

The light from the maid's candle flickered over the desk, and the girl turned back to Honoria, now clutching the coverlet desperately to her chest.

'There is nothing there,' Clara said.

And nothing *was* there. Honoria stared at the spot where the dark shape had been, the thrum still buzzing heavy in her head.

'That noise, then. Can you hear it, Clara? Can you?'

The poor girl was chalk white. 'I hear nothing, ma'am.'

'You must!'

'I do not!'

In that moment the noise stopped. Stunned at the sudden silence Honoria pressed her hands to her ears, testing them, and Clara stared at her mistress in distress.

Christmas Eve brought with it a blinding sun that hung low in the blue sky and set the snow twinkling. The harsh light streamed in through the bay window of the shop onto the large table in the middle of the floor, lavishly bedecked with garlands of spruce and ivy. In the centre stood the wassail bowl and platter of mince pies Honoria's girls prepared every year, and so it was that The Golden Fan was full of customers taking advantage of the merriment and festive cheer.

Some had come in for last-minute purchases, ladies who had yet to find a fan for the ball. Indeed, the shop was humming with expectation at the joy such an event would bring, and when the Whiting carriage appeared on the other side of the square the ladies excitedly fluttered their newly purchased fans.

Honoria watched and listened to it all with a horrid sense of detachment, exhausted as she was; she had not been able to sleep another wink the previous night after being woken by that dreadful shade, and while it did not return, nor the strange smell, nor that peculiar thrumming sound, she had tossed and turned. At last Honoria chose to light a candle and commit to the task she had intended for later that morning, to sew the painted rose husk onto the carved bone guards and sticks. It took some hours of painstaking stitching before she was done, the sky turning burnt orange as she had lain down her tools and announced the fan to be complete. And what a beauty it was – despite her shaking fingers that fumbled the needle Honoria's work was exceptional, perhaps even the best she had created in her long and illustrious career. Mayhap it was the emotion attached to the fan that gave it its brilliance, that very *personal* connection which contributed to its beauty. Whatever it was, Honoria had no doubt that Amelia Whiting would be pleased.

It was that very girl who crossed the town square at that precise moment. The low sun made her strawberry-blonde curls gleam, and without meaning to Honoria glared at her across the shop floor.

'Mrs Joseph?' said Miss Peters then, crumbs of mince pie dusting her collar. 'Are you quite well?'

Honoria had jumped at the woman's fingers on her sleeve, and it took a moment for her to recall herself and pin a smile to her face.

'I am merely tired, madam, that is all.'

The old woman nodded in understanding. 'You and your girls have worked tirelessly this past month. It is no wonder you feel fatigued. You shall be glad of the rest, I expect.'

'Quite so, quite so.'

Miss Peters hesitated, pressed Honoria's arm. 'What with Mr Joseph gone, I suppose you shall be spending Christmas alone?'

Her words hung between them, all the more awkward for they had been overheard, and Honoria pressed her lips just as Miss Whiting entered the shop. The elderly lady ducked her head.

'Forgive me, Mrs Joseph, I had not meant to pry. But it's frightful cruel to spend the day by yourself.'

'I shall be perfectly contented,' Honoria said, though despite the assurance her stomach gave a sickly twist.

What if the shadow were to return? What if she were not to be alone after all?

She forcibly cleared her throat.

'I dare say I shall enjoy it all the more for the solitude.'

Miss Peters let out a breath, heavy with brandy from the wassail bowl. 'If you wanted to spend the day with us, I would not object in the slightest! My sister and I would be pleased to receive you.'

The unexpected kindness made Honoria's eyes water.

'I thank you. But I'd prefer to be on my own. I'm sure you understand.'

'Of course,' Miss Peters nodded, 'of course,' and, with a troubled look on her wrinkled face, she stepped out of the way to make room for Amelia Whiting.

The young woman was dressed in crimson, round cheeks flushed with cold. Honoria was reminded of something else red and picked at the memory of its dried crust under her fingernail.

'Is my fan ready, Mrs Joseph?' Amelia gushed, eyes gleaming with excitement. 'Is it ready as you promised?'

Honoria turned away. Almost reverently she reached for the wooden box set on the shelf behind the counter and placed it on the glass between them. Instantly Amelia Whiting grasped it in her hands, a greedy look on her pretty face, and opened the lid with a flourish.

The fan nestled in bone-white silk. Closed as it was, only the topmost elaborate carvings could be seen until its new owner took it from the box and spread the delicate leaves wide. There was a gasp of admiration from the other customers as Miss Whiting held it to the light streaming through the bay window, and in the sun's rays every intricate detail revealed itself on the bleached bone: the swirling vines, the pointed thorns, the curling tendrils; the miniature roses interspersed with tiny circles to create a lattice effect. Then, of course, the painted leaves between its sticks: the pumice had reduced the skin to a smooth finish which gave no hint as to what it had been before, adorned now with painted green leaves and golden feathers. And there, in the centre, two glorious yellow roses.

Yellow for infidelity, one for each adulterer.

Honoria watched the play of emotions on the girl's face. Wonderment, admiration. Satisfaction.

'Oh,' Miss Whiting breathed. She raised her gaze to Honoria's. 'It is beautiful. Just what I had hoped for. And the carvings! So delicate! However did you do it?'

A memory came to her then. Ruched skirts exposing a pair of shapely stockinged legs. Animal grunts, whimpering sighs. Benjamin's breeches down by his ankles, his horsehair wig askew . . .

'With pleasure,' Honoria said softly, and this time her smile was genuine. 'With great pleasure.'

Honoria sent her girls back to their boarding house just after two, when the winter sun no longer seeped into the shop but had sunk below the trees, dying the sky honeyed gold. For a long while she lingered, fearful of Widow's Walk and those awful crunching footsteps, but when the day slipped into dusk she finally turned the key in the lock. She would *not* be frightened, Honoria told herself sternly. Nothing, after all, could be worse than what she might find at home.

Snow had begun to fall, heavy fat flakes that landed on the brim of her bonnet. Honoria walked as fast as she could across the town square and reached the gate to the lane just as the snow became thicker and faster. Within seconds Honoria could barely see the path in front of her, but there was no other way home – through Widow's Walk she must go, and with a chest unbearably tight she stepped down into the narrow lane.

The sound came almost immediately, but this time Honoria did not bother to call out. Instead she tried to ignore that dreadful crunching and concentrated simply on putting one foot in front of the other.

'Eternal rest,' she whispered, starting up her prayers for the widows in the graves on the other side of the hedge, as if speaking to them might appease the creature which hounded her down Widow's Walk.

'Grant unto them, O Lord, and let perpetual light shine upon them.'

Crunch, crunch. Crunch, crunch.

Honoria felt tears upon her cold cheek.

'May they rest in peace. May they rest in peace!'

Crunch, crunch. Crunch, crunch.

On down Widow's Walk she went, into the driving snow. She had kept a fine pace at first, but in the cavern of the tall hedgerow the way was dark and Honoria was slowed down by the flurry. The fear she had been so determined to keep at bay began to sneak its way into her heart, wedging itself there like a fist.

Was this her punishment? she thought wildly, as the footsteps continued to match her own. Was this her deliverance?

Crunch, crunch. Crunch, crunch.

She raised her eyes, despairing, squinted into the night. Surely the gate was near? Surely, oh surely, she was at the end? Crying in earnest now Honoria pressed on, wiped the wetness of snowflakes and tears from her eyes, and then she saw it: the spindles of the gate mere yards in front of her. Sobbing in relief Honoria rushed forward to greet it . . . and the toe of her boot caught within her skirts.

With a loud cry she stumbled. In desperation she held out her arms, tried to prevent the fall, her hands finding hedgerow. The sharp fronds of holly poked viciously through her gloves, stabbing her fingers like knives, and the pain caused her to let go. When she hit the ground Honoria gasped, both at the cold and in relief, for the snow had cushioned her fall.

The crunching stopped.

On the ground Honoria lay still and panting.

I must get up, she thought. I must reach the gate, the bridge, home!

She became aware then of breathing, and not her own. It came from the other side of the hedge, directly by her ear at ground level. The breath was just like the sigh of before, a heavy bellowed release that – now she listened to it, actually *listened* to it – sounded . . . Honoria raised her head.

It sounded like a snort.

The sound stopped. A single crunch. Another breath.

Unsure now, Honoria scrambled up from the ground, her dress and cloak covered in snow. Ignoring the stinging pain in her fingertips she reached the iron gate, pulled it open. On the other side she turned to the right rather than straight across to the bridge, where the hedge came to an end and met the low wall of the churchyard. Honoria looked over it . . . and laughed.

A pony stood on the other side of the wall. A pony! She laughed again, her relief swift and warm like a balm. The creature that had been following her was nothing more than Mr Samuel's cob, left to roam in the churchyard, and it had simply followed her journey down the hedgerow, innocent as you please!

'Oh, heavens,' she breathed. Honoria reached out her hand to rub its muzzle; warm, solid, as real as she. 'Were you keeping me company all this time?'

The pony tossed its mane, gave again that same snort, and Honoria laughed once more.

What a silly fool she had been! To frighten herself half to death on account of a pony! She scratched the cob behind its ear and, quite convinced now all her troubles were the result of nothing more than her over-active imagination and the anxiety of these past weeks, Honoria almost skipped across the bridge toward home.

Clara had set the fire burning strong in the bedchamber and Honoria sat in front of it, a blanket over her knees. The maid had exclaimed when her mistress came in, her clothes damp and heavy from her fall, but Honoria – good humour restored – waved her off.

'Never mind me,' she said. 'You get off with you now, back to your parents. They'll be expecting you.'

Clara, pale-cheeked, watched Honoria nervously. 'Are you sure you'll be all right here on your own? I can stay if you want me to.'

Honoria shook her head. 'I promised you Christmas Day off and you shall have it. I'll not be accused of being a harsh mistress. Just bring me a nice cup of tea, and get home before the snow prevents you.'

'But I feel so dreadful leaving you all alone. After everything that has happened . . .'

'Nonsense,' Honoria assured. 'I shall be perfectly content.'

So Honoria sat in her armchair by the fire, letting the heat of the flames seep into her clothes. Clara had insisted she change, but it would be a pointless exercise when she would only get dirty again. She still had a job to do, after all. Instead Honoria waited patiently, resting her head against the back of the chair.

It would be so easy to sleep. No doubt she needed the rest. It had been a trying few weeks, these past days especially. The worry of discovery, compounded by the urgency of completing her commission for Amelia Whiting on time . . . Honoria thought of the girl now, preparing for the ball at

Larkshood Manor. She hoped it would not be postponed on account of the weather, for it would be a damned shame if all Honoria's efforts had gone to waste. She could picture the girl perfectly, strawberry-blonde curls bobbing in the candlelight, wearing a gown of gleaming yellow silk or emerald-green satin, the new fan hanging from her wrist or fluttering in front of her face . . .

Honoria considered the romantic language of fans. Would Amelia use it to coquettishly hide her eyes? Would she place the tip of the fan to her heart? Or perhaps she would open the fan slightly and wave it. Each gesture meant something different, and Honoria smiled. How pleasing to think Miss Whiting might use an old lover to attract a new one!

The fire crackled in the grate, a steady thrum. Slowly, Honoria raised her head from the back of the chair.

A steady thrum.

The sound began as a low pressure in her ribcage which grew louder and louder, yet she could not hear it – no, this was a sound Honoria could *feel* with every part of her body except her ears, a strange electrical pulse. The warmth, the ease which she had felt lulled into, was extinguished as fast as a blown-out candle, and, swallowing hard, Honoria gripped the arms of the chair, turned her gaze to the bed.

She sucked in her breath.

There was an imprint on the coverlet. No shadow, no dark shade. Just a shape.

'Here you are, ma'am,' said Clara, arriving with a tray. On it was a teapot, cup and saucer, the sugar bowl, and a small dish of steaming stew. She set the tray down on the table next to Honoria, and promptly began to pour. 'I know you said you weren't much hungry, but I couldn't go without leaving you something. Oh, Mrs Joseph! You look awful pale.'

Honoria stared at Clara. The girl held the teapot over the cup, watching her mistress. Shaking herself, Honoria blinked.

'It's nothing,' she said slowly. 'I dozed off and you frightened me, that's all.'

Clara's face cleared. 'Well then, that's fine. Here,' she added, handing Honoria her tea. 'This shall perk you up.'

Honoria took it with a hand that shook so much she spilt some of the tea into its saucer. Clara's brows drew together.

'Are you sure you're quite well, ma'am?'

'Perfectly, Clara. Go on, get along. Please send my regards to your parents.'

The maid hesitated a moment, but it was clear she wished to be gone and so she said, 'There's a small goose already cooked for you in the larder. All you need do is warm it tomorrow. Tatties and greens too, with a little plum pudding for after if you've room for it.'

Honoria inclined her head. 'Thank you, Clara.'

The maid hesitated again.

'What is it?'

Clara twisted her fingers. 'It's the cellar, ma'am. The strangest smell is coming from it, you see.'

'Smell?'

'Yes, ma'am. Like gone-off meat, rotting fruit.'

Honoria teased the pleat of the blanket. 'A dead rat,

perhaps,' she replied, 'though I did not notice anything this morning when I brought up the firewood.'

'But—'

'I shall check again tomorrow, just in case, but you'd best not disturb yourself. Whatever it is, it shall be gone by the time you return.' Honoria cleared her throat. 'Now, get off with you. Merry Christmas.'

Clara seemed to want to say something more, but at length the maid dipped her knees. 'Merry Christmas to you too, Mrs Joseph.'

Honoria waited until she was quite certain Clara had made herself scarce before leaving the bedroom. The pressurised sound had disappeared with the maid, and Honoria wondered if she *had* in fact dozed off, just like she claimed. Well, if that were the case it simply would not do. Honoria had too much to be getting on with to succumb to sleep, no matter how much she needed it.

Removing the key from her pocket, she went down to the cellar and unlocked the door. The barrel she kept the body parts in Honoria had moved to the very back in hope the stench of decay would not reach the rest of the house so quickly, but while the odour had been subdued by the cold Clara managed to mark it. Still, as Honoria told her, by the time she returned there would be no trace of Benjamin Joseph left to smell.

It took over an hour to dispose of him. Only later, once Honoria had washed and changed into her nightclothes could she eat her cold stew, her mind rested, finally at peace. Yet sleep did not come swiftly, as Honoria hoped it might. Instead, she lay staring at the ceiling of the four-poster. The room was dark, the fire having burnt down some time ago, but through a chink in the curtains Honoria could see the snow was coming down in earnest, a true blizzard that was sure to prevent Lord Whiting's guests from attending the Yuletide ball. Amelia Whiting would not be using her fan tonight, but somehow, now, that no longer mattered; Honoria had instead the satisfaction of knowing her husband was dead (how she rejoiced the night she put the riffler through his chest!), and that his mistress would not realise each time the fan pressed against her bow lips she was kissing the skin off Benjamin's back.

Beside her the bed sank. Honoria shot up, clutching the neck of her nightdress. A putrid smell invaded her nostrils, a smell so strong she could taste it on her tongue. How had Clara described it?

Like gone-off meat, rotting fruit.

And the sound. The sound! That started up too, filling the room with a terrible thrum. Clammy with terror Honoria tore herself from the bed.

Tripping over the hem of her nightgown she ran to the door, and when she discovered it was locked panic took her completely. The thrumming sound was deafening now; pushing her palms to her ears she turned, and Honoria's scream of horror caught dead in her throat.

On the bed was a dark shadow. Very slowly it began to

move across the coverlet, the darkness curling about the bedposts, and Honoria heard the sound of claws on wood. As the shadow slipped to the floor the moonlight sneaking between the chink in the curtains shone upon it, giving the shade corporeal shape, and Honoria watched in horror as it crawled like a toad along the floorboards. She knew what it wanted, knew it meant to tear her to pieces and send her scraps to the Devil as a just reward for her treachery, and Honoria could do nothing except watch it come toward her, that creature with revenge in its glaring eyes.

That creature with Benjamin Joseph's simian face.

For poor Clara the shock of discovering her mistress' body ruined her Christmas entirely. The snowdrifts which had settled so thickly across town had prevented her from coming to the house until well past midday, by which time Honoria Joseph's body was stiff with both rigor and cold. The fire was dry, the goose uneaten, the wooden post of the bed deeply scratched, as if an animal had set its monstrous claws upon it. But that was not what scared the maid so frightfully, for Honoria's face was a terrible sight to behold – her mouth twisted in a silent scream, her eyes bloodshot and staring, her hands raised as if warding off a terrible foe.

Fist clamped to her mouth to stem her whimpering, Clara rushed for the doctor, and despite the maid's most abject insistence (*my mistress was frightened to death, I'm sure of it!*), it was later said that Honoria's mind and heart had simply failed, the weight of heartbreak too heavy for her to bear. No wonder, too, for it was generally thought that Benjamin Joseph really had treated her very cruelly indeed. And so, while her husband was still thought to be fit and healthy, living somewhere in London as merry as you please (*'twas the Devil's parlour, that place, a perfect fit for him!*), the people of the town thought it a kindness to consider the man as good as dead. And so it was that the body of Honoria Joseph, proprietress of a prosperous fan shop in a small but affluent town located in the mid-counties of England, was buried at the far end of the churchyard, in the last and most lonely spot against the towering hedgerow that ran alongside Widow's Walk.

CAROL OF THE BELLS AND CHAINS

Laura Purcell

Rain beats drearily against the high windows. The fire hisses and wavers beneath a dripping chimney. Abigail thanks each sound; they mask the silence that falls as she enters the servants' hall and takes her place at the table. She is trying to count her blessings; there's always something to be grateful for. One: warmth and shelter on a rainy evening. Two: the pleasant servants' hall with its vaulted ceiling, a sideboard full of china, shining copper pans. Three: the plate of mutton, peas and potatoes set on the table before her.

She plaits her fingers together as the butler says grace. Even with her eyes closed, she senses the hostile glare of the lower servants upon her. Once the prayer is finished, she picks up her cutlery and keeps her gaze trained on the food. A low level of conversation is permitted, but experience has taught her that a governess has no friends; not even Martha the nursemaid, with whom she works closely. Abigail moves in a class of her own: impoverished gentlewoman. Unequal to the family, yet never truly one of the staff.

Beside her, the housekeeper and the lady's maid chatter about the approach of Christmas.

'Mrs Arden has been so good. She's letting me take three

days off to visit my father – you know how bad his lungs have been.'

'That's nice. You'll have earned your time away by then, what with all the parties you'll be dressing her for.'

'So many social engagements this year! I thought the mistress might host less, in her condition, but no such luck. Now I have to take all her ballgowns out at the seams . . .'

Abigail sips politely at her drink, but it goes down the wrong way. Pain burns in her gullet, makes her eyes water, and despite her best efforts to smooth the matter over, a splutter emerges from her lips.

Everyone stops eating and stares.

The housekeeper narrows her eyes. No doubt she thinks Abigail interrupted on purpose. 'You've not requested leave of absence over the holiday, Miss Scott?'

Abigail dabs her mouth with a napkin and shakes her head. Who would she see? Only her sister Deborah, another governess. There's no love lost between them. Even if they could meet, they have no house to gather in and precious little to celebrate. Their days of skating and sledging throughout the winter are long gone.

The lady's maid sniffs. 'A governess is hardly needed over Christmas. Not like the rest of us. *She* won't be sweating in the kitchen or sewing till her fingers ache. She'd do better spending Christmas with her kin and leaving the little ones to enjoy the holiday unchecked.'

'Young Master Edmund will be so excited,' the housekeeper agrees indulgently. 'How those big blue eyes of his shine!'

'A beautiful child. But I must confess a soft spot for Miss Judith. She was the mistress's first.'

The housekeeper cuts her mutton with care, covertly eyeing Abigail. 'I dare say *you* favour Master Gilbert above all your pupils, Miss Scott? He is the clever one. I don't suppose you ever need to correct *him* on his sums.'

Abigail fights to control her facial expression. 'I do not have favourites amongst the children.' A tinkle sounds through the scrape of cutlery. Abigail watches the bells on the wall, sees which one vibrates. *Schoolroom.* She pushes back her chair. 'Excuse me.'

It's both a disappointment and a relief to leave the hall and mount the servants' staircase. Abigail's still hungry, having managed only three mouthfuls of her meal, yet she's keen to get away from the staff.

Not that the children treat her with kindness. Chaos reigns in the schoolroom. Three-year-old Edmund squirms in Martha's arms, his fists flailing, small feet pounding her stomach. *Those big blue eyes* the housekeeper praised simmer with fury.

'I'm sorry,' Martha gasps. 'I didn't summon you. He kept pulling the bell, I couldn't get him to stop.'

'It looks as if you needed me, anyhow.'

Martha scowls. Abigail didn't mean to offend her, but surely the nursemaid can't imagine she's coping well alone? All the chairs have been removed from their desks to construct a fort in the corner. Dark-haired Florence nestles in the centre, reading – at least her occupation is unobtrusive. Her elder, fairer sister Judith draws on the moist window panes and Gilbert is up on the desks, leaping between them like islands in a stream.

'Stop that!' Abigail cries. 'Gilbert, get down at once. You might fall and break your neck.'

He ignores her. At six years old, he's more than ready for the transition to masculine clothes and his own tutor. He looks grotesque, like an overgrown infant with his curls and his billowing smock.

Conversely, Judith is ten yet wears the provocative expression of an adolescent. She turns from where she has written *Miss Scott smells* with her fingertip. 'See, Edmund? I *told* you not to ring the bell. Now *she's* come back.'

'And just in time too,' Abigail snaps, pulling her away and folding the shutters across the window. 'Enough artwork, young lady. You were supposed to be practising "While Shepherds Watched Their Flocks".'

'I *know* it already. I play that piece for Christmas every year. A good governess would teach me something new.'

Abigail lets her insolence pass, focusing instead on the flitting form of Gilbert. What if he slips? The Ardens won't tolerate the slightest bruise upon their precious heir. She catches him mid-jump, taking a knee to the chin for her pains. Coppery blood fills her mouth; she swallows it and sets Gilbert down.

'Why do you always spoil my fun?' he pouts. 'You're so *dull*!'

'Desks are for writing on, not for climbing,' she says thickly.

Gilbert fists his hands onto his hips. 'Desks are for writing on, not for climbing.' He mimics her voice with uncomfortable precision. 'Well, next year I'll be breeched and free of all you silly women. Then I can do as I please.'

She won't be sorry to shear off those curls, dress him like a gentleman and relinquish him into the hands of a tutor. In fact, she can barely wait.

Stoically, Abigail tries to place the desks in their proper order while Martha carries little Edmund back to the nursery. Without being asked, eight-year-old Florence begins to dismantle her fort and pushes the chairs beneath their allotted desks. Abigail told the housekeeper she didn't have a favourite amongst the Arden offspring. She lied.

'Come now, children, enough of this silliness. Did none of you even *look* at the story I left you with? Who can tell me a single fact about St Nicholas?'

'I read the story,' Florence says softly, retrieving the book from the corner. 'St Nicholas was a kind man. He gave money to three sisters, so their parents didn't have to sell them into slavery.'

'Yes! That's right. Good girl, Florence. See, St Nicholas rewards nicely behaved children. Next time you're tempted to shirk your studies, you ought to think about all the presents you'd like to receive from him on St Nicholas Day.' Her eyes move between the well-fed, finely dressed scions of wealthy parents, wondering what else they could possibly desire from life. 'Do you know what St Nicholas brings naughty boys and girls? Only lumps of coal.'

There's plenty more she can say on this topic, for Abigail is mistress of many tales. Her own nanny was a refugee fleeing Napoleon's armies; she escaped with no luggage except a mental repository of stories designed to scare young children witless. Nanny would threaten the Ardens with Krampus, but Abigail restrains herself. Nanny's frightful yarns are only to be used in cases of emergency.

Judith appears to read her thoughts. 'Were you a good child, Miss Scott?'

Abigail smooths out her skirts. 'What makes you ask that, Judith?'

She grins nastily. 'Because St Nicholas didn't help you, did he? You were sold into servitude. That's why you work for us now.'

Mrs Arden's chambers are stifling, in body as well as spirit. Rosewater saturates the rugs, hangs alongside the curtains and seeps into the wallpaper. The mistress wears a protective gown and mask while the maid powders her hair; Abigail is forced to breathe through her nose instead.

'So? What have you to tell me?'

Mrs Arden likes to see her discomforted. The mistress took an aversion to Abigail early on, simply because the master treated her in a friendly manner. It wasn't *flirting*, but a jealous wife like Mrs Arden will always make mountains out of molehills.

'Miss Judith wishes for a silver-backed mirror,' Abigail recounts, her voice squeezed tight. 'And some red ribbons. Master Gilbert has asked for his own signet ring. Master

Edmund craves confectionery, and Miss Florence . . .' She swallows, nearly chokes on powder. 'Well, I haven't been able to ascertain what Florence desires for St Nicholas Day.'

Mrs Arden waves a hand. 'Oh, that does not signify. Any old thing will do for Florence.'

Resentment burns in her chest alongside her smothered coughs. 'Florence is a good child—'

'Precisely. She will not complain.'

'But—'

'That will be all, Miss Scott.'

Abigail dips a curtsey. What lies they tell the young about the festive season! She's been bleating on about St Nicholas, but the truth is this: bad people are continually rewarded, while the good are ignored, even at Christmastime. It's enough to break anyone's spirit.

She slopes back towards the nursery where the children will be finishing their breakfast. High-pitched laughter jangles and sets her teeth on edge. It's strange, how the giggles of one child are delightful, yet a group of them together sounds like savages cackling. What she hears now isn't merry at all.

She opens the door to see the breakfast table lying abandoned. Martha chases Edmund, whose jam-tipped fingers threaten to mark the wallpaper. The other three children are strangely grouped. Florence sits cross-legged on the floor, her eyes blank, a doll pulled onto her lap. Either side of her, like a pair of bookends, are Judith and Gilbert. They're laughing so hard that they can barely stand straight.

'What is so amusing?' she demands. Judith tries to whip a hand behind her back, but Abigail seizes her wrist and extracts a sheet of paper. 'What is this?'

Florence hunches into herself. 'It's mine, Miss Scott.'

'I didn't steal it from you!' Judith gasps through her giggles. 'I found it under her pillow, Miss Scott, so you can't blame me.'

Abigail is certain that she can and *will* blame Judith. Her eyes skip over the careful penmanship. What she has confiscated is a letter: Florence's letter to St Nicholas.

I wish Papa would notice me and sit me on his lap. I wish Mama would call me pretty like she does Judith.

Her heart drops. She shouldn't read this; the poor child's privacy has already been violated.

Yet Gilbert has no such qualms. He's committed the contents to memory already and mimics his sister's voice. 'Please help me, kind St Nicholas. I don't have any other friends.'

He really is a little turd.

Florence seeks solace in the worn face of her doll. It's perhaps her lack of tears that hurts Abigail most of all. She can feel the child's raw embarrassment as if it's her own. It once was.

Giving Judith and Gilbert all her attention now – even negative attention – will only compound the problem. What Florence craves is obvious from her letter. Abigail bends down to her height. 'Come with me, Florence. I want to speak with you.'

Meekly, Florence stands and follows her into the small bedroom the girls share. She curls up at once on the mattress, her doll pressed tight to her chest. Abigail perches on the end of the bed. If only there were words to make this better! She is twenty years older than Florence, yet she cannot teach her how to secure love, or how to stop the others from mocking her.

It was the same when Abigail was young: Deborah performing each task effortlessly, while she struggled to glean even a husk of praise. Desperation made her look ridiculous. No one seemed to value her until Roger came along . . . But she couldn't hold on to his affection, either.

'I am so sorry this has happened to you. You don't deserve to be laughed at.'

'It doesn't matter,' Florence mumbles into her pillow.

'It does. And while I don't have the right to comment upon your letter, I will say one thing. You *do* have friends. You shall always have a friend in me.' Florence sniffles. She looks so like her father. Abigail aches to touch her, to hug her, but it isn't her place. 'I will take your note and make sure it reaches St Nicholas before the sixth.'

'No!'

'Why not?'

Florence squirms. 'It was stupid. St Nicholas won't help me. I'm not a good girl.'

'Yes, you are! It's a pleasure to teach you. You are the most—'

'If I was a good girl, I wouldn't hate them.' Florence

clutches at the doll, her small face pinching. 'I try not to but . . . I do. I hate all three of them.'

Who can blame her? Abigail wants to confess that she hates them too, that she loathes the staff, that she detests Florence's mother. But she gives a governess's answer. 'Loving others would not be a virtue if everyone were easy to love. At this time of year, we must bear with those we dislike. I will talk to your siblings about their behaviour. You need not attend lessons today, if you prefer.' Abigail stands up from the bed, but Florence moves quickly to clutch at her skirts. 'What is it, child?'

'I put up with them all year round. Does St Nicholas see?'

Abigail's smile feels false, a betrayal. She knows very well the girl will receive no material reward for her behaviour. People will always incline to her elder, prettier sister, despite her sharp tongue. 'Yes. You'll reap the benefits of your kindness one day, Florence. Maybe not now, but later.'

'Do you promise?'

She hesitates for longer than she should. 'Of course.'

The sixth of December. Dark clouds spread across the sky like patches of damp over a wall, while the wind ravens about the house. Ash has blown from the fireplace and scattered over the schoolroom floor in a poor imitation of snow. Abigail bends to sweep it herself, rather than summon the maid. The windows drip; the sentence *Miss Scott smells* rises once more.

Downstairs, the children will be opening their St Nicholas Day gifts, but it doesn't feel much like a holiday. There's something oppressive in the air, the metallic taste that heralds a storm. Abigail sorts her books and music sheets, wondering what throwaway trifle Mrs Arden bought for Florence in the end. Nothing personal or expensive. It seems to be the same in every family: the eldest sister reaps the best of everything.

Abigail realises she's grinding her teeth. It's foolish. Yesterday's unpleasantness has opened old scars, brought her own childhood into clear and bitter focus. Her parents always favoured Deborah above her, before they died. Their preference made no difference; both girls wound up as lonely governesses. But the important point is this: Deborah will forever be the favourite now. Abigail can never change their minds.

A quarter of an hour later her pupils file into the schoolroom merry and rosy-cheeked; or at least three of them are. Judith sports her new hair ribbons and Gilbert is wearing his signet ring. Young Edmund sucks on peppermint rock, cradling a toy boat in one arm.

'What did you receive?' Abigail asks Florence as they take their seats.

Wordlessly, the girl produces a nutmeg grater, shaped like a shoe, and places it on her desk. The local pedlar tried to sell Abigail a similar gewgaw when he came to the servants' hall.

'Bad luck,' Judith sneers. 'Even though she wrote St Nicholas that *lovely* letter.'

Something gives way in Florence's expression; for a moment, Abigail's certain the sisters will come to blows.

But Florence seems to master it, clenching her hands into fists instead.

She has more self-control than Abigail would in her position. Enough is enough. *Someone* needs to fight back against these little wretches, even if Florence can't.

'We're not going to learn about St Nicholas any more,' she announces briskly, moving to the centre of the room. 'You've shown me you're old enough to learn the other side of the story.'

'The other side?' Gilbert repeats, sceptical.

'Oh yes. Everything casts a shadow, even St Nicholas. Today I'm going to tell you about the one who follows him on his rounds.' She pauses for effect. The name hovers on her tongue, sharp with danger. 'Krampus.'

Silence.

'Is that some kind of cat?' Judith quips.

Abigail returns an icy stare. 'Hush! He mustn't hear you say such a thing. You need to be careful not to upset him. Be very, very careful.' She's never been able to hold their attention before, but now they stare, waiting for her words. 'There are many names for Krampus. Some call him *Père Fouettard*, others *Zwarte Piet*. He has no Christian name, because he's the opposite of a saint. Can anyone tell me what that is?'

The hush seems to prickle. 'A . . . devil?' Florence ventures.

Abigail nods. 'A demon.'

Judith's smirk withers on her rosebud lips.

'He may walk upright like a man, but Krampus is no

mortal. In place of his feet are the cloven hooves of a goat. *Clip, clip* they go across the ground – not that you would hear them coming. Your ears are filled with the clanking and jangling of his chains. Thick iron chains, hung with bells, which he dragged up with him from Hell. Think how strong he must be, to pull them always in his wake!'

Edmund drops his stick of rock.

'Black hair coats his skin. Horns sprout from his head. Come, Gilbert, give me your slate, I shall draw you a picture.' She sketches hurriedly, feeling reckless, powerful. The chalk squeals and makes Gilbert jump. 'See, here? A goat has flat teeth for chewing grass, but not Krampus. These are his fangs and his long, pointed tongue.'

'What does he do?' Judith breathes.

'Consider it logically. St Nicholas comes to reward, so Krampus must come to . . . what?' There's a twinkle in her eye, a quirk to her lips; she's enjoying this too much. The children are already frozen in their chairs, yet somehow Abigail can't stop herself. 'He comes to punish, of course.' She adds a sack, stuffed with branches, to the monster's back. How easy it is to illustrate her childhood fears! The images flow straight from her brain into her fingertips as if they've never gone away. One forgets pleasant dreams, but not nightmares. 'If you are lucky Krampus will simply beat you with birch branches and sticks. But if you've been really naughty . . . if, for instance, you've been cruel or unkind to those weaker than you . . .' She shakes her head and titters. 'You'll go into the sack.'

'What's in the sack?' Edmund bleats.

She pushes away a memory: how she used to wake up, gasping for breath, dreaming she'd been smothered inside that sack. 'The sack itself isn't important, it's merely a means of carrying the naughty children away. Of course, no one really knows what happens to them after that . . . Some say they are drowned; some say Krampus eats them. Others believe that he simply takes them back to Hell with him. What do *you* think happens?'

Edmund bursts into tears. His cherubic face, crumpled in terror, brings her first pang of remorse. She'd been aiming at Judith and Gilbert, not him.

'Don't snivel!' Gilbert snaps at his younger brother. 'Be a man. There's nothing to fear.'

'Oh, aren't you afraid?' Abigail asks, conversationally.

'No,' he blusters. 'If anything bad was going to happen, it would have happened last night. But it hasn't. We've been rewarded, see?' He raises the hand with the ring. 'All these presents. St Nicholas visited us last night, not Krampus, because we're good children.'

Abigail cocks her head. 'Are you?'

'Yes!'

She does her best replica of Judith's nasty smile. 'I pray for your sake that is true.'

A gale is blowing outside, whooping around the grounds and rattling the trees together like dry bones. The hunting dogs howl from their kennels. Air squeezes through the cracks in the window frame, agitating the curtains. Abigail pulls the bedcovers up over her neck.

The children will be so afraid. She remembers stormy nights in the nursery at home, the visceral fear she and Deborah shared. That was, at least, one front upon which they were united. They would comfort each other without judgement when bad dreams came. Now she's inflicted a similar terror upon the Arden children. Wilfully. Frightened those she was charged to protect. Shame sits thick in her throat. What sort of woman *does* that?

Wind barrels down the chimney, making the fire judder. The flames cast a hectic light. Abigail tries to console herself with the fact that she and Deborah survived their fright; Nanny's stories caused no lasting damage. Judith and Gilbert *needed* taking down a peg or two. Isn't it better that the check should come from her, their governess, than from some stranger in the future? All kinds of excuses spring to mind, but in her heart she knows her conduct is indefensible.

There's a light tap against the door. The handle works up and down. Something pats against the wooden panels, seeking admittance.

Absurdly, she sees a flash of Krampus's black hooves. 'Hello?' she calls.

'Miss Scott?'

Florence. Abigail gets out of bed and crosses the cold floorboards to unlock the door. The child looks smaller and helplessly thin in her nightgown. 'Whatever's wrong? Why aren't you asleep?'

Florence twists her hands, firelight playing across her pale skin. 'I'm . . . I'm afraid.'

Another artificial smile. 'A big girl like you, afraid of the wind?'

'No! Of Krampus.' Guilt presses on her chest like a flatiron as Florence adds in a whisper, 'I heard his bells and chains. He's outside my window right now!'

Abigail bends down to the child's height, takes her by the shoulders. 'He isn't there, Florence. The story I told you this morning, that was . . .' She trails off. What can she say? That it was designed to petrify Judith and Gilbert? That she didn't stop to think how much she might upset Florence and Edmund in the process? 'Krampus is just that: a story. Make-believe.'

Florence's dark eyes, her father's eyes, brim with tears. 'May I sleep with you tonight?'

Abigail's chamber is small, her bed narrow, but she's brought this predicament on herself. 'Of course you can.'

Slight as Florence is, she takes up most of the mattress. Abigail has to curl her body around the child's lightly trembling frame. If she closes her eyes, she can imagine herself elsewhere, in a cottage of her own, snuggled up with the daughter she never had. That life might have been hers. She and Roger would have been married for five years by now, were it not for her betrayal. An act of rashness, the same rashness that prompted her to tell the story of Krampus to the Arden children . . .

Strange. Florence was right: as Abigail drifts towards

unconsciousness, the gale does sound a little like discordant bells.

'What about the adults?'

'Hmm?'

Florence's voice vibrates through her back as she speaks. 'When adults are naughty, who comes for them? Are they punished, too?'

'Yes,' she yawns, not heeding the question. 'Yes . . . I suppose that's only fair . . .'

Florence waits for more, but Abigail has fallen asleep.

It must be time to rise; Martha's voice travels through the walls from where she's scolding the boys in the nursery. Light presses against Abigail's closed eyelids, shifting red and yellow. She puts out a hand for Florence, finding only an indentation in the mattress.

'It's come right down!' Groggily, she opens her eyes. Florence stands at the window, silhouetted by cold, white light. 'Look, Miss Scott!'

She climbs out of bed, wincing as her bare feet meet the chill floorboards. Florence has already pulled the curtains aside and pinned them behind their holdbacks. The lawns no longer stretch green behind the house; they're awash with shrivelled foliage. Every crisp, paper-brown leaf that had clung on into December has been blown down, along with sticks, birds' nests and entire branches. Florence points over near the lake, where a birch tree has snapped in half like a matchstick. Its limbs sprawl, arachnid, into the water.

'Oh dear! I hope no damage was done. The wind must have been blowing very strong to break a trunk.'

Florence presses her nose to the glass. 'Maybe it was Krampus, gathering his sticks?'

'Nonsense. I told you last night, he's just a story.'

She'd hoped to do away with the Krampus business and start afresh today, but it seems there's no escaping him. As soon as they're dressed and step out into the corridor they meet Martha, carrying sheets. Yellow stains make a silent accusation against her.

'Master Gilbert wet the bed,' Martha huffs. 'He's never done that before!'

Gilbert? Abigail would have expected it of Edmund, not him. Yet even the eldest boy is only six, she reminds herself – young enough to lose control of his bladder through fear. Her cheeks warm. She can feel Florence looking at her.

'We had better check on your sister,' she says with forced brightness. 'Judith slept all alone last night.'

'It wasn't very nice of me to leave her, was it? I thought Krampus was coming and I just ran.'

Abigail swallows. 'Fear makes us do strange things.'

But Florence didn't *just run*, as it turns out. The door handle refuses to budge, forcing Abigail to produce her keys. Evidently Florence had the foresight to close the door and lock it behind her.

'Judith?' Abigail calls. 'Are you decent?' There's a low whimper. The lock yields and she cracks the door open.

An acrid aroma overpowers her: wood smoke, coal dust,

urine. Choking, Abigail stumbles further into the chamber. If she could breathe properly, she would scream.

The bed curtains are torn to ribbons, the posts a tally of scratches and splinters. Judith lies on top of the covers. Her hair is tangled with burrs and, although the fire has burnt out, her skin flushes an angry red.

Abigail pulls Florence into the room and closes the door fast behind them. 'What happened?' she manages to gasp.

Judith only snivels.

Florence's eyes are like saucers. 'I told you Krampus was outside the window,' she breathes.

Abigail approaches the bed and tries to touch Judith, but the girl shies away. Her arms look raw, covered in lashes and prickles. 'Who did this to you? How could . . . The door was locked!'

Judith bursts into fresh tears.

No one must see this. How would Abigail explain it to the maids, to the mistress? She can't explain it to herself. Nonetheless, those wounds need to be washed and dressed. She'll have to fetch supplies without drawing attention, give out that Judith is sick . . .

'Florence, stay with your sister. I'm going to get some medicine.'

Florence shakes her head vigorously. 'I don't want to stay in here! What if Krampus comes back?'

'He won't . . . he can't . . . he isn't even real!' she cries, slipping from the room and locking the girls in.

Her mind turns cartwheels. What is she doing? Surely it

would be wiser to seek help, to sound an alarm? Someone has hurt the child and they must be caught . . . Yet it happened on her watch. The Ardens might dismiss her for negligence.

She walks blindly down the corridor, lost in thought, bumping into Martha as she returns from the kitchen. 'Tell the boys lessons are cancelled,' she mumbles. 'Judith is unwell.'

She doesn't wait to hear a response. Doesn't contemplate what she'll do if the mistress asks to visit her poorly child. Her overpowering instinct is to conceal what's happened, as if she were to blame. Deep down, didn't she want this?

She told Florence that Krampus couldn't have hurt Judith and technically that's true. But the question is left hanging, swinging back and forth like a sword over her head: who on earth did?

'Keep that fire blazing hot!'

'But I'm sweltering!' Florence complains. She's removed every article of clothing except her shift and her petticoats, which cling to her with sweat.

'That's good,' Abigail says from her position by the bed, tending Judith's wounds. 'We want heat. If the fire's burning strong enough, no one can come down the chimney.'

The chimney *must* have been the point of entry into the chamber – the door was locked, the windows shuttered. But who could have been climbing up on the roof, in last night's wind? They'd have to anchor themselves, if they didn't want to be blown away with the roof tiles; they'd have to be weighted with something heavy like . . . Like chains.

Judith winces as Abigail's cloth peels back a flap of skin. There's no bleeding, at least. Judith's thrashing is nothing that time and a bit of salve can't heal. Physically, she'll be fine, which is more than can be said for the four-poster bed. How will she prevent her employers from seeing the damage?

Florence prods the flames with a poker. Sparks leap like luminous fleas. 'Krampus came from Hell,' she muses gravely. 'A bit of fire won't stop him.'

He isn't real. He *can't* be real. Abigail dampens her cloth and realises her hand is trembling; it sends water rippling to the edges of the basin. 'What did you see?' she asks Judith again.

'Nothing!' the girl moans fretfully. 'I *told* you. The fire was out. I just heard the chains, dragging over the floor, then the cracking wood . . .' Tears choke her. 'Then I felt pain.'

'Why didn't you scream?'

'I couldn't!' Judith splutters. 'I reached for Florence but she wasn't there!'

Florence makes no defence. Abigail understands only too well; she once treated Deborah the same way. It had been *her* idea to skate on the millpond, *her* need to win that pushed them further than they could safely go, but when the ice started to splinter she'd made a dash for it, leaving Deborah stranded with a leg either side of a long crack. She didn't *mean* to abandon her.

She shakes off the memory. 'And you definitely heard

chains? Not a voice, not anything that could help us discover who attacked you?'

Judith regards her as if she's run mad. 'Krampus attacked me. *You* should know, you brought him here! You told him we were bad children.'

Abigail shudders at the idea of herself holding an audience with Krampus. Giving the demon a teacup to nurse between his cloven hooves, sharing her grievances, as if they had anything in common.

Krampus was always the name she feared above all others. She used to hear his bells in her sleep, picture his sharp teeth parting to unleash a long, serpentine tongue that probed inside her ears. Of all Nanny's myths and legends from the Continent, he was the one that clung to her like dirt. *Could* there be any truth to the tale?

'I didn't think Krampus was real, Judith. I just said it to frighten you. And he's meant to come on the night of the fifth! I can't have . . . I can't have *summoned* him, by telling the story? Could I?'

In other circumstances she'd suspect the children of playing an elaborate trick on her. But no child could do this! Judith wouldn't submit to such mistreatment for a lark – she's barely submitting to Abigail's ministrations now.

'It's your fault,' Judith insists again.

She thought she'd be satisfied, seeing this arrogant girl taken to task, but instead she feels nauseous. 'I'll make you better,' she promises. 'This will heal. You'll see.'

'I want Mama,' Judith whimpers.

'No! Your mother won't believe you,' she says hurriedly. 'She'll say a servant must have hurt you, she'll bring the constable! Don't you see, I have to keep you here until you're healed, until I can fix this bed somehow . . . This has to be our secret.'

Judith eyes her with mistrust.

Florence pushes a log on the fire. 'But I don't want to stay in here!' She repeats, 'I don't want to sleep in this room! What if Krampus comes back?'

Judith gives a little sob.

'He won't come back,' Abigail avers with more confidence than she feels. 'But I'll remain with you. The boys will be safe in the nursery with Martha, and I'll sit in the chair and keep watch over you tonight.'

As though she would be any match for a demon! If Abigail saw Krampus, she'd scream herself hoarse. But that is the curse of being an adult: she must always talk as if she is in control of the situation, as if she is not just a terrified child at her core.

'You'll stay awake all night?' Florence asks doubtfully.

She nods. How could she possibly sleep, after this? 'All night. I promise.'

At first, it's simple: fear keeps Abigail vigilant. She's primed to run, to fight, she can barely remain in her chair. Her body tenses with every crack from the fire, every sigh of the mattress as the girls turn over in bed. Wind soughs through the debris it pulled onto the lawn last night, weaker now but honed to a sharp and chilly point. It's as though the temperature drops in sympathy each time Abigail's stomach plunges with dread.

She wishes Deborah were here; only Deborah would understand the enormity of this. *He's real*, she wants to shriek at her sister. *He was always real.*

Her dry eyes sweep the corners, watch the shadows cavorting. No matter how much wood she piles on the fire, it won't light the entire room. There's always a dark patch where vague shapes seethe and then melt, as if they were never there at all.

The children sleep, exhausted by pain and terror. She listens to their shallow, even breath, so different from her own. She's near to panting. Her keen senses overpower her: her heart beats a wild tattoo and her vision starts to swim.

In another hour, the constant anxiety has devoured her reserves of energy. Her body can't maintain this level of intense watchfulness. Her eyes seem to burn along with the fire. Slowly, her chin droops. The heat is becoming soporific. Abigail shakes herself. This won't do. Is she really so weak? It's only one night. She has to stay awake. She promised Florence . . .

She wakes with a snort. Disorientated, she casts around and realises with horror that she's failed. She fell asleep! But the fire is still blazing and the children lie peaceful. Except . . . something has altered.

She makes straight for the bed, blinking, certain what she sees must be a shadow. It isn't. Black marks are smeared across the sheets and the girls have been lightly peppered with coal dust. She raises a hand to check them for injury – stops. The soot is upon her too, all over her fingers, as if Krampus has seasoned her for a meal.

Footsteps in the corridor outside. Abigail's throat closes up. Now is the moment to act, to protect the children. She turns towards the door, spreads her trembling arms in a pathetic shield before the bed.

A knock. 'Miss Scott?' In her turmoil, it takes a moment to recognise Martha's voice. The knock comes again, more urgently, and Abigail fumbles with her keys to open the door. The nursemaid stands, hair unpinned, a glass globe lamp illuminating her worried face. 'You weren't in your room. What have you been . . .' She frowns, clearly confused to see Abigail looking like a chimney sweep, but her own concerns are more pressing. 'Never mind. Where is Master Gilbert?'

'What?'

'Master Gilbert,' she repeats. 'He's not in his bed. Please tell me he's with you.'

Abigail shivers despite the heat. 'Oh, good Lord.'

Martha swears. 'Where's he gone? We have to find him. Help me find him!'

Abigail hesitates to leave the girls, but what can she do? She closes the door on them, locks it tight.

'Where could he have got to?' Martha frets. 'If he's gone outside, at this time of night, the mistress will have my guts for garters!'

'He . . . might not have ventured far.' It doesn't sound

like Abigail's voice. She wants to cry, to scream at Martha that Krampus has taken the child, but somehow she finds herself going along with the search, as if Gilbert has simply run away.

Martha hisses. 'Ouch! What in the name of—' Her lamp flickers as she bends to rub her foot. She's stepped on a pine-cone, puncturing the skin. Pinecones are strewn all the way down the corridor. 'How did this happen?'

'Give me the lamp.' Abigail casts light in the direction of the schoolroom. It's as bad as the wreckage in the grounds outside: every piece of winter foliage decorating the house has been torn down. Prickling holly, green needles, blistering berries of mistletoe. Winding through the mess is a trail of black hoofprints. 'Dear God.'

She takes off, moving faster than Martha can in her night-gown and bare feet. A wet, green scent rises as she crushes leaves underfoot. There's another smell, equally festive and out of place: pomanders. As she nears the schoolroom, she sees the ornaments the children made last week: the cloves pulled out and scattered like shrapnel; the oranges eviscer-ated, leaving nothing but deflated sacks of skin hanging on the banisters.

The schoolroom door is closed. A sooty handprint covers the brass knob. Swallowing hard, Abigail yanks it open.

The flame twists and stutters inside the lamp. Someone has raised both the sash windows, letting the biting wind sail in. The door leaps out of Abigail's hand to slam against the wall. She jumps with a shriek just as Martha catches up.

'Master Gilbert!'

Martha snatches the lamp and plunges inside the room. By the wild, capering light, Abigail can see the Arden heir, bound across a desk by chains. He looks like a spit pig, with a lump of coal wedged between his teeth instead of an apple.

'Help me!' Martha cries, tugging at the heavy metal links. Sleet jangles on the roof; the wind picks it up and flings it through the windows. 'Miss Scott! Help!' Abigail takes a step forward as Martha works the coal loose from Gilbert's mouth. A tooth comes with it. He retches and his vomit flows as black as sin. 'What happened?' Martha keeps asking, but the boy trains his bloodshot eyes on Abigail.

A bell rings.

'It's for you,' Gilbert croaks.

Another tinkle, another, then another; it sounds as if all the servants' bells in the house are swinging back and forth. Abigail drives her fingernails into her palms. Nothing feels real, and yet this is all horribly familiar. It's her worst nightmares come to life.

She runs back down the corridor, slipping on leaves, catching her skirts on holly. Downstairs, the staff are beginning to wake. This racket will bring the master and the mistress before long, and how will she possibly explain?

Suddenly, the sight of the girls' bedroom stops her in her tracks. The door stands wide open. All the air seems to leave her lungs. The fire blazes, but the bed is empty. Abigail dashes to the nursery where the bell tolls on, knowing in her heart what she'll see. Sure enough, there's only an imprint left in Edmund's cot.

'Oh God, oh God.' She never intended this. She can't think now *what* she wanted, why she was ever angry with the children. All she recalls is her own youth: the misdemeanours she cannot sponge out, the iniquities for which she can never atone.

There's a servants' staircase that runs from here, past the kitchens and outside. It's the only place Abigail can think of to go. If Krampus has removed the children from the house, he must have taken them *somewhere* . . .

Maybe she'll see him, a fearful shape silhouetted on the rooftop. Or maybe she'll be able to catch up with him as he toils his way across the estate, chains clanging, sack writhing. Would he go to the lake? Drown the poor little Ardens? She doubts she'd be able to stop him, but she has to try.

It takes all her strength to open the door against the force of the wind. Sleet falls in earnest now, needling at her skin. Instead of melting as it hits the ground, it bounces back and wheels into shapes. Although the moon shines full, Abigail can hardly see anything beyond the mass of white specks hurtling this way and that. She ducks her head and pushes forward, accepting each stinging ball of sleet as a penance. Why oh why did she tell Nanny's story and bring this down upon them? She should never have let the children's ignorant cruelty make her cruel in turn. Judith and Gilbert are brats, certainly, but they are young. They might improve in time. Doesn't Krampus consider that?

Doesn't he see how arbitrary it is to exercise judgement on characters not fully formed?

Abigail can scarcely feel her feet. Her ears ring with cold and her teeth are starting to chatter. Sound swirls about her with the sleet. She studies the ground: leaves, sticks, fast-settling globs of ice. But just ahead is a flattened patch; something heavy has swept this way. She can only raise her head an inch or two against the wind, yet it's enough to glimpse a trail of broken twigs, leaves swept aside and grazes in the dirt where an object has been dragged.

A choking odour builds as she follows the trampled path. Bitter dust that sits heavy on her lungs and pokes its fingers down her throat. Through a flurry of white, she makes out prints resembling a pair of horns: the spiked tracks of cloven hooves.

Her body quivers from cold and fear. It's too late to turn around and she has no idea where she is. Near the stables, perhaps, or the leaves heaped for burning? Surely nowhere else on the estate could produce this stench of rot?

A shape looms in the distance. It's low to the ground but wide, with a decided hunch at the centre. Abigail hopes against hope that it's some kind of rock or boulder, rather than the object she expects to find.

In a few more laboured steps, all hope of pretence expires. The damp earth beneath her feet is scored from where a cumbersome burlap sack has been hauled to the edge of the lake and abandoned.

'Florence!' she calls. The wind snatches her voice and carries it away. 'Edmund? Judith?'

The sack's belly swells full. Big enough, fear whispers, for three children to be gathered inside. But there's no movement, no twitching. Whatever lies within is motionless.

'No, no.' Abigail edges closer, covering her nose and mouth against the smell. Sleet settles on the rough burlap. Even so, she can see the dark, rusty stain seeping through.

Falling to her knees, she crawls to close the remaining space between her and the sack. Mud drives under her fingernails, tears burn against her cheeks, but what does discomfort matter now? Nothing matters in the dark shadow of her crime. She has done this. Abigail.

Her numb fingers struggle to untie the strings and open the sack. Perhaps she ought to prod at it or poke it first, but she'd rather see the horror than feel it. Those small, cold, lifeless limbs. A little head, never to rise from its slumber.

With a rip, the ties give way. Abigail retches from the stench: coal, decay and something sickly sweet, as if all the sugared treats of Christmas have soured. Trembling, she eases the mouth of the sack apart.

She expected to see blood and frozen corpses, but she can't see at all. The inside seems cavernous and interminably dark.

'F-f-florence?' Holding her breath, she bends closer, peeks right in. Nothing but darkness. 'Edmund?'

The sack is empty.

Abigail pauses for a moment, dumbfounded, unable to piece her thoughts together. She doesn't hear the clanking until it's right beside her ear: weighty metal links falling fast upon each other and, high above them, the absurdly cheerful tinkle of a bell.

She opens her mouth to scream, but something pushes her hard from behind. The stench of the sack fills her lungs, her nostrils, her mind, until it is all that remains.

Dawn rises across the Arden estate in serene tones of coral and peach. Birds return to the shattered remains of their nests, twittering softly, while a few ducks venture back on the lake.

Lights already blaze behind every window in the house. Dogs bark, servants shout. Mr Arden himself, still clad in his banyan and slippers, heads a procession of men. He's stopped bellowing his children's names in case the servants hear the raw desperation that's crept into his voice.

Gilbert's gabbled account of last night makes no sense. The poor boy's imagination must have warped his attacker into some kind of monstrous goat form . . . It still doesn't explain why the kidnapper took the other children and left him behind.

A thin mist rolls off the lake and over the sugared landscape. The ground has frozen hard as iron. Even if the little ones haven't been crushed under the mass of fallen branches, they will have caught their death of cold. It couldn't have been the governess who took them, could it? An act of petty revenge for his rebuffing of her advances? They say Hell hath no fury like a woman scorned . . .

'There!' the groom shouts.

Miraculously, the fog parts and exhibits a sight too good to believe: three small figures, holding hands. They shiver, gravely observing an object by the water's edge.

Mr Arden starts forward, banyan flapping around his legs. 'My darlings!' Edmund breaks free and flies to him. In a moment, he's scooped the precious boy up into his arms; he is cold, so cold, but whole, safe. Mr Arden fights back the swelling tears. Judith screams, 'Papa, Papa!' and throws her arms about his waist. Only Florence remains a little apart, quivering like a greyhound, eyes pinned to the lake.

He sees now that the object on the shore is a large, unpleasant sack, stuffed full to bursting. Were the house-breakers seeking valuables after all? Nothing was missing.

'I thought he was coming for us,' Florence breathes in a rush of mist.

'Who, child? What on earth happened? What is in that sack?'

She turns wide eyes, full of wonder, at him. 'He wasn't here for us! He wanted her.'

'Florence, what are you talking about?' She always was an odd fish. 'Tell me what is in the sack!'

But a footman has already gone forward to inspect the baggage and his face is grim. Mr Arden notices the reddish patches oozing through the burlap, the hovering flies. For some reason he can't name, he wants to tell his servant to stop.

Yet before he can issue the order, the footman parts the lips of the sack, and his own burst open to release a terrible scream.

ABOUT THE AUTHORS

Kiran Millwood Hargrave is a poet, playwright, and the author of several award-winning books for children and young adults. Her debut novel for adults, *The Mercies*, was a *Sunday Times* bestseller and won a Betty Trask Award. Kiran lives in Oxford with her husband, the artist Tom de Freston, and their rescue cats, Luna and Marly.

Laura Shepherd-Robinson's first novel, *Blood & Sugar*, won the Historical Writers' Association Debut Crown and the Crimefest/Specsavers Debut Crime Novel award; and was a *Guardian* and *Telegraph* novel of the year. It was also shortlisted for the Crime Writers' Association John Creasey (New Blood) Dagger and the Sapere Historical Dagger; the Amazon Publishing/Capital Crime Best Debut Novel award; and the Goldsboro Glass Bell; and was longlisted for the Theakston's Crime Novel of the Year award. Her second novel, *Daughters of Night*, was a *Times*, *The i* and *Guardian* novel of the year. It was shortlisted for the Historical Writers' Association Gold Crown; the Theakston's Crime Novel of the Year; the Fingerprint Awards Historical Crime Novel of the

Year; and the Goldsboro Glass Bell; and was longlisted for the Crime Writers' Association Gold Dagger.

Andrew Michael Hurley is the award-winning author of three novels: *The Loney*, *Devil's Day* and *Starve Acre*. *The Loney* won the Costa First Novel Award, Book of the Year at the 2016 British Book Awards and was hailed as a modern classic by the *Sunday Telegraph*. Andrew lives and writes in Lancashire.

Imogen Hermes Gowar is the author of the *Sunday Times*-bestselling *The Mermaid and Mrs Hancock*, which won a Betty Trask Award and was shortlisted for the Women's Prize and the *Mslexia* First Novel Prize, amongst numerous others. Imogen lives and writes in Bristol.

Natasha Pulley is the *Sunday Times*-bestselling author of five novels: *The Watchmaker of Filigree Street*, *The Bedlam Stacks*, *The Lost Future of Peperharrow*, *The Kingdoms* and *The Half Life of Valery K*. Her first novel won a Betty Trask Award and was an international bestseller. She lives in Bristol and teaches creative writing.

Elizabeth Macneal is the author of two *Sunday Times*-bestselling novels: *The Doll Factory*, which won the 2018 Caledonia Novel Award and has been translated into twenty-nine languages, and *Circus of Wonders*. Elizabeth is also a potter and lives in London with her family.

Bridget Collins is the award-winning author of numerous novels for teenagers and two for adults: *The Binding* and *The Betrayals*. *The Binding* was a *Sunday Times* bestseller, shortlisted for various awards including the Waterstones Book of the Year, and was the number one bestselling debut fiction hardback of 2019.

Stuart Turton's debut novel, *The Seven Deaths of Evelyn Hardcastle*, won the Costa First Novel Award and the Books Are My Bag Readers Award for Best Novel, and was shortlisted for the Specsavers National Book Awards and the British Book Awards Debut of the Year. A *Sunday Times* bestseller for three weeks, it has been translated into over thirty languages and has also been a bestseller in Italy, Russia and Poland. His second novel, *The Devil and Dark Water*, was chosen as a best books of 2020 pick by the *Sunday Times*, *Guardian*, *Daily Mail* and *Financial Times*.

Jess Kidd was brought up in London as part of a large family from County Mayo, and is the award-winning author of four novels: *Himself*, *The Hoarder*, *Things in Jars* and *The Night Ship*. In 2016 Jess won the Costa Short Story Award and published her first book for children, *Everyday Magic*, in 2021.

Catriona Ward is an American-British horror novelist whose work has been highly praised by Stephen King. Her debut, *Rawblood*, won Best Horror Novel at the 2016 British Fantasy Awards, was shortlisted for the Authors' Club Best

First Novel Award and a WHSmith Fresh Talent title. Her second novel, *Little Eve*, won the Shirley Jackson Award 2018, was a *Guardian* best book of 2018 and won the August Derleth Award for Best Horror Novel 2019. Catriona is the only woman to have won the August Derleth Award twice. Her short stories have appeared in numerous anthologies. Catriona's third novel, *The Last House on Needless Street*, was published to acclaim in 2021.

Susan Stokes-Chapman grew up in the historic Georgian city of Lichfield, Staffordshire, but now lives in north-west Wales. She studied at Aberystwyth University, graduating with a BA in Education & English Literature and an MA in Creative Writing. Her debut novel, *Pandora*, became an instant number one *Sunday Times* bestseller, and in 2020 was shortlisted for the Lucy Cavendish Fiction Prize as well as longlisted for the Bath Novel Award.

Laura Purcell is a former bookseller and the author of seven novels, including *The Silent Companions*, which won the WHSmith Thumping Good Read Award 2018, and *The Shape of Darkness*, winner of Historical Crime Book of the Year 2021 at the Capital Crime Fingerprint Awards.